This book is dedicated to John,
Suzy and Chris, with love

... and he looked for judgement, but behold
oppression; for righteousness, but behold a cry.

Isaiah 5:7

Faith is the Bird that Sings to the Dawn
while it is still dark

Kabir

PROLOGUE

New Year's Eve

'Put down the gun, Thomas.'

Lorimer kept his eyes fixed on the man who was standing at the other side of the bedroom, arms clutched around the whimpering child, the gun pressed against her pale blonde curls.

Thomas Blackburn's eyes were red-rimmed, devil's eyes, staring at the tall police officer who had dared to enter the house where bodies already lay sprawled and bloody.

'She's your little girl, Thomas,' Lorimer said softly, willing himself not to shift his gaze and succumb to the temptation of glancing at the toddler caught in the man's vice-like grip. 'It's Lauren. You don't want to hurt her, do you?' Lorimer's voice sounded steady as he spoke, though it belied his true feelings. Inside, his stomach was churning, the smell of blood filling his nostrils.

It was imperative that Blackburn heard the voice of reason, the policeman's calm reassuring words posing no threat to the wild-eyed gunman. The sound of his voice had lulled many a criminal into a false sense of security over the years though nothing in Lorimer's experience had truly prepared him for a moment quite like this.

'Stay back!' Thomas Blackburn lifted the pistol away from the side of Lauren's head and waved it towards the detective superintendent. 'Stay back or I'll shoot you as well,' he cried.

Was that a note of desperation Lorimer could hear? The voice beginning to crack under the strain of what he had done? Was this the moment when a deranged husband and father would suddenly break down and weep?

It was a split-second decision, an instinct telling the detective to defy the gunman's command.

Despite the body armour, Blackburn could easily kill him with one shot to his face. If this gamble all went horribly wrong, Lorimer could be making a widow of his beloved wife.

Thoughts of Maggie were brushed aside as Lorimer shifted his weight, preparing to step forward and put out his hand, ready to accept the gun.

The child wailed as Blackburn gripped her harder, a shrill piercing cry.

Then, as Lorimer took one step forward, the world exploded in a mass of red as the girl's screams were silenced by the blast.

He watched in horror, unable to move, as Blackburn put the gun into his own mouth and fired, the air filled with noise and gore, spattering the policeman as he stood helpless and trembling.

'Your baby,' he cried, dropping to his knees and reaching out his hands to touch the child's body. 'Your baby . . . '

He stared at the place where the man had been, now an empty space filled with the acrid smell of gun smoke.

Lorimer was only vaguely aware of the sound of running feet entering the room and the feeling of hands under his arms lifting him up, tears blurring his vision, the moment already replaying in his head.

CHAPTER ONE

This city was all his, Gallagher told himself, swinging round to face the huge window overlooking the rooftops of central Glasgow. St Vincent Street swept upwards past the busy shopping thoroughfare to the graceful old office buildings where rows of well-tended window boxes were displayed from early springtime right through till the first frosts of winter. Even today, on this cold February morning, he could see traces of greenery and a few ornamental cabbages brightening up the grey walls as he looked down at street level. It was a part of Glasgow that had not seen too many changes, the business district still housing the premises of lawyers, accountants and insurance companies, those who could afford the high rents that these smart four-storey blocks commanded. The façades had remained the same for several generations although in many cases the interiors had been drastically altered to reflect the changing tastes of those whose money could buy these sorts of surroundings, as well as to accommodate so many new technologies.

The man swivelled in his captain's chair to gaze appraisingly around his spacious office, admiring the pictures in their gilt frames hanging on the walls. Several Glasgow artists owed their success to the businessmen and women who had bought up their paintings to furnish spacious boardrooms and reception areas, the displaying of such artworks testament to the standing of those buyers who could afford them. His own interest had begun with the sort of clever craftsmen who could fake any sort of thing he wanted. For a price. But he'd discovered that it was not just some of their under-the-counter work that had interested him.

Jack Gallagher stood up, coming closer to stare at a particular painting. It had caught his eye one day as he'd hurried down Blythswood Street, pausing at a gallery whose double-fronted windows always showed the best of contemporary art.

The picture had made him stop for a moment, its swirling autumn colours reminding Jack of the days long before he was rich, when a day tramping over the hills with his father had seemed the best thing that life could offer the young boy. Gallagher was far from being a sentimental man but the painting had drawn him into the gallery, the desire to own the piece for itself stronger than the knowledge that it was by a renowned artist whose work commanded a hefty price tag.

Now it was his and he could look at it whenever he felt inclined, though somehow he had never quite recaptured that first sensation of being back on the hills again, his own innocent youth lost for ever. Still, he enjoyed the landscape and took pleasure in knowing that he had made a good investment.

And Jack Gallagher knew what was value for money. His drug dealers got what they paid for, mostly over the market value, but then he refused to have anything to do with the shoddier goods that had flooded Glasgow recently, stuff that was cut with no end of rubbish. His clientele appreciated that, Gallagher knew, and paid accordingly. His thoughts turned to his first visitor of the day, the man who always came early in the morning before the city was properly awake. Like all of his clients, Charles Graham paid in cash. Not shabby used notes but sleek bundles of fifties wrapped in clear plastic bags as if he was averse to dirtying his hands with the money. Graham was a careful type; all he had ever given was a PO box for an address, something that tickled Gallagher's curiosity but he grudgingly admired. If Jack Gallagher knew your real home address that was tantamount to having a hold over you as long as you chose to live there. It would not be the first time by a long way that a couple of his thugs had paid a visit to one or other of the boss's dealers who had been tardy with their payments. But he knew instinctively that Graham was higher up the food chain than those shadowy types on his payroll. And today Gallagher was particularly interested in the man's visit and not just because Graham paid a little over the odds for quality product. He'd done the man a couple of good turns since they'd met and now it was time to call in those favours. Blackburn's death and the media circus that had surrounded it had created problems, one of which he hoped could be solved by his early-morning client.

Gallagher looked at his watch, the Rolex fastened to his wrist just another symbol of his success, another object that he took for granted nowadays and, like the painting, it too had lost that first thrill of ownership. The man should be here at any moment. He frowned. Jack Gallagher wasn't a man that you kept waiting. *Punctuality is a mark of good manners*, he remembered his father telling him. Gallagher's frown deepened into a scowl. Had the memories conjured up by that painting come back to haunt him? His mouth turned up in a grimace that was almost a smile. Nobody would ever make him go back to these old days when he was a ragged boy plodding after his father. Other memories came flooding back; the cramped space in the Gorbals tenement, the stink of his own unwashed body as he'd sat amongst the other kids at school, the rapping on the door as the rent man came to demand his money, children all kept quiet and fearful behind their mothers' skirts as the banging got louder. No, he'd never go back there again. He'd made his money, ruthlessly trampling on the dreams of his impoverished parents as he'd taken the road that led to this fine office high above the city streets.

CHAPTER TWO

Lorimer groaned as he turned in the bed, feeling the weight of the duvet across his ankles.

Waking up was the worst moment of the day.

For a few brief seconds he would simply be aware of the physical things, the warmth of the bed, the hazy light coming from the space between the curtains, his gummed up eyelids ...

Then the images kicked in, reminding Lorimer why he was here, unshaven and alone in bed, long after his wife had left for work.

Details flooded back, small things that had seemed so insignificant at the time. Lauren Blackburn's grubby toy rabbit, clutched in the child's small hand; the way the flower-patterned curtains had sagged against a broken rail; the paint stains on the gunman's jeans ... the bodies of the woman and her two boys, blood seeping out of their gunshot wounds; then the explosive noise as the child was killed just feet away from his face ...

It has been recommended that you take extended leave, the deputy chief constable had told him as they had sat together in the Scottish Crime Campus out at Gartcosh. There had been a look in the man's eye that brooked no discussion but by then Lorimer had almost welcomed the thought of turning his back on the job that had led him into that house.

The briefing meeting in the days that had followed was a mere blur now, the trauma risk assessor talking quietly, gathering the facts about the incident, the forms to fill in a necessary reminder of why he was off on the sick.

He closed his eyes but it was no use. The scene of carnage returned, the sounds of the child's cries louder than ever, as if begging him to save her from the madness of her distraught father. Night after night he had woken to the scream that was his own voice and the arms that had enfolded his shaking, sweat-drenched body, Maggie soothing him like the child she had never held.

He'd been lucky, they had told him, those serious-faced colleagues who had taken him out from that place. Blackburn could easily have blown him away before turning the gun on himself.

Lucky was the last thing the detective superintendent felt right now, a groan escaping his dry lips. His body felt heavy, his head aching as though he were coming down with a virus. *Lethargy. Inertia*, he'd tried to explain to the doctor when she had asked him to describe how he felt. It was as if he had been whacked senseless by these intangible forces, words that had hitherto been absent from the vocabulary of who he was. The woman had nodded her understanding. It was normal to feel like that, she'd told him. It would pass, given time and treatment, she'd promised.

He closed his eyes then opened them again, terrified that the images would return if he allowed himself to fall asleep.

The familiar *hrrrum* then a thump on the duvet signalled Chancer's arrival. Lorimer put out a grateful hand, feeling the cat's soft fur under his fingers, reverberating purrs a reward for caressing his ears, tickling that special place under his chin. He leaned back, his body relaxing for a moment as the world was filled with softness, the pillow behind his head cool against his damp hair. It was fanciful to imagine that the animal could sense his anxiety and had come to offer comfort; Chancer was simply taking advantage of a warm body to snuggle into, that was all. The big orange cat would turn around and around until he was comfortable then lick his fur and settle down with a sigh to sleep. It was a routine that had become established ever since Lorimer had been at home, the cat happily accepting the change to their domestic arrangements.

Lorimer yawned, acknowledging the drowsiness that was making him sink back into the comfort of his warm bed, resigned to the sleep that drew him down once more.

It had been a quiet New Year's Eve to begin with. The city streets were crammed with shoppers bagging their final December bargains, the post-Christmas retail frenzy at its height, women of all ages desperate to find the perfect outfit to wear on this special night of the year. Later, of course, the police would have the usual drunks to contend with and the violence that too often followed. That was only to be expected in this city where an inflammatory remark about a rival football team could result in a knife between the ribs. By the time the bells had heralded the new year, the officers who were on duty would be looking at the declining spaces in their cells, wondering what to do when yet more offenders were brought in off the streets.

Detective Superintendent William Lorimer did not expect to be part of this, however. His day was meant to end mid afternoon when he would meet Maggie at her favourite coffee bar over in the West End where they would enjoy a relaxing hour or so before heading home. He had been congratulating himself on managing to finish a pile of paperwork that had been bothering him for weeks; the sense of satisfaction at having completed this task on 31 December had made the detective arrange the stack of papers neatly together then lean back with a sigh, a smile playing about his mouth. A glance at the clock on the wall opposite his desk reassured him that there were less than two hours before he could make good his escape and join his schoolteacher wife. They had enjoyed a couple of days with each other over Christmas but the New Year's break would see them together right up until Maggie had to return to work.

The smile on his face faded with the peremptory ring of the telephone.

'Lorimer,' he answered at once, his brows darkening as he listened. 'On my way,' he said shortly, gathering up his jacket and heading out of the office.

The haste of his passing caused the top sheets of paper to rise in a sudden draught, spilling across the detective's desk and landing upon the floor where they would lie in disarray until other hands came to pick them up.

Down at ground level the detective superintendent was handed the body armour, a bulky Kevlar vest that he strapped on as soon as he was inside the police van. Uniformed officers who were trained for this sort of incident sat in two rows behind him, weapons by their sides, all faces solemn, no words spoken amongst them.

Intelligence had it that gunshots had been heard coming from a family home, the gunman identified by neighbours as Thomas

Blackburn, the father of a young family of three kids. The houses on either side of the Blackburns' terraced house had already been evacuated and the area cordoned off to await this armed response unit.

A serious look from the chief firearms officer was all that was required for Lorimer to understand the gravity of the situation that lay ahead of them all. It would not be the first time that Lorimer had been asked to confront a gunman and perhaps his reputation for keeping a cool head in dangerous situations was the reason he was here now, sitting beside the driver as the van lurched around the city streets towards its destination.

The road had been deserted as they had arrived, armed officers spilling out and ranging themselves around the property at various vantage points. None of them wanted to end the year having taken aim and fired at another human being; each and every one would be pinning their hopes on the man who strode towards the front door and pushed it open, disappearing inside. All eyes were trained on the windows above, from where the sounds of gunfire had come.

Lorimer had called up the stairs first. 'Thomas! Are you there? This is Detective Superintendent Lorimer speaking.' His voice had fallen woodenly in the confined space but he had the sensation that someone was listening.

'Thomas, I'm coming up the stairs now,' he called out, then, grasping the handrail, he stepped carefully up, hearing the creak of the wood under the worn carpet. There had been only time to ascertain the layout of the house: two bedrooms upstairs with a small bathroom facing the top of the stairs, the living room nearest to the front door, access via the kitchen from the back door that led to a garden. Lorimer stood two steps below the landing, the bathroom door slightly ajar in front of him. Was the gunman there? Watching and waiting?

11

'Thomas, it's time to come out. There's no place to hide any more,' Lorimer said, his voice deliberately sympathetic as if he could relate to how this crazed man was feeling.

The silence was broken by the sound of a child whimpering. Lorimer took the last steps to the landing, turning his head to the left to see the bedroom door ajar, the body lying where it had fallen.

There was no movement from the woman who was face down on the carpet, a red stain pooling from a wound around her head. Lorimer glanced at the dark hair shiny with blood. Whoever she was, he knew that this woman would never see another new year again.

A quick glance behind him gave Lorimer time to read the names on the other bedroom door: *Brian*, *Michael* and *Lauren*, plastic nameplates that had been stuck one above the other, the girl's name the lowest of the three. That door too was partly open and Lorimer took three quick paces towards it, pushing it open with his gloved hand.

The boys were lying across the bed, the arms of their bloodied corpses spread out as if in supplication to the rescuers who had come too late to save them. Lorimer turned away, sick at the sight of these two wee boys, their lives cut so short. *By their own father?*

His feet retraced their path to the other room where the cries of the little girl were growing louder.

It was either an act of complete bravery or utter stupidity to push open that door.

Thomas Blackburn stood with his back to a cupboard, one hand encircling his baby daughter's shoulders, the other holding a gun to her head. For a brief moment the two men stared at one another. Blackburn's eyes were frantic as he gazed at Lorimer.

Crazed with drink? Appalled at what he had already done? Or simply astonished to see the audacity of the tall man who had entered the room?

'Put down the gun, Thomas.'

CHAPTER THREE

Charles Graham stepped into the street and smiled. He had listened to Gallagher's proposal carefully, frowning occasionally to hide the rising excitement that threatened to show in his face. It would have come sooner or later, he'd told himself. Jack Gallagher wasn't the kind to give with one hand and forget to take back with the other. Give him his due, Gallagher had handed over the faked paperwork without question, for a considerable sum it was true, but that was to be expected from the man at the top of Glasgow's drug hierarchy. The old woman was becoming a liability, the big man had told him. And could Mr Graham see his way to doing something to help him out? His smile widened. Mr Graham certainly could. They'd shaken hands on it, two businessmen who had reached an understanding of one another's value.

Supply and demand, that was the mantra that had been dinned into him by his economist stepfather from an early age. *There will always be a need for doctors*, his mother had agreed and so the years of grinding study had begun as soon as her only child was at secondary school. These had been painful years, his poor reports resulting in rows at home then long hours of private tuition that had allowed the boy to gain sufficient passes to study medicine at university. *A sacrifice*, he'd been constantly reminded, the money poured into his education bleeding out of the household, denying him things that other children took for granted: a new bicycle at Christmas, school trips abroad, fresh uniforms each new session instead of the ill-fitting trousers (that had to last) constantly shaming him.

His grin twisted as he crossed the city street. Not all of those years had been wasted, though, had they? The student who had been kicked out of his medical course after failing everything in his first year was now a success if his bank account were anything to go by. That was how everyone measured success nowadays. It didn't matter a toss if you had a string of letters after your name so long as you had the trappings of wealth, he told himself, thinking of the spacious modern apartment that he now owned outright. No mortgage, no money worries.

His grin widened. Aye, the old man had taught him about supply and demand all right. He had found a way to supply those folk who wanted to ease their suffering relatives into the next world. He chuckled as he tried to imagine what his mother and stepfather would say if they'd still been alive to see the way his life had turned out.

Because, as his visit to Gallagher had proved, the demand for putting people to sleep just got bigger all the time.

Gallagher swung on his high-backed chair, rereading the latest letter. Stupid bitch, he thought to himself, fingers ready to crush the papers into a ball. She'd threatened to go to the papers; *kiss and tell*, she'd written, as though he had been in a clandestine relationship with the old biddy; the very thought of it made Gallagher feel sick. But Ellen Blackburn's threats were dangerous and her removal would not come a moment too soon. Getting rid of the old bag should have been easy enough but Gallagher had needed something that looked more natural than a bullet in the middle of her forehead. Her son, Thomas, had been useful in that regard, a hired thug who never flinched when it came to brute violence. Gallagher sighed. Nobody would have been surprised when he took a gun to the wife but to kill all three of the weans ... that was bad even by his own standards. It was little wonder that the auld yin had gone off the rails a bit but to come crawling back again and again to Blackburn's boss as if it was somehow his fault that the family had been blown away ... ach, it was a pain in the tonsils.

Jack Gallagher looked again at the note in his hand, the badly spelled letter threatening to go to the papers unless more cash was put into her hands. On a regular basis. Who the hell did she think she was?

There were other ways to deal with a nuisance like this, he told himself. Nothing that would leave a mark on her ageing body, of course: he wasn't that daft. A small trace of a smile tugged at the corners of his mouth as Gallagher looked at the file on his desk. Charles Graham was an unlikely executioner but the services he had outlined at their meeting had impressed Gallagher. He'd even dropped a hint to the effect that he wasn't above carrying them out himself. He liked the way that Graham had set out the scheme, evading the law and keeping his identity a secret. Gallagher had already guessed that Charles Graham was not his real name. After all, hadn't he provided some fake papers for him in other names? Besides, the young man didn't look like a Charles, far less a Charlie, but he doubted if he would ever discover the man's true identity.

His smile broadened as he thought once again of the idea they had discussed, its simplicity very pleasing.

It would serve two useful purposes: to test Graham's resolve and to shut the old woman up for good.

He clutched the letter and squeezed it into a ball then tossed it towards the waste-paper basket. It hit the rim and fell noise-lessly onto the carpet. Gallagher frowned then pursed his lips. He wouldn't miss her and hit the wall, that was for sure. And the beauty of it all was that she'd never see it coming.

The man stared out across the city, wondering if there were other ways to stem the tide of interest into his business affairs. Perhaps it was time to put a little pressure on another man who had become his ally.

CHAPTER FOUR

January had heralded the usual spell of wet and blustery weather, sudden gales dislodging slates from countless roofs, blowing down trees across roads and railway tracks, keeping ships in harbour while the seas boiled with an angry rage against these island shores. William Lorimer had become aware of every change in the temperature, his frequent glances into the grey skies confirming what the weather girl on the screen of his television had predicted. He hadn't become addicted to the TV soaps, as Maggie had hinted with a forced smile. Nor had he watched the more serious programmes, like the reruns of all the David Attenborough nature documentaries. Other people's fictional daily dramas failed to capture his interest and he baulked at seeing yet another cheetah or lion tear its prey to bits across a dry and arid landscape. Instead he sat flicking from one channel to another, sometimes keeping his gaze fixed to a game of rugby or football but mostly absorbing the items of news across the globe, filling his mind with images of folk far worse off than himself: the immigrants who had left their homes behind and travelled with nothing but that final shred of hope in their tired eyes; the streets of foreign cities bombed to bits, smoke rising from unnamed buildings where bodies of the dead were no doubt concealed; and then the relief as a smiling man or woman stood by a map explaining what was really happening in his own little part of the world and what sort of weather the viewer might expect.

He had tried to explain this to the woman from TRIM, the trauma risk management assessor, who had given him a sympathetic smile as she had nodded. 'Your own world has been turned upside down,' she'd explained. 'It's little wonder that you have a desire to cling to something that is predictable, like a meteorological report.'

He didn't tell her how he sat in the armchair staring at the screen for hours on end, unshaven, too weary to be bothered getting dressed, the dressing gown that Maggie had bought him for Christmas now grubby and stained.

Today was the same as every other day since Detective Superintendent Lorimer had been sent home on sick leave from his job in Glasgow. He had slept fitfully, waking several times with those dreadful images as strong as ever, his body crying out for sleep. Then, as daylight filtered through the curtains he had woken at last, groggy from the medication that was meant to give him some hours of rest: Maggie already gone, the school day begun.

The mug of tea slopped over onto the tray, making a liquid beige puddle as he staggered towards his armchair. He glanced at it in a moment of self-disgust then sighed, slumping down and reaching for the remote control. Between bites of toast and marmalade he flicked from one channel to another until a newscaster appeared on the screen, the view of Westminster behind him. Lorimer tuned out the discussion between the TV journalist and the politician, gazing instead at the skies above the river Thames, marvelling at the sun shining through a cloudless blue.

Outside his own sitting room on the south side of Glasgow the rain beat down relentlessly, battering the glass of the window as if demanding to be let in. He hadn't seen so much as a shred of blue sky in weeks, *not even enough to mend a sailor's trousers*, as his granny used to say. The memory of her voice made him smile for a fleeting moment. Then it was gone, like all his family had gone. His father when he'd been a boy, his mum, suddenly, during his final year at high school then all of those little babies . . .

Why, why why? he'd cried out so often in anguish.

It was a question that Dr Rosie Fergusson had partly answered once the post-mortems on all five family members had been carried out, DNA tests taken. *The little girl wasn't Blackburn's*, she'd told Lorimer. *Maybe that was a reason for tipping him over the edge?* A jealous husband, a wife who'd cheated and (as the neighbours told police officers afterwards) had been about to walk out on him and take the kids. It was such a sad, familiar story, but one that gave Lorimer no relief.

He felt the tears begin to fill his eyes and brushed them away with an impatient hand. Self-pity was not part of who he was. Or at any rate, it had not been part of the man he used to be. Nowadays the slightest thing could make him well up, a rush of emotion making him shake and sweat as though a fever had entered his bones. *It will pass*, the doctor had reassured him. *It just takes time.* And he had clung to these words, memories of himself as he had once been flickering across his mind like the images on his TV screen. One day soon he would be the commanding, purposeful person that he had always been, the doctor had promised. Yet, as he sat huddled into the armchair, eyes fixed on the television, Lorimer began to doubt that he would ever be fit to resume his work again.

*

The waiting room struck him as a cold place to be, blue chairs in rows of four, like airport seating, some back to back, their wipe-clean surfaces like the vinyl flooring, sterile and cheerless. No human mess would be allowed to remain on these shiny surfaces, any trace of bodily fluids removed swiftly before the next lot of patients could sit down.

He put a hand to his face, remembering. The moment when the blood and matter hit his skin, just below his eyes, dripping down. His hands had been scarlet with bloodstains as he'd lifted them up, his clothes damp when they'd hauled him off that floor.

He looked at his watch and frowned. His appointment was already twenty minutes late and Lorimer wondered what sorts of illnesses had kept his GP back this afternoon.

His eyes were drawn to them first because of their chatter, two small children playing around their mother's feet. One of them seemed quite absorbed by the leaflets he had picked up from a nearby table and was looking at them solemnly, though he was far too young to be able to read any of the words. The other little boy was concentrating hard on threading a row of wooden balls along a series of twisted wires, his face utterly focused on the task.

Despite himself, Lorimer found that he was smiling at the pair of them, their innocence immediately banishing his darker thoughts. What sort of father would he have made?

The boy with the leaflets let some of them fall onto the floor.

'Oh-oh,' he exclaimed. Then, slowly and carefully, the child began to pick them up one by one, laying them back in a neat pile, not in the least fazed by his laborious task.

Lorimer watched him, fascinated. Was this the sort of deter-mined patience that *he* needed? Was this what the doctors were trying to help him to do? See the pieces of his life scattered around him and enable the detective to pick them up again?

21

'William Lorimer.' The doctor was suddenly in her doorway and Lorimer stood up, the children behind him forgotten as he made his way into the surgery once more.

Maggie Lorimer closed the car door with a sigh. Coming home was not her favourite time of day any more. Seeing her dishevelled husband sprawled in front of the television, dirty mugs strewn around the floor, was becoming hard to take. That appointment on Monday up at Auchterarder couldn't come a moment too soon. The facility was said to be first class, officers who had come a cropper one way or another benefiting from different types of intensive therapy. And, she realised with a rush of shame, she'd welcome a few days all on her own.

She had thought nothing could have been worse than the case from last year when her own cousin, David, had been one of the victims of Quiet Release, that end-of-life scam. But in some ways this was harder to endure.

He was sitting in front of the television, all right, but dressed in clean jeans and a warm sweater, only one mug left on the carpet by his side. Maybe things had begun to improve? Maggie pulled off her scarf and coat.

'I'm home,' she called, forcing a note of cheerfulness into her voice, and walked through to where her husband was sitting.

'Missed you,' he murmured, getting up and enfolding her in his arms. 'It's been a long day. Waited ages at the surgery to see the doctor.'

Maggie gave a sigh as she let herself be clasped to his chest. It had been a long day for her, too, with a departmental meeting that had become acrimonious, the newest member of staff in the English department at school a rather loud-mouthed woman who seemed to object to everything that was proposed for the forthcoming diet of exams. Once, Maggie would have poured out all her tales of woe about what was happening at Muirpark Secondary School and he'd have listened, offering an opinion or a humorous remark to defuse her tension. But now Maggie Lorimer bit her lip, telling herself that her husband had so many things on his own mind it was unfair to burden him with her troubles.

'Didn't you manage to sleep ...?' The question was out, sounding like an accusation before she could stop herself.

The long sigh and shake of his head was all the answer that Maggie was going to get. He'd taken the prescribed medication at the beginning, in expectation that a return to work would quickly follow, that these nightmares would suddenly end. But of course they hadn't and the sickness, the retching each morning, made everything worse instead.

She'd tried to ask him about it. Just once. But after listening to how he felt as his face had been spattered with warm blood and the bits of human wreckage, Maggie saw that such questions only made him flinch so hadn't asked again. Some nights when he woke screaming she could see her husband's hands scrabbling at his skin as if the blood and flesh of the Blackburn man and the baby girl were still clinging to him. It didn't help that Maggie was teaching *Macbeth* to her fifth-year class, the image of the haunted woman that was Lady Macbeth unable to cleanse herself from guilt blood constantly returning to her mind.

But her husband had done nothing to feel guilty about. He'd been brave, was going to receive a commendation for his efforts to stop that crazed gunman. Who could have done any more?

So Maggie forced a smile and patted his arm. 'Cuppa?' she asked, already walking away from him towards the kitchen.

CHAPTER FIVE

Water dripped sullenly down the tenement walls onto the cracked, weed-infested ground and the shape below. In the darkness it looked like a heap of rubbish discarded by folk in a hurry to leave, a mound of unwanted bedding perhaps, left to rot beside the other detritus that clogged the narrow pathway. But to his practised eyes it was the very thing he had been seeking.

A swift foot to the rounded shape produced a squeal of protest and a guttural oath.

'Hush,' he said, bending down and prodding the man's arm with one gloved hand. 'Don't make such a fuss.'

'What is it you want?' The words came out like a groan.

'Ha!' He pulled on the man's coat collar, forcing him to his knees. 'I know what *you* want.' He gave a mirthless laugh.

A pair of eyes looked at him out of the gloom of the night, desperate eyes hollowed with an endless yearning.

'Want to feel better?' he asked softly, knowing as he spoke what effect his words would have. Like a conjurer, his fingers dipped into the darkness then suddenly reappeared holding a small object aloft.

The eyes never left the small packet, the damp head nodding even as the drug addict's arms scrabbled his filthy quilt around his body once more.

'Well, get up and come with me. I've got everything you need.'

The man on the ground lifted up a bare arm, a flag of surrender, letting himself be pulled to his feet.

'Nice and easy,' his captor said, one arm slung around the addict's back, guiding him towards the mouth of the alley. 'Don't want anyone to hear us, do we?'

The sodium glow from the street lamps was blurred, thick fog making it impossible to see anything but the wet pavement beneath their feet. Nobody would mark their passing. And nobody would miss another homeless man on the city streets.

It was too easy.

Supply and demand. He could supply what this derelict creature longed for. And all he demanded in return was his soul.

CHAPTER SIX

Castlebrae appeared like any other large country house hotel from the outside, the grey stone and grey drive softened by evergreen shrubs and trees, lawns stretching out of sight. Perhaps in the summer months there would be beds of flowers but now, on this February morning, the facility appeared rather daunting; its black door within a pointed archway shut fast, no daylight yet reflected on its many windows. Lorimer had heard good things about the centre, however. Every year thousands of officers made their weary way to Auchterarder, a pretty town in the Perthshire countryside, seeking recovery from their injuries.

And yet, as he pulled into the car park in this murky winter light, William Lorimer felt that he really shouldn't be here at all. This was a police treatment centre for officers injured, usually in the line of duty. Not for folk like him. His hand hovered over the button that would kill the engine of the big car. Should he stay or should he take off down the drive again? Still, what was waiting for him back home? Night after night of seeing the same images, feeling the spatter of warm human debris across his face, hearing those gunshots reverberating in his brain. His second

TRIM assessment had not shown any improvement from the initial visit at the beginning of January and so here he was, with the last option open to him.

With a sigh of resignation his fingers reached out and the murmuring sound of the Lexus was silenced. A quick look outside told him that it was a bitterly cold day. Leaves that had fallen months ago swirled around the car park, the wind sweeping them up against a heavy sky that promised snow. Lorimer shivered despite the warm Shetland sweater that Maggie had urged him to wear. As he pulled open the door he could hear the rustle in a nearby beech hedge and feel the cold against his face as if nature were warning him to make haste and head indoors.

He pulled on his navy blue overcoat, then, gathering up his bag, turned towards the main entrance, head down against a sudden gust of wind. The Lexus blinked once as Lorimer pointed his key fob towards it. When would he make the return journey for good? he thought with a pang, suddenly regretting the days ahead when he would be forced to lie down in a lonely, impersonal bed away from his Maggie. Would two weeks here really be enough to banish these horrors inside his head?

A voice answered the ring of the doorbell and Lorimer pushed open the security door and entered a small porch opposite a stained-glass inner door.

The door closed behind him with a bang as the wind caught it and Lorimer found himself in a brightly lit hallway with a curved reception desk to one side. It fulfilled his initial expectations: this was just a hotel by any other name so far.

'William Lorimer?' A woman behind the desk rose to her feet and smiled, coming around with outstretched hand. 'Welcome to Castlebrae.'

Lorimer took the proffered hand. It was warm, like the woman's smile.

'May I ask you please to sign in?' She beamed again, handing him a sheet of paper with the centre's logo at the top. 'And I need you to make an appointment with the nurse.'

His raised eyebrows brought a swift response.

'It's customary procedure to have an initial assessment,' she assured him, 'then your programme for therapies and down time can be worked out for the duration of your stay here.' Her eyes left him for a moment and Lorimer turned to see an older man approach. The fellow immediately picked up his bag and motioned Lorimer towards a wide staircase.

'Welcome to Castlebrae,' he said, echoing the friendly receptionist. 'I'm Jimmy Rae. Anything you need during your stay with us, just come to me and ask. Even if it's just for a wee blether,' he added.

Lorimer stared, unsure how to respond. Who exactly was this person who now strode ahead of him? Mid fifties, maybe older, he mused, assessing the man. An ex-cop? A doctor of some sort? Or was he just assisting the woman behind the desk? For once Lorimer's powers of detection failed him as he puzzled over the question. For an older man he was certainly fit, not stopping to take a breath at the half-landing, where a patterned-glass window provided a barrier against the gloom outside.

'Here you are,' Jimmy said, leading him through an archway and into a bright, spacious room. 'Room twelve. Nice westerly view of the hills.' He placed Lorimer's bag on the luggage stand and looked at the tall detective. 'I hope you'll be comfortable here. Just ask if there is anything you need, anything at all. Now,' he fished in his jacket pocket and brought out a sheet of paper, 'here's all the details you need for your stay. There's a plan of all the facilities and a list of mealtimes plus, of course, your weekly planner.' He peered at the sheet of paper in his hand. 'Your appointments with the therapists and counsellor are all in the morning. It'll be up to you to fill in whatever classes you want to take in the afternoons. You're back home at the weekend. Everybody leaves fairly sharp on Friday afternoon,' he said. 'Though we like you to be back in good time the following Monday to pick up with your programme.'

'Okay.' Lorimer agreed. He'd signed up for two weeks and he wasn't one to dodge commitments. Besides, this might be his final chance to find the healing he so desperately sought.

'The phone is for your own use or to contact any of us at any time,' Jimmy continued, looking at Lorimer with an understanding smile. 'And that includes the wee small hours,' he said firmly. 'The staff here are on duty twenty-four seven.' His smile widened and he gave a chuckle. 'Just like any police force in the country.'

Then, giving Lorimer a pat on his arm, Jimmy turned away. 'I'll leave you to settle in,' he said. 'Coffee- and tea-making are here in your room but there is always a cuppa being served in the residents' lounge.' Then Rae gave a glance at his watch. 'Do you want to come down now to see the nurse or would you rather have a rest first?'

'Make it a little later if that's okay.'

Rae looked down and and scribbled a time on the sheet of paper then handed it back to Lorimer.

'Eleven o'clock?'

Lorimer gave a wintry smile, looking at the appointment scheduled on his personal timetable. 'Aye, fine, thanks.'

Then he was gone, leaving Lorimer alone in the room. It was pleasant enough, he told himself as he took off his coat, trying to lose the feeling of despondency that threatened to descend. A white-covered double bed, a two-seater sofa, and a television. With the pale oak wardrobe and matching chest of drawers, full-length curtains in shades of apricot and sunrise red, it was a room that felt warm and welcoming. Probably designed to be that way, his cynical inner voice suggested. He pushed open a door to reveal the en suite bathroom complete with bath and overhead shower, tiles gleaming, paintwork pristine white.

He would sleep (or try to at any rate) nearer to the windows where he could indeed see the faint outline of distant hills presently obscured by the low dark clouds. Shades of green from the lawns melted into the variety of conifers and leafless oaks marching into the distance. He felt a sudden prick behind his eyelids, gratitude towards whoever had selected room twelve for their newest patient.

Lorimer lay down and closed his eyes, a familiar weariness making him long to sink into the oblivion of sleep. He kicked off his shoes and turned onto his side, tugging the duvet so that he could slide under its soft downy folds. Visions of the road he had travelled came back to him, the sound of traffic still a murmur in his ears. He pulled the cover over his face, blotting out the emerging daylight. Just a wee lie down, he promised himself . . . then, as though the leaden clouds outside were enfolding the man in their shadows, his eyes closed and sleep took him at last.

Jimmy Rae had seen miracles happening in this place: men and women who had been wheeled through these doors had walked out with a spring in their step and a smile of wonder on their faces. It was his job to return these broken police officers to their duties and he had had many years of satisfaction in being able to do just that. Officers whose bodies had been damaged in car crashes or who had been injured by an assailant in the line of duty had come here to find the sort of treatment they needed. Sometimes it took many months for an officer to regain his or her mobility but the therapists were a dedicated lot who never gave up on a single patient. And there was that other sort of brokenness that Jimmy saw; the spirit of an officer, who had witnessed more than a human being should ever see, plunged into the depths of despair, rendering them unfit for the job. Post-traumatic stress disorder was a factor commonly enough known about in the armed forces but the police service also saw its fair share of victims.

Superintendent Lorimer was not unique in suffering from the ghastly things he had seen in the course of his job, though he would be treated here at Castlebrae as if he were a special case. Because that was how each and every single officer was regarded. Jimmy had taken in the thin, pale face, the cold fingers clasping his own, the haunted blue eyes darting around the reception area as if looking for a way to escape. And he felt the rush of compassion that came with every new patient who entered the big house.

Lorimer rubbed his chin as he sat up, blinking. It took just a second to remember where he was, the room around him unfamiliar. Outside, the day was still dull and grey. A quick look at his watch told him that he had less than ten minutes before the appointment with the nurse that was to take place downstairs. He slipped into the bathroom and splashed water on his face, towelling it vigorously, then padded out to find his luggage still unpacked lying by the side of the bed. *Wear comfortable clothes, preferably sports gear*, the letter had informed him and he quickly rummaged in the bag by his side, slipping on tracksuit bottoms and an old rugby shirt then pulling on his ancient trainers.

This is it, Lorimer told himself, his jaw clenched as he closed the door behind him. This is where it all begins.

The male nurse was a friendly type, his Glasgow accent immediately putting Lorimer at ease. His interview mostly meant running through questions about his general health and fitness followed by the sort of routine examination he'd come to expect. *No problem with blood pressure*, the man had remarked as if that was something Lorimer ought to be proud of. Yet it served simply to reinforce the feeling that he was a fake, a phoney, someone who was taking up precious space here in this splendid building.

'You're not alone in requiring treatment for a non-physical injury,' he told Lorimer, his eyes crinkling at the corners as if he found this to be a source of some amusement. 'We regularly have crash victims here.'

'Crash victims?'

'Och, that's what I call them. It's not unusual for road traffic cops to find themselves suffering from traumas.'

'I'm not a traffic cop ...'

The nurse smiled. 'Aye, I know. But you've had a different sort of crash, haven't you?'

Lorimer didn't answer. What words could he have used to describe the night terrors and subsequent weakness he had endured?

'Lack of sleep?' the nurse hazarded.

'Yes,' he sighed.

'General feelings of being run-down and listless?'

'That too,' Lorimer admitted.

There was a pause then the nurse drew his chair a tiny bit closer as though he wished Lorimer to confide in him.

'Any notions of doing away with yourself?'

'What? Are you serious?' Lorimer sat back, shocked by the question.

'We have to ask to see if you present any risk to yourself.' He shrugged. 'Our aim is to make you fit to return to active duty. And that includes finding out what goes on in here.' He tapped the side of his head and gave Lorimer a grin.

'I've ... I've not had any thoughts like that,' he began, biting his lip and shifting uneasily in his chair.

'It's no crime if you have,' the man answered. 'But we just need to know so we can take best care of you while you're here.' He eyed Lorimer with a look that bordered on sympathy. 'Lots of folk come here with the idea that their career in the force is all washed up, that they're no use any more. It can lead them to rather depressive ideas, know what I'm saying?'

Lorimer nodded slowly. It was a bit of a revelation to find that his was far from being a unique situation. And he listened carefully as the younger man went through the programme that he would be following, a programme that included complementary therapies and relaxation workshops as well as t'ai chi sessions.

'Oh, and you'll be seeing the patient adviser at least once each week, beginning tomorrow. Here's the plan for your stay,' he added, handing Lorimer two pages with several slots already blocked off. 'Afternoons are for your own recreation but we hope you'll make use of the gym and the pool.'

Lorimer took the sheets, adding them to the file he had brought from his room.

'Did Jimmy mention the welcome meeting? It's at five o'clock and you'll be expected to attend with all the other newcomers.'

*

Lorimer slipped back upstairs to room twelve afterwards, deciding that was where he would spend time before lunch. Outside, the clouds had cleared away and a weak band of sunlight filtered across the horizon, a lemon wash of colour against the misty grey hills. What he would give to be out there again, boots on and a pack upon his back! He turned away, gnawing at a ragged fingernail, the familiar sense of lethargy dulling his senses. He'd been a fit man before all of this ... would he ever find the strength to climb another hill?

The morning's activities seemed to have stripped him of every last bit of energy that he possessed and yet the room seemed suddenly confining so that he decided to take a walk around the centre to familiarise himself with its layout instead of his plan to linger here on his own, away from the other officers.

It was, he'd tell Maggie later, a state-of-the-art place to receive treatment. The new swimming pool and gym facilities were better than anything he'd ever come across and it was a humbling thought that each and every officer who paid a small amount every month out of their salary was entitled to this experience.

As he passed by the reception desk on his way to the dining room, Lorimer noticed that there were people arriving all the time, a week's luggage placed by their feet as they signed in. He looked up as another patient entered, a woman on her own pushing herself in a wheelchair, her streaky blonde hair messed up by the wind, pale cheeks temporarily pink from the exertion of making it along from the car park. What was her story? he wondered, trying not to stare.

The lunch he selected consisted of a very nice pumpkin and orange soup and a spicy chicken wrap. Lorimer was surprised by how hungry he was as he sat down at an empty table.

Here and there men and women of all ages were gathered but it was obvious who were the newcomers and who had been at the centre for some time by the way little groups were formed. He wasn't ready to make polite conversation with strangers, he told himself. Not yet. Happily no one came to sit beside the tall brooding stranger and he was able to wander back upstairs, his feet leading him to room twelve as though by instinct.

A sigh of relief escaped him as he closed the door and leaned against it. Well, he was here now and he ought to make the best of it. Should he fish out his swimming stuff and head back downstairs to that enormous pool? For a moment he was tempted by the idea of sinking under the greenish water. But the moment passed as he yawned and sat back down on the bed, pulling the duvet across his body. Just a little rest, he told himself. A few minutes' shut-eye, that was all ...

He woke with a jerk and sat up, suddenly aware of the darkness outside. What the hell was the time? Blinking stupidly, Lorimer saw that the digital clock read four fifty-five. He must have slept for hours ... The thought amazed him, then, in a rush, he staggered to his feet. He had to be out of here now or he'd miss that welcome meeting. And there was no way he wanted to be the conspicuous latecomer.

In minutes he was hurrying down the main staircase and following other new patients along the corridor that led to the conference room.

The meeting consisted of the presentation of a short video and a welcome talk by Jimmy Rae, who, they learned, was the person in overall charge of Castlebrae. During the video, Lorimer glanced at the other officers seated close by him; men and women dressed casually in sweatshirts and jeans for the most part, no obvious signs of their injuries apart from the ones whose hands grasped arm crutches. And the blonde in the wheelchair, her hair now tidily drawn back in a clasp. Some of them asked questions afterwards, practical things for the most part, *Where's the nearest pub?* bringing a wave of laughter from the other new arrivals.

'Okay, folks, that should give you some sort of overview of what goes on here,' Rae told them before handing over to the fitness supervisor who went over fire safety and the house rules (no booze in the centre, he told them with a grin, but they could go down the village pub so long as they were all back by midnight).

There was a new sense of camaraderie as they allowed Jimmy Rae to shepherd his new arrivals into the dining room, sitting where he directed them in a manner that Lorimer found intriguing. Jimmy had evidently thought out a seating plan for these men and women and Lorimer was suddenly interested to see who would be next to him, since his own place was near the end of a table.

'Hi, I'm Karen,' the blonde woman said, as she wheeled herself to the place next to his, her voice betraying her Irish accent.

'Lorimer,' he replied.

'That your first name?' she asked, head to one side, intelligent grey eyes regarding him thoughtfully.

'No, that's William. Or Bill,' he offered reluctantly. 'But most folk just call me Lorimer.'

'The Old Bill,' Karen laughed. 'Isn't that what they call us down south?' She gave him a hesitant smile. 'William's a good name, though, so long as you don't shorten it to Billy in certain places where I come from.'

Lorimer returned her smile then picked up a water jug and filled their glasses.

'We get to pick our meals for tomorrow,' Karen reminded him. 'Wonder what we'll be having just now? I'm hungry after all that exercise. Did you find that pool? Wicked, isn't it?'

The meal passed slowly, Lorimer's appetite deserting him as the woman chatted about her injuries and the road traffic accident that had eventually brought her here. His own reason for being at Castlebrae was not something he wanted to share, he decided, feeling distinctly uncomfortable. Karen was the sort of officer who deserved to be here at Castlebrae, whereas the old feeling of being an imposter came over him once again. Couldn't he just have gritted his teeth, picked himself up and got on with the job?

It was a relief when dinner was over and he could escape back to the sanctuary of his room, leaving Karen to chat to one of the other women who were heading into the lounge for coffee.

His room was blessedly quiet after the buzz of voices in the dining room. Lorimer let out a sigh. Was this how it was going to be? Making the necessary small talk then coming back to lick his wounds? What a coward he was! He bit his lip, aware of the silence that was now more oppressive than comforting. A silence he knew could easily be banished by joining other people downstairs.

But it was the comfort of disembodied voices that he needed, not the demands of social interaction, so he reached out and grasped the TV console. He leaned back onto the rumpled pillows, glad of the colours and light streaming from the screen. The digital clock beneath the television displayed 18.45 in red numerals. He'd watch the last of the local news programme then give Maggie a ring, Lorimer decided.

He wasn't really listening, didn't hear the words of the golden-haired reporter who stood outside the hospital ward, but he did sit up a little straighter as he saw the uniforms of the nurses passing by and the porter who was wheeling a patient in the background.

For one split second the man appeared on his screen, giving a glance towards the camera. Then he was gone.

Lorimer blinked, the remote control suddenly in his hand. *It couldn't be*, he told himself. It wasn't possible. He was imagining things. The voice inside his head scoffed at the very idea.

For a moment he sat staring, thinking hard. Once the programme was over he could capture it again on replay. Then he would see if the man who had turned his head towards the television cameras was indeed the elusive person that the police had sought in a case that had ended with so many people dead and damaged.

One look at the remote told him a different story. This wasn't his own television set. There was no facility to replay the programme.

A sudden panic filled his chest and he stood up, cursing himself for being in this place.

Maggie. He had to call Maggie.

Hasty fingers sought his iPhone and he waited impatiently as the number rang out.

'Hello?'

'It's me.'

'What's wrong?' Maggie replied suddenly, picking up on his tone.

'Something happened,' he began, wishing that he were standing with her, breathing into her hair.

'What?'

'Something I saw on television. On the news, actually.'

'Uh-huh?' Maggie asked, her tone wary.

'The man we never caught,' Lorimer said quickly. 'The one we suspected was behind Quiet Release. I saw him on the television. Maggie, you've got to record it for me. Replay the six o'clock news. Please. It's important!'

'Of course, darling,' she said heavily.

'Sorry, but I must go. Just in case they replay that bit . . .'

Maggie tried hard not to weep as she put down the telephone. She'd do as he asked but it would be a pointless exercise, just one more demon attacking his poor brain. *And yours*, a little voice added.

The gloom outside seemed to have seeped into the house and Maggie moved towards the window, drawing the heavy winter curtains against the night. But no amount of effort could keep the black thoughts from invading her mind, thoughts that had been brought back with her husband's call. She'd hoped to forget it in time, that case from last year when many vulnerable patients, including her own sick cousin David, had been targeted by an illegal organisation that had sought payment from relatives in return for ending those patients' lives. It had concluded with several arrests but the mysterious man behind it all had never been found. The police investigation had come far too close to home and even now David's brother, Patrick, was awaiting trial for assaulting his wife, the woman who had paid a substantial sum in order for David to be given a fatal dose of morphine. At least poor Patrick had been given bail and was still able to run the family farm, a place that Maggie had loved in her childhood.

Now here was Bill imagining that he had seen this elusive

killer! It was so much nonsense, she told herself. His brain was telling him things; but it wasn't his fault, Maggie reasoned, it was the post-traumatic stress that had wrought such a change in her lovely husband. She bit her lip, yearning for the strong man who'd held her and comforted her to be back once more, the feeling of loneliness and despair bringing tears to her eyes.

CHAPTER SEVEN

Lorimer strode eagerly along the corridor to where the man sat behind his desk.

'William. You feeling better already?'

Jimmy Rae's face lit up as their newest patient approached.

'I did have some sleep earlier,' Lorimer admitted. 'But that's not what's important right now. I've seen something on television that needs to be reported.'

'Come and sit down.' Jimmy stood up and waved a hand at the chair next to his own. His expression had changed. He was looking at Lorimer with a wariness that made the detective suddenly impatient.

'Listen. Forget for a moment that I'm suffering some kind of breakdown, will you? Last year I was involved in a major case where an illegal end-of-life gang was exploiting sick and elderly people. We've got several of them behind bars but we never found the person behind it all.' His words came out in a rush and he could hear the strain in his own voice, the pitch heightening as he relived the images he had seen.

'Calm down,' Jimmy told him, one hand on Lorimer's sleeve. 'Take your time.'

Lorimer snatched back his arm, ready to glare at the man. Then he sighed.

'Sorry. I'm a bit keyed up, that's all. What it is ... ' he found Jimmy Rae's eyes and held them with his blue stare, 'I just saw that very person on television. A clip about something in a hospital. Wasn't paying that much attention. But I know it was him. I never forget a face,' he added firmly.

Jimmy believed that. This earnest man staring hard at him was full of passion for his job. He'd met his sort before: police officers whose inbuilt integrity held them accountable to right every wrong that came their way. Jimmy felt a flash of pity for the gaunt man beside him. Maybe he was right. Maybe the man on the TV *was* the culprit who had escaped justice. But it was far more likely that William Lorimer was experiencing a delusion, shifting his focus from the nightmares that haunted him. Jimmy had seen it happening several times to patients like this, anxiety eating away at their very souls, grabbing any chance to plunge back into the maelstrom of the job that was police work.

'Have you had a coffee since dinner?' Jimmy asked. 'You could tell me more about this while we sit in the lounge.' He rose to his feet with a smile that he hoped Lorimer would take for complicity.

The centre director watched the tall man's shoulders slump and his head nod in acquiescence. *He knows I don't believe a word of it*, Jimmy thought as he led Lorimer along the corridor towards the residents' lounge where a fire was burning brightly in the grate. This man was nobody's fool. He'd probably seen as much of broken humanity as Jimmy had himself, though from a different perspective. A man like William Lorimer was a huge asset to Police Scotland and Jimmy Rae was determined to restore him to the job fit and well.

*

The strong black coffee was sour in his mouth. He'd mumbled scraps of information about Quiet Release, hearing his words hesitant and uncertain. How could this man understand his desperation to link what he had seen on that TV screen with the team back in Glasgow? Rae's job was all about healing. Lorimer got that. Did the man have any inkling of what it was like to be intent on hunting down a criminal who had wreaked havoc on so many lives?

Lorimer was a good judge of people, his detective skills often guessing at their occupations or personalities from the different ways they spoke or behaved. But this man was a bit of an enigma. For a start he looked too old to be working at a full-time job. His white hair was still thick and his eyes keen and yet, now that he saw him up closer, Lorimer would have put him somewhere in his late sixties, far older than he had seemed at first glance. But, apart from laughter lines around his eyes, the face was calm and smooth, a veritable testament to the powers of therapy.

'What's your own background, Jimmy?' he asked, laying down his cup and looking at the man across the table. 'Have you always worked in places like this?'

Jimmy threw his head back and laughed.

'Goodness me, no!' He tilted his head as he regarded Lorimer thoughtfully. 'I see you didn't read up on the brochures we sent you,' he said, eyes twinkling. 'Maybe you should pick one of them up and make it your bedtime reading. That'll give you the answer you want.'

'Oh?' Lorimer's eyebrows rose in a gesture of enquiry. But Jimmy Rae shook his head. 'Read it and see,' he said. 'Now, how about one of these cakes? The apple tarts are home-made and the pastry just melts in your mouth.'

*

Lorimer smiled despite himself as he folded the brochure and lay back against the pillows.

So. Jimmy Rae had been a military man. Lorimer wondered what his story had been. The early years of serving overseas must have opened the man's eyes to a huge breadth of humanity. *Retrained in medical therapy*, the brochure had explained. But not *why*, something that Lorimer would like to have found out. Perhaps he would simply ask him if the occasion arose. *Married with grown-up children, hobbies including hill walking*, Lorimer had read. A man after his own heart, then, if he enjoyed the hills. And of course, having been an officer in charge of squads of soldiers, Jimmy Rae was probably as perfect for this job as it was possible to be. No wonder there had been a twinkle in his eye! And he'd wanted me to read this for myself, to think about it, rather than be told first-hand how his life had panned out, Lorimer thought. Jimmy hadn't wanted the conversation to be about himself, but about his patient. About Detective Superintendent William Lorimer.

And suddenly Lorimer saw that this white-haired man was every bit as dedicated to his job as he was himself. Instead of investigating a case and seeing it to a satisfactory conclusion with the meting-out of justice, Jimmy Rae welcomed each new patient and ensured that his staff worked with them until they were fit and well enough to return to active service. Well, perhaps he'd help him to achieve this aim. But first he had to speak to someone who would listen to what he had to say and do what he asked.

Kirsty Wilson pulled away from her boyfriend's embrace as the telephone rang.

'Oh, just leave it . . . ' James Spencer's Geordie voice drifted off as Kirsty bent to pick up her mobile. He knew that she would never do that. What if she were being called out on an emergency?

'Hello?'

James watched as Kirsty's eyes opened wide in surprise.

'How are you?' she asked, unable to hide the note of concern in her voice. Then her fingers clasped the phone a little tighter as Kirsty listened intently for several minutes while her old mentor explained the situation.

'Yes,' she said at last. 'I can do that. Leave it with me, sir.' She looked down at the floor, her expression solemn then rang off, merely saying, 'Bye, sir,' though in truth there was a lot more that Kirsty wanted to say.

'Who was that? Do you have to go out?' James asked.

'Last person I imagined,' she began. 'It was Lorimer.'

'What? But he's off on sick leave,' James protested.

'Aye, but he's seen something he wants me to follow up,' Kirsty said, sinking back down onto the settee and letting herself be folded back into her boyfriend's arms. 'And in a few minutes we can see it for ourselves.' She picked up the remote control and flicked on the television, eyeing the menu that would allow her to catch up on the earlier programme.

It was several minutes later that she managed to freeze the image and turn to James.

'Well?' he asked, his dark eyebrows raised in expectation.

'I think he's right,' Kirsty told him. 'But heaven alone knows how I'm going to persuade the powers-that-be to reopen the case.' She sighed.

The image facing them was blurred and ragged at the edges. But the moment captured was enough for the detective constable to know that it was the same man who had been sought during the Quiet Release case several months ago.

'Who is he?' James murmured, following her gaze.

'We never knew,' Kirsty admitted. 'That nurse, Mary Milligan, identified him as the bogus doctor who had been around the hospital.'

'But she was off her head!' James grinned. 'Wasn't she the one who practically threw herself at the police?'

'Aye.' Kirsty gave a sigh. 'It's some sort of syndrome. You can ask Solly about it. He knows the correct term for it. Attention seeking. Wanting to be part of the investigation when you are the culprit.'

'And she pointed the finger at her own associate? That's mad!' James shook his head in disbelief.

'We were never sure if she simply picked out a person at random or if he really did exist. But there were all sorts of signs that there was someone else behind it. Someone who was pulling the strings.'

'A man who could manipulate that crazy nurse,' James added, staring at the TV screen.

'A murderer,' Kirsty muttered darkly. 'And maybe he's still at it. After all,' she said, letting the image unfreeze and the figures move once more. 'Look where he is and what he's wearing.'

It was obvious that the background was a hospital corridor. Nor was there any doubt that the figure melting into the background was wearing the green overalls of a hospital orderly.

CHAPTER EIGHT

He put the uniform onto a hanger and placed it on the hook behind the door, fingering it for a moment.

The smile on his face broadened. His parents had wanted him to become a doctor and in a way that was what he had become. Even if the transition was only temporary and the job to be done demanded far more disguises than simply donning this garment and pretending to be part of a huge hospital staff.

Mary had almost blown it for them, he remembered, the smile dropping from his handsome face. Her recklessness had cost them several of his associates, men who had been useful but who were now behind bars, their protests that they didn't know the real person behind Quiet Release bringing the full weight of the law upon them.

It had taken time to rebuild the scheme, to stockpile sufficient quantities of the drugs that would end so many people's lives, but he was confident that he could pick up the threads of his organisation. He was already weaving his web of hope and promise among those who were weary of having to dance attendance on relatives who were a drain on their finances as well as their precious time. They listened to the sympathetic orderly who wheeled his patients around the hospital, encouraging them to talk about their problems, offering sympathy. He knew what persuasive words to use, how they wanted so badly to be rid of their responsibilities without feeling guilty about it. Paying him a large sum could ease their consciences, of course, as if by sacrificing their own savings it made everything okay. And of course he would give them all such reassurance, beguiling them into the belief that what they were doing was for the good of their loved ones.

Love! He snorted as he turned away from the door where the green overalls hung. Mary had imagined herself in love with him, the stupid fool! But it had been enough to make her do his bidding, though she had gone too far, almost unmasking him at the end. And she still did love him, he supposed, taking all the blame upon herself. After all, despite her incarceration in Scotland's high security mental hospital, he had heard that Mary Milligan had changed her story, insisting that he didn't actually exist. And that suited him absolutely fine.

Like many handsome men, Detective Superintendent Mark Mitchison was not averse to staring at his own reflection. His smile was sincere as he glanced at the face in the rear-view mirror for a few seconds and then turned his attention back to parking his car in the staff car park at Govan police station. Life was good, Mitchison told himself as the Porsche Boxster drew to a silent halt, the noiseless door opening as he stepped out of the luxury car. He wasn't the only police officer who liked fast cars, he knew, eyes trailing across the vehicles parked inside the walls next to the large red-brick building. There were Audis and Mercs among the bog standard Hondas and Fords but none of them was a patch on his own baby, he decided, letting his gaze linger for a moment on the gleaming paintwork. And if anyone ever queried how he had come to drive an expensive car like that, he simply shrugged, grinned and told them that a single man had to spend his money some way, didn't he? That shut up most of the guys who struggled with mortgages and childminding fees but Mitchison knew there were still murmurings about the head of Govan CID who enjoyed a lifestyle that most could only yearn for.

He was just yards from the door when the vibration in his inside pocket made him stop, the smile fading as he reached for the mobile.

'Mitchison,' he said sharply, noting the caller ID immediately. 'I'm right outside the office,' he added, his voice dropping to a whisper. 'Can you call me back later?'

Anyone seeing the man in the light grey suit thrusting the phone back into his pocket might have wondered if he had received bad news, such was the scowl on his face. In truth, it was the intrusion that had darkened his mood, reminding him only too well exactly how he had come into the trappings of wealth that he enjoyed. Jack Gallagher wanted something. He had sensed that in the man's voice. And when Gallagher called it could only mean trouble.

CHAPTER NINE

If only he didn't feel so tired, Lorimer thought, rolling onto his other side. The overwhelming feeling of exhaustion had taken its toll, the need for sleep rendering his once fit body limp and weak. *Hammered by inertia*, he'd described it, as if the lassitude that had reduced him to this shadow of his former self was somehow a powerful force. And always he wanted to sleep, to sink into a slumber so deep that no dreams could touch him.

Tomorrow it would be his birthday and he had already determined to surprise Maggie and take her out for a curry over the weekend to celebrate. The Shish Mahal, he told himself, turning again, pulling the thick duvet around his body. It had been their favourite place to enjoy Asian food ever since university days when they would stroll down to Gibson Street and share a meal together. Now the restaurant was firmly established around the corner in Park Road, close to Solly and Rosie's home and a few minutes' walk from Kirsty and James's flat.

His thoughts turned to his friends and when he had last seen them. Solly had been attentive afterwards, visiting often and listening to Lorimer stumbling to explain just how he felt. The psychologist had not tried to offer advice or probe into how he was feeling, simply being there seemed enough, yet Lorimer wondered now what the professor of psychology had made of the breakdown. Did he and Rosie discuss it? Had Solly ever spoken quietly to Lorimer's doctors? Yet wasn't the whole aspect of confidentiality supposed to be ingrained into these professionals? He tossed in the bed, anxiety making him grind his teeth as he imagined all sorts of scenarios.

Then he stopped. Solly might be able to help in other ways. Could he use his contacts to get him in to see Mary Milligan? If he were to begin to follow up the trail of that face he had seen on the television then he should surely start with her. The weekend for his birthday might be stretched a little, after all.

With this new idea in his mind, Lorimer lay staring into space, his thoughts turning back to the unfinished case that had left him with such a sour taste in his mouth.

Professor Solomon Brightman put down the phone with a sigh. Maggie had explained the whole thing to him and he had felt her pain, listening to her voice. The human voice gave away so many clues as to how a person was feeling, he mused, something that Lorimer had learned in his job too. But what if he was correct? What if the image that the detective superintendent had seen this evening really turned out to be that of the mysterious man that Mary Milligan had claimed him to be? Solly thought back to the woman who had worked in Glasgow's biggest teaching hospital. Mary was originally from the islands. *Fey*, Kirsty had said at first, *fanciful*. But the woman now committed to Carstairs Mental Hospital was suffering from something far more dangerous than an overactive imagination. She had killed in cold blood. For gain, yes, but more for the thrill that such deeds had given her. She had flirted with the truth, ingratiating herself into the investigation in a manner that had thrown the whole team off the scent. And all the time Mary had been in a liaison with the man behind the entire scheme, something that she continued to deny.

When the telephone rang again, Solly raised his bushy eyebrows. It was coming on for ten o'clock, a bit late for any social calls, surely, unless poor Maggie Lorimer had wanted to talk some more.

'It's you!' The professor could not keep the surprise out of his tone.

'Sorry. Is it that late?' Lorimer apologised. 'Can't sleep for thinking about something . . .'

'The face you saw on tonight's news programme?'

'You saw it too! Solly, what did you think?' Lorimer's voice was suddenly eager, more like the person he had been before that fateful Hogmanay.

'No, sorry, I didn't see it. Maggie called me.'

'Oh.' The single word fell heavily between them, his friend's disappointment tangible.

'Perhaps there will be a repeat on the ten o'clock programme,' Solly suggested mildly. 'I could tape it for you if you like?' he added.

'Would you? There's just a wee basic telly in this room. Though I did ask Kirsty if she could find it on hers.'

'You have been busy,' Solly murmured, wondering at the animation that he could discern in Lorimer's reply.

'Will you ring me back once you've seen it?'

'It may not be shown again,' Solly warned. 'Don't sit up all night waiting to hear from me. If I don't ring back by eleven then you'll know it hasn't been on.'

'Oh, I'll be watching it here, don't you worry,' Lorimer told him. 'And if I see that face again I'll expect you to call me right away.'

'And if you don't . . . '

There was a pause then Lorimer's tone dropped once more. 'I'll speak to you tomorrow,' he said gruffly. 'I've a favour to ask.'

Solly sat silently in the comfort of his West End home, imagining the other man propped up in the bed at Castlebrae, staring at the television screen in despair. Whatever it had been that his friend had wanted him to see had not been shown again; a small piece of local news, not worthy of being repeated on the later programme, other events having overtaken it in importance.

Lorimer would call him tomorrow, Solly reminded himself. And he wondered just what sort of favour it was that the man wanted.

DC Kirsty Wilson lay awake, listening to the soft breathing coming from James slumbering beside her, her mind too full for sleep. Lorimer was right. The image of that man was definitely the person Mary Milligan had identified as the mystery doctor. She'd swear to it in a court of law. And if the police were to reopen the case and hunt him down, perhaps she would have to do just that.

CHAPTER TEN

He was awakened by the cries of geese flying overhead, a sound that had him out of bed in one bound, pulling aside the curtains to see their arrow-shaped flight in the morning light. The dawn was a promise of brightness to come, layers of mist obscuring the treetops, pink and pearly grey melting together with a haze of blue high above. He watched the birds until they were out of sight, heading for some feeding grounds, no doubt, their purposeful wing beats a marvel to his eyes. It was something, he supposed. A little bonus of being so far away from the city. And a gift for his birthday. Perhaps he might take a walk outside, follow the pathway the birds had taken, see if he could find where they had come to land. Lorimer hadn't thought to bring his high-definition binoculars to this place. But now, with the thought of his birthday celebrations at the weekend, he resolved to bring them back here to Castlebrae next week.

Sitting on the edge of the bed, he closed his eyes, remembering. Solly hadn't phoned back but perhaps that was just as well. He could imagine that the psychologist would take sides with Jimmy Rae and the people here at Castlebrae. *He'd be reluctant to do anything that would impede your recovery*, a little voice insisted.

And that was surely true. Solly only wanted the best for his friends. He wouldn't want Lorimer to scratch the itch that was this unfinished business with Quiet Release, but to concentrate his energies on becoming fit and whole again.

What a name! Lorimer thought of the scheme that had lured so many vulnerable people into making decisions about the end of other folks' lives. *Quiet Release*. It had a certain ring about it, a reassurance of peacefulness, of letting go of the pain and troubles of this life. He was clever, whoever he was, this man who had dreamt up the whole business. Perhaps that was something to ask Mary Milligan if he were lucky enough to be permitted access to the woman. Who thought up the name? The Englishman who had pretended to be the long-lost son of one of the elderly victims in order to gain her fortune? Yet he had denied all knowledge of the start of the business. They knew from his interrogation that he'd been brought in by the old lady's Glasgow lawyer, the pair of them cooking up the scheme together, a scheme first suggested by Mary Milligan and her mysterious doctor companion. But Mary was denying all knowledge of an accomplice now, something that Lorimer simply did not believe. There had been too much evidence that another man was involved. And somewhere in the depths of the Scottish Crime Campus there were traces of DNA from several murder scenes waiting for a match.

His mind was spinning with thoughts of the case and he realised that the mist had lifted from the pine trees and he could see their outline more clearly. If only it were as easy to see through the darkness that covered this problem, he told himself, a sudden weariness making his shoulders sag. He yawned and slumped back onto the bed, wondering what lay ahead. Would they want him to play these mind games he'd tried on the computer? Or would it be more like the counselling he'd already received from the person to whom he had been referred by the police?

'All I want is to sleep,' he murmured aloud, yawning once more. 'Just let me sleep.' But the memory of that sheet of paper with his personal programme printed on it made him sit back up with a groan. He'd do whatever they asked of him. It wasn't in his nature to be bolshie when folk were doing their best to help him.

Lorimer's mouth twisted in a faint grin. Well, he was going to be a bit of a nuisance to his colleagues back in Police Scotland, wasn't he? And he already had young Detective Constable Kirsty Wilson on his side.

Kirsty had been awake long before the dawn light, these February mornings cold and murky, short winter days bringing a sense of gloom to the city. Everyone on the underground platform was silent, many staring at their mobile phones, busily texting before their day's work properly began, others peering into the black void as though willing the subterranean train to arrive.

She'd told Lorimer that she would do whatever she could but now, in the pale reality of the morning, Kirsty felt far less confident of any success. There were fewer people to whom she could turn for help these days. Her dad, DI Alistair Wilson, was retired from the force, away with her mum on an extended holiday to the United States, and Lorimer, to whom she had often turned for advice, was the very one who now sought *her* help! There had been changes all through the service lately; Sir Robert Caldwell, the Chief Constable, had also retired along with several of his deputies and the most senior officers in Police Scotland were men and women Kirsty had hardly ever met. Besides, her recent transfer to the Govan Division in Helen Street had left the young woman feeling isolated. There was no other officer that she knew well enough and her immediate superior was a taciturn individual who seemed to barely tolerate Kirsty's presence. She needed someone who would authorise a continuation of the investigation into Quiet Release yet, standing on the platform, listening to the rumble of the approaching train, Kirsty realised she hadn't the foggiest notion whom she should turn to. This morning, however, she was going back to Stewart Street for a meeting. Maybe there would be someone there she could talk with?

It was Sadie who gave her the idea. The elderly woman pushing the trolley full of baked goods around the various police stations every morning had become a friend. Sadie Dunlop had known her dad for years, and Lorimer of course, and had never minced her words with any of the police officers. *See them wantin' me tae be politically correct?* she'd once declared to Kirsty. *Ah'd like tae see them try!* And so, despite the older woman's predilection for speaking her mind and sometimes crossing the bounds of what was considered acceptable, Sadie Dunlop was fondly tolerated as much for her direct wit as for her excellent scones and cakes.

'Aye, wee yin.' She sidled up to Kirsty, stopping the trolley at an angle so that the young woman could peer into the layers of goodies. 'What's yer fancy the day? I've a couple of Danish pastries left. Used tae keep them for His Nibs . . . ' She tailed off and Kirsty turned to see the old lady sniffing into a handkerchief. 'Aye, well, mibbe we'll no' see him back here ony mair.'

'Don't say that, Sadie!' Kirsty rejoined. 'I'm sure he'll be back once . . . '

'Once he's got over his breakdown?' Sadie frowned. 'D'you really think so? Och, I don't know.' She shook her greying curls. 'Can't imagine our man falling ill . . . like *that*,' she added in a tone of disgust.

'Sadie!' Kirsty remonstrated with the older woman. 'That sort of thing can happen to anyone. The shock of just being there, never mind how it all happened, would be enough to affect the bravest person. Besides,' she lowered her voice, 'I think it was the fact that Blackburn had killed all his wee children, you know what I mean? He and Mrs Lorimer tried to have a family for years. So many stillborn babies, my mum told me,' she added.

Sadie's frown cleared suddenly. 'Oh, my God!' she exclaimed, hand to her throat. 'I never realised ... Oh!' She leaned against the wall as Kirsty stood and looked at her. 'You just dinna expect it from a *man*, though, do you? I mean, being kind o' depressed an' that.'

'That's nonsense, Sadie,' Kirsty protested. 'Men have just as many deep-seated anxieties as women. Maybe more. I mean, we at least can get stuff off our chests by talking to each other about things whereas men tend to bottle it all up. Think they ought to do the stiff upper lip. Not the healthiest thing to do, I'm told.'

'Still. *Lorimer*.' Sadie shook her head again. 'Who'd have thought it?'

'Well. He actually phoned me last night,' Kirsty confided. 'And he sounded pretty much his old self, if you ask me.'

'Oh, aye?'

'Can you keep something to yourself, Sadie?' Kirsty glanced along the corridor to make sure nobody else was listening in to their conversation.

The vigorous nodding was all the reply that the detective constable required to unfold the tale of Lorimer's call and the revelation about the television sighting.

'What are you going to do, wee yin?' Sadie asked at last, her eyes now wide with interest.

'I don't know,' Kirsty confessed. 'There's nobody in the senior

58

ranks that I feel able to talk to. So many changes.' She shrugged. 'So many new faces, especially where I am in Govan.'

Sadie looked thoughtful for a moment. 'Maybe not,' she said at last. 'Do you remember the name Niall Cameron?'

Kirsty frowned and shook her head. 'I'm not sure. Should I?'

'Ach, you'd just be a bairn back then.' Sadie smiled. 'Niall was one of Lorimer's most promising young detective constables. Like yourself.' She gave Kirsty a sly nudge with her elbow. 'Came from one o' they Hebridean islands, cannae remember which one,' she continued. 'Anyway, the lad's done all right for himself. Rose up the ranks. Like Lorimer did himself at that age, come tae think of it. Anyroad, he's a DCI now at thon specialist place. You know, where they just cover all the murders an' that. Must be part of your own building, eh?'

Kirsty could not repress a grin. 'You mean the MIT,' she said. 'Major Incident Team,' she added, seeing the older woman's puzzled expression.

'Aye, that wan.' She looked intently at Kirsty. 'Why don't you have a word with Niall? He always thought such a lot of yer man.'

'Everybody does,' Kirsty replied stoutly.

'Oh, no, not everyone.' Sadie shook her head. 'I could tell you a few tales out of school about one or two who didn't always see eye to eye with our Lorimer. But I'm sure you've heard things from your dad at one time or another.'

'Not really,' Kirsty confessed. 'Frankly, I can't imagine anyone not getting on with Lorimer. He's . . .' She paused, wondering how to describe the man who had originally inspired her to join the police force.

'He's a one-off,' Sadie finished for her. 'And I'll be the first to give him a big hug when he comes back to work, wait and see.' She rose and wiped away a tear from the corner of her eye.

Grasping her trolley handle the old woman began to move off once more. 'Nobody appreciates ma Danish pastries like he does,' she mumbled, leaving Kirsty staring in her wake.

DCI Niall Cameron, she thought to herself. No, it wasn't a name she remembered but then officers could be moved from one division to another quite easily, especially when promotion beckoned. The recent reshuffle had seen Kirsty's own transfer across to the city's Southside. Her dad had just been lucky in being part of Lorimer's team for so many years. If Dad were around she might have asked him about DCI Cameron. Kirsty looked thoughtful for a moment. 'Thanks, Sadie,' she murmured to herself.

'Maybe that's the very person I need.'

Several hours later, Kirsty clicked through the pages on her computer screen until she came to the one she sought.

DCI Niall Cameron BA, she read. A graduate, unlike herself, Cameron had fast-tracked through the service. Plus he'd been part of a training programme at Tulliallan, the police training centre, to help new recruits. Good for him, Kirsty thought, in a spurt of admiration. That sort of dedication made her like the man already.

She sat back, wondering what he was like. The thumbnail photo showed an attractive face, the smile somewhat amused as if he were sharing a joke with the photographer. It was a face she could warm to, Kirsty realised.

And at that moment she made up her mind. She would make discreet enquiries about DCI Cameron then see if she could arrange to speak to him about the possibility of taking the Quiet Release case a step further.

*

He was taller than she had expected, not quite Lorimer's height of six foot four, and DCI Cameron was of a slimmer build, his face all angles as though carved from stone. But there was nothing cold about his expression as he shook Kirsty's hand.

'DC Wilson, please come in,' he said, the voice soft and lilting, a dead giveaway of the Lewis man's roots. It was a lovely voice, Kirsty thought as she sat opposite, shaking her head at the offer of tea or coffee. The other desks in the room were empty, she was glad to see, the three detective chief inspectors that shared this office out on some MIT business of their own.

'You mentioned Lorimer in your email,' Cameron said, sitting forward and eyeing her with interest. 'How can I help?'

'You know he's off sick?'

'I had heard. Horrible business,' Cameron said. 'Still, it can happen to any officer any time. We take all sorts of risks in this job, don't we?' He smiled a lopsided sort of smile as if his own experience in the police service had given him some hard knocks. 'Nobody's immune from any sort of upset, even those who believe themselves to be the most hardened of souls.'

Kirsty relaxed a little. This was exactly how she had felt herself, though there were still those who murmured about the detective superintendent being less than the invulnerable figure he had become in so many minds.

'Now, I am sure this visit has nothing to do with Detective Superintendent Lorimer's rehabilitation,' he went on, a shrewd look in his clear grey eyes.

'You're right, though if you can help me then maybe you'd be helping him too.'

She paused for a moment then began to describe the case from the previous year, the patients who had been murdered, the suspects who were now in custody and the one person who had made his escape: the mysterious doctor.

'Lorimer saw him on television,' Kirsty said, watching Cameron's face closely. 'On yesterday's early evening news programme. I recorded it on catch up. And I think he's right.'

'Go on,' Cameron said, one hand stroking his chin thoughtfully, a gesture that reminded Kirsty for all the world of Solomon Brightman, though the man opposite her was clean-shaven, unlike Solly.

'I wanted to know if it would be possible to reopen the case. But I wasn't sure who to ask,' she finished, looking up at the tall man hopefully.

'Why come to me?' Cameron frowned for a moment. 'I wasn't on that case.'

'I . . .' Kirsty stopped for a moment. 'It was Lorimer who headed it up, really,' she said. 'I was involved to quite an extent when I was at Stewart Street and so was DS Len Murdoch, but he's retired now. Just last week, actually,' she added, thinking about the man who had been her mentor at the start of her CID career.

'And there have been lots of changes recently,' Cameron said quietly. 'I can see your dilemma.' He paused for a moment, staring past Kirsty as though he were seeing something in his mind's eye.

'As it happens I've got a meeting at Gartcosh tomorrow. I'll see what can be done. But I have to be honest, the present budgetary constraints are making it very hard for any cold cases to be reopened, no matter how recent they might be. I'm sorry to sound negative, but that's just the way things are at the moment. Politics.' He shrugged, as if Kirsty ought to understand by that one word how difficult her task might be.

'Well, thanks for seeing me,' she said, feeling a wave of heat flush her cheeks as she stood up. 'It was good of you to spare me the time.'

'Listen,' Cameron raised his hands, 'I'd give as much time as I could if it would help Lorimer. He's . . . ' He tailed off and gave Kirsty a crooked grin. 'He's a bit special, isn't he?'

Lorimer was feeling anything but special as he walked along the corridor to the waiting room where he was to meet his patient adviser. He was just one more officer in a long line of casualties, he told himself. One more troubled mind affected by the job. In fact, as he watched the woman approach him, a small smile of welcome on her face, he could detect lines of weariness around the eyes and the mouth, lines that were exaggerated by the woman's hair being drawn back in a tight knot at the back of her head.

'Hello, I'm Christine,' she said, taking a step forward and clasping his hand.

'Hello, Christine. I'm Detective Superintendent William Lorimer.' He offered his hand which she took, giving it a squeeze. 'But you can drop the Detective Superintendent and just call me Lorimer.'

'We don't use ranks here anyway,' the woman replied. 'Didn't Jimmy tell you?'

Lorimer hesitated. Was that something he had missed during the welcome meeting? Had his attention slipped as he'd looked around at his fellow sufferers, wondering what had brought them all to Castlebrae?

'Shall I call you William?' she asked, 'Or Bill?'

'No, Lorimer will do, thanks,' he replied, wondering if his insistence meant that they were getting off to a shaky start.

'Okay,' she replied, but the slight lift of her eyebrows told him that this woman would prefer to be on first-name terms with her patients.

'Did you have a good journey here?' she asked as they walked back along the corridor to her office, listening politely as he returned her question.

'Fine, thanks. Left early from Glasgow yesterday so no problems with the traffic.'

She stepped back to let him enter a small room where three chairs upholstered in kingfisher blue were angled around a small coffee table. Christine ushered Lorimer towards them.

No sitting across the table, he thought, noting the avoidance of a confrontational and formal setting. The only desk was a working one placed against the wall, a telephone to one side and a kettle on the other. She wants me to feel comfortable in her presence, he reckoned, the years of experience in observing body language and in drawing out people in different interview situations coming to the fore.

The table held a water jug, a glass and a box of tissues, Lorimer noticed. And he suspected that the box of Kleenex was not for patients with a runny nose but for those who might break down and weep, something he'd done far too often lately.

'What we're going to do this morning is quite simple,' Christine began. 'You talk, mostly, and I listen.' She gave a small smile and looked at him intently, a look that made him drop his gaze.

She's not sure about me, Lorimer realised. What has she heard? What did she expect? His eyes slid to her left hand where he saw the white space where a wedding ring had been worn. That told its own story, didn't it? What was this woman's life like outside the treatment centre? Did she have kids of her own with the normal strains that any domestic life could bring? Yet whatever her own background, Christine seemed to be focusing all her attention on the man beside her, something that made Lorimer feel a little uneasy.

These inner questions were brushed aside as the therapist moved her chair so that she was facing him.

'How did you sleep last night?' she asked.

'The usual.' He shrugged. 'Well, maybe better than at home, to be honest. At least I didn't wake up screaming,' he added with a hollow laugh.

'Is that something you normally do?'

He nodded, avoiding her penetrating look, ashamed all at once to be opening up his mind to this stranger, yet desperately wanting to unburden himself. She was looking at him as if she could see right into his soul and suddenly he felt treacherous tears prick against his eyelids.

'That's something we will try to address, Lorimer,' she said quietly. 'But first tell me what you think about yourself and about your future.'

My future? he thought, unconsciously twisting his hands together. Was there one with Police Scotland?

'I feel a bit of a fraud, to be honest.' He smiled thinly. 'When I look at all the officers here who really need help . . .'

'You don't count yourself as needing help?'

He shrugged and avoided her gaze. 'Not as if I've been injured in the course of duty,' he mumbled.

Christine shook her head. 'You've undergone a significant trauma, and what that means is that your body is showing a normal reaction to an abnormal experience.'

She made it sound so straightforward. An abnormal experience. It had been that, all right.

'Suppose so . . .' he agreed reluctantly.

'What about your wife?'

Lorimer relaxed immediately, the hint of a smile around his eyes. 'Och, Maggie's just marvellous. Supports me no matter what sort of cases we're going through.' His face fell as he remembered the murder of her cousin in that nursing home. 'She's had more to put up with than most, though,' he admitted, sighing. 'Poor lass.'

'That's good to hear that she is behind you. Was she happy about you coming here, then?'

'I think so,' Lorimer replied, 'especially if it makes a difference. It's been hard for her. I've been so tired. But that's pretty much how I feel most of the time, and very unsettled. The images ... well, it's not just images ... there's always that sound, the child crying—' He broke off as his voice became husky and to his dismay Lorimer found that he could hardly swallow, the desire to weep overwhelming him.

The counsellor waited, her face bland and expectant, not full of sympathy, something Lorimer was grateful for. Sympathy would just weaken his spirit, he realised.

'I ... I find it hard to block out the sound even after I wake up. It's usually silent and shadowy in my room. Just the noise of my wife's breathing beside me. Too quiet. Like an empty stage waiting for the actors to come on and I know they're there, waiting in the wings. I know that if I let myself sleep again, they'll return and the whole nightmare will happen over and over again. That sound ...' He closed his eyes tight and remembered. 'It was so loud then ... the gunshot stopped her cry ... her wee body was on the floor in front of me, her face all ...' He shook his head, not wanting to remember.

'Okay. Let's not go there again,' Christine said quietly. 'Talking about it will only bring it all back and what we want for you is not experience that over and over again.' Her voice was firm. 'Have you come across the MoodGYM yet?'

The change of subject made Lorimer sit back and raise his eyebrows. 'What's that?'

'It's an online form of cognitive behaviour therapy. No need for a person to ask you any questions. It can help with different forms of depression in that it shows you the way you feel and how these feelings result in behaviour.'

'You'd rather I spent time alone with a computer?'

Christine smiled, the lines on her face softening, her eyes displaying a genuine sympathy at last. 'Not at all. Maybe you can carry that out at home, not while you're at Castlebrae. Here you will have one-to-one sessions with me and the other therapists; it all adds up to your recovery. Meantime, you'll be given some medication that should help to give you a bit more sleep. You look as if you need it, frankly,' she added kindly. 'Jimmy wants you to get out into the grounds for some fresh air as well as a few sessions in the gym, so that your body wants to take a proper rest. We take quite a holistic approach here, you know,' she said. 'Mind and body are so inextricably linked. But I think you know that already, Lorimer.'

He's stricken by the waste of it all, Christine wrote as she sat in her office over a cup of coffee. *Easy to understand why, poor man. He and his wife have never been able to have a family. Saw that in his GP's notes. Needs a lot of rest and some fresh Perthshire air.* She looked out of the window at the rain clouds sweeping across the midday skies. Christine gave a sigh. Bill Lorimer had seen some bad stuff in his time as a police officer. Like so many she had seen in her years here at Castlebrae. More than most folk would ever see in a lifetime.

'Well, we'll send him home feeling a lot better in a couple of weeks,' she said aloud now, returning her gaze to the computer screen and the confidential notes that only she would ever see. She glanced down at the paperwork on her desk, suddenly noting the detective's date of birth.

'Ah, it's your birthday today,' she said softly. 'Poor man. You'd much rather be back home with that wife of yours, I imagine.' Then, as she recalled those troubled eyes and that furrowed brow, the patient advisor smiled. Best present you could have is getting over all of this for good, she thought. And she would play her part in William Lorimer's recovery.

CHAPTER ELEVEN

Looking down at his hands he saw how still they were. No nerves, despite the pounding sensation in his breast. He'd have made an excellent surgeon, someone had once remarked, a long time ago, but the words had been spoken drily, almost as a criticism of his character. *Cool, detached* and *disciplined* – these were all words written in various school report cards as his teachers had sought to make sense of the quiet boy who kept himself a little apart from the rest of his classmates. And he'd had his parents to thank for that. The strict upbringing in that house, the loneliness he'd forced himself to ignore and the joy that he had eventually found when he'd taken those first lives.

As a small child he had enjoyed tormenting flies then snuffing out their very existence, mashing them to spots of black pulp on the dry pavements. The opportunity for progressing to larger prey had been difficult but not impossible; a couple of the locals had never found their beloved pets after they had gone missing, small bodies buried far from home. Thankfully, his stepfather had a mild form of asthma that made having a dog or cat out of the question. How would he have coped seeing an animal day by day, his hands itching to choke the life out of it?

He'd killed so often since those days and yet the thrill of taking a life had not diminished.

He looked at his hands again, surprised to see that the fingers were curled into fists. He unclenched them, sighing lightly.

There were things to be done: the briefcase to be packed with all that he required for the task he'd been set, that address over in the East End to be reconnoitred, a suitable disguise thought up. Now he had to still the rising excitement he felt surging inside and call up his resources of calm for this new death, the woman across the city blithely unaware that her time on earth was coming rapidly to an end.

CHAPTER TWELVE

Lorimer sat on the edge of his bed. This would be the second night that he was to spend in Castlebrae and already it felt as though he had been away from home for a lot longer. He had changed into sports clothes and joined the t'ai chi class that afternoon; anything to take his mind off the face that he had seen. And, for the time he had been in the class, it had worked. Concentrating on the movements and on his balance had had the effect of making Lorimer feel better than he had for weeks, though he was not quite sure why.

The laptop sat opened on the dressing table, its screensaver a woodland vision of autumn foliage, something to calm the spirits, perhaps, he thought, wondering who had chosen that particular image. He'd tried the online mind programme Christine had mentioned but had quickly given up. Maybe another time, once he was back home for good.

The headache had begun with the strain at the back of his neck, travelling up and across his skull until the throbbing reached his eyes. Now all he was left with was the option to take the prescribed pills and try to sleep or to leave his room and seek out a fellow sufferer. The notion of having to talk to another police officer, some stranger who was here to heal and mend, was swiftly dismissed. And it was really far too early to turn in, though the skies outside his window were already as black as pitch.

Maggie would be at home, a little voice reminded him. Then he was across the room, fumbling in his jacket pocket for his mobile phone, suddenly desperate to talk to his wife.

For a few moments the call rang out and his mouth turned down, the idea that she might be out somewhere and he would be unable to make contact dispiriting him even further.

'Hello?' Maggie's sweet voice was there and Lorimer's heart swooped with a sudden joy.

'It's me,' he said, his voice gruff with emotion.

'Well, hello, you!' she exclaimed coyly. 'Missing me?'

'Oh, Mags, if only you knew how much!' he replied softly, turning onto his back and staring at the ceiling.

'I called you earlier. Did you get my voicemail? Anyway, happy birthday, darling!'

'Oh, sorry, must have missed that somehow. Strange not to be with you . . .'

'How's it all going?'

He heard the note of hesitation as she posed the question and immediately felt a wave of guilt. What on earth had this poor woman been going through? She'd never once complained about his depression, his moping around the house whilst she had been busy working as usual.

'It's fine,' he lied. 'They're a great bunch of people up here. All experts in their field.' Well, that was true at least, Lorimer told himself, if you believed the blurb on their website. Though to be fair every one he had met so far had seemed genuinely caring about his recovery.

'Did you want to do anything special this weekend?' he asked. 'Since I'm away today on my birthday. Once I'm home on Friday ... do you have plans ...?' He stopped for a moment, uncertain what else to say.

'Hello? Are you still there?'

'Yes.'

'Thought we'd been cut off just then,' Maggie said, a tone of relief in her voice. 'Sorry you didn't get that voicemail. You know I never forget your birthday. Isn't that what husbands are supposed to do to their wives?' she countered with a giggle in her voice.

'I've never forgotten your—' He broke off, realising that Maggie was teasing him now. Had he become so grim that he failed to hear a joke? The idea troubled him for a second and he tried to stifle a sigh so she wouldn't hear him. 'Just three more nights here then I'll be back to see you,' he reassured her. 'A long weekend back home. Everyone leaves Fridays and comes back next Monday morning to take up here as they left off.'

'And you're sure everything is okay?'

'Yes, like I said, everything is grand. Really.' He paused, wondering how to tell her about contacting DC Kirsty Wilson. 'I've got loads to tell you but it can all wait till I'm home.'

'What do you fancy doing? A meal out to the Shish?'

'We'll see,' he replied. 'Right now I'd be happy to settle for a night in with you all to myself.'

There was a different sort of silence between them now, the sort of silence that comes when no words are needed.

'Miss you,' she said softly.

'Miss you, too. See you soon, love. Bye.'

He clicked off the phone and lay back, one arm cushioning his head. They had often been apart in the course of Lorimer's work, sometimes for several days at a time if the job entailed travelling far from home, but this felt different.

What sort of life had Maggie endured being married to him? Did her colleagues pity her for the long hours that he spent on the job instead of doing things that other husbands did? Going out to the theatre, down the local pub or just staying in cuddled up together watching the telly? And they'd never had any children. Had that been his fault? Was there something in his genetic make-up that had determined these poor babies would never be born alive? Maggie had never laid the blame at his door, though. And they had both lamented each lost child right up till the day that she'd had to have a hysterectomy. By that time Maggie had decided that even the consideration of adopting a child was too late for them. What had he given her, then, to make up for a loss like that? Nothing, he told himself. Nothing but grief and now she was saddled with a husband who couldn't even do his own job properly.

She'd be better off without me, an inner voice whispered and Lorimer turned on his side, his eyes catching sight of the bottle of pills that lay on his bedside table. A glance at the windows made him blink. The brass rod that was fixed across each pane of toughened glass told its own story: something to prevent a patient from opening the window and throwing themselves down on to the ground below. That male nurse's question hadn't been so daft after all.

Then, as suddenly as it had entered his thoughts, the wave of self-pity was brushed aside. That wasn't the sort of man she'd married. And he still had things to do in this life. Beginning with seeking out the man whose face had caught his attention on that TV news programme.

*

74

Being a hospital orderly was fine for a short while. It had enabled him to blend in with the other staff and chat about the patients as he went about his work. Not just tasks required by his contract of employment but the real job of ingratiating himself with the visitors, whispering ideas into their heads.

'All right, darling?' He smiled warmly at the old lady lying back on her heap of pillows, still groggy after her spell in the recovery room. 'Won't be long till we get you back to your own bed,' he promised, his reward a faint smile from the patient as she drifted in and out of sleep. She wouldn't want to chat, the way she was right now, he thought, coming to a halt next to the doors of the hospital lifts.

Some of the patients were only too glad to have a conversation with the pleasant young man who was wheeling them to and from the different wards. It was easy to engage them in chat, especially those who appeared a bit nervous about being in hospital in the first place. He'd heard confessions from men as well as women about their fears; how they dreaded going under the surgeon's knife, how they'd felt so powerless once the anaesthetist's needle had slipped into their veins.

His eyes would stray to their wrinkled skin, his hands twitching with sudden desire. To be alone with them for just a little while, enough time to place his syringe into their unresisting flesh ... to watch that last breath ...

He wheeled the old lady into the lift and touched the control panel, smirking a little; nobody would believe the thoughts being harboured by this nice-looking orderly.

Often he was glad of the green coveralls, their anonymity suited him so much better than the disguise he had adopted before. People looked at a doctor, despite changes in health regulations. Nowadays, rolled up shirt sleeves replaced the white coat and stethoscope around the neck, something that he regretted. The loss of a white coat seemed to have robbed these professional men and women of their gravitas. Anyway, being looked at was something he could do without. Once he had re-established his scheme there would be no need to push these trolleys around the maze of hospital corridors. He had almost everything in place, and the stockpile of necessary drugs was greater than ever.

Quiet Release was finished now but there were other ways to access those who wished their loved ones a swift exit from this world, ways that nobody would ever dream of.

'Here we are, Greta,' he cooed, glancing at the plastic name-tag on the patient's wrist as the door pinged open. 'Get you back to bed again,' he murmured, wheeling the trolley towards the geriatric ward.

A spasm of annoyance made him shudder for a moment as he regarded Greta Thomson's blue-veined arms lying outside the covers. How many of her family would rather she were dead and buried, saving them all the bother of hospital visits and the trouble of finding the right care home with all the expense that involved? One quick injection and it would be all over. Couldn't they see that?

He suppressed a grin as the nurse came forward to take charge of her patient. Just as well plenty of them saw things his way, he told himself, thinking of the luxury penthouse flat that was waiting for him after this shift.

'Thanks, Gordon,' the nurse said as he left the room, ready to wheel the empty trolley back downstairs.

It wasn't his real name, of course. He wasn't stupid enough to do that. But let them call him Gordon for as long as he was working here. He felt the lanyard flapping against the pale green material of his uniform. Gordon, Tony, Steve … he'd picked names that were easily forgettable, names that could belong to anybody, though 'Charles Graham' was a name he used only rarely and never in a place like this. His fists clenched as he remembered Charles Graham, the man who had made his life a misery. Well, he'd seen to that all right, hadn't he?

As he waited for the lift once more, he shut his eyes, remembering the rundown tenement building where he had lingered for a brief moment. To his chagrin, Ellen Blackburn hadn't been at home that day. But it would happen soon, he'd promised Gallagher. And, once he'd rid the drug lord of this particular problem, perhaps it would be time to discuss the next step in his bid to resurrect his campaign of death.

'Gordon Smith doesn't exist any more,' the man said.

'I hear what you're saying, Mr Graham,' Gallagher replied. 'What are you asking me to do about that?'

There was a pause then Gallagher heard a soft chuckle.

'I'm sure you have *connections*,' the voice told him. 'We don't want anyone muddying the waters at this stage, now do we? Don't want any link between the *real* person and any friend of yours still using that name?'

Gallagher raised his eyebrows though there was nobody to see the gesture of surprise as he clutched the mobile a little more tightly. The man's voice was smooth, not a hint of ingratiating himself with the drug boss even although Gallagher knew when a favour was being asked. The whole scheme of resurrecting this Quiet Release business depended on each of them trusting the other, though at the end of the day it would be Gallagher, not Graham, who would be calling the shots.

'No, of course not. You can leave it with me.'

Jack Gallagher's mouth twisted into the semblance of a grin as he cut the call. There were different ways for a man like him to keep the law from interfering in his business. He leaned forward and tapped the keyboard a few times until it brought up a familiar name. A swift email should do the trick. Better by far to have a directive coming from *inside* the police.

A few moments later Gallagher smiled as the cursor clicked on Send. It was in their best interests to keep that case closed, he'd written. And, if this particular cop knew what was good for them, they'd heed Jack Gallagher's words.

CHAPTER THIRTEEN

Was it being in a different environment? Lorimer wondered, sitting up and blinking at the grey light filtering through the gap in the curtain. Last night he had not dreamed about Blackburn or the child's final scream for help, a cry that had rent his heart asunder. Yesterday's stress management workshop had seemed so ordinary at the time, he remembered. Yet it seemed to have had the desired effect. Especially at the end when these words had appeared:

And remember: no life, save one that has ended, is free from stress . . .

That was something Lorimer had grasped, like a drowning man clutching at a lifeline thrown into the water before it covered his head. Stress was there at every turn. And sometimes it could be helpful. Yet the incident in Blackburn's home had been a tipping point, perhaps. He had seen too much blood, too many bodies, lives taken by violence in ways that nobody should ever witness in one lifetime.

His sleep had been bereft of the horrific images from New Year's Eve but that did not mean he had slept without any other pictures in his mind. Other cases had left their mark, no doubt, but Lorimer's sleep had rarely been troubled by any of them for long. Now, as daylight dawned on this early February morning, he took stock of the people who had touched his life in so many ways, triggered by the fragments he could recall about that one strange dream.

He had been running across a field, chasing after a man, desperate to catch him before something dreadful happened, what exactly wasn't clear in the dream. And there was a knife, a blade, flashing in the air above him, ready to drop onto his head if he didn't put up an arm to ward it off. Then the knife changed into a thin black figure and it too was trying to escape from his clutches. He'd heard his own breathing coming in gasps, louder and louder, a pain blooming in his chest.

Lorimer had woken up then, shaking, sure that he had been about to die in the dream. *But it was only a dream*, his more sensible self assured him.

So many times he had chased after real criminals. And caught them. People who had tried to outwit the forces of the law and been grasped by his own outstretched arms. Like the man with a predilection for underage sex who had lured several young women to their death, that trafficker in human misery and, more recently, the hired ned who had been part of the end-of-life scam that was Quiet Release. And, of course, there had been others. Was the dream part of a subconscious voice that was trying to tell him to regain his former fitness? Right now, sitting on the edge of the clinic's bed, Lorimer knew he could no more chase after a fugitive than fly in the air. This depression had left him weak and feeble; sometimes it felt as if a plug had been pulled, draining all of his strength away. No wonder Jimmy Rae had encouraged him to take part in the exercise classes.

Lorimer yearned all of a sudden to talk about this, but not to the patient adviser with her steady gaze. Not just yet. At that moment he knew exactly who would listen without passing judgement and yet who might offer some sage advice.

Professor Solomon Brightman closed the door behind him and turned up his coat collar against the morning drizzle. Rosie had taken the day off work, some bug or other having made her sick all through the night, and so he took the walk across the park towards the University of Glasgow on his own rather than hand in hand with his wife. Rosie's office was only five minutes away from his own and their daily walk together over the hill of University Avenue was something that the professor cherished. Sometimes she was out of the house long before her psychologist husband, days or nights when she was on call to attend scenes of crime. As the head of the department of forensic medicine, Dr Rosie Fergusson had many duties: being with an investigation team to examine a corpse when a sudden suspicious death occurred, performing post-mortems on the victim and giving evidence in court were just three of the tasks she regularly had to face. Solly's own days were much more regulated by comparison. The timetable was planned months in advance though the students themselves gave the job a variety that never ceased to delight him. Occasionally Solly would be summoned to a divisional headquarters and asked to join a major incident team, his expertise in criminal profiling a useful tool when it was needed.

His eyes fell on the grey-green turf on either side of the path. There were no signs yet of winter releasing its grip, no small shoots of a burgeoning spring. He shivered, glad of the heavy tweed coat, as a gust of cold wind shook a spatter of raindrops onto his dark curls from the overhanging branches of a tree. Quickening his stride, Solly turned his thoughts to the day ahead and to his spacious office where he would boil up a kettle and take a warming drink of herbal tea before his first tutorial session.

Solly hurried to catch the green pedestrian light and crossed over to University Gardens. A quick glance upwards showed the stained-glass windows of his office that looked out over the crest of the hill and the old university buildings, the place that Solly now whimsically regarded as his second home.

He sighed as he took off his damp coat and hung it on the wooden coat stand, leaving the cashmere scarf around his neck for the time being. He fingered its soft fabric, remembering the moment when he had unwrapped it on Christmas morning, the gift (ostensibly from his little daughter, Abby) something to be treasured.

Soon the professor was standing at his window, a steaming mug of fruit tea in one hand, horn-rimmed spectacles pushed up on his forehead to dissipate the steam on their lenses. Down the hill he could see the corner of the grey building where the department of forensic medicine was housed and his thoughts returned to his beloved wife and her sickness. Should he call her yet? Or leave her to sleep?

As if in answer to his thoughts the telephone began to ring.

'Professor Brightman.'

'Solly. Are you busy right now?'

'Lorimer? Good gracious. Are you all right?' Solly laid down the mug of tea and sank into the ancient leather armchair next to the telephone table. His friend's voice betrayed a definite edge. Anxiety? Solly suddenly felt the need to find out more.

'Thought you were still up in Perthshire?'

'Only for another day or so. I'm coming down on Friday then I'm back here all of next week. I think it'll only be a few days ... ' He tailed off, doubt in his tone.

'I was thinking about you as it happens,' the professor mused, his eyes catching sight of the calendar on his wall. 'The seventh. That was your birthday, wasn't it? Congratulations. I remember that party a few years ago. The full moon ... mmm ...'

'Yes, well, nothing like that this year,' Lorimer sighed. 'But that's not why I called. There's something I'd like you to do for me if you can, Solly.'

There was a pause and the psychologist sensed the policeman's reluctance to come right out with his request. He's going to ask me something he thinks I won't like, he told himself.

'It's about Mary Milligan,' Lorimer began. 'She's still in Carstairs, I take it.'

'Ye-ess.'

'Solly, I'll come straight to the point. I want back onto the Quiet Release case.'

'But you're off on sick leave,' Solly protested. 'You're not supposed to be doing anything like this.'

'Oh, I've passed the information about seeing that man on to the correct quarters, don't worry about that,' Lorimer assured him.

But the swift riposte did not fool the psychologist for one moment. Lorimer was up to something. Solly waited for a moment longer, considering. His friend's voice was different; gone was the dull, slurred speech that he had heard too often on his visits since these shocking murders on Hogmanay. That was a good sign, of course. But what, exactly, did Lorimer want him to do?

The answer, when it came, brought back the memory of that woman who had killed in cold blood, sending a chill down the professor's spine.

'Can you arrange for me to visit Mary?'

*

Lorimer put down the telephone, his hands shaking. Solly had agreed to accompany him to the state mental hospital on Saturday. Lorimer would pick up his friend and drive them both across the countryside to Carstairs. Solly had a free morning as it happened, he'd told Lorimer, so would be able to come with him. Whether that was true or not, Lorimer didn't know. He'd sounded sincere enough but then he'd grown to distrust anything people said, he realised. Was Solly just humouring him? Was he in cahoots with the therapists in this place, perhaps? And at this very moment likely calling them to relate their recent conversation?

Lorimer ran his hands through his hair. What was happening to him? Why did he have to look for ulterior motives in everything? It was stupid to feel so paranoid! he told himself crossly. Solly would help him just as young DC Kirsty Wilson was trying to help him and not because of his medical condition but because they surely knew that it was the right thing to do.

'I'm sorry, but that's their final answer,' Niall Cameron told her.

'But why?' the young woman protested, hands on the detective chief inspector's desk, apparently forgetting for a moment that she was addressing a much more senior officer.

'Mostly budgetary constraints, as I suspected,' he replied slowly. 'Though I think that the person who vetoed reopening the case might have had some more personal reason for thwarting our mutual friend.'

'What do you mean?'

Niall Cameron sighed. 'That's not something that I can tell you, I'm afraid, DC Wilson,' he answered, a shadow clouding his fine features. 'And I'd thank you to keep this to yourself.' He looked her straight in the eye until he saw the young woman nod in agreement. 'I'm afraid you will just have to accept that there is no way the case can be taken forward without far more evidence to back it up.'

'Oh.' Kirsty's face was downcast and Niall felt a sudden pang for the younger officer. *She cares about him a lot,* he told himself. *And so do I, but my hands are tied here.*

As he ushered her from his office, DCI Cameron experienced a surge of anger against the woman who had slammed down the request. Chief Superintendent Pamela Crossan, a woman who was rumoured to have had several affairs with fellow officers, was not one of his favourite people. And when he had been leaving her office he had almost bumped into another officer, one who was believed to have graced Crossan's bed at one time. The fair-haired detective superintendent was a man he saw occasionally at the Helen Street station, since it was Mark Mitchison who headed up the CID branch at Govan. The deliberate gesture of letting him pass as the door lay ajar and the smirk on the other man's face had been suggestive as if to say *you, too?*

But then he had stopped and come closer, a strange expression on his face as if he was trying to place DCI Cameron. The sickly scent of his aftershave had made Cameron's nostrils twitch.

Superintendent Mark Mitchison had never liked Lorimer for some reason best known to himself, and now that Mitchison was in the running for an even more senior promotion he could afford to throw his weight about a bit. Cameron recalled the sneer in the man's voice and his curled lip as he'd spoken about Lorimer.

You used to be one of Lorimer's boys, didn't you? Cracked up, hasn't he? Couldn't stand the pace? Ah, well, don't suppose he'll be back any time soon unless it's for some pen-pushing job.

Cameron had recoiled at Mitchison's obvious delight in Lorimer's breakdown. That was why the other man had stopped.

Mitchison had evidently associated Niall with Lorimer from the old days when he and Lorimer had been after the same job – a job that Mitchison had been given, to everyone's surprise. And now he simply wanted to gloat over his old rival's distress. Schadenfreude. A right nasty word for the way some folk gained pleasure at another's misfortune. Well, Niall Cameron's own Hebridean upbringing had taught him that cruel things spoken of others might just come back to haunt a person. What was it the Scriptures said? *Cast your bread upon the waters and it will return unto you.* It usually meant that doing a good deed would bring prosperity into your life. But did the opposite apply?

He glanced out of his office window at the sky. A shaft of weak sunlight was struggling to emerge from behind those rainclouds, reminding Cameron that there was a higher force for good. A smile appeared along his mouth. If the Lorimer he remembered was even half the man he used to be then he doubted whether Chief Superintendent Crossan's directive would stop the detective superintendent from finding out what he wanted to know.

'I'm really sorry, sir.' Kirsty's voice sounded so sincere, so humble, that Lorimer wanted to give her a hug. She'd done her best, probably stepping out of line for him, even.

'It's all right, lass. I can understand. Happens all the time,' he said, trying to make the DC feel better. But that wasn't true, was it? Cold cases from way back could be reopened at any time given further evidence; he'd had first-hand experience of that himself.

'Take care, sir. We miss you,' she blurted out and Lorimer blinked, sudden tears starting in his eyes.

'Och, I'll be back to torment you all before you know it,' he said gruffly. 'Bye, now.'

She was a good girl and a fine officer, Lorimer told himself. And he really should not have put her in a difficult position. Still, it was heartening to know that someone else was on his side, someone who could verify that the face on that recorded TV clip was in fact the same man they had been seeking during the Quiet Release case.

Lorimer sat on the edge of his bed, staring out at the cloud-filled skies above the naked trees. If the powers that be had turned down Kirsty Wilson's request then so be it. He'd do it by himself, he decided. Or with a little help from a friend.

CHAPTER FOURTEEN

'Saw you on the telly the other night, Gordy.' The blonde-haired nurse addressed the porter as he passed by the nurses' station. 'Your five seconds of fame!' she exclaimed.

The man stopped abruptly, the empty trolley that he was wheeling squeaking to a halt.

'What did you say?'

'The telly. Has no one mentioned it? Couldn't miss *that* handsome face, could we?' She paused then turned away to sneeze into a handkerchief. 'Sorry. Think I'm going down with a cold. It was on the six o'clock news the other night. Something to do with waiting times. Again.' The woman made a face as she stuffed the hanky into her pocket. 'Wish they'd just leave us alone to get on with our jobs,' she grumbled, hands laid flat on top of a pile of patient files.

There was a silence as the man stared at her, his mouth open in a moment of disbelief.

'What?' She tossed her head and frowned at him.

'You really saw me on television?' he asked slowly.

'Come on, it's no big deal,' the nurse snorted. 'Hardly going to make you a celebrity now, is it?'

The porter turned away and resumed his journey along the corridor and around a corner to the bank of lifts that were designated for the theatre, leaving the nurse staring after him, a frown on her face.

'Strange man!' she whispered under her breath. 'Thinks I fancy him, does he? That'll be the day!' Then, for no apparent reason, she gave a shudder that was nothing to do with the impending virus.

His hands gripped the metal bar tightly as the lift descended. Had he even noticed the television cameras? The man calling himself Gordon Smith closed his eyes, trying to recall a moment when a camera had been pointed in his direction. But nothing came to mind. The place was always so busy nowadays, patients and visitors milling about at each level of this enormous hospital, many trying to find their way to a particular department, that it would have been fairly easy for a TV news crew to take some long-range shots without people noticing.

But if that stupid nurse had seen him, then who else might have caught a glimpse of his face? Not Gallagher, he hoped. He didn't want anything to jeopardise the resurrection of Quiet Release now that he had secured the cooperation of Glasgow's biggest drug boss.

His teeth ground together. It was too dangerous to remain here any longer. He had spread his poison well, he thought as the lift doors opened and he walked back into the daylight, but the fate of these patients could no longer be in his hands. It was time to move on, disappear from sight and leave only the ideas he had planted behind him.

But before the handsome orderly left this place for the last time there remained one final task that he was determined to carry out. He'd known about it for weeks now, watched as the nursing staff went about their routine of replenishing stocks. It was not as if he needed it but the temptation to take it from under their noses was a challenge he didn't want to resist. And, besides, if Jack Gallagher ever began to dilute his product, there would be sufficient high-quality morphine for several of his own future clients.

He was only being nice to her, Staff Nurse Audrey Dickson told herself as the good-looking porter passed by and dropped a lascivious wink. Nobody usually gave a girl like her a second look. Audrey pursed her lips and tried to concentrate on the paperwork on her desk. There were several discharge prescriptions waiting to take to the pharmacy and she would need to go down with one of the other nurses to hand them in. Audrey gave a sigh. The security was tight but that was all to the good. Her mind flashed back to the incident when a nurse had been caught putting prescriptions for temazepam into her local chemist after forging a hospital doctor's signature. Struck off from working in any UK hospital after that, Audrey remembered. Well, it would never happen up here. The protocol was so strict that it was a wonder any of the poor patients ever got their drugs before they left the wards to go home.

She lifted her eyes to the cupboard where the controlled drugs were kept, her hand straying to the two keys in her pocket. Marjory MacKellar usually had the other one but she was off sick today, the flu spreading like wildfire around so many of the staff. Well, she'd just have to take one of the other nurses with her instead, Audrey decided. The younger ones needed to have the experience of doing it some time, she supposed, flicking through the daily roster. Caitlin. Audrey frowned. It would have to be her deputy, Caitlin, the young girl who still looked as though she should be in school uniform instead of her nurse's blues. At least the lass was dependable; never off work for even a day since she'd qualified and begun working in this ward.

Audrey was just sliding off her stool when she looked up and saw the porter returning along the corridor, but this time he slowed down and gave her a warm smile that made the nurse tingle in places that made her blush.

'You're looking very fresh today, sister,' he said, tilting his head to one side and looking at her with those dark eyes.

'Staff nurse,' Audrey replied automatically then she gave a giggle. 'Why did you think I was a sister? Can't you tell the difference?'

The porter gave her an appraising glance. 'Of course,' he murmured. 'It's just that . . . ' He hesitated, leaving Audrey curious to know what he had been about to say.

'What?'

'You've got such an air about you,' he continued. 'Something that none of the others seem to have.'

'What d'you mean?' Audrey gave a little shiver as he continued to stare at her in a way that was not completely comfortable.

'You're the sort of woman that a guy would look up to,' the porter said, wagging a finger as if to emphasise the point. 'I bet all the doctors are mad about you,' he added with a sigh.

Audrey giggled again. 'Get on with you!' she exclaimed, feeling the heat infuse her face.

'Come on, don't tell me you haven't got a boyfriend amongst them . . . ?'

His question had brought him closer to Audrey's desk and she could see that the look in those large brown eyes was wistful. Surely he didn't think . . . no, that was absurd . . .

'You wouldn't ever have time to share a coffee with a humble porter, I suppose?' he asked, still gazing at her with a longing that took Audrey's breath away.

'I . . .' She hesitated then saw him drop his gaze and look at his watch.

'I'm off this shift in an hour. Does that tie in with one of your breaks, Staff Nurse Audrey Dickson?' he asked, a wicked smile around his lips.

He'd gone to the trouble of finding out when she took her break! Audrey raised her eyebrows in astonishment. Maybe he really did fancy her . . . ?

'The coffee shop on the ground floor?'

The nurse found herself nodding, too full of amazement at this invitation to speak.

Gazing after him as he loped along the corridor, Audrey blinked in disbelief. She'd fancied the guy for ages, ever since he had appeared on their wards. He was well spoken, obviously educated, and she was curious to know what a man like that was doing being a porter in a place like this. Well, perhaps she was about to find out once they'd sorted out this latest drug consignment.

He'd watched and waited for days until he knew the routine by heart. This ward rarely kept more than thirty phials of morphine, he'd discovered. They were all signed in and out by two people in the controlled drugs book with the names of the patients receiving them, dates, times and quantities remaining after the necessary amounts had been taken for use. It was a very secure system. He had watched while the pharmacy technician had brought the locked cases of drugs to the wards and counted them out with one of the trained nurses, usually someone like Audrey, the very overweight thirty-something with mouse-coloured hair that always seemed to be escaping from an untidy knot at the nape of her neck. She was efficient, though, he had seen that easily enough. And she kept one of the keys to the controlled drugs cupboard, which was why he had been so keen to make her like him. The virus that had already closed some of the wards in this block had taken its toll on several of the staff and he had overheard Staff Nurse Dickson bemoan the fact that she was carrying both keys around with her till the younger nurse came on duty, something that was against the rules.

He was ready to make his play for her now, smoothing a hand over his dark hair. A crease appeared between his eyes as he felt the balding patch at the crown of his head. Girls liked bald men, though, didn't they? The ones who shaved their scalps. He gave a shudder. That wasn't going to happen to him, though. If he really was losing his hair then there would soon be enough in his bank account to pay for anything he wanted, including a hair transplant.

One hand stroked the beard that he had grown over the past few months. That would have to go. As soon as he was out of here with the drugs then he'd take time to shave it off and return to the person he wanted to be next: the person who was going to visit Ellen Blackburn.

I'll see you after work, he'd whispered as she had buttoned up her uniform, hardly daring to look up at his face. Now, back in the ward, Audrey felt as though what had happened between them was visible for all to see; she felt a wave of shame pass over her but it was mitigated by a sense of pride.

She wasn't just *big Audrey*, the lumpen girl that nobody wanted. She was a desirable woman with curves that fascinated a passionate man. He hated the stick insects, as he called them.

That's what he had told her over their coffee, nodding as a couple of visitors had passed them by, a glamorous pair of girls whose endless long legs and sweeping hair extensions had made Audrey sigh. *They're not real*, he'd said. *Not a real woman like you*. And then those eyes had bored into her and they'd left their coffees unfinished and headed back upstairs, the knowledge that something special was about to happen between them.

The red light came on as he opened the cupboard but the hand that grabbed the large box was in and out in seconds and the light was extinguished as soon as he placed the pair of keys back into the double lock.

Nobody would look twice at the porter as he passed through the corridors, the folded blankets concealing the box of drugs.

CHAPTER FIFTEEN

Jimmy Rae watched as the big silver car left the forecourt. He sighed and shook his head. Had he done the right thing? It was all very well helping to make the man fit for his return to duty, but to collude in the case that Lorimer was so keen to have reopened, well, maybe he had overstepped a line there. The white-haired man chuckled to himself. It had actually given him a little thrill to be involved, if he were to be honest. Taking a video clip on Lorimer's mobile phone of the rerun of these television images seemed such a small thing to do. Yet that action might well have serious repercussions and he could only hope that none of them would be to the detriment of the tall detective whose car was now out of sight.

The journey from Auchterarder to Glasgow had raised Lorimer's spirits, the clouds lifting in wisps above the glens, the hazy winter light luminous against the crags of distant snowy mountains. Behind the wheel of the Lexus was a place he always felt comfortable, the big car eating up the miles as he drove south. His hand strayed to switch off the heated seat; being too hot made him sleepy and Lorimer did not want to come to grief on this stretch of icy road. The gritter lorries had been out early and he had noticed the crunch beneath his wheels where extra salt had been spilt across the motorway.

Soon he had left the flatter plains of Sheriffmuir behind and was approaching the city of Stirling, its proud castle gazing down on the Carse below, the great golden hall dazzling in a shaft of sunlight. The motorway was reasonably quiet at this time of day, rush hour past, and the Lexus sped along on the outside lane practically all the way towards the city.

When the familiar skyline came into view, Lorimer heaved a sigh of pleasure. He was coming home to Glasgow, his own city, the place where he belonged. Tonight he would be with Maggie and tomorrow they would awake, twined in one another's arms. But then there was work to be done and the faint smile that had crossed the detective's face vanished as he contemplated the visit to come.

It had been a long and tiring day, the sort of day that every teacher experienced from time to time, the kids restless and distracted no matter how hard Maggie Lorimer tried to engage their attention. *They need their half-term break*, her friend Sandie had declared as the two teachers had strolled out to the staff car park together. And it was true that these short winter days seemed to leach all the energy from both pupils and teachers. She'd welcome the time off when it came.

Maggie sighed as she heaved her bags into the passenger seat. It was all very well being long-suffering but her husband's illness had taken its toll on her too and there was no one at home to pick up the pieces whenever she felt a bit down. Before, she and Bill would chat about their work, grumble a little perhaps to get things off their chests as husbands and wives do. Lately she had felt so alone, the house too quiet, the evenings stretching out hour after weary hour. Her class marking was up to date and she had read all the books that had been Christmas gifts so, really, she ought to be looking forward to welcoming him home this evening, shouldn't she?

Would he want to go out? Or would she reheat the pot of home-made chicken broth and sprinkle it with fresh parsley? As she drove towards the Clyde Tunnel, Maggie's thoughts were on what else her husband might enjoy for his birthday dinner. A small smile crept onto her lips as Maggie recalled his previous birthday. He was a passionate man, though that side of their life had been sadly neglected since the tragedy on New Year's Eve. Perhaps if she were to light some candles, put on her sexiest nightdress ... The smile faded and she heaved another sigh. Well, that remained to be seen, didn't it?

Her heart lifted as she saw the silver car in the drive. He was home! At once all her reservations disappeared and Maggie was out of her car in seconds, rushing to open the door, to see him again.

'Hi,' she called out. Then she was in his arms, enfolded in the familiar hug that always made her feel cherished and special.

'Happy belated birthday, darling!' she murmured. 'It's good to see you.'

For a moment she looked into his eyes, knowing that she meant every word, yet fearful just what she might see there. Was he any better for the few days' treatment at the Perthshire centre? Or were these demons still lurking beneath the surface?

'How are you?' The question was out before she had time to think.

He turned away from her and strode towards the kitchen.

'I'm okay,' he said. Then, 'Cup of tea? You look like you could do with one.'

'Thanks.'

'Quite a lot's been happening, actually,' he said over the noise of the water filling the kettle.

Would he tell her about the treatment? she wondered.

'Told you about the TV clip, right?'

She nodded silently, her spirits plummeting once more. Surely he wasn't going to hark back to that?

But his voice was continuing behind her.

'Sent an email to Kirsty, asked her to compare the image to the one we have on record.'

Maggie shook her head silently. At least DC Kirsty Wilson would be able to show her former mentor that he was fantasising.

'And she confirmed that it was him!' Lorimer's voice held a note that Maggie hadn't heard in weeks, an excitement that made her look at him properly as he turned away from the kitchen.

'Really?'

'Says there's nothing they can do right now, though. Only to be expected.' He smiled with a shrug. 'Still, it's a start . . .'

A start of what? Maggie wanted to ask but one glance at those blue eyes gazing into the distance was all she needed to know. It was as if a light had been switched back on, the animated expression on his face, something that she'd missed for far too long.

'And Solly and I are going to Carstairs tomorrow. To interview Mary Milligan,' he added, a smile creasing his face.

'But why . . . ? If they aren't going to reopen the case . . . ?'

Then he was sitting beside her on the sofa, one arm slung around her shoulder, drawing her closer to him.

'Maybe they won't have to,' he said softly. 'Maybe I'll just poke around a bit myself, see what I can find. The old brain needs something to keep it occupied,' he laughed.

Maggie's mouth curved in a smile as she rested her head on his shoulder, feeling his fingers trail through her hair. It was as if the past few weeks had never happened. Was it the treatment he had been receiving that had wrought this change? Or was this sighting of the man they had sought in connection with the Quiet Release case a catalyst of some sort to bring back the man she knew and loved?

Later, listening to the rise and fall of his breathing, Maggie felt the deep peace that always came after their lovemaking. Perhaps the terrible nightmares would return to make him rise, screaming, as they had done for the past weeks, but something inside told her that tonight her beloved husband would sleep a dreamless sleep and wake to a brighter dawn.

CHAPTER SIXTEEN

Glasgow seemed to be blanketed in a pall of featureless cloud, the dampness seeping into his bones as Lorimer stepped out of the warm car. He had been lucky to find a parking space on University Avenue and he hurried to the meter, thrusting coins into the slot, shivering a little as he waited for the ticket to appear. He had stopped wondering long ago why Solly had never learned to drive, deciding that it was probably safer for other road users; his friend's mind constantly on things unseen, never the road ahead of him.

Soon he was loping across on a green light and heading towards the terrace where Solly awaited his arrival. The professor didn't normally come into his office on Saturdays but he'd asked Lorimer to meet him there instead of at their home across the park.

By the time Lorimer had entered the building his hair was wet from the misty drizzle and he left damp footprints on the stone steps leading up to the first-floor office.

'Solly?'

Pushing open the door, Lorimer's eyes roamed over the spacious room that appeared to be empty.

Then, as if he had conjured himself out of thin air, Solly stood up behind a large armchair next to one of his walls of books, brandishing a silver teaspoon in one hand, a huge grin on his face.

'Found it,' he exclaimed. 'I've been looking everywhere for that one. It was underneath that bookcase,' he continued, as if the explanation was important. 'Fancy a cup of tea?' He waved the teaspoon as if it were a magician's wand.

'Aye, why not, we've got time, haven't we?' Lorimer replied, glancing at his wristwatch.

'Oh, I think so,' Solly said, vaguely. 'She's not going anywhere, after all. And it would be a good idea to discuss how you are going to present her with this new evidence. I cleared that with her doctors, by the way.' He looked at the detective quizzically. 'You were intending to tell her what you saw, weren't you?'

Lorimer raised his eyebrows slightly. 'More than tell her, as you know,' he said, tapping the pocket where his mobile phone was tucked away. 'Now, how about a nice strong brew, Solly? None of your fancy herbal stuff for me,' he went on, deliberately changing the subject.

And, if he noticed the smile on the bearded psychologist's face as Solly turned to lift the kettle and take it to the sink, Lorimer might have remembered how it would be well-nigh impossible to fool this man.

The State Mental Hospital sat on the outskirts of Carstairs, an inoffensive Scottish village set deep within the countryside, its rail link to the main cities giving no clue to what lay close by. Apart from the name. The very word 'Carstairs' sent a shudder through even the most hardened soul, the knowledge that the inmates included those whose deranged mental conditions had resulted in unspeakable crimes.

The windscreen wipers swished back and forth, unable to clear the persistent drizzle that smeared their view. Outside all was dank and murky, the winter grasses a dull beige, leafless trees stark and skeletal against the sullen skies. Lorimer slowed down as they reached their destination, already preparing himself for the intense security that separated them from the people within the building looming ahead.

It seemed to take an inordinate length of time to cross the remaining security checkpoints; the airport-style body scans, as in any prison, the need to be photographed and hand over identification in the form of his warrant card, and then the seemingly endless barriers between the reception area and their final destination. For once, however, there was no need to hand over his mobile phone since Solly had explained to Mary's doctors what it contained.

Now Lorimer and Solly were seated in a surprisingly light and airy room, its barred windows screened by patterned glass, the walls painted in a soothing shade of primrose yellow that looked as if the decorator had recently finished. Lorimer sniffed the air, but there were no residual paint smells. Perhaps this room was rarely used, he thought, observing the corners to look for any scuff marks, the sorts of evidence that could be seen in any police interview room in the land. The table and chairs were, however, fixed to the floor, a precaution that anyone would take in a place where violence could suddenly erupt and a piece of furniture be used as a missile against the staff.

He was stretching his long legs under the table when they brought her in. Both he and Solly stood up at once, gazing at the woman who was being escorted between two orderlies in light blue uniforms.

Mary Milligan had changed since he had last seen her, Lorimer realised. Her previously ginger hair was two-tone now, the natural dark roots having grown in, making her complexion paler than ever. The sweetheart-shaped face was drawn and gaunt, shadows beneath her eyes speaking of some inner turmoil, perhaps?

'Hello, Mary,' Solly said.

The woman stared at each of them in turn as if trying to remember their faces. Then, as if a veil had been lifted, she grinned.

'Oh, it's you,' she said to Solly. Her smile slipped a little as her gaze shifted to his companion. 'What brings you here, Lorimer? A social visit, is it?' Her eyes narrowed as she regarded him, and the detective wondered not for the first time just what was going on in Mary Milligan's disturbed mind.

She was an obsessive attention-seeker, of course, Lorimer reminded himself, and their visit would serve to make her preen with self-importance, something that he might well use to their advantage.

'You're an important person, Mary,' he said, allowing his mouth to turn up in a slow laconic smile. 'Surely you know that?'

The woman stared at him fixedly then sat down heavily on the chair next to Solly. 'What d'you want?' she mumbled, head down, arms folded across her chest in what he recognised as a protective gesture.

'We want to help you, of course,' Solly replied gently. 'We all want that, Mary.'

'Aye.' She nodded absently as though she had hardly heard him.

'We wanted to talk to you about a *friend*,' Lorimer continued. As he emphasised the word, Mary sat up a little straighter and nodded silently.

'Don't have many friends in here,' she said, then gave a hollow laugh, the despair in her voice chilling Lorimer's blood.

'But you have a friend out there,' Lorimer persisted, tilting his head towards the glazed window panel.

He leaned forward a little so that she was caught in his blue gaze.

'I've seen him, Mary,' he said softly.

The woman's reaction was immediate. Her body stiffened as she unfolded her arms, crossing them over her breasts, fingertips gripping the shoulders of her blouse. Then she began to rock back and forward, her lips pursed as though to stop a cry from escaping.

'He's working again, Mary,' Lorimer went on, his eyes never leaving her own. 'I saw him in Glasgow. Did you know he was still there?'

The woman shook her head wildly, teeth pressed so hard into her lower lip that Lorimer thought she might draw blood.

'He hasn't been to see you?' Lorimer feigned surprise. 'That's not very nice, is it, Mary? I mean, you were lovers, weren't you?'

The woman's hands came down, each knuckling her eyes, then there was the sound of a long indrawn breath.

'He doesn't exist,' she whispered at last. 'I told you before. He isn't real.'

'But I saw him, Mary. I saw him in a hospital,' Lorimer replied.

'What?' The hands were down flat on the table top, the woman's mouth wide open in an O of disbelief.

'And we have trace evidence that shows there were two of you in Frankie Bissett's flat, Mary. We know you didn't kill him on your own,' he told her, his tone quite matter of fact, deliberately non-threatening.

The former nurse looked from Lorimer to Solly as if for reassurance that what she was hearing was all lies.

'He's right, Mary,' Solly told her. 'And the police will find him, you know, whether you are willing to give him up or not.'

She sat back again, regarding them in turn, a look of cunning returning to her eyes.

'This is all bullshit,' she said. 'You're making it up.'

'Are we?' Lorimer let the question hang in the air until he saw the doubt return to her face.

Then, drawing out his mobile phone, he turned it towards her and pressed a button.

The image flickered across the screen, the face of the hand-some man turning to the camera.

He watched the woman's face as every last vestige of colour drained away.

Then she began to scream.

CHAPTER SEVENTEEN

Audrey sat, head bowed, as the two officers began to question her. She wouldn't look up at them, not now, lest her eyes give her away. She'd dropped the keys somewhere, she'd told them, haltingly, when they'd spoken to her at the hospital. A terrible mistake. That was all. But now, in this dingy interview room deep in the heart of the city, Audrey knew that the mistake she had made was to let her passions rule her better judgement; something that she could not possibly allow again. But would they believe her as she told her story for a second time? And, worse still, would they force her to relive the awful truth?

Charles Graham pressed the buzzer and waited, his reflection on the smoked-glass door giving a vague impression of a well-dressed businessman. Nobody seeing him standing there would remark on any similarity to Gordon Smith, the hospital orderly who was at this very moment being sought by police for the theft of a large quantity of drugs from the Queen Elizabeth hospital. Gone was the beard and floppy hairstyle that had endeared him to the nurses on the wards as well as the elderly women he'd wheeled along those endless corridors. In their place was a clean-shaven man with dark hair swept back from his pale fore-head. This man had the appearance of money; the well-cut suit and silk tie, the Burberry raincoat draped across his shoulders and a pair of highly polished brogues that spoke of old-fashioned class. And these were not simply props, chosen to give a certain impression on this cold Sunday morning; they were things that he had selected carefully, wanting to clothe himself in the trappings of affluence as he took a further step in his ambition to become one of the wealthiest men in this godforsaken city.

'Mr Graham, good to see you.' Gallagher was across the room in three strides, the large, callused hand taking his visitor's in a grasp that was meant to show this newcomer the sheer brute strength of a man whose very reputation struck fear into so many around the city of Glasgow.

'Call me Charles, please.' The younger man smiled easily, inclining his head in the merest suggestion of a bow.

Gallagher smiled back. 'Take a seat,' he ordered, gesturing Graham into the easy chair by the window, watching as he crossed one leg over the other, looking perfectly relaxed in the office where so many others had cowered in fearful respect.

There was something about him that intrigued the older man. That handsome face, clean-shaven now, the cool way he sat, hands clasped as though it were he and not Gallagher who was about to call the shots. Not arrogance, exactly, but a confidence that the older man grudgingly admired.

Ellen Blackburn would never suspect a man like this.

Lorimer whistled as he placed the steaming mugs of coffee on the tray beside the plate of croissants, warmed for a few minutes in the oven. Maggie had bought these as a special treat for his birthday weekend, he realised. And yet it would be her treat too, he had decided, rising while she still slept. Breakfast in bed together was a Sunday thing, or a holiday thing, a rare occasion at any rate. For a moment his thoughts returned to the woman in Carstairs: had she ever sat in bed beside that handsome bearded man sharing a breakfast tray? The idea seemed absurd, somehow, that criminal folk could enjoy the same delights as he and Maggie did. But why not? She had been smitten by him to the extent of covering his tracks, even denying his very existence to protect him. But he couldn't bring himself to believe that the feelings he and Maggie shared were remotely like that relationship. Mary Milligan's love was tainted and he doubted that it had been truly reciprocated by the man he still sought.

As she opened her eyes to see him standing there, Maggie breathed a sigh of sheer pleasure.

'This is nice.' She smiled, struggling to sit up, pulling the duvet to cover her naked breasts. 'Thank you.'

'My pleasure,' he whispered, dropping a kiss on her forehead.

Maggie watched as he stood up and handed her the tray. The gesture was unexpected and all the sweeter for that. Having him at home with her was all she wanted but to be spoiled with a Sunday morning breakfast tray gave her so much more than Maggie had anticipated. It gave her hope, she realised, carefully taking the tray from his hands so that her husband could hang up his dressing gown on the back of the bedroom door and come back into the space beside her. He looked stronger now, she told herself, the determined jawline and those muscular shoulders. Another little smile twitched the corners of her mouth as she remembered their lovemaking from the night before. Could it be possible that this Castlebrae place was making a difference already? She watched as he took a mug of coffee and placed it on his bedside table, his hand quite steady.

The fragrant scent of the coffee wafted between them as they sat there together. She felt his warm fingers entwining her own. *I love you*, he'd whispered into her hair as they'd lain together last night, their passion spent. But now there was no need to speak, the companionable silence and that smile in his blue, blue eyes more potent than any words could utter.

CHAPTER EIGHTEEN

Ellen Blackburn's tragedy had brought sympathy from her friends and neighbours, despite the fact that the woman had rarely been liked in the street where she lived, a stone's throw from the old Duke Street jail. She'd been fêted by the press at the time, given interviews in the front room of her upstairs tenement flat and enjoyed more attention from strangers eager to hear her history than from anyone in her own family. But now the interest had tailed off, the story of her son's killing spree yesterday's news, and Ellen was feeling frustrated that nobody was calling at her front door any longer.

It was that frustration as much as anything else that had led her to seek out Jack Gallagher and demand more money from Glasgow's notorious gangster. The thought of Thomas never coming around any more, a brown envelope thrust into her gnarled fingers, ate into her. No, she'd get what was rightfully hers, Ellen had decided. If Thomas hadn't done that terrible thing . . . well, he'd still be coming every other week to help eke out her paltry pension, wouldn't he? And, in a twist of logic, it made sense to her that Jack Gallagher should be the one to recompense for that lack.

She was watching a television programme where young girls spent time swishing around in wedding frocks, humming and hawing about whether this one or that was the perfect dress for their forthcoming nuptials. Ellen, who had never worn the white frock (being up the duff with Thomas and only too glad to accompany his father to Martha Street for a registry office wedding), drank in the details jealously, feasting her rheumy eyes on what seemed like acres of expensive tulle, though she really hadn't a clue about the price, being unable to understand the conversion rate from US dollars. When the doorbell rang, Ellen gave a start, since anybody arriving ought first to press the security buzzer at the main entrance to the flats. She smoothed her hair and shuffled along in her bedroom slippers, one eye on the shadow that obscured the glass lintel at the end of the hallway.

She slipped on the chain before opening the door and stepped back to get a closer look at the man standing on her doorstep, a briefcase in one hand. He was a good-looking guy, younger than her Thomas and dressed in a smart charcoal suit under his navy raincoat. His clean-shaven face looked down on her with a smile.

'Who the hell are you?' she growled, expecting to be told that she was receiving a visit from one of God's own people, either the Mormons or Jehovah's Witnesses.

'I'm Mr Graham. Can you tell me if Mrs Blackburn is at home, please?'

'Aye, she is an' ye're lookin' at her,' Ellen rasped, curiosity making her hand hover above the chain. 'What d'ye want? If it's the *Watchtower* ye're sellin' I'm no' interested,' she snapped, ready to slam the door shut on the handsome face.

'No, no, not at all, Mrs Blackburn. I'm here at the request of

Mr Gallagher. He asked me to bring something to you.' The smile and the expression of warmth in his eyes made Ellen hesitate for just a moment. This wasn't one of Gallagher's usual goons. This guy was smart, more like a person from a real office than the type of heavy she used to see hanging around with her Thomas.

'I need you to sign some forms,' the man went on, patting the soft leather briefcase. 'If I might come in for a few minutes?'

Ellen gave a grunt of acquiescence and slipped the chain back to allow the fellow entry to her home.

'C'mon through tae the living room,' she muttered. 'Suppose ye'll be wantin' a cup o' tea?' She was secretly pleased now that it looked as if Gallagher were bending to her demands. Aye, you couldn't put one over on Ellen Blackburn, she told herself, leading the way into a room that smelled of years of cigarettes and stale carry-outs.

'Tea would be lovely,' her visitor agreed, in a voice that folk like Ellen described as 'posh' though it was simply the product of a good education and had a Glasgow accent of its own, sounding not unlike the nice blokes off the Scottish news programmes. It was that 'decent' voice as much as anything that let the old woman lower her guard. She busied herself with pouring water into a kettle and setting a couple of clean, unchipped mugs on a tray.

'D'ye take milk an' sugar?' she shouted through from the tiny kitchenette.

'Yes, both, thank you. Do you need a hand?'

Suddenly he was standing behind her, one hand on Ellen's shoulder. 'Allow me, please,' he said, in a tone as smooth as milk chocolate, so Ellen stood aside, watching in amazement as the fellow poured boiling water from her own kettle and set the teapot on a tray along with the mugs, sugar basin and the opened half carton of milk. Ellen blushed suddenly, wishing she'd thought to pour it into a wee jug but for the life of her she couldn't think when she'd last seen a milk jug in this flat.

She followed him back through then sat down, staring at him as he poured the tea and handed her a mug.

'You don't mind . . . ?' he asked, still with that smile on his face, and Ellen shook her head in wonderment at this apparition of gentility that had descended on her shabby little home.

'Terribly sorry to hear about your misfortune,' he remarked as they both settled back to drink the tea. 'I was never acquainted with your son.' Ellen nodded. Nobody who looked like that had ever been in Thomas's company except for the polis and even they didn't measure up to this man.

'Now, let's get down to business,' Graham said briskly, bending to one side to retrieve the briefcase and setting it on his lap. 'I need you to sign these consent forms.'

'What am I supposed to be consenting to?' Ellen asked archly. 'Something worth my while, I hope?'

Graham simply smiled in reply and took out a sheaf of printed papers. Then, laying them on the table, he stood up and came around Ellen's chair as if he were about to go through whatever stuff was written on the documents, guiding her from his position at her shoulder.

She screwed up her eyes at the closely written script, not paying attention to the movement as the man drew out the rubber gloves from his coat pocket and slipped them on.

Ellen gasped as the pad was pressed across her nose and mouth. She wanted to gag and for a few seconds her fingers scrabbled upwards.

But the smell and a humming noise in her ears made her slump

113

into her chair. Then there was a dizzying sensation of falling through space as the room disappeared into eternal blackness.

It was the work of seconds to render her unconscious.

Slowly he removed the chloroform pad and came back around the chair, feeling with his fingers for a pulse. He smiled. She was still alive. But not for much longer. Then he began the work that he had intended to carry out all along, measuring the dose from the phial and inserting it into the syringe. He plunged it into an unresisting vein, leaving the syringe to dangle from her withered flesh.

With a huge sigh he settled back in the chair he had so recently vacated, watching the rise and fall of her breathing until the final gurgle and gasp let him know she was gone.

Eyes gleaming, he grinned, smoothing fingers down towards the bulge in his trousers. He could feel the hardness in his groin and shook his head with a laugh at his own body's reaction. It had been so long, so long since he'd watched that very last breath disappearing.

A doctor is all powerful, his stepfather had said, and, as ever, Mum had agreed, casting glances between her husband and her son as if to affirm the words. *He has the power of life and death in his hands*, Dad had continued gravely.

His smile was tinged with a sort of regret, the closest he ever came to feeling anything resembling grief: if only he could have let them live to see how successful he had become, their clever boy!

When he was entirely satisfied that there was nothing more of life in the old woman, he took the mugs back through to the kitchen and rinsed them carefully under the tap, drying each one in turn and putting them back in the cupboard beside the others. No trace would be left in this place to reveal *his* presence, though he had left the plastic box with most of the other used needles lying on the floor next to her chair. If anyone was bothered enough to look a little further they might find prints that matched those of a dead man, Gordon Smith, another drug victim. And if they tried to make a link they would assume that Ellen Blackburn was just a user like these street people. It was a perfect way to cover his own tracks, he thought with a smile.

A quick search around the flat produced what Gallagher had instructed him to retrieve. The letters from the gangster were stuffed into a magazine rack beside the television set and he found the banknotes in a china jar next to the tea caddy in her kitchen. *No way will these be traced back to any bank account with my name on it*, Gallagher insisted. He stuffed both letters and bankrolls deep into the bottom of the briefcase before looking at her one last time.

Whoever came in here next would find the old lady lying in her chair, head bowed forward as though she had simply fallen asleep. The overdose of drug would tell its own story: a woman so stricken with grief that she had sought consolation in too much opiate.

The newspapers would have a field day, of course. But Ellen Blackburn would not be there to enjoy that final episode in her story.

115

CHAPTER NINETEEN

The snow that had begun as tiny swirling flakes, almost invisible at first, was now a whirlwind of white, whipping across the windscreen of the Lexus and smearing his vision.

Lorimer glanced at the temperature: it was two degrees below. The skies ahead were massed with snow clouds, visibility decreasing with every mile as he drove back towards Auchterarder. Maggie would be heading for work now, the Glasgow school still open despite the forecast of more snow and the possibility of everyone being sent home early, their half-term break beginning sooner than expected. It would not be the first time that teachers had struggled into work only to be told to go back home again. But Maggie Lorimer was not the type to give up easily and with so much course work still to be covered before the May exams, she would want every minute with her pupils. Still, as he slowed the big car down to twenty-five miles an hour, his thoughts were with his wife and the precious hours they had spent together.

I could give it all up, you know, he had murmured into her hair. *Find a different sort of job.* Maggie hadn't said a word but the sad little smile and shake of her head had told him all that Lorimer needed to know. She was the sort of wife that every serving officer ought to have, he told himself now. Not only did she support his choice of career, Maggie understood the problems that came with this job. Even now. *Especially* now.

For a time he had felt stronger, her arms around him, her sweet body close to his own. Yet, the further he drove from her, the old sense of weakness returned. His head ached as though the low pressure in the skies above were bearing down upon him. What good would it do him to return to the treatment centre at Castlebrae? The frown between his eyes tightened. Wasn't everything changed? And would he ever be fully fit to return to the rigours of police work?

Suddenly the tyres slipped and slithered as the car began to skid and Lorimer took his foot off the accelerator, steering into the whiteout.

It was tempting to touch the brake but he guided the Lexus forward, peering into the mass of dizzying snowflakes falling from the skies. Ahead there was no sign of another vehicle, no twin red tail-lights to follow. A swift glance in the rear view mirror told him that there was not one other car behind him. The sense of claustrophobia caught at his throat, a rising panic that needed to be subdued if he were to come out of this smothering cave of white that was closing in on him.

Slowly, slowly he drove along the barren stretch of road. Where the hell was he anyway? Visibility was down to mere feet, any road signs rapidly obscured by the snow. And how far had he to travel before the turn-off that would take him to Auchterarder? He pressed the radio button, hoping for a traffic update, but all that came through was a murmuring buzz of sound.

Lorimer had been in bad snowstorms before. Once it had taken him seven hours to drive from the Borders back to Glasgow, snowdrifts ten feet high on either side almost blocking the roads. He took deep breaths, deliberately calming himself. Focus, he told himself. You're not in any danger yet.

He blinked hard, concentrating on the patch of road ahead. It was warm inside his vehicle, there was a bottle of water tucked into the side panel of the door and a shovel and rope in the boot, things that he kept there every winter as a matter of course. If it came to the bit he'd call the emergency services. If his mobile found a signal, he reminded himself wryly.

He slowed down once more as the hills became steeper, straining to see where the road stopped and the grass verges began, the white shapes of bushes now buried beneath the falling snow. Round this next corner, shouldn't there be the sign for the turn-off? His back was rigid as he leaned forward, the windscreen wipers laboriously shifting icy sheets from the glass, allowing Lorimer glimpses of the way ahead.

The lights in front of him appeared out of nowhere, two red spots, one higher than the other, making Lorimer touch the brakes.

'Dear God!' he exclaimed aloud. Then his eyes focused on the car that had skewed off the road and was lying at a dangerous angle, its wheels almost off the side of a steep overhang that plunged down to the fields below.

Only taking time to switch on his hazard warning lights, Lorimer pulled himself out of the Lexus and stumbled across to the vehicle, fastening his coat as he went. The wind spat icy needles onto his skin as he plodded through the snow and he had to blink away huge flakes that landed on his eyelids.

The vehicle was completely covered in white and his first instinct was to wipe away the snow that had masked the nearest window.

Then he saw her.

A woman, slumped forward, motionless, head resting on the steering wheel. He caught sight of grey curls escaping from an old lady's woollen hat.

Lorimer tugged at the door, the effort to yank it open making his arm ache as the wind howled around him, threatening to pull it out of his grasp.

He wedged his body inside the door, hands fumbling off his gloves, shoving them in a pocket.

The skin at her neck was still warm and he breathed a sigh of relief as he felt the pulse beating. Still alive, then. But what were the extent of her injuries? And how the hell was he going to get them both out of here?

It was then that Lorimer noticed the lights on the dashboard and realised that the engine was still turned on. How long had she lain here? Long enough for the vehicle to be covered in snow, he thought. At least the car didn't feel particularly cold, though with the driver's door wide open it would chill the injured woman soon enough.

He closed the door carefully, and headed back to the Lexus.

With one eye on the vehicle tilted precariously over unknown depths of snow, Lorimer pulled out his mobile and rang the number that he hoped would bring relief. His teeth were clamped over his lower lip as he waited for the familiar ringtone. Then he exhaled a sigh as a voice responded to his call.

Any neck injury might be made worse should he try to move the woman, he reminded himself, but the possibility of her suffering hypothermia was equally dangerous. *Keep her warm*, the voice on the line had advised. But it was impossible to enter the passenger side of the other car and putting his own weight next to hers might topple the vehicle completely upside down. No, there was only one thing for it, Lorimer decided as he wrenched open the driver's door once again, snowflakes fluttering in and settling on her inert form. Carefully he bent over the woman's body and unclipped the seat belt. Then, cradling her head with his left arm, and bending his knees to take the strain, he lifted her up against his chest.

He curled her into him, protecting her face from the icy onslaught as he staggered under the weight of her unconscious body. Each gruelling step back to the Lexus was fraught with the danger of slipping but at last he was there, reaching out with frozen fingertips to open the passenger door. Lorimer felt a sharp pain in his lower back as he braced himself against the door then bent to lay the old woman gently against the heated seat. He slammed the door shut, cutting off any further entry from the gusts of snow then staggered around to the other side of the Lexus.

In moments he was beside her, his coat off now, placing it over her and tucking it in to keep out any draughts.

Upright and warm. The phrase came back to him suddenly, a grim smile tugging at the corners of his mouth. Wasn't that what his gran used to tell him? Each time her birthday had come around she'd say it: *So long as I'm upright and warm it's a time to celebrate.*

The sound of voices made Lorimer start. He turned, seeing the old lady beside him, his coat still around her, the face pale but not the parchment white that he associated with death. He must have fallen asleep, he realised, as the voices came nearer and lights shone through the gloom.

'You all right, there, sir?' Lorimer heard as he opened the door a couple of inches.

'Aye. Can you see to this lady here? She's the one who's been in the accident,' he replied, pushing the door wider and stepping out into a white world of brightness.

The snow had stopped and everything was quiet except for the sounds from the police Land Rover.

'Okay, sir, we'll take it from here. Can you just give my colleague your name and address and answer his questions for us?'

The next few minutes were a blur of activity as the old lady was carried to the waiting vehicle, ready to be taken to the nearest hospital.

'Your coat, sir,' a uniformed police officer handed Lorimer the navy cashmere overcoat and he took it, suddenly grateful for its warmth.

'You did a grand job, there, sir. Keeping her warm like that.' The officer nodded in approval as he slid in beside Lorimer, his high-visibility storm coat bulky against the passenger seat.

'Maybe it was because I was well trained.' Lorimer smiled.

'Oh?'

'Superintendent William Lorimer, Police Scotland,' he replied, taking out his warrant card and showing it to the man whose eyes widened in surprise. 'I'm on sick leave at the moment. Just heading back to Castlebrae,' he explained.

'Goodness,' the man murmured, glancing from the warrant card to the tall man with the piercing blue eyes. 'What were the chances of someone like you turning up just when that old dear needed help, eh? Strange old world, isn't it?'

There would be a tale to tell later; how he met the detective out on this barren stretch of road, this small act of heroism one more story to add to all of the rest.

*

121

It was, indeed, a strange world, Lorimer thought as he drove slowly up to the treatment centre some time later, the speed bumps hardly noticeable under the snowfall. Everything sparkled under the watery sunlight, each angle of the building softened by the blanket of white. As he walked across the well-gritted path from the car park, Lorimer looked up at the sky. The snow clouds had disappeared and now the air was tingling under a pale winter sky. It was hard to believe the snowstorm that had enveloped him was gone, leaving the world quiet and calm. He had felt the ache in his back as he'd lifted his bag from the rear seat of the Lexus. But his mind was no longer fogged by doubts. It was a relief to be here once again and he was ready to submit to whatever treatment he needed.

Somewhere an elderly lady would be receiving help for her injuries; somewhere that Land Rover and its officers would be patrolling the roads to keep folk safe. For wasn't that what their job was all about?

He breathed in the cold, crisp air, a renewed sense of purpose filling his senses.

Somewhere out there, too, was a man whose face he had spied on that television screen, a man who remained free to carry out his evil deeds.

As Lorimer's glance fell from the skies to the sweeping hills below, his jaw tightened in a determined line. No matter what happened, he was going to find that man.

CHAPTER TWENTY

Rosie swallowed hard. After all these years she ought to be inured to the smells that wafted up from decomposing bodies but this morning her stomach heaved at the very sight of the itinerant whose corpse lay on her operating table. She breathed in slowly behind the green mask, taking her time, exhaling until her diaphragm tightened.

The man had been found by the Riverman, George Parsonage, beneath one of the bridges that spanned the Clyde, face down in the mud, vomit-stained clothing a clue to his death. Had he choked? Or had the final substance with which he had abused this poor emaciated body been enough to kill him? A post-mortem examination was mandatory in any sudden death that might or might not be suspicious and it was not for the pathologist to determine which dead body was more deserving of her attentions. Each one had been someone's wee boy or girl, Rosie was wont to tell her students. Someone just like you, perhaps, she'd remind them. A victim was someone whose chance at living had been taken away from them. But sometimes they had ended their own lives, by mischance or by sheer carelessness, the drug high that they wanted being worth the risk of death. Was this what had happened to this poor soul?

The lungs were tubercular, a sign that whoever he had been, his way of life pointed to the damp, cold streets. Too many like this man had graced her metal table; homeless creatures whose lives had been ruined by drink or drugs. Well, she sighed, wrinkling her nose, there were no external signs of damage to his body apart from the scabs and sores created by perpetual use of a hypodermic needle. It would be up to the toxicologists to give a final say in what it was that had actually killed the man.

Rosie stood beneath the shower, grateful that the last autopsy had been performed for the day. It was always a sad business to carry out a post-mortem on a nameless person, as if death had swept everything away including their very identity. Sometimes no one even claimed the bodies of these folk from Glasgow City Mortuary.

A yellow sticker was pasted next to details kept in the log book, a reminder to the pathologists and technicians that the corpse might be HIV positive and present some danger even after death.

Her hand slid over her stomach as she soaped her skin. The memory of that nausea returned and for a moment she stood still, as though listening for something. But in truth, it was only her unspoken thought. And, as Rosie continued to run her fingers across her abdomen, her lips parted in a small smile of wonder.

DC Kirsty Wilson sat back and stretched her arms wide. She'd finished the paperwork about the body found by George Parsonage, the Glasgow Humane Society officer. Now it would be up to the scientists to decide on the ending of this particular story. A drug death, she expected; a story that was all too common nowadays, whether in the city or anywhere else in the country. *Drugs are the scourge of the modern age*, she'd heard her dad say often enough. And he was right.

Her thoughts wandered to her father. He'd been upset to hear about the detective superintendent's breakdown and, like others, found it hard to come to terms with the strong, resilient character of Bill Lorimer crumpling under the events of New Year's Eve. *He isn't a superhero*, she'd heard DI Jo Grant say. *He's just flesh and blood like anyone else.* But there had been murmurings too, comments about the man being unable to hold down his position again, as though a mental or emotional breakdown somehow stigmatised a person for life.

He's finished! she'd heard DC Jean Fairlie declare when Kirsty had returned that day to Stewart Street, a remark that had made Sadie Dunlop glare at the woman.

Would the medics up at Castlebrae be able to mend that broken mind? Kirsty had googled their website, listened to the testimonies of officers whose careers had continued after various trauma, both mental and physical. Surely he would come back to them? She found herself clasping her hands tightly together as though praying to some unseen deity. Well, perhaps she was. And if there *was* a God in heaven watching everything that went on down here, surely he would help Lorimer to full health again.

'Did him in, didn't he?' The man hunched inside his tattered coat spat on the icy ground.

'How d'ye make that out?' the other man mumbled through teeth that were black and broken.

The tramp drew closer and pulled his companion into a darker corner of the underpass as though afraid to be overheard. 'It was him, I'm telling ye,' he hissed, his shaggy head turning this way and that, rheumy eyes bright with fear.

'Naw, why wid he do that?'

'I think it wis cos Gordy telt him stuff.'

'Whit kinda stuff?'

'Gordy telt me,' he began, then, drawing closer to the other tramp's face he whispered, 'He telt me that man paid Gordy for his ain self.'

'Eh? Whit kind o' nonsense is that? His ain *self*?'

'Thon beardie man wanted tae use Gordy's name, an' that. Wanted to know where he used tae live, all sorts of stuff.' He shivered suddenly. 'Could've been mine: Tam McLachlan. Or yours, Seamus O'Halloran.' He shot the other man a look. 'Said he'd pay him in kind ...'

'Ah ...' There was a pause as the two men regarded one another, a silent understanding passing between them.

'He took away his *identity*, Seamus,' Tam said at last, the words coming out like a sigh. 'So,' he continued slowly, 'naebody knows it wis Gordy's body that wis found by thon Parsonage fella. The one that pulls them out the river.'

'You mean the polis don't know who Gordy is, then?'

Tam McLachlan nodded slowly, considering. 'Do you think we ought to tell them?'

It was one of those times that Lorimer would have enjoyed, DC Wilson thought, remembering her mentor's words: *I don't believe in coincidences*, he'd told her often enough. And yet here was one that she had almost stumbled upon by chance. They had been fortunate to have been paid a visit from one of the old tramp's drinking buddies, Tam McLachlan, a poor-looking creature who had told them his name and given the dead man's last known address. It had puzzled her, that old man's ruined face: hadn't she seen him somewhere before? But her memory had refused to yield up any connection and now DC Wilson was sitting in the driver's seat outside a nondescript tenement flat, pointing to the paragraph from the hospital admin records.

'*That* Gordon Smith? You've got to be joking!' the detective sergeant beside her exclaimed, eyeing the young woman with a look that bordered on disbelief.

DC Kirsty Wilson stifled a sigh. Her current boss, Detective Sergeant McCrone, was gazing at her as though she were a schoolgirl, not a fully fledged detective in Police Scotland. 'We can't deny that it's the same flat, sir,' she told him, trying to keep her tone as neutral as she could. 'The victim who died as a result of an overdose was called Gordon Smith. The old man had been evicted from here a while back. And it was exactly this address that the hospital orderly of the same name gave to his employers.' She watched his expression as the DS took in her words. McCrone was a heavily built man in his forties, his pockmarked face and thinning hair were two of his less attractive features but it was that sneering voice that grated most on the younger officer. McCrone or Moanie (a soubriquet that Kirsty had learned almost as soon as she had been posted to this division) snatched the paper from Kirsty's hands and turned away as though he needed to read it for himself. They'd all been referring to the fugitive as Gordon Smith but it seemed that the DS was personally affronted by the hospital orderly's duplicity.

Can't you see he'd stolen the dead man's identity? Kirsty wanted to yell at him as she raged to herself. That was the same address that other old derelict had written when he had paid a visit to the city mortuary and asked his note to be passed to the police.

'Well, that explains a lot, doesn't it?' McCrone turned back to her, the familiar curled lip a sign that she recognised. 'Explains why *you* couldn't find him. Lets you off the hook,' he added, smirking, as though the concerted search for the hospital thief was somehow down to Kirsty's ineptitude. 'Mitchison will need to know, but I shan't mention your name, hen.' He stopped and tapped the side of his nose. 'This is a job for the big boys, no' for wee lassies.'

Then he turned to give a tug at the seat belt, leaving the detective constable staring at his back for a moment, wishing that she had never left Stewart Street and the comforting presence of Detective Superintendent Lorimer.

CHAPTER TWENTY-ONE

The therapist had asked him a few questions about his general health before allowing him to lie face down upon her narrow bed. Lorimer had closed his eyes, partly out of embarrassment that a pretty young woman was beginning to massage his back but mostly because of the languorous feeling that had crept over his whole body.

You might go to sleep, she had warned him, something that Lorimer doubted. But now, the hands that swept across his shoulder blades, circling the places where tension had become rock hard, seemed not to be a part of the therapist at all, as if they somehow had a life and energy of their own. There was a sensation of mild pain as she kneaded the rope-like muscles on the back of his neck, her strong fingers probing deeper and deeper to rid his body of the knots of stress that had built up over the past few weeks.

Weeks? The question came to his mind. Hadn't he been experiencing tension headaches for months now? Perhaps this morning's events had simply compounded the strains on his over-weary body. And mind.

Would they let him know how that elderly woman was? He

hoped so, picturing her in some hospital bed, being tended to by caring professionals, like the young woman whose thumbs were making circles above his shoulder blades. It wasn't just his fractured mind they were trying to mend, Lorimer thought, yawning as he turned his head to one side.

He let his arms fall either side of the narrow bed, a sigh escaping from him as the scents and warmth in the darkened room made him relax into a drowsy half sleep. Images of the deep snow and the tilted car blurred as he began breathing heavily.

'How're you feeling?' Solly glanced down at his wife, their fingers linked as they crossed the road to Kelvingrove Park.

'Fine,' she answered airily, but a small smile and refusal to look up at his eyes made Solly begin to wonder.

'You're ...?' He stopped on the pavement, blissfully unaware of the students who were milling around them. 'Rosie!'

She was nodding her head and grinning now, shyly, as if her secret was only to be shared with him.

Solly clasped her to his body. 'I can't believe it,' he whispered. 'When did you find out?'

'I did a test today,' Rosie admitted. 'Explains a lot, though, doesn't it?' she added ruefully, patting her stomach.

Solly beamed at her and took her hand in his once again. 'Right, soon as we're home you're putting your feet up, okay?'

'Sure,' Rosie laughed. 'I can just see Abby agreeing to that!'

'Leave that young lady to me,' Solly answered. 'I aim to spoil you properly this time,' he warned her.

They strolled hand in hand through the park, the dusk muted to the colour of sapphires against the city skyline. Their breath was ghostly in the frosty air and Solly looked down as they stepped along the path, anxious now to avoid any icy patches

130

that might cause his wife to stumble. Such precious cargo that she was bearing . . .

'We had the tox report on that itinerant. Did I tell you?' Rosie began.

'The one George Parsonage found near Glasgow Green?'

'Aye. Strange sort of overdose,' Rosie murmured. 'High quality morphine. Not the sort of thing you'd expect to find on a street person. Wonder where that came from?'

Solly squeezed her hand. Once she was home he wanted Rosie to forget the job for a while, sit back and relax, bask in the wonder of her pregnancy, shut out the world for a time. Matters of other lives and deaths could wait their turn.

He watched the pair of them slouch under the railway bridge, hunched into their ragged coats, collars turned up against the fog that had descended on the city.

'Looking for me?' He smiled as they turned the corner in the direction of the river. They recognised him, all right, despite the fact that his hair was shorter and he was now clean shaven.

The one called Tam refused to look him in the eye, he noticed. Well, that was hardly surprising given his betrayal. Gallagher had told him that the police had been nosing around the old tramp's former flat; but they would find nothing to link him to this creature. He stared at the other one who was trying to grin, dodging from one foot to the other in a shambling sort of dance. It was obvious from his behaviour that the tramp needed a hit.

'Seen anyone interesting today?' he asked, tossing his words lightly into the frozen air.

'Naw,' Tam replied then spat on the ground as if that were a full stop on any further conversation.

'Never mind,' the man said with a laugh. 'I'm in a generous

mood tonight. Thought you lads might need a wee bit of fire in your blood, eh?'

The pair of them stopped at once, Tam eyeing him with suspicion (because he'd got rid of his beard, perhaps?). But the older man, Seamus, sidled up to him with hope and expectation in his rheumy eyes.

'How much?' Seamus grunted, his hollow cheeks sharpened by the shadows from the street lamp.

'You can pay me back in kind,' the man grinned. 'Tell me about yourselves, eh? I'm sure both of you have interesting stories.'

'You've got to be kidding us,' Tam growled. 'Why'd you want to know about a couple of old fools like us?'

The younger man shrugged. 'People can make it worth your while if you've something to sell.'

'What?' Seamus looked at him properly now, his eyes like a pair of stones. 'What're you saying? What have we got tae sell that's worth anything?'

'We thought—'

But whatever Tam had thought was silenced by his companion's elbow suddenly in his midriff.

'Aye, sure, pal, what d'ye want tae know?' Seamus nodded, moving closer, his gaze searching the young man for signs that their reward was forthcoming.

'Ah, later.' The young man smiled. 'After you've told me everything about your lives,' he added, taking a small electronic device from his coat pocket and flicking a switch. 'Right, now who's going to begin?'

'Here.' The packet was slipped swiftly from one hand to the other. Then he looked at them in turn with a slight smile on his handsome face. 'Enjoy.'

Then, leaving them to unwrap the drugs and savour the anticipation of a night of bliss, he turned on his heel and walked back towards the city and its brightly lit restaurants and bars where nobody would remark upon a well-dressed man making his way towards Central Station.

These two would be no loss to anyone. In fact, wasn't he doing society a favour in ridding it of such undesirables? he asked himself, his polished shoes leaving marks along the damp pavement. Maybe he'd make use of their identities one day, maybe not, he shrugged. Under the lamplight his smile curved into a grin. The poison that would soon be flooding their veins would not take long to finish them off. But it would be a painful and brutal end.

Just a pity he wasn't going to be there to watch as they took these final gasping breaths.

CHAPTER TWENTY-TWO

T am McLachlan was not a man to weep over another's misfortune but he had felt the hot tears slide down his cheeks as Seamus gave one final twitch then slumped to the floor.

The old man had been too eager, Tam told himself, bundled in his overcoat some hours later. But, in truth, even as he had spun his own web of lies into that man's listening ears, he had known all along that he was going to let Seamus be his guinea pig. He rewrapped the empty phial into the cloth and stuffed it into Seamus's pocket, his fingers clumsy under the heavy gloves; careful to ensure that no traces of his own identity would be discovered. Let the polis figure that one out when they found him in this dump, he thought viciously. Whatever this dealer in other people's identities had supplied was meant to finish them both off. But Tam McLachlan had been patient enough to wait and see.

He aimed a kick at the inert body lying at his feet, a surge of rage coursing through him. Stupid, stupid old fool! Should've listened to me, Tam thought. But, hadn't he half believed the fellow himself? That charming smile and the plausible tone of voice. Lulling them into a false sense of security. Just like he'd done to Gordy. And now, Seamus.

Well, he wouldn't be getting away with any more. Not if he could help it.

Tam shivered suddenly. Who was he kidding? If the man found out that he hadn't taken the lethal drug, then he'd be after him without a second thought. Once upon a time he'd have been able to contact DS Murdoch but that door was closed to him since the big detective's retirement. There had been that wee lassie cop ... the one who'd taken his details, hadn't she been Murdoch's sidekick a few months ago? But to put his trust in a slip of a girl like that?

No, it was time to clear off out of this city with its creeping shadows and night-time terrors. But, even as he began to consider ways to effect his own escape, Tam McLachlan knew a deep longing to avenge himself on the smiling young man who had infiltrated their underworld.

CHAPTER TWENTY-THREE

'It's becoming a *tad* more complicated,' the man told his colleagues with an engaging smile.

There was a collective sigh from the men and a solitary woman seated around the long table. Despite his undoubted charm, Superintendent Mitchison was not their favourite senior officer by a long way, his deliberation and adherence to the rule book now legendary. But someone had asked him to pass on a message from on high and here he was. Their own detective super, Lucy Renton, had been off sick since her stroke and was unlikely to be replaced any time soon and the general thinking amongst the team was that Mark Mitchison would be selected to take her place. He might have been excused his rather pedantic way of handling cases if he had been better at relating to his colleagues but the detective superintendent always appeared to be a bit aloof, a cut above the others here in Govan police station, rarely joining his colleagues for a pint at the end of a long day, though he would always put a decent tab behind the bar when the occasion arose.

Police gossip said that the fair-haired man who stood over them, arms folded across his chest, was the spoiled only son of elderly parents who had given him a private education in one of the city's more illustrious academies despite their Glasgow council scheme background. But most believed that he'd inherited money: after all, who among them could afford a car like the white Porsche that roared into the staff car park each day?

It was, thought Niall Cameron, staring at his superior officer from his place at the far end of the conference table, a wonder that the detective superintendent had progressed as far as he had in his career. He could not recall any outstanding cases attached to Mitchison's name, and yet he had managed to climb the promotion ladder somehow. Was it true that other officers' successes had contributed, Mitchison taking credit for cases that his subordinates had solved? *Talks the talk but cannae walk the walk*, one of Cameron's fellow officers had commented in a moment of disgust. Listening to him now, Cameron found it hard to imagine the well-groomed DS out there actually chasing criminals. Like the cases he'd seen with Lorimer.

His thoughts wandered to the man who had been his mentor some years back. What was he doing now? Was it possible, as someone had suggested prior to this meeting beginning, that he was looking for a change of direction after his spell at Castlebrae? *Something less onerous*, he'd heard Mitchison declare with a laugh after a rare interdepartmental meeting. But no one had joined in the apparent mirth, their respect for the officer who'd risked so much then come to grief on New Year's Eve leaving Mitchison alone to smile at his own attempt at humour.

As the superintendent droned on, DCI Cameron watched him carefully. There was no enthusiasm in that good-looking face as he spoke about the need for care when handling the current situation. His blond hair was expertly coiffed and the silk tie perfectly knotted but these were small vanities that Cameron found distasteful. It didn't look right, somehow, on a police officer. Like his predilection for designer suits, his well-laundered shirt cuffs displaying their trademark gold links, the perfect triangle of yellow silk handkerchief emerging from his breast pocket. Again, his thoughts turned to Lorimer whose dark hair always seemed in need of a haircut, his overcoat unbuttoned as his long strides took him to wherever a case dictated.

'Any questions?' the voice asked. Mitchison's eyes travelled around the table, coming to rest at last on the figure of DCI Niall Cameron, who had been thinking such treacherous thoughts of his superior. Had they shown on his face? Niall wondered.

'Gallagher can't be allowed to run his empire the way he wants.' Cameron spoke at last, making all the others turn to stare at him.

'The way I see it, we need to crack his technology,' he continued. 'Only way we're going to find out where the supplies are coming from and who's bringing them in.'

'Hacking isn't an option,' Mitchison replied swiftly. 'The press would come down on us like a ton of bricks.'

'The press don't need to know,' the woman next to Cameron growled under her breath.

'We've got plenty of civilians who could infiltrate his system,' Niall persisted.

'Not an option.' Mitchison shook his head dismissively.

'What about *increasing* surveillance? He's bound to step out of line one way or another,' a different voice suggested.

Cameron looked at the police officer who had spoken. DCI Frank Tweedie didn't often contribute at meetings like this, the older officer marking time till retirement later in the year. But something had prompted him to speak out now and Cameron wondered why.

'Oh, we'll certainly keep an eye on him but there is no need for a round-the-clock watch on the man or his business,' Mitchison said, the dismissive tone in his voice making Tweedie redden.

CID can handle it from here on in, was the unspoken inference. Did the man in charge of this meeting see himself in charge of the MIT team already? Cameron wondered.

'If that's all then you'd better be getting back to your respective cases, gentlemen. And lady,' Mitchison added with a mock bow towards the only woman DCI seated at the table before sweeping up his papers and leaving the room.

Cameron stood up with the others with a sigh and a shake of his head, ready to follow them out. But a hand on his arm held him back.

It was DCI Tweedie, one of his fellow officers and a man he both liked and respected. Sharing a room with the other detective chief inspectors brought them closer together, especially in the midst of an A-rated case where everyone was at pains to follow things through. And the expression on his face as he nodded towards the officers drifting away suggested that he wanted a private word with Niall.

Tweedie waited until they had all left then closed the door of the briefing room and returned to where Niall Cameron was still standing at the far end of the large oval table.

'He's got to be stopped, you know,' he growled, ushering Cameron into a dark corner of the room.

'Gallagher? Of course he has—' Cameron began, but the hand that clutched his sleeve tightened.

'Not Gallagher,' Tweedie hissed, then turned as if to check that no ears were listening. 'It's Mitchison I'm worried about.'

'Mitchison?' Cameron frowned, puzzled. 'What d'you mean?'

Tweedie breathed in sharply then stared at the younger man

for a while as if assessing him. 'Listen, Niall. I'm off in just a few months. But it doesn't mean I'll be past caring what happens to this police force of ours. Or what goes on inside it.'

'Meaning?'

'Meaning it isn't just Mr Big, Jack Gallagher, that needs to be watched.'

Cameron looked over the other man's head at the door shutting them off from the officers who had assembled round the conference table. Somewhere on the other side of that door Mark Mitchison was going about his favourite business of making Police Scotland a more efficient and streamlined organisation; at least in his own little kingdom of CID, this part of Glasgow's G Division being housed in the same building as the Specialist Crime Division. But the constant carping from the higher echelons about overspending was beginning to hurt the major investigations, not to mention the cold case units that were perennially short of money and manpower.

'Aye.' Tweedie nodded. 'I've had my suspicions for a while but there's been nothing to prove. So far. But a keen pair of eyes like yours might spot something that others could miss.'

'What are you suggesting?'

Tweedie gave him a tired smile. 'If Mark bloody Mitchison doesn't come to grief along with Gallagher by the time I hand in my warrant card then I hope you'll take up where I leave off.'

'You think he's *bent*?' Cameron whispered.

'Certain of it. Why d'you think he's been procrastinating about keeping tabs on the biggest bastard in Glasgow?' Tweedie glanced behind him once again, a fearful look in his eyes. 'It's not the first time he's made us back off from Gallagher. I've thought for a long time that he might be in Jack Gallagher's pocket but saying it out loud would've got me the push long ago.'

'So, what do you want me to do?'

'Watch and listen, young 'un, watch and listen.' Tweedie loosened his grip on Cameron's sleeve. 'But be careful who you trust. Mitchison's got influence and could make your life a misery if he wanted.'

He let out a long exhalation then let his shoulders relax as he sat back in the chair at his desk.

It would be all right. Gallagher would need to pay for this, though, he thought, closing his eyes and imagining the drug lord's grimace as he named his price for protecting him. Some of these MIT officers upstairs were getting too close to the man's organisation and keeping Gallagher one step ahead of them was becoming more and more of an effort.

At forty-nine he was a bit too young to retire from the Force but the idea of it appealed to Mark Mitchison right now. Okay, so his pension would take a hit, but the money he'd made from his partnership with Gallagher would keep him in clover for years to come.

Perhaps it was time to sever links with the gangster altogether? One wrong move and everything he had built up could come tumbling down around his ears and Mark Mitchison had no intention of spending any part of what remained of his life in prison.

A hacker, Niall Cameron thought, once he was back at his own desk in the room he shared with three other DCIs, including Tweedie. Mitchison's words came back to him. Perhaps that was the answer. And, giving a smile, the DCI took out a battered notebook from his inside pocket and leafed through its contents. *Some things are best kept secret*, he remembered Lorimer telling him when he'd first given Niall Cameron that hard-covered note-book. *Not everything needs to be kept in a computer.*

It was as if he could actually hear his former boss's voice in his ear sounding encouragement as Cameron's finger stopped on a particular name in his contacts list. Then his smile widened into a grin. Why not pay this person a visit? Something might come of it and, if nothing did, it would still be good to catch up with someone he hadn't seen in a fair old time.

The front window of the shop was stuffed full of mobile phone cases and pictures of reconditioned computers placed carefully against laptop bags, nothing of any value that could be grabbed in a raid. What was most valuable within these premises was the knowledge that its owner kept inside his head; knowledge not just of every make of computer or how to fix them but, more importantly, how to enter their hidden depths. A hacker, some might call him, but the DCI knew that Paul Doherty was far above involving himself in the sort of games that mere hackers played. Government officials had entered these premises discreetly, only to come back on a different day, leaving with valuable information. He'd been wooed by different administrations over the years but Doherty preferred the anonymity of his little shop in Paisley High Street. And the freedom to take on whatever jobs came his way.

The door gave a ping as the detective chief inspector pushed it open, then a rattle as he closed it behind him. There was nobody behind the cluttered desk that separated the shop from the workroom behind a half-opened door but from the faint sound of a voice Cameron guessed that Paul was on the telephone to a customer. Sure enough, the figure of a dark-haired man dressed all in black appeared in the doorway, mobile pressed to his ear.

The quick glance at the newcomer to his shop became a grin as Doherty clocked who it was, then, with a nod and a silent mouthing *just a minute*, he disappeared once more. Cameron found that he was grinning back, pleased to see that his friend hadn't changed much. Doherty still had the long-haired hippy look that he'd adopted at university, whilst the man from Lewis had grown into the habit of wearing a smart suit under his ancient waxed jacket. Doherty had been the life and soul of every student party back then, Cameron content to follow in his flatmate's wake, his own preference for sobriety never a hindrance to a good night out. Like many clever people, Doherty had enjoyed the extra-curricular activities of student life to the full whilst apparently doing little coursework. An illusion, of course, since he'd obtained a double first in Maths and Computing Science. Cameron had seen his fellow student's light burning well into the wee small hours in the weeks before the final exams as he'd sat up night after night himself, determined to make a success of his four years at university. Then the police force had come beckoning for Niall Cameron and in the intervening years it seemed as if Eugene Paul Francis Doherty had disappeared from everyone's radar, only to reappear as the proprietor of this tiny shop.

Cameron looked around him as he waited for his friend to re-emerge. The walls of the shop were fitted with locked glass cabinets displaying a variety of expensive hardware but behind the desk that separated the two parts of the premises were open shelves stacked full of boxes from floor to ceiling. Anyone entering the place with the intention of making a quick grab at some of that stock would have to vault the desk and deal with the wiry man dressed in black. Cameron smiled to himself, remembering the impression that some of the lasses used to have of Paul as a weedy type, his scraggy haircut and painfully thin body belying the man's true physique. Doherty had come from a long line of sportsmen, his grandfather having been a member of the British Olympic weightlifting team. But Paul had chosen martial arts as his own sport and woe betide anyone who tried to take a loan of this quick-footed creature.

Last time they had met, Cameron had arrived at the shop in answer to a hasty phone call, only to find a would-be robber out cold on the floor and Paul standing over him with a bemused expression on his face. He'd sorted it out, but not before Doherty had explained the exact tactics he had employed to disarm the intruder and send him flying across the shop.

'Sorry about that.' Doherty was suddenly back behind the counter. 'Was on a call with a customer who couldn't understand what was wrong with his computer.' He shrugged. 'Wasn't anything wrong at all. Guy just didn't know enough about the software.'

He tilted his head and regarded Cameron with a faint smile. 'Well, Chief Inspector, to what do I owe the pleasure of this visit? Need a new laptop, maybe?' He glanced to the side of the shop where a variety of new models lay side by side, the price tags fixed to the tops of their screens.

'Hi, Paul.' Cameron stretched out his hand and clasped the other man's slim fingers in his. 'Good to see you,' he began. 'No, sorry, I'm not in the market for anything like that.' He hesitated and glanced around him. 'Don't suppose you still have a wee kettle in that back room of yours?'

He was rewarded with a wide grin and a knowing look. 'Aye, maybe I do,' Doherty answered, clearing a space on the wooden countertop to reveal a hinged section that he lifted up. 'Just go on through,' he nodded, 'I'll lock up for a bit.' He moved gracefully past the policeman to turn a key in the front door and flip the sign to CLOSED.

'So,' Doherty bent forward to refill his mug from the large teapot, 'you're looking for a hacker?'

Cameron winced. 'I wouldn't put it like that,' he protested. 'Nothing illegal ...'

Doherty grinned up at him from under his floppy fringe of hair. 'It's okay. I do it all the time. But only for the good guys,' he added, his expression suddenly serious. 'There have been times when I've been asked to cross certain lines, y'know? By folk whose business I don't want in any shape or form.'

'Like?'

'Like your man Gallagher, for one. Told his messenger boy that I wasn't up to standard with what he was asking for. That I was just a poor salesman, nothing more.' Doherty's grin returned.

'Aye, right!' Cameron scoffed. 'And he believed you?'

'Well, he's left me alone since then. Must have found someone else who didn't have so many scruples about working for scum like that.'

'Don't suppose he gave you any email addresses?'

Doherty shook his head. 'They're not that stupid. Anyway, tell me what your own IT boys and girls have got on him so far.'

DCI Cameron sat back, stretching his long legs under the table and proceeded to fill in his friend with the information about Jack Gallagher and his extensive drug empire.

'It's all the more galling that we lack the resources to infiltrate his business. These men are all up to speed with the latest technology. Keep in touch with a secret network of mobile phones, probably bug their own employees.' Cameron looked down at his hands, shaking his head. 'It's not just them keeping ahead of the law that bothers me, though.'

'Oh?' Doherty stared at him.

Cameron looked back at this man who had become something of a legend in the computing underworld, wondering just how much to reveal.

'It's how they do it,' he said at last, his voice dropping to a whisper.

Paul Doherty turned back the sign on the shop door, his eyes on the retreating figure of his old friend. Niall Cameron was as straight as a die and he wondered just what it had cost him to come and ask for help when there were such resources at his disposal within Police Scotland nowadays.

It might be a dangerous game to hack into the drug baron's network but the very idea was appealing, possibly because of the risks involved. The detective chief inspector would return if and when Paul had anything to report. Meantime their only contact would be by telephone. He'd text the agreed code word to let the detective know to visit as soon as he could. Doherty smiled as he entered the back room once again, glad that business was quiet enough to allow him to begin a search that might lead to some very interesting discoveries.

CHAPTER TWENTY-FOUR

We take a holistic approach here, Lorimer recalled the woman telling him. It was a phrase that had slipped easily from several lips. And it covered a range of activities, as he was finding for himself as he performed yet another sit-up, the weight between his hands making the action that bit more difficult. So far the course had involved a mixture of physical activities and one to one counselling with relaxing massage thrown in for good measure. Now, as the days continued, Lorimer could feel a change in his body. Gone was the lethargy that had made him slump into his armchair at home and he was surprised to find that he was even sleeping better at night. *All that fresh air*, Maggie had joked on the phone. And yet he hadn't been out and about as much as he had hoped, the snowy conditions preventing the longer walks he had wanted to take.

One place that he did intend to visit was the sensory garden, despite the bushes and plants being wreathed in their blanket of white. It was across from the main door and at first he had thought it was simply part of the landscaping until he'd read the sign, *Catherine Gurney Sensory Garden*.

He sat up at last, deciding that he had enough time to take a walk there after his shower.

The air around his head was like a halo as the cold hit his still-damp hair but the drop in temperature was actually invigorating after standing in the hot water. A bit like the Finns would do in their saunas, he told himself, lengthening his stride to cross the distance between the main building and the sensory garden. The trees above him were frosted, catching the weak February sunlight and silvering their bare branches into something magical. A curving path led Lorimer around and away from the world outside and into a place that was at once sweet-smelling and mysterious, the box hedging fragrant as he ran his gloved hand to scatter the snow from the foliage. At the end of the path lay a small shrine where a smiling Buddha sat, oblivious to wind or weather. It was too cold and wet to sit here now but Lorimer imagined that it must be a place where damaged souls could come in warmer weather to contemplate whatever injuries had brought them to Castlebrae.

They'd thought of everything, he realised, looking up at the faint blue patch beyond the spreading clouds; even the spiritual side of things. It was little wonder that the notion of *souls* had come to him, standing here: this was a place where healing took place on so many different levels, just as they'd said it did. He breathed in and then out again, the sharp cold making him stand straighter, taller, his breath a faint cloud in the icy air. *How are you feeling?* Maggie had asked and he'd replied with the ubiquitous answer, *fine*. But now, standing here under a canopy of darkening sky that threatened further snowfalls, Lorimer had to acknowledge that he was not just fine, he was actually better.

A few steps back along the path made him see other things

148

too, not just the different perspective of this garden with its snow-covered beds. As he made to leave, there was a pergola in front of him, something he'd not really noticed on his way into the garden. An inscription carved into the wooden structure made him stop and read.

MAKE TIME, CHERISH TIME,
WHILE TIME LASTS FOR ALL
TIME IS NO TIME WHEN TIME HAS PAST.

Lorimer read the words again and again, his thoughts racing back to the scene in the Blackburns' bedroom. The father who'd stopped time for his entire family. The little child who'd screamed in his arms, begging for the chance to live.

And his own time? He was forty-five years old now. How was he spending his time? Recuperating in this place while other men and women did the work of policing his beloved country. But wasn't that the whole point of this message? Wasn't he making time to recover? And cherishing time?

His thoughts went back to Maggie. How little time they spent together! Should he be tempted to give it all up? He had excuse enough now for an early retirement, although it would cause a deep dent in his pension. He shook his head, knowing that this was not a serious option, yet resolving to make more time for the woman in his life who meant so much to him.

For all time is no time when time has past, the last section warned the reader. He might have been the one on whom Blackburn turned his gun. That might have been the moment when all time was extinguished for William Lorimer. But he'd been given a second chance to recover and reflect on what the next step in his life would be.

The image of a bearded man in the green uniform came into his mind. That was his allotted task, to find him and to put an end to whatever misery he was creating in the world.

The dining room was almost full by the time he reached it. Looking around, Lorimer wondered where to sit this time. His mind was still full of the images from the sensory garden and he was reluctant to be drawn into a conversation with any of the chattering officers, no matter how friendly they were, so he took his tray of food across to where a young dark-haired fellow was sitting on his own, staring out of the window at the snowy landscape, his plateful of food neglected on the table.

The other man started a little as Lorimer sat beside him.

'Is it all right if I join you . . . ?' the detective superintendent asked.

'Go ahead,' the officer replied, his pale face turned momentarily towards Lorimer.

But there was a hint of reluctance in the younger man's demeanour, something that almost made Lorimer lift his tray and leave.

'This your first week?' Lorimer asked softly and watched as the other man nodded silently.

For a few minutes Lorimer concentrated on spooning the home-made soup into his mouth, glancing from time to time at the back of the man's head as he stared moodily out of the window.

'They're an amazing bunch of people here,' Lorimer offered. 'I didn't think anyone could have changed the way I was when I came in here, you know.'

'Injured on duty, were you?' The man turned and looked Lorimer up and down for a moment.

'You could put it like that,' Lorimer agreed. 'Something happened during a case that messed with my head.' He shrugged. 'I didn't consider myself injured at the time, or even when I came here last Monday. But I see things differently now.'

'How's that?' The dark eyes watching him narrowed into a frown.

'Our minds can be battered and bruised just as much as our bodies. More so in our line of work when you consider the things we see, the stuff we have to do . . .'

'That's an interesting way of putting it – just how I feel. Battered and bruised. But there isn't a mark on me to show it,' the officer added bitterly.

'That doesn't mean it's any less painful, does it?'

The young man nodded and sighed. 'Try telling that to my boss,' he said. 'He says I'm just a wimp. Told me to pull myself together or give up the job.'

'Anyone I might know?' Lorimer asked lightly.

'Och, I really shouldn't . . . Oh, what the hell. Guy called Mitchison, Govan CID. Superintendent Mitchison.' He spoke the name as though it disgusted him then turned to Lorimer. 'Do you know him?'

Lorimer raised his eyebrows and nodded. 'We've run into one another from time to time,' he said slowly. 'Our paths haven't crossed for a good while, though, I'm happy to say.'

The young officer grinned and stuck out his hand. 'I'm Aaron.'

'Lorimer. Pleased to meet you.'

'Lorimer? *That* Lorimer? You're the guy that smashed that end-of-life scam! I read all about that.' Aaron's eyes had lit up for an instant then he frowned again. 'But what on earth are *you* doing here?'

'I guess I'm here for the same reason as you are, Aaron. To find some sort of healing so I can get back to work,' he answered lightly.

'And have you?' the younger man asked doubtfully.

'Oh, I think so. Listen, forget what Mitchison and others say. Your health isn't just about what's visible on the outside. I've learned that much in the few days since I arrived. Stick in at your programme and you'll see what I mean.'

'Aye, well . . .'

Aaron nodded and picked up his fork then began to eat the food on his plate.

Lorimer smiled to himself: that was you just a short week ago. But since being at Castlebrae he'd found that depression affected so many officers. And was it any wonder? Hopefully this young man would be brought back from the grim places in his soul and returned to Police Scotland ready to take up his duties once more.

Then, as he recalled the senior officer who had belittled the man's condition, he stopped eating for a moment. Mark Mitchison was not the sort of man Lorimer would want to be serving under on his own return to work. He recalled the superior expression, something that spoiled the man's good looks, and that annoying, affected accent. Some years ago Mitchison had been selected for promotion instead of Lorimer, much to the displeasure of Lorimer's colleagues, and the fact still rankled a little. However, he rarely saw the other officer since they were in different divisional headquarters and the detective superintendent was glad of that.

He glanced back at the young man at his side. Would Aaron cope back at work with someone like Mitchison bearing down on him? Or would he buckle under the man's lack of insight?

Hopefully he would find the strength to resist any barbed remarks from Mitchison or anybody else ignorant of what really went on in a person's mind. Castlebrae did its best for those who needed healing but there were other challenges to face when they left this place for good.

CHAPTER TWENTY-FIVE

Detective Constable Kirsty Wilson hummed beneath her breath as she drove across town to the city mortuary. It was another freezing day and the traffic was slower than normal, drivers cautious after the latest snowfall that had frozen overnight. The gritters had been out since way before daylight and Kirsty could hear the tyres hissing through brown slush, darker twin tracks on the road left by the earlier commuters. Beside her in the passenger seat the family liaison officer sat, staring out of the window, glancing behind from time to time at the passenger in the back of the Honda. They'd finally tracked down one of Smith's relatives, someone who was grudgingly willing to confirm the dead man's identity. It had been a matter for the Fiscal to decide, of course, but the decision from the Crown Office was that the previous identification by a fellow itinerant might not be sufficient. Besides, there had been no one to claim the body and give it a formal burial. Until now.

Gordon Smith's cousin, Ida Gemmell, had not been happy at the idea of uniformed cops turning up at her home and so they had picked the woman up at the bus stop nearest to her house in Drumchapel.

'Nearly there,' Kirsty told them, turning into the car park next to the city mortuary. She had to remember that what to her was becoming a routine was a new and upsetting event in the life of the woman who was scowling in the back of the Honda, probably full of nervous anticipation at what lay within these grey stone walls.

The family liaison officer took Ida Gemmell's arm as they walked through the building to the viewing room.

'Mrs Gemmell?' The three women turned at the sound of the Irish voice. It was Dan, the pathologist.

'Sorry, Dr Fergusson can't be here to see you. Off sick, I'm afraid.'

Kirsty raised her eyebrows, wondering what had happened to make the director of the department take time off. Rosie was never ill.

Dan escorted the woman towards a small window. 'No need to go into the room where he is,' he said gently. 'You can see everything you need to on this TV screen.'

Ida Gemmell looked up at the older man and sighed, her relief almost palpable.

'Thank God fur that,' she muttered. Then, as though it had been a slip of her tongue, she crossed herself and nodded, ready to take a look at the cousin who had been reduced to living on the streets.

The pathologist pressed a switch and the curtain moved back, revealing a television screen and the image of a man lying still on a white bed, the sheet pulled up to his chin.

'Aye,' Ida said shortly. 'That's oor Gordy.' She shook her head and then wiped away an invisible tear from the corner of her eye. 'Looks a sight better in death than ever he looked when he was alive, pair bugger.'

Kirsty and the family liaison office exchanged glances behind the woman's back. What a way to be remembered!

The rest of DC Wilson's day passed in trying to piece together the time between Gordon Smith's eviction from his old address and the day that his body had been discovered. How had he spent his days? And how on earth had that bearded man managed to appropriate the identity of a down-and-out? The bogus hospital orderly had certainly never lived there, that fact confirmed by every neighbour they had spoken to. All sorts of questions were turning around in Kirsty's mind as she made the connections between the thief who had taken all these drugs and the man lying in the mortuary.

She closed her eyes for a moment, images from the previous year's case swimming into her brain. Her first job as a detective constable under the mentorship of DS Len Murdoch had not been without its surprises. The gruff DS had given Kirsty lots to think about back then.

Suddenly she remembered. Tam McLachlan! She knew where she had seen the man before. That old pub in the East End of the city, what was it called? The Big Yin, that was it. He'd been one of DS Murdoch's informants, an old alkie who'd been only too happy to give them information for a few drinks. Dear Lord! How that old man had fallen into bad company since then. He was out on the streets now, in that half-world where men and women shifted from hostel to hostel, sleeping rough when they had to, sharing needles in darkened derelict rooms . . . No wonder she hadn't recognised him! And yet the old man had come forward to identify his friend, not afraid to talk to police officers. And now Kirsty understood why that was.

Was it possible that she could find him again? And would he

open up to her the way he had with DS Murdoch during last year's case?

Lorimer stood up from the edge of the bed where he had been sitting and looked out of the window, the mobile phone still warm in his hand. *Be careful*, he'd told Kirsty. *Don't let yourself be caught between doing your job and keeping me in the loop. Not that I'm ungrateful, of course . . .* He'd added that in case she had thought him harsh. But in truth he was concerned for the young woman. She knows what I'm up to, he thought, a grim little smile softening his mouth. The case back in Glasgow simply concerned the detection of a thief who had stolen a quantity of morphine from their biggest hospital, not the pursuit of the ringleader of Quiet Release who had escaped their clutches. But, if he could make them see that this person was one and the same, would the case be reopened after all?

DCI Niall Cameron had advised Kirsty that there was not the will to do that and she had passed this on to him. Lorimer knew enough about the working of Police Scotland to recognise that there were more constraints than mere budgetary considerations at work here. Someone didn't want him meddling in the case again. And, as he stared out at the expanse of white covering every feature of the gardens, the detective superintendent began to wonder why.

If there was any particular point that he could identify as making a change it had come during the Pilates session, he thought later. Had it been the need to focus on his breathing? Or the way the class simply relaxed at the end, encouraged by the visualisation exercise? That might remain a puzzle unless he simply asked the female instructor about it but in some ways having the question answered wasn't as important as knowing that a difference had been made. It was funny to think that he'd actually felt taller as he'd walked along the corridor to the treatment room afterwards for his next appointment.

And he'd felt happier, less anxious about talking to the other officers or, indeed, to the therapists themselves.

Now it was Friday and he was heading to his second session with Christine, the patient adviser to whom he had opened up about the Blackburn case. That had upset him at the time and he had shifted the blame onto the woman when, thinking back, she had actually deflected his reliving of the trauma. Hadn't the upset actually come from his own attitude about it? His anger and frustration that he'd been unable to save the little girl? Had he blamed himself? That was a question he was more able to face today, Lorimer realised. The patient adviser had focused more on where he was now and what he wanted for his future. She'd be pleased, he thought, to find how far he had come on his journey from the sad and weakened man who had walked through the door at Castlebrae.

The past few days had made him calmer and the nightmare had not returned again. *So far*, a treacherous little voice reminded him. And he felt physically stronger too. Swimming lengths in that magnificent pool and putting himself through a strict regime in the gym was beginning to pay off. Perhaps, he thought with a faint smile, the simple equation between exercise and better sleep was all that it had taken to make him feel this good.

Christine Russell smiled at the man sitting beside her. This second session had been more than she could have hoped for. His whole demeanour told her more about his state of mind than any words. Lorimer was relaxed, one leg crossed over his knee, sitting back in the armchair, a mug of instant coffee in one hand. Gone were the heightened shoulders, the tension so apparent around his neck area, the tired lines around his eyes.

'So, you're looking forward to leaving us later on today?' she teased.

'Ach, if I could stay on and spend time in the gym and the pool then I'd not be in a hurry to get back to work,' he laughed, gazing at her frankly with those amazing bright blue eyes.

'And none the worse for Monday's adventure?'

Lorimer smiled at her and ducked his head modestly. 'Oh, I just happened to be the right person at the right time, that was all.'

Christine raised her eyebrows a little but said nothing. He'd arrived back soaked through and exhausted after having hauled the old woman out of her snowbound vehicle. And yet he'd made no fuss about it whatsoever.

'May I ask how you feel about yourself now, Lorimer?' she asked, though the question was surely academic. It was easy to see the change in this man. He was even quite a dish now that he had lost that haunted look. Lucky Mrs Lorimer!

'Much better, thanks,' he replied. Then he paused and tilted his head a little, as though considering what to say.

'I have to be honest and tell you that I didn't really give myself much hope when I first came here.'

Christine nodded slightly. She'd heard that so many times before but for this man as for the others it was a new experience.

'I thought there was no way I'd be so eager to get back.'

'To work?'

He nodded and smiled a lazy smile that made the patient advisor feel a warm glow of satisfaction.

'There's a particular case I'm anxious to resume. Nothing to do with the incident on New Year's Eve,' he added, the smile slipping a little. Yet his voice was firm as he spoke and there were no telltale signs from his body language that gave her grounds for concern. No, this one was going to be all right.

'That's what we aim to do here,' Christine reminded him. 'Try to return you fit and well for active service. And, we hope, to give you a better future. After all, I think you've learned quite a lot about managing stress and the relationship between your physical and mental fitness.'

She stood up and smiled at him. 'I'd be happy to see you again any time, you know, but somehow I think we won't meet again.'

The woman turned away for a moment, one hand up as though to prevent his leaving. 'Oh, I nearly forgot,' she apologised, bending down and rummaging in a capacious bag. 'There's something I wanted you to have.'

She thrust a red parcel into his hands and smiled. 'Call it a belated birthday present. You can open it when you get back home. Take care, now.'

CHAPTER TWENTY-SIX

'Kirsty rang,' Maggie told him once she had disentangled herself from his embrace. 'She sounded quite excited. Any idea what that might be about?' She watched her husband's expression.

'Not sure, but I'm hoping it'll be about the Quiet Release case. Sorry,' he added as Maggie made a face. It still rankled that her own cousin had been a victim too.

'Go on, call her back. I've got stuff to do in the kitchen. Lasagne.' She threw him a smile over her shoulder, gratified to see his grin at the mention of one of his favourite meals.

'DC Wilson?' Lorimer asked as the familiar voice gave a tentative 'hello'.

'Yes, is that you, sir? Are you back home? How are you?' The young detective's questions came tumbling out in a breathless rush.

'I'm an awful lot better, thanks, Kirsty. The folk in that place really do know their stuff. If anyone ever asks you about it, tell them it's worth every penny of the pittance taken out of our salaries.'

'You sound different, more like your old self,' Kirsty answered cautiously.

'Well, let's hope so. I'm going back to work on Monday,' he said with a laugh.

'That's good news, sir,' she said.

'Was that all? Did you just ring to see how I was keeping?'

'No, it's just ... I was worried that I ought to have told someone about Tam McLachlan.'

'You mean you didn't pass that on?'

'No, sir, I thought ... well, I was anxious that it would be you taking charge of the case again ...' The girl's vice tailed off, sounding miserable.

Lorimer stifled a sigh. It was important that Kirsty Wilson didn't keep information like this to herself and by the sounds of it she was anxious that something positive would be done now that she had made this vital link. She needed to know how important it was to follow such matters up as quickly as possible. Time lost in the wake of a criminal incident could determine whether or not a culprit was ever caught.

'Are you on duty right now?' he asked, aware that his tone was a little sharp.

'Yes, as a matter of fact I'm in the Govan office till after six o'clock tonight.'

'Well then, you need to talk to whoever is in charge of the Queen Elizabeth inquiry. Tell them you may have someone who might give us more information. Who's on this case, anyway? Anyone I know?'

'It's DS McCrone, sir. And he's already away out of the office. Long weekend because of the school half-term,' she explained.

'Anyone of DI level or above still there?'

'We-ell, I could see who's about.' Kirsty sounded doubtful.

'And, of course there're always senior officers upstairs in the MIT.'

There was a momentary silence then he could hear her breathing hard. 'Could I talk to DCI Cameron about this, sir? I already approached him when we saw the man on the TV last week so at least he knows about that.'

Lorimer thought for a moment.

'Okay,' he said at last. 'See if you can find Cameron. And let him know I'm home. I'd be happy to talk to him about this case if he wants.'

'Right, sir. I'll do that and have him get back to you.'

Lorimer ended the call and looked across the room to the open-plan kitchen where Maggie was busy grating cheese to stir into a sauce. It never really stopped, did it, he mused; the intrusion of crime into his life at any hour of the day or night.

'You all right, darling?' he asked softly, coming up behind his wife and encircling her waist with his arms.

'Yes, I suppose so,' Maggie answered with a sigh. 'Is that case being reopened then? Is that what Kirsty called about?'

Lorimer nuzzled the back of her neck. 'Ach, it probably will be, but I might not have any part of it. Depends how things pan out,' he said vaguely.

'William Lorimer!' Maggie turned and shook her head at him, the wooden spoon waving in her hand. 'Do you really think I'm as daft as all that? You're like a dog with a bone! You'll never let this one go if you can help it, I know you too well for that!' She made a face then began to laugh. 'Go on, pour us both a drink. At least that will keep you from driving anywhere else tonight!'

Kirsty looked out of the windows at the car park. It was a dreich, cold Friday night and so many officers had headed for home.

Would DCI Cameron be among them? she wondered as she headed along the corridor until she found his office. There was a light showing under the door and so she knocked and waited.

'Come in,' a voice commanded and she opened the door to see the detective chief inspector seated at his desk, apparently engrossed with some files on his laptop.

'Ah, DC Wilson.' Niall Cameron's face broke into a smile as he rose and extended his hand towards her. 'How nice to see you again. Or is it?' His smile dropped to a frown as he looked at the girl. 'Nothing wrong, I take it? Lorimer all right ...? Here, sit down, won't you?'

'Thank you, sir.' Kirsty sat on a plastic moulded chair opposite the senior detective. 'I spoke to DS Lorimer a wee while ago and he said to tell you he's back home and is starting work again on Monday. He sounds fine,' she added.

'I'm glad to hear that,' Cameron replied with a sigh of relief. 'So, what brings you to me this evening? Not just a social call to tell me how our mutual friends is faring, I guess?'

Kirsty smiled in spite of herself. He was a good detective, she realised, as the man gazed at her with interest. Like Lorimer himself, DCI Cameron had the knack of reading a person's body language and hers probably told him that she was in a state of some excitement.

'Well, sir, it's like this,' she began. 'I think I may have found someone ... I mean I should have told DS McCrone ...'

Kirsty swallowed hard then told the man how she had come to recognise the old tramp after he had identified the body of Gordon Smith.

'When did you make the connection, DC Wilson?' he asked in a tone not unlike that which Lorimer had used.

'Very recently, sir,' she admitted in a small voice. 'Detective

Superintendent Lorimer told me that I ought to have taken it straight to DS McCrone, but I—'

'You wanted to let Lorimer know first,' Cameron interrupted her. 'I understand,' he told her, but one eyebrow was raised in a sign of disapproval, making Kirsty want nothing more than to sink into the carpet and disappear.

'I should have . . . ' She bit her lip.

'Well, maybe no great harm's been done, as it happens,' Cameron said smoothly. 'Is DS McCrone available over the weekend, do you know?'

Kirsty brightened a little. 'No, sir, he's gone away for a few days. The rest of the team are all working on the hospital case trying to locate this bogus Smith character. See, the hospital porter used the identity of the down-and-out man, this poor guy who was found dead.'

'And was it a suspicious death?'

'An overdose of morphine by the looks of it, sir. He was a known addict.'

'So this orderly chap then filches a quantity of morphine from the Queen Elizabeth and disappears,' Cameron mused. 'But was it before or after the robbery?'

'Sir?'

'The addict. Was he found dead before or after the hospital robbery?' the DCI repeated patiently.

'Oh, days before, sir.'

'And now we know that this is the same person who was identified by Mary Milligan when she was supposedly helping us with our enquiries into Quiet Release.' Cameron's expression changed and he looked more intently at the dark-haired young woman sitting beside him. 'You made the arrest if I recall correctly, DC Wilson.'

Kirsty felt her face redden. 'Yes, sir. Just happened to be in the right place at the right time,' she claimed modestly.

Cameron threw back his head and laughed. 'Way I heard it you were tanking it up that road like a Formula One driver!'

'Well, I don't think anyone would've booked me for speeding, sir, not when I caught up with her, anyway.'

'Let's see what I can do with this, DC Wilson,' he said at last. 'I can look into past records of where McLachlan lived, see if we can find him again.' Cameron looked at Kirsty then smiled, his eyes crinkling at the corners. 'And, if we do, then maybe he'll be happy to have a new cop buy him the occasional drink,' he said, nodding at Kirsty in a meaningful way.

Social media was the way to go, Graham had assured him and Gallagher had to admit that the younger man had a point. There were fewer ways to be traced, he'd insisted, and any Twitter accounts could easily be shut down if the wrong sort of questions began to be asked. Graham had impressed him with his knowledge of IT systems and the intricacies of the internet, something that Jack Gallagher preferred to leave to his underlings. *Too old to be bothered with all of that*, he'd told his accountant when the woman had suggested that he familiarise himself with stuff like spreadsheets. He didn't like to admit it but sending an email was about the extent of his involvement with computers. Gallagher had always liked communicating by telephone, listening to the reaction of whoever was on the other line as he browbeat them with his commands and, often as not, with his threats of what would happen if his orders were not carried out to the letter. But this young man who had entered his world could be something of an asset. Decent-looking guy, too, well dressed and not pushy, the sort of man he'd wanted to be at that age, Gallagher realised. Though, if he were to be honest, the rough edges would never be smoothed away no matter how much money he spent on clothes and fancy cars; Jack Gallagher was what he was: a Glasgow gangster who'd pulled himself up the hard way, ruthlessly trampling on anyone weaker than himself in order to reach the top.

The other asset that Graham was bringing to their tentative partnership was his ability to change, chameleon-like, into these different identities. Gallagher hadn't asked where they'd come from even as he arranged the fake paperwork, though he had a fair idea that each of the names were those of dead men.

Pity he hadn't brought any muscle with him, Gallagher thought. *I work alone*, the guy had claimed. And he'd certainly carried out the hit on Ellen Blackburn without any fuss.

Like Gallagher himself, Graham was careful and he'd never been caught.

And hell would freeze over before that ever changed.

CHAPTER TWENTY-SEVEN

Paul Doherty lifted his black leather jacket off the chair and sauntered out of the tiny back office, whistling along to the music sounding through his earbuds. It would have been fun to see where Niall Cameron worked but the DCI had warned against meeting anywhere that might compromise their secret investigation and so he was not heading into Glasgow to the Govan office but walking down from his own small premises.

A chill wind blew along Paisley High Street, scattering crisp packets and discarded betting slips from the bookies next door as Paul set off down to the centre of the town, glancing this way and that. Even in his own lifetime the place had changed. What had once been a prosperous, bustling town was now suffering the effects of the sprawling malls that bordered the banks of the Clyde in nearby Renfrew. Charity shops had sprung up like weeds to replace the traditional bakers' and butchers' shops; even the High Street Woolworth's had vanished along with Arnott's, the town's oldest department store. It had meant a cheaper rental for the IT specialist but it still tugged at his heart when he looked around, remembering the crowded streets of his youth.

Still, some things never changed, Paul thought, as the ancient abbey came into view. That particular building must have seen more changes than he could imagine over the hundreds of years since people first entered for worship.

Paul grinned to himself. It had been Niall's choice for a meeting place, of course, as he remembered that his friend was a devout Christian, though perhaps not so rigid in his beliefs as some of his fellow islanders. A teetotaller, Niall had never minded the ribbing he'd got at university when he'd chosen orange and soda over pints of lager. And it had always meant that he'd been their designated driver so the lanky lad had been popular, though his quiet manner and good humour alone had naturally endeared his fellow students to him. It was no surprise, really, that he had joined the police after graduation, a clean-cut lad like that; honest as the day was long. And no wonder that he'd made something of his career. He'd always been a good listener and, Paul realised looking back, Niall Cameron had been pretty adept at sussing out his fellow man, even then.

What, Paul wondered, would the senior detective make of the findings he had to bring to this clandestine meeting? And how would it chime with Niall's suspicions about the officer whose files Paul had hacked?

The coffee shop adjacent to the main part of the abbey was quiet, the afternoon tea ladies either deciding it was too cold to venture out or reluctant to travel homewards in the gathering dusk. Paul chose a table that faced towards the door so that he would see Niall Cameron arriving.

'Hello, you're here,' a melodious voice proclaimed behind him.

Paul swung around in surprise as Niall sat down beside him. 'Where did you spring from?'

Niall Cameron gave a slow smile. 'Thought I might as well

spend a few minutes in there,' he said, indicating the door that led into the church. 'Have you been in recently?'

Paul shook his head. 'Not in years . . .'

'It's a wonderful place.' Niall sighed. 'Worth having a look even just for the stained glass. Though I imagine it would be better on a sunny day . . . all that light streaming through . . .' he mused.

'Well, we're here now. Want to order a coffee?'

'I'll get them. Something to go with it? The home baking looks pretty good.'

'Och, if they've got a flies' cemetery that would be ace,' Paul replied, craning his neck to see the display of cakes and biscuits by the counter.

Minutes later he was biting into the soft pastry packed with dark fruit, aware of his friend's amusement.

'Ach, some things never change, Paul,' Niall laughed. 'Seems like yesterday we were lining up at the uni canteen and you were begging them to keep you a flies' cemetery.'

'And they always did. Good women succumbed to my charms even then!' he declared, wiping the sugary crumbs on his plate and licking them off his fingers.

'Now,' Niall leaned forward and looked intently at the dark-haired man, 'have you found anything?'

Paul kept his face straight and watched as Niall shook his head. 'Nothing?'

Then, unable to suppress the grin any longer, Paul nodded slowly.

'You wee rascal! Nearly had me there!' Cameron laughed. 'Right,' his expression growing more serious, 'what do you have for me?'

Paul glanced around as if to check that there were no elderly ladies earwigging at the nearby tables then he drew a tiny object from the inside pocket of his jacket.

'Here.' He slid the memory stick across the table and Niall Cameron covered it with his hand.

'What've you found?' the DCI whispered.

'Correspondence between your man and Gallagher,' Paul said quietly, watching the other man's reaction.

Niall Cameron sat back, his lips parting in surprise. 'It was that easy?' he exclaimed.

Paul made a face. 'No, it wasn't easy at all, pal. It took me days to crack Gallagher's secure codes and then some. He's either IT-savvy or he's got an expert that encrypts all his emails for him. This guy's taking no chances,' he declared. Then he tilted his head to one side questioningly. 'What's your interest in him anyway? Gallagher? You never mentioned what sort of case you're on.'

'No, Paul, I didn't,' Niall replied softly, pocketing the memory stick. 'And that's the way it's going to stay. For your own good.'

Paul Doherty raised his eyebrows. 'Well, I know his reputation. Not a nice man, is he?'

Niall shook his head. 'Is there any way he could find that you've been hacking his files? Any way he can trace it back to you?'

'No.' Paul shook his head. 'I used a reconditioned laptop and a bogus identity. The whole thing's been fragged and taken back to factory condition now.'

Niall Cameron tapped his pocket. 'So this is the only evidence I've got?'

Paul grinned and shook his head. 'Oh, I kept a back-up, of course. So, if you ever lose that one, you'll know where to come for its twin.'

*

Lorimer felt in his pocket for the memory stick as he crossed the car park at the Scottish Police headquarters at Gartcosh. He'd made several copies of that clip from the television since returning home to Glasgow, the face of the mysterious bearded man travelling with him all the way from Auchterarder. But, as yet, few others had seen the copies.

The security area loomed ahead and he was buzzed through in record time, his warrant card glimpsed by the on-duty officer whose job it was to vet every single person who walked though these high gates whether they were visitors or simply coming to work. The detective superintendent was under no illusion why he was here this Monday morning, however. The email from the deputy chief constable had been terse and to the point. If he was fit to return to duty then there were things to discuss. But first he was to be carefully assessed by an independent patient adviser brought in from a private health company.

Lorimer's thoughts turned to Christine, the lady back in Perthshire who would no doubt be preparing for her own sessions with officers whose traumas had curtailed their ability to serve. She'd given him a present as he'd left, hadn't she? A package wrapped up in shiny red leftover Christmas paper. But he'd yet to open it and see what it was. A book, he guessed, something about cognitive behaviour, perhaps? Maybe he'd open it tonight once all of this palaver was finished and he was given his new orders.

The building never failed to impress him, its steep-sided walls etched in long lines that reflected the pattern of DNA markers, something that civilian visitors might never realise. Sweeping his glance upwards Lorimer thought that they gave the place a certain gravitas. Once inside he strode across the wide, open hall, the floors above like canyons teetering high in the air, a valley between the entrance and the far end of the building, breakout areas visible for all to see where men and women from as many as eighteen different establishments could mingle. It was not just a home for police officers, far from it: Gartcosh held the most envied forensic resources in Europe as well as some seldom-visited areas where highly trained personnel kept watch on terrorist behaviour. *The public would sleep better if they knew what goes on in there*, he'd told Maggie after his first visit to that particular department.

'Detective Superintendent,' a voice greeted him and Lorimer turned to see a familiar figure standing by the lifts. 'What brings you here? *Well*, I hope?'

The look on Mark Mitchison's face; that trace of curled lip and the sneer in his voice brought back the words of his fellow patient from Castlebrae. And then the man smiled, all charm, it seemed, though Lorimer thought he detected something of a smirk on the handsome face as the numbers above the lift doors descended to ground level.

'Very well, thank you,' he replied blandly and yet, despite himself, Lorimer's hand went to his pocket as though to ensure that the USB stick was still safe. There was something about Mark Mitchison that had always made him uneasy and the fact of his being here, now, was not helping Lorimer one bit. He clamped his teeth together as the other detective superintendent entered the lift, noticing that he didn't bother to ask what floor Lorimer wanted. He reached out and pressed the button then turned away, ignoring the man as best as he could.

'Hear you were at Castlebrae, isn't that right?' Mitchison whispered. 'Too bad you fell ill like that.' He shook his head. From anyone else these words might be construed as sympathy but from this man they sounded merely disparaging.

Lorimer could smell a heavy male perfume of some sort wafting from the other man. The pungent sickly odour seemed to fill the small area they occupied, making him all the more aware of the confined space. He clenched his teeth even more, eyeing the numbers as the lift rose to the floor that he wanted.

'Are you hoping for a change of direction now? Something a little less onerous, perhaps?'

Mitchison just couldn't help being patronising, could he? Lorimer thought. Even though both men were the same rank, Mitchison evidently felt superior to the man standing next to him.

Stupid bastard. You know nothing about the sorts of traumas some of your officers have gone through, do you? Lorimer wanted to say, deliberately keeping his eyes from making contact with Mitchison. How on earth had Aaron, the officer he'd met at Castlebrae, coped with a man as insensitive as this?

Lorimer found himself clenching and unclenching his fists. He would love to throw a punch at that smooth chin even if just to see the other man's expression. *But Mitchison wasn't worth the bother*, a little voice reminded him, a voice that suddenly sounded like Christine Russell's.

With a ping the doors opened and Lorimer stepped out, the fresh air hitting him like a welcome relief from the claustrophobic smell within the lift.

He didn't look back as he walked away, but was that the sound of mocking laughter he heard behind him as the doors of the lift shut once again?

The patient adviser, a white-haired woman in her mid fifties, smiled as she led him back along the corridor to the stairwell that overlooked the atrium. 'So glad that you've had time to recover,

Superintendent Lorimer,' she said, shaking his hand warmly. 'Back to work as from today, then?'

'Looks like it now you've given me the all-clear,' he countered. 'And I can tell you I'll be very glad to be doing something useful again.'

'I think from what I heard that you were quite useful to a certain elderly motorist during your stay in Auchterarder.' She twinkled at him. 'Quite the hero, it seems.'

'Och, don't believe everything you hear.' But the patient adviser merely raised her eyebrows and smiled again over her half-moon spectacles as if to acknowledge Lorimer's modesty before turning back and heading towards the room where they had spent the last hour discussing his progress.

Well, that's that, he thought, one hand moving to his inside pocket for his mobile. A quick text to Maggie to let her know that he had passed the assessment and was now heading back to work. *Might be a bit late, will let you know*, he wrote, grinning at the words he had written to her so often in his career. He paused at the rail that overlooked the huge sweeping canyon of levels below, his hand fumbling the object in his coat pocket: yes, he'd get back to Stewart Street as soon as he could, but first there was someone he needed to see.

Deputy Chief Constable Caroline Flint glanced out of the window at the clouds scudding by and, despite the warmth of the room, she shivered. London was enjoying temperatures of sixteen and more, the crocuses were covering the parklands all over the capital and yet here winter had still to lose its icy grip. Her recent promotion had not been a step that Caroline had taken lightly though most women in the force these days would have bitten her hand off for a chance to be at this level in Police Scotland. There were not many officers from the Met up here these days though the journey north had been worth it for a few people in years past.

She thought of the detached house and its empty garden, a new-build in a village outside Glasgow, comparing it with the Surrey cottage that she and Gregory had let out on a long lease, then heaved a sigh. It would look better in the summer months when the bare trees put out their leaves and she and her husband had spent weekends planting annuals from the garden centre. He had looked on this move to Scotland's largest city as an adventure, or so he had said. But did he really feel like that now? Before Christmas they had been so occupied with packing up and saying goodbye to friends that Caroline had hardly noticed whether her husband's enthusiasm had waned or not. And she had been so busy since taking on this new role that she'd never thought to ask. Ten years her senior, Gregory Flint was glad to have retired from his position in the city law firm, his sights firmly on the opportunities to see more of Scotland and its out-door delights.

Caroline glanced over the wintry landscape, pale grasses blowing sideways as a bitter wind flattened them. Somewhere out there he was climbing a hill, knapsack over his shoulders, a walking pole in each mittened hand.

A second sigh was cut short as Caroline heard a rap on her door.

'Come in!' Her throaty voice, the result of a sixty-a-day habit, boomed across the room.

The door opened to reveal a tall, dark-haired man whose blue eyes fixed on her the moment he entered the room.

'Detective Superintendent Lorimer, ma'am,' he announced.

There was a small moment as they looked at one another and Caroline wondered just what he saw. A tired, older woman who had reached the pinnacle of her career? *He* looked his age anyway, mid forties, she knew from his file.

'Lorimer.' She smiled and reached out a welcoming hand, glad to feel the strength in his grasp. 'Come and sit down. D'you want a coffee or anything?' she asked briskly, hoping that he would decline. She'd rather concentrate on what he had to tell her than be bothered with cups and saucers.

'Thanks, but I just had one,' he replied, a hint of smile around his lips as though he had guessed her thoughts.

'Right, then, let's begin.' DCC Flint folded her hands and placed them on the lap of her black skirt. 'You spoke to me on the telephone about that case from last year. I remember it,' she added, looking at him intently. 'We gave you a bit of help at our end. The so-called banker, wasn't it?'

'That's correct, ma'am,' Lorimer replied. 'We managed to arrest all but one of the gang.'

She watched as he made a face.

'The one we believe to be behind the entire operation,' he added.

'And you think he may be stirring up the same sort of business again?'

Lorimer nodded. 'We think he was sometimes posing as a doctor, sometimes a community nurse, and now he appears to have been working as a hospital orderly. Under an assumed name.'

'Gordon Smith,' Flint said. 'Yes, I read your report when you sent it yesterday. Made interesting bedtime reading,' she added with a wry smile. 'So, Lorimer. What do you want me to do about it?'

He leaned forward and placed a small object into her hand. 'I think you may wish to have a look at this, ma'am.'

Caroline took it between her finger and thumb and turned it over speculatively as though it might explode at any moment.

'And this contains evidence?' she murmured.

Lorimer nodded. 'You'll see that the man behind the Queen Elizabeth hospital robbery is one and the same as our man from Quiet Release, so I think there are grounds to reopen the case.'

'With you heading up a team from Stewart Street? Was that your idea?'

'With your permission, ma'am,' he said, his blue eyes watching her own.

Caroline sat back and stared at him. She was willing to bet that this man had broken a few criminals in his day with that blue gaze. There was something she wanted to trust about that face. And yet the rumours had reached even DCC Flint's ears. Was he fit to be given such responsibility so soon after his rehabilitation? She recalled the nasal voice of that fair-haired fellow, Mitchison, a man to whom she had taken an instant dislike when he'd tried to charm her. That sort of thing simply didn't cut it with Caroline Flint. Her years as an undercover officer had made her good at seeing the real person beneath the façade; it was one of the strengths that had put her where she was today, she thought as she inserted the memory stick into the computer.

'How about we give the case over to the MIT?' she suggested a few minutes later. 'See if a crack team can hunt this person down?' She waved a hand at the screen with its image of the bearded man.

She watched closely as Lorimer stifled a sigh and tried not to chew his lower lip. *He wants this to prove himself as much as to finish the job,* she thought suddenly.

'If you say so, ma'am,' he replied at last. But she could see the disappointment in these blue eyes as they shifted away from her stare.

'With you heading up the team, of course,' she added slyly. 'Superintendent Renton is unlikely to come back from her sick leave, I'm afraid, and her job will be up for consideration as soon as she decides on a retirement package. Detective Superintendent Mitchison has been covering for her. *Temporarily*, you understand.' She watched Lorimer's face as her words sank in, hoping that he had noticed her emphasis on Mitchison's role, and Caroline Flint smiled faintly as though she could read the thoughts behind that serious expression: was she offering him another job? A chance to head up the MIT?

'I believe you know one of the officers there: DCI Cameron?' the DCC continued smoothly. 'I think perhaps you'd find him very useful in putting a team together. What do you say?'

The man's raised eyebrows were almost comical as he looked at her in surprise.

'You, of course?'

'Very well, then. I'll let Stewart Street know that you've been seconded over to Govan at my request and Superintendent Mitchison can be relieved of the extra burden of his current duties,' Flint replied, standing to show that the meeting was now over.

Lorimer tilted his head and regarded her with the ghost of smile as though he in his turn were trying to guess what was inside her mind at that moment.

'Thank you, ma'am,' he said, clasping her hand once again.

'Nothing to thank me for, Lorimer. It isn't going to be easy. But then, I suspect you aren't really one to look for an easy berth, are you?'

She smiled at him properly now and was rewarded with a grin that changed instantly from a solemn expression to one that lit up his whole countenance.

Yes, Caroline told herself as she closed the door on the tall detective. She liked the cut of this one's jib, all right. And she had a notion that Detective Superintendent William Lorimer was a man who'd be a good friend if ever she needed one.

CHAPTER TWENTY-EIGHT

Money, Solly had told them. That was what had been at the root of the entire Quiet Release case. There were only a few motives for murder, really, he told his students. Jealousy, desire for power and greed being three that he had seen most in his years as a criminal profiler. Every one of the people behind Quiet Release, including Mary Milligan, had strenuously denied being the person that had administered the lethal injections and Solly had pondered long and hard about the mysterious bearded man, the one who had escaped. Why not delegate the task of injecting morphine to others, particularly a health professional like Mary? The question that had troubled him at the time returned once more to tax his brain. The simple answer was that this person actually *wanted* to take away the lives of his victims. And not, Solly believed, through any altruistic instinct. Oh, goodness me no, he thought, stroking his beard as he sat beside the window of his office. That would be to endow him with some sort of pity. And he was certain that this individual lacked any empathy whatsoever for his fellow man. The psychopathic personality was one that he was certain fitted this man's profile and the professor was beginning to toy with the idea that this man *enjoyed* the act of killing simply because it gave him power over the moment of life and death.

What sort of childhood produced a person like this? Had he been the only son of domineering parents, forced to do things that he didn't want to? Kicking against an authority that he yearned to escape? Or maybe he'd been one of several kids, striving for attention, wanting to make his parents notice him. Well, weren't most teenagers like that for a time? Rebellious phases were natural but few ever led to a longing to take the lives of other people.

Money had become a secondary motive for the notorious Dr Shipman's killing spree but evidence pointed to the fact that the general practitioner had rarely benefited financially from murdering his patients. No, the man had lusted after the God-like power to decide when a person was to die, a megalomania so intense that it was estimated there may have been more than two hundred and fifty victims, though he was charged with but fifteen deaths.

What had Shipman's background been like? Solly turned his thoughts to a lecture that he had given recently on the subject. Shipman had been the son of a devout couple, the mother dying when Harold had been in his teens. *He'd* been the one to give her morphine to release her from her pain, Solly reminded his students, a statement that always elicited a gasp from the audience.

Perhaps they needed to look a little further into the past, to investigate the background of doctors whose parents had died when they were young. Or was that the best way to go? Solly sighed, imagining the nightmare of tracking that sort of information down. What if . . . ? His thoughts raced around as he tried to focus on his subject and what little they knew about him.

When he'd been spotted by Lorimer on that national news

programme the bearded man had been acting as a hospital orderly, not as a qualified medical person. And he'd been seen that early morning last year outside the home of an elderly victim, posing on that occasion as a district nurse.

What if, unlike Shipman, he wasn't a qualified doctor at all, but had some knowledge of medical training? Solly tapped a pencil against his even white teeth, a memory twitching in his brain. Hadn't he'd compiled some information from the internet, intending to write up lecture notes on the subject? There had been a medical student who had been kicked out of his course here at Glasgow University but had returned under an assumed name, trying again and again to obtain his degree. A local chap, if he remembered correctly. It had been a newspaper sensation at the time, opinion divided between those who thought the fellow a dangerous crank and those who felt sorry for his failed efforts to become a doctor.

What if a sense of failure had led the man behind Quiet Release to carry out these acts of killing? Was he trying to prove something? To his parents? To a society that had rejected him? Solly heaved a sigh. He could follow a line of thought like this all day and still it was all conjecture. But the pattern of behaviour was a sort of evidence after all. And he was beginning to see that this was a very dangerous individual who would never stop killing, especially now that he had obtained such a large quantity of morphine. Just where, wondered Solly, would he strike next?

CHAPTER TWENTY-NINE

Why did he not simply buy a ticket to some warm part of the world and live out his life comfortably overseas? Yet the notion of such enforced idleness lacked appeal. Wouldn't he be better to head for a country further north, like Denmark, where he could continue his work? Now, here was a place that attracted him. The Danes were sensible folk, after all, and he could see them sharing his vision for an end-of-life strategy. He stood staring moodily out of the picture window that overlooked the River Clyde, his penthouse apartment giving him a panoramic view south-west of the city. Today the distant hills were obscured by low cloud and the water below him was being blown into squally waves as the fierce wind ran across its leaden surface.

What was he doing here in Glasgow? There was no sense of nostalgia for his home town, nothing like that to keep him here, after all. Both of his parents were long gone and he had no siblings or offspring tugging at his coat-tails. And as for a woman ... well, he could find one anywhere he chose. Not that he relished the thought of a long-term attachment. Having a woman stay here, cluttering up his domain, did not appeal in the slightest.

Mary Milligan was one of the few that had stayed with him

overnight, but caution had made him move away from that previous flat in the West End after she was committed to the State Mental Hospital. He'd taken advantage of a quick sale by a Glasgow footballer, who was heading to the big time down south, and moved here in the weeks before Christmas, a slack period for the estate agent who was eager to meet his price. And if the man's eyebrows had been raised when he'd paid with a briefcase full of cash, then that was too bad. The bloke could think whatever he liked.

He could tell that the persona of Charles Graham had charmed Gallagher, all right, and he smiled as he saw his clean-shaven reflection in the dull glass. Was that what was keeping him here? The thought of doing business with the gangster? Had he even felt a thrill when Gallagher had approved his ideas? Not really, he admitted to himself. It was a bit of fun to play the part but he knew deep down that what really kept him here was a pull of a different sort.

His list was growing week by week, these vagrant addicts, all on the lookout for drugs, whose identities he aimed to secure for his own use. They would do anything for a fix, anything at all. And once they had outlived their usefulness he would take pleasure in putting them to sleep, one by one, thus ridding the city of more undeserving mouths to feed.

The image of that old woman in the East End flat came back to him and he clenched his fists, imagining it all again ...

His fingers twitched as he remembered wielding the syringe, plunging his poison into the tired old veins and watching closely until that last gasp took Ellen Blackburn from the world. He wanted to do that again. And again ...

Turning away from the rainswept view, he began to plan how he would ensnare his next victim.

CHAPTER THIRTY

'You've got to be joking!'

Lorimer was sitting in the staff car park at Govan police station listening to his friend. 'There is no way on earth that resources could be found for an investigation into something as tenuous as that, Solly.'

There was the customary silence from the professor of psychology and Lorimer waited, frowning despite being used to the other man's lengthy pauses in conversation. He drummed his fingers on the steering wheel, casting a glance at the digital clock. There were still several minutes before the officers inside the building expected to greet him. Lorimer gritted his teeth, then remembered what he had been told at Castlebrae about releasing tension. He breathed in and out then held his breath for a count of four.

'You don't mind, then, if I look into that myself.' Solly's voice came back to him but he heard no sign of a question there.

'So long as you're careful not to muddy the waters, Solly. And report back to me personally with anything you find, okay?'

He could imagine the smile and the nod from his friend as he cut the call. It would not be the first time that Professor Solomon

Brightman had conducted a little unofficial investigation. Police Scotland had been glad of the expert services of the profiler in some cases of multiple murder, but there had been other times when his friend had stepped out on his own, intent on pursuing a line of thought without the least regard for his time and trouble, never mind his own safety.

Lorimer knew only too well what skills his friend could bring to a situation like this where they continued to seek the man behind Quiet Release. He just hoped that the men and women inside this building would be as prepared to throw their resources into finding him at last.

The Major Investigation Team brought together a group of police officers experienced in handling serious crimes. MIT West was the biggest of the three specialist crime units north of the Border and could go anywhere in Scotland at a moment's notice, should a major incident occur. The last time he had been with them had been that fateful afternoon on 31 December, but if the new DCC had her way, this might well be his place of work in the future.

Lorimer heaved a sigh. The incident at Blackburn's home was something he could cope with now, his nightmares gone. Though he doubted whether he could ever truly forget the sound of that child crying in her father's arms. *You lost your own children*, one of his therapists had remarked and he recalled the gentle look of understanding in her eyes. It was at that moment Lorimer had realised the truth about his breakdown. It hadn't just been about the Blackburn children dying. That small massacre had stirred up the pain he'd forced down after every time Maggie had lost one of their babies. Now it was just the two of them. *And Abby*, a little voice reminded him, making him smile at the thought of little Abigail Brightman, the child who had become their goddaughter.

'Lorimer!' A tall man standing the reception desk turned as he entered and gave a lopsided grin.

Lorimer smiled back. 'Niall Cameron, well, well, well. I was told I'd find you here.'

'Great to see you, sir.'

As Cameron shook his hand Lorimer noticed the wedding ring on his finger.

'Married now? I hadn't heard.'

'Lass from back home,' Cameron replied. 'Eilidh's a nurse at Gartnavel. In the oncology unit.' He made a face. 'Met her when my uncle was down for treatment. Poor old soul passed away a couple of years back. Never did make the wedding.'

'And you're both living in Glasgow?'

'Aye, over in Knightswood. Handy for both of us. I just skip through the tunnel every morning.' Cameron looked at his former boss. 'And how about you, sir? How are you keeping?' His Lewis accent was tinged with a concern that was reflected in his deep grey eyes, these straight dark eyebrows raised as the DCI asked the question.

Lorimer could see how the years on the job had changed the younger man. His dark hair was now flecked with grey at the temples but that pale Celtic skin was still smooth and unblemished.

'I'm fine now, thanks. And ready to get back to work.' They stepped away from the desk and Cameron led him towards a bank of lifts.

'You've done well, though. DCI at your age? That's pretty good going.'

'Fast-tracked.' Cameron grinned. Then he narrowed his eyes as he regarded Lorimer. 'You couldn't have been much older when we first worked together?'

Lorimer gave a self-deprecating laugh. 'Och, they must've been hard up for folk when they promoted me.'

'Not how I heard it. DCI at thirty? Doesn't happen often. And I've just been promoted, as it happens. Thirty-six next birthday,' he admitted.

'Good, good,' Lorimer nodded. 'Now, you've set up the computer for me? Everything's ready to show them?'

Cameron grinned. 'Yes, sir. And I can't wait to see their faces.'

The lift arrived and its doors opened with a ping. Both men stepped back to allow three other plain-clothes officers to leave before they entered and Cameron pressed the button.

Once the doors had closed with a sigh, Cameron turned to Lorimer, grasping his arm.

'Sir, there's another matter I want to discuss with you. Something that needs to be spoken about in private,' he said hurriedly. 'Can you spare the time after this meeting?'

Lorimer blinked in surprise at the change in the Lewis man's tone. He detected something urgent in the man's voice and the solemn expression in Niall Cameron's eyes told him that he had been waiting for the moment when they were alone in the lift together to ask his question.

So. Was it something that he didn't want anyone else in this building to overhear? Something he had been waiting to share with his old boss?

'Sure. House for an Art Lover?' he suggested. The famous Charles Rennie Mackintosh design across in the park was now an upmarket restaurant and popular wedding venue but both men remembered the case from long ago that had ended not far from its doors.

'So long as it's somewhere quiet,' Cameron replied, nodding at Lorimer as the lift door opened.

The officers around the table all looked up as Lorimer entered the room with DCI Niall Cameron. He cast a glance around, noting a few familiar faces and several that he had never seen during his career.

One man, older than the rest, stood up and beckoned Lorimer to the end of the table where a vacant seat was obviously waiting for him.

'DI Jim Isherwood.' The man shook Lorimer's hand, a firm once up and down, looking intently at the taller man as if reading his face for any sign of weakness. Then he gave a smile and a nod that seemed to signify that he was satisfied with what he could see. 'Glad to have you with us, sir,' he said. 'Superintendent Mitchison isn't here today so I will pass on whatever we discuss since it impinges on one of his ongoing cases.'

Lorimer refrained from making any comment. He was under no illusion that DS Mitchison, who headed up the CID here in Govan, would enjoy scuppering his plans to renew the Quiet Release case. Cameron had told Kirsty Wilson as much, though perhaps not the fact that Lorimer and the superintendent had been at loggerheads for a very long time. However, CID had no jurisdiction over the affairs in the MIT and Lorimer had no intention of bringing the man anywhere near this team.

Isherwood made the introductions and Lorimer nodded a greeting to the men and women around the table, giving a special smile to those whom he already knew, like Frank Tweedie, a DCI who had joined up around the same time as his friend, Alistair Wilson, Kirsty's father. Tweedie was old-school, a wee terrier of a man who was known for not letting go of a case until he'd collared his man. Lorimer smiled again; Frank Tweedie would be on his side, of that he was certain.

'Good morning,' he began, standing at his place at the head of the table in the briefing room, the white screen behind him.

'I'm Detective Superintendent William Lorimer and I'm here today to explain to you why we are considering reopening the Quiet Release case.'

There were glances amongst the officers and a little murmuring but the moment he raised a hand, Lorimer had their full attention.

'I'd like you to look at the following pictures,' he began, turning to the screen and clicking the remote button.

The face that appeared on the screen was of a bearded unsmiling man, the security photo taken from the hospital records office, a now familiar image given that it had been distributed to every police station in the country.

'The man who styled himself Gordon Smith,' Lorimer remarked. 'A predatory individual who stole a huge quantity of morphine from the Queen Elizabeth.' He let the image linger for a moment longer then replaced it with another picture.

'Now, look at this, please,' he said and clicked once more.

The subject, unaware of a television camera pointed in his direction, was in the background, wheeling a hospital trolley, his upper body and face quite distinct, the frame frozen to capture the moment.

'He had no idea that he was being caught on camera,' Lorimer told them. 'It was completely by chance that I happened to see this on the BBC evening news.'

He turned to face the screen once more.

'This next picture is one that has been kept from last year, the Quiet Release case,' he told them, flicking the button and looking at the image on the screen. That it was the same person in the black-and-white picture was obvious as a collective murmuring broke out.

'Same man I saw on that programme. A matter of days before he swooped on the hospital drugs,' Lorimer remarked. 'We had no evidence last year that this was anyone special. One of our culprits identified him as a bogus doctor but her testimony was severely flawed, partly due to her mental instability. We never could be certain that she wasn't making it all up, choosing a stranger at random from the CCTV recordings.'

'But now you know she was leading you to him.' Frank Tweedie spoke up.

'Perhaps she was. It's hard to be sure,' Lorimer admitted. 'Mary Milligan suffers from a complex disorder that makes her want to be the centre of attention.'

'Even when she takes the risk that she might be found out?' a female officer commented, her voice sounding puzzled.

'Especially then,' Lorimer broke in. 'That's one of the quirks of her condition. Something we could never have guessed at the time.'

'So now we know she was telling you the truth.' DCI Cameron nodded.

'She was telling us a truth of sorts. Gambling with the notion that we would never find this man. And she was right' – he made a face – 'until now.'

Lorimer stood at the doorway, shaking hands with the members of the team who had attended the meeting. Every single officer had shown his or her approval for reopening the case, something that he had honestly expected, given the new evidence tying the bogus porter with the mystery man that Mary Milligan had fingered then later claimed to have invented. Would they be able to obtain any DNA from the hospital to tie the man calling himself Gordon Smith with the unidentified samples still lingering in the lab at Gartcosh?

The wind that had howled all night and swept the leaves into corners had dropped just a little as Cameron and Lorimer walked from the car park to the restaurant at the House for an Art Lover. The pale building seemed to float as Lorimer gazed upwards, white clouds scudding against a powder-blue sky, making him slightly dizzy.

'We came here for the Christmas night out,' Cameron remarked as he held open the door. 'Bit pricey but the food was good.'

Lorimer nodded, already looking towards the tables by the window for a place where they might talk without being overheard by other patrons.

'Over here,' he said, nodding towards a corner that looked out over the grassy bank towards a door set into a high wall. They could always stroll around the walled garden if they needed somewhere else to talk in private, he thought.

Cameron sat with his back to the huge picture windows facing the entrance.

He wants to see everyone who comes into this place, Lorimer thought, his curiosity whetted for what the DCI wanted to disclose. And he was interested to find out why Cameron was so intent on keeping this meeting private.

They ordered soup and open sandwiches with a pot of tea to share, then Lorimer sat back and folded his arms.

'Thanks for sparing the time, sir,' Cameron began.

Lorimer merely raised his eyebrows and smiled as if to indicate that it was no bother, though in truth there was a lot to do now that he had obtained the go-ahead from the DCC to temporarily head up this MIT team.

'It's good to see you again,' Cameron went on. 'How is Mrs Lorimer?' He gave a half smile. 'I heard on the grapevine that her cousin had been one of the Quiet Release victims.' His smile dropped.

'Aye, that was a bad business,' Lorimer replied. 'Still, we hope to tie up all the ends this time. But I don't think that is why I'm here. Am I correct?' he asked, looking at the man across the table.

Cameron leaned forward, glancing up as though to check nobody could overhear him though the nearest customer was a man reading his newspaper several tables away.

'It's like this, sir,' he began and Lorimer saw the movement in his throat as Niall Cameron swallowed nervously. 'I've been doing a bit of investigating on the quiet.' He hesitated and looked at Lorimer. 'One or two of us have been concerned about some of the decisions made by a senior officer. So ...' He bit his lip before continuing. 'I asked a friend of mine to do an internet search on this officer. I know it was unorthodox,' he said quickly, 'but it's proved to be pretty conclusive.'

'What do you mean? And who's the officer you have worries about, Niall?' Lorimer frowned. This was serious indeed if an honest type like Niall Cameron had gone outside the jurisdiction of Police Scotland to hunt for information about a fellow officer.

'It's to do with an ongoing investigation into Jack Gallagher's business, really.' Cameron sighed. 'DCI Tweedie and I weren't happy about the way it was being handled. There were just not enough resources going into surveillance and we began to ask ourselves why.'

'Go on.'

'My friend is something of an IT whizz,' Cameron explained. 'Sometimes works on a freelance basis for different government departments.'

He paused for a moment before continuing.

'I gave him permission to access some of our secure files.'

'Dear God!' The words were out before Lorimer could stop them.

'I know, I know.' Niall ran his hands across his thick dark hair. 'It wasn't what you'd expect from me. But we got a result,' he whispered, eyes shining as he leaned closer. 'Turns out this officer has been in a – how can I put it – a close relationship with Gallagher.'

'You mean he's in Gallagher's pocket?' Lorimer's frown deepened, the shock on his face making the younger man sit back a little.

Cameron managed to nod in answer to the question.

'And just who is it we're discussing, may I ask?' Lorimer continued, his voice low, the tone icy.

'Someone you already know, sir,' Cameron said, looking into Lorimer's blue gaze without flinching. 'It's Detective Superintendent Mitchison.'

The timing of their lunches arriving could not have been better as far as Lorimer was concerned and it was not just the hot bowl of butternut squash soup that he had to digest. The two men ate in silence, Lorimer dimly aware of his companion casting glances his way but he did not want to talk right now; all he wanted was to think about the way forwards. Using a civilian to rake up muck about a fellow officer was bad enough but to find out it was a man in Cameron's own building who was in cahoots with a known gangster could blow up in all of their faces if it wasn't handled carefully.

'You have concrete evidence of Mitchison's goings-on?' he said at last, shoving his plates to one side and picking up his teacup.

'Yes, we do,' Cameron assured him. 'And it's clear enough from the emails between the pair of them that our man's been feeding Gallagher titbits of information to allow him to escape our clutches time and again. Also,' Cameron leaned closer, 'there are some serious amounts of money being paid into a bank account in his name. Not the one that his salary's paid into,' he added with a grin. 'He's not been that stupid.'

Lorimer remembered the incident at Gartcosh and how the detective superintendent was always so sharply dressed. And Mitchison had set his face on further promotion, he knew. Was there ... could there be ... other senior officers who were on Gallagher's payroll? The thoughts wheeled around his brain as he sipped the tea.

'Sit on this for now, Niall,' he said at last. 'Mitchison may not be the only one that Jack Gallagher's targeting.'

The DCI's eyes widened. 'You don't think ...?'

Lorimer shrugged. 'We don't know yet. But maybe your arrangement with that friend could be extended a little? Ask him to see if he can find any other officers' names in Gallagher's correspondence.'

'Then what?'

Lorimer sighed deeply. He was asking himself the same question. 'We'll see,' he replied vaguely. 'But when it comes to the crunch a report will have to be made to Professional Standards.'

Niall Cameron nodded. 'I thought of taking it all to them myself, but then I wondered if you might advise me to do something different.' He gave a faint smile, his grey eyes crinkling at the corners. 'And you have.'

CHAPTER THIRTY-ONE

The Big Yin had been named after one of Glasgow's favourite sons, a man of many talents whose life had begun on the shipyards and taken him all over the globe, his talent for music and swift repartee endearing him to millions. Billy Connolly had once set foot inside this establishment, the local worthies insisted, but stepping into the spit and sawdust interior of the East End pub, DC Kirsty Wilson felt such claims were grossly exaggerated.

The barman was slouched over the counter with a copy of the *Racing Post*, hiding his face so that Kirsty had to clear her throat to catch his attention.

'Aye, what'll it be?' the man asked heavily, his reluctance to lay down his paper only too apparent.

'I don't want anything to drink, thanks,' Kirsty told him sharply. 'I just want to find someone.'

'Oh, well, in that case maybe you want tae borrow a telephone directory,' the man guffawed.

Then, as Kirsty whipped out her warrant card and stuck it close to his face, the barman's mouth opened in an O of understanding.

'Tam McLachlan,' she said firmly, never taking her eyes off the barman for a second. 'I've spoken to him in here before. You'll know where to find him.'

'Auld Tam?' The barman straightened up and looked at Kirsty with something she recognised as a natural wariness, a distrust of the polis that might make this a wasted visit.

'Aye.' She nodded. 'Len Murdoch used to buy him a drink or two.'

At the mention of the former detective sergeant's name, the barman leaned forward.

'Len sent you?' he whispered.

Kirsty thought for a split second. To tell a lie might get her somewhere but that went against her nature.

'I need to find Tam,' she insisted quietly. 'Before he comes to any harm.'

'What's the auld rascal been up tae noo?' The barman attempted a smile but it faded swiftly as Kirsty's glare told him that this was a serious matter.

'Where would he be?' she asked again.

The barman glanced over her head as if checking to see if anyone was listening to their conversation but the bar was practically empty; just a couple of pensioners playing draughts in one corner and a man wearing a yellow reflective jacket, his dark cap beside his pint. A lollipop man, Kirsty decided, nobody that could be a threat to the suddenly skittish barman.

'He got turfed out of his old place,' the barman whispered. 'Been on the streets, last time I heard, pair auld bugger.'

Kirsty felt her heart plummet. So, she thought, he could be anywhere . . .

'Thanks,' she said and began to turn away.

'Haud on, hen,' the barman hissed. 'You might want tae try

the mission. Glasgow City Mission, Brown Street. D'you know where that is?'

Kirsty nodded. 'Next to the MOD?'

'Aye. Last time he wis in here he telt me he'd been goin' there fur a wee warm-up during the day. No' jist fur the food at teatime.'

Kirsty gave a shrug. 'If he's that down on his luck then how come he managed to find enough money to buy a drink in here?' she asked.

It was the barman's turn to raise his shoulders. 'Search me,' he replied.

Kirsty leaned closer to the counter. 'When did you last see him?'

The barman shook his head. 'Cannae mind exactly. But ah think it wis afore his pal got pulled out the river. Your lot'll know mair aboot that, eh?'

Kirsty nodded and then fished in her pocket and produced a crumpled fiver.

'One for yourself,' she said, laying it on the counter top along with her card.

The barman gave her a slow smile. 'Ah dinna drink, hen, but ah'll pit it oan a cuddy,' he laughed, picking up the paper again as Kirsty turned to leave. 'An if ah see yer friend who shall I say wants tae see him?'

Kirsty pointed to the business card then looked the barman in the eye. 'And I'll expect a phone call the moment you lay eyes on him, okay?'

She could feel the man staring at her all the way out but there had been a different expression and Kirsty knew a small moment of victory as she recognised it as respect.

*

'Crikey, that's a big quantity to find in someone like that,' the woman wearing a white lab coat commented as she sat at her computer recording the findings of a toxicology test.

'What d'you mean?' The girl next to her turned to ask.

'Well, says here that Seamus O'Halloran was an itinerant. Found in some backstreet stone dead. But, see the result ...' The lab assistant swung the screen around so that her colleague could see.

'Good grief! How did a poor old soul like that get his paws on such a quantity of high-grade morphine?'

'Good question. And not the first one either. There was that other tramp who had OD'd on a massive dose, d'you remember?'

Her colleague nodded. 'What d'you think? Is someone doing a vigilante exercise? Ridding the city of its vermin?' The girl shuddered in disgust.

The lab assistant frowned. 'It's an old man you're talking about,' she chided the younger woman. 'Not some piece of rubbish.'

The woman turned her screen back and resumed typing up the toxicology report. It was none of their business what happened now but she would keep her ears open for any developments: Rosie Fergusson was good at relaying interesting bits of news, especially when a case proved to be less than straightforward.

'Seamus O'Halloran. Was identified by a pal of his when we had him in for the PM. Same old chap that came by before, Tam McLachlan,' Rosie told Kirsty as the girl prepared to babysit for the evening. 'He was in and out of the office in a heartbeat. Something else you might want to know, though. We had an intriguing tox report like the one from your other itinerant,

Gordon Smith. Very high quantity of morphine in the blood, enough to have killed a horse, I imagine.' She gave a weary shake of her head. 'Anyway, I'll leave you to it. Her ladyship is sound asleep, by the way. Exhausted after a heavy day at nursery.' Rosie laughed. 'So you and James should have no trouble with her tonight.'

'Oh, Abby's never any bother. We like playing with her, don't we?'

Kirsty turned to her boyfriend who stood nodding his agreement.

'Aye, the wee lass is fine with us,' he assured Rosie. 'Loves stories being read to her. *My* job!' he said proudly. 'Likes a northern accent, probably,' he declared, deliberately exaggerating his Geordie tones.

'Okay, well thanks again. We won't be late back. It's just a lecture we both need to attend tonight. I'm introducing my guest speaker and Solly wanted to hear him speak.'

At the sound of the front door of the Brightmans' flat closing Kirsty flopped down on the comfortable settee and patted the seat cushion beside her.

'Interesting tox result,' she began, glancing at her boyfriend. She had said nothing to James about her plan to track down the old tout but now she knew for certain that it had been Tam McLachlan who'd identified Rosie's latest post-mortem case.

'Aye,' he agreed. 'Do you think the two deaths might be linked somehow?'

'Well, Rosie certainly seems to think so and the Crown Office will have to be kept informed as it looks like a possible development. I mean,' she broke off to pick up the mug of coffee that Rosie had poured earlier, 'what sort of down-and-out gets expensive gear like that? You don't expect them to be injecting anything much. Too damned costly.' She sipped her coffee, thinking hard about the man who was being sought by the MIT. Could he be the one who'd supplied those drugs? James would love hearing all about her theories, Kirsty knew, but she hesitated to reveal them just yet. 'Dad used to tell me that once upon a time they picked up the jakeys off the suspension bridge on a weekend. Meths drinkers, most of them. Used to mix methylated spirits with milk and take it through a straw, would you believe!'

'So,' James asked again, 'how did these two guys get high-grade stuff like that?'

It was a question that was asked several times the following day. The elusive Gordon Smith's link with the first dead tramp, from whom he had stolen both name and background details, was a matter for further investigation by members of the team now. And the fact that another dead, homeless drug addict had been found with a similar MO ran a shiver of excitement through the MIT.

Seamus O'Halloran had been known by several of the police officers as an occasional thief and registered addict, his house long since repossessed by a mortgage company, his family refusing to have anything more to do with the old man. It had been his friend and drinking companion, Tam McLachlan, who had made the official ID at the city mortuary. So far, none of the dead man's relatives wanted to claim his body for burial. And Tam had not left any address worth having.

That in itself was interesting, DC Wilson thought as she pored over the documentation they already had at their disposal. Tam had been in and out of the mortuary in double-quick time, Rosie had mentioned. The address he'd given turned out to be bogus, making Kirsty wonder just how Tam really spent his days and nights now. Was he in dosshouses and hostels, perhaps? She sat back and thought for a moment. The folk in Glasgow City Mission were on the side of the angels; maybe she would just give them a call and see what they might tell her.

The mission had been the recipient of the Christmas charity collection back at Stewart Street, Kirsty recalled. It was one of the places that genuinely helped those that were down on their luck with nowhere to stay and no one to care.

A telephone call was not enough, she'd decided after some deliberation, and so now she was driving through the city streets, noting the changes to so many places, new tall edifices of glass and steel rubbing shoulders with the solid sandstone buildings. Some of the newer office blocks were pretty ghastly, she had always admitted to herself, yet whenever she looked up at places like the green dome of the Mitchell Library, the University Tower on the skyline or Rennie Mackintosh's Art School tucked away in Garnethill, Kirsty felt her heart lift. Glasgow prided itself on these architectural gems: 'Look up' being one of the commands made by every good tourist guide, but today Kirsty could only admire the streets from ground level as she headed for the mission.

There was one free parking space outside the building and Kirsty shivered as she left the warmth of the car and scampered around to the main entrance. For a moment she paused, reading the notices fixed to the glass doors.

Under a simple yellow sign proclaiming HE IS RISEN were the words:

Drug taking/dealing will not be tolerated in or around our building.

Police will be called if necessary.

For once she would have been glad of the uniform, its presence commanding a sort of respect that helped in many ways. The man who stood talking to a wee tub of a woman wearing a printed pinny did not appear to notice the newcomer to the ground floor of Glasgow City Mission at first. That was okay by her, Kirsty thought, taking the time to look around at the stacks of folded chairs and the formica-topped tables where several men were seated in what was evidently a dining room. She tried not to catch any eye that was staring her way, glancing around the room instead.

A Che Guevara image of Christ wearing the crown of thorns caught her attention.

MEEK. MILD. AS IF, the caption read. Was that the sort of image the people in the mission saw? A strong revolutionary who could turn lives upside down?

Kirsty waited patiently until their conversation was finished, just overhearing scraps of what was being said.

'Aye, ah c'n hear ye a'richt, Matthew. Ah'm no' cornbeef. Twenty pun o' tatties an plenty o' ingins. Therr's enough meat left ower tae mak a guid load o' stovies fur a'body,' the woman declared, her little eyes fierce as she stood, arms across her ample bosoms, glaring at the man.

'Fine, Betty, fine. I'll leave it all up to you, then,' the man replied, holding his hands up in a gesture of submission that made Kirsty want to giggle. The sight of that wee wifie standing up to the man who was probably her boss would stay in her mind until she could relate the scene to James later.

The woman stomped off, leaving the man raking a hand through his thatch of brown hair as he turned with an exasperated sigh.

It was only then that he seemed to catch sight of Kirsty.

'What can I do for you, my dear?' he asked, smiling as he came forward to welcome her. Yet there was a puzzled look on his face as his eyes made a swift appraisal of the smartly dressed young woman who had arrived with no appointment. Not the usual sort of customer, his gaze seemed to suggest.

The warrant card changed all of that.

'DC Wilson, Police Scotland,' Kirsty told him briskly, noting the questioning look and the way the man's shoulders straightened at the sight of her card.

'Matthew Girdwood.' The man stretched out his hand and Kirsty clasped it, feeling the warmth as he shook it. 'What can I do for you, DC Wilson?' he asked, gesturing her to a quiet corner of the room.

'I'm looking for a man named Tam McLachlan. I believe he frequents the mission?' she began.

'Yes, we know Tam. He's one of our regulars.' Girdwood nodded. 'Comes in most days – so many of them have nowhere to go and this weather drives them in, to be honest,' he said, turning to the huge glass windows where they could see the first flakes of snow beginning to fall.

'He's not in any sort of trouble. That is, we aren't looking to arrest Tam for any misdemeanour, but I think he may have placed himself in some sort of danger,' she told Girdwood.

The weary smile and shake of the man's head indicated that Girdwood had heard this sort of tale too many times before.

'Drugs, I suppose? Dealers making menacing threats? We do our best to keep that sort of thing at bay,' he added, pointing to the sign on the glass door.

'I'm not at liberty to say,' Kirsty said stiffly, trotting out the standard phrase. 'I met Tam some months ago and again more recently when he identified a friend of his who had died in suspicious circumstances.'

'Like I said, he is a regular here. Nice old soul, really. Far too fond of the drink, but you'll know that, of course,' he continued, his eyes meeting her own as if he were assessing Kirsty's motives for being there.

She held his stare then saw the crinkles appear at the edges of Girdwood's eyes and mouth as he grinned and for a moment Kirsty felt as if she had passed some sort of test.

'Come on through,' Girdwood told her, standing up. 'I think Tam might be upstairs just now.'

And in answer to her puzzled frown he added, 'Dinner's in an hour or so, once Betty's stovies are ready, and they all make sure to be here in plenty of time.' He nodded towards the group of men sitting at the tables. 'We cater for about a hundred and sixty every evening. Place closes at ten but before that we hope to involve those who come to have food with prayer and a time to talk.'

Tam McLachlan started when his rheumy eyes took in the young woman who accompanied the centre's director.

'Hello, Tam.' Kirsty smiled as she sat in a vacant chair at the table where the old man sat. 'Remember me?'

He blinked once then nodded silently, still staring at her. 'Murdoch's wee sidekick,' he said at last. 'How is he? Haven't seen him around.'

'Detective Sergeant Murdoch's retired, Tam. I'm sure he'd be delighted to know you were asking, though,' she replied, a twinkle in her eye.

'Huh, that'll be shining bright, lass. Murdoch was good at wheedling things out of me, so he was.'

'And you were happy to oblige for a few drinks, weren't you, Tam?'

The old man shrugged. 'Nae drinks in here. A' teetotal so they are.' He feigned disappointment, rolling his eyes to heaven and catching Matthew Girdwood's glance.

'And that's the way we'll stay,' Girdwood told him. 'Drink's ruined so many lives, Tam, your own included,' he added seriously.

'Aye, well. Mibbe the young lady here wants a quiet word with me, Matthew,' Tam said pointedly and then gave a mock salute as the centre director left them alone and walked back to his office.

'Nice man, that,' Tam told Kirsty as he watched Girdwood's retreating back. 'Wants to save us all, of course.' He gestured to words painted in red against the white wall.

I HAVE LOVED YOU WITH
AN EVERLASTING LOVE;
I HAVE DRAWN YOU
WITH LOVING KINDNESS

He gave a shrug as if to say *what a hopeless task* then turned back to give Kirsty a questioning look.

'That's kind of why I'm here too, Tam,' she began.

'Dearie me, you want to save my soul, lassie?' He sat back in his chair, raising his hands in mock astonishment.

'I think I want to do a wee bit more for you this side of Eternity first,' she declared, leaning closer to the old man. 'Let's begin with Gordon Smith, shall we?'

CHAPTER THIRTY-TWO

The archive material produced exactly what Solly had feared; list upon list of names of student drop-outs, year after year. He had googled *student who falsified his name to become a docto*r in his search engine and that had at least put flesh on the bones of his faint memory of that astonishing case. A young seventeen-year-old boy who had been forced to relinquish his place at university to study medicine had changed his name more than a decade later, spent a year at a Glasgow secondary school, nobody questioning the man who still looked like a teenager. He'd continued the deception all through that school year and then had begun his medical studies, only to drop out a short time later. The hoax might have continued right up until graduation, though, Solly thought. The fellow had got away with it until his identity was discovered and the press had splashed the story across every front page.

What if . . .

He was sitting in the bay window of his spacious office, oblivious to the comings and goings of students down below in University Gardens, pondering the idea that had begun to germinate in his mind. Whoever the stranger was, he had taken on a different identity to become not only a hospital porter but also the guise of a district nurse (although that probably hadn't required being in the company of any other medical professionals: nobody else in the district where he had taken an old lady's life had ever seen or heard of a male community nurse). Then he had been a so-called doctor, according to part of Mary Milligan's original testimony, but anything she had told them could be discounted as seriously flawed due to her state of mind. Or could it? Solly believed that Mary had told them half-truths. It was hard to gauge the man's age from the photographs. A beard put years on you, as Solly well knew. He'd often been taken for far older than his age, especially during his student years, something that had been a bit of an advantage whenever he'd presented an academic paper to men and women far ahead of him in age and experience.

What if . . . he thought again and grinned. There were ways of changing an image with a few clicks of a mouse button if the correct software were at one's disposal and he thought that for someone up at Gartcosh, the Scottish Crime Campus, this would be the work of a couple of moments.

His smile was still in place a few minutes later, the email and attachment sent whizzing through the ether to the person he had in mind. By the end of today he might well have a face to put to one of the hundreds of names on his list. It would be time-consuming and require patience but Professor Brightman was a patient man and never minded taking his time to winkle out a piece of evidence that could give him the result he wanted. Lorimer would be grateful for any sort of help in this investigation, he knew, and meantime he would continue thinking about the profile of a killer whose nefarious skills suggested at least some sort of medical background.

*

Lorimer was thankful for the cooperation of the men and women on the MIT team but now they had to make a concerted effort to discover just who this man was and what involvement he'd had with the late Gordon Smith, a known addict who had fallen on hard times.

They'd given Lorimer a room of his own in the Govan head-quarters, nothing fancy, but it had the advantage of looking out over Helen Street rather than the staff car park. And there were trees there, several dark silhouettes of crows decorating their bare branches. Should his time here be prolonged in any way Lorimer knew he'd enjoy seeing the leaves unfurl from tightly closed winter buds, and maybe even swathes of yellow daffodils heralding spring. Still, he hoped to be finished here long before that and return to his duties across the city at Stewart Street once more. Meantime, there were several things with the investigation that had to be worked on: during Superintendent Renton's absence he was responsible for the management of the entire MIT team as well as their ongoing cases; something that would keep him chained to this desk until late every night. Poor Maggie, he thought with a sudden qualm of conscience.

A knock on his door made Lorimer turn from the window to see DCI Tweedie enter the room and close the door quietly behind him.

'Sir, you wanted to see me ...' Tweedie began.

'Aye, Frank, sit down.' Lorimer gestured towards a chair. 'Think there's something we need to discuss,' he said, his eyes catching the older man's.

Tweedie nodded, looking away from the blue stare, then took a seat opposite the detective superintendent.

'Cameron mentioned he'd told you about our ...' He paused

for a moment, obviously keen to choose his words carefully. 'Our *disquiet*,' he added at last.

'That is a matter that has to stay completely within these four walls,' Lorimer said grimly. 'Nobody else can know about it, understand?'

'Oh, you don't have to worry about me.' Tweedie gave a weak grin. 'I've got far too much to lose ...'

'That's exactly what I am worried about,' Lorimer replied lightly. 'You've got a pension to think about. Few more weeks till you retire. Why muddy the waters now?' He sat back, regarding the other man thoughtfully, steepling his fingers together against his chin.

Tweedie gave a frown. 'Because I didn't want to leave here with something like that on my conscience. Knowing that ... a certain senior officer ... might be on the wrong side of the law isn't a matter I could live with.' He shrugged. 'Simple as that, really.'

'So you confided your fears to DCI Cameron?'

'Straight as a die, that young man!' Tweedie declared. 'Knew that my concerns would be safe with him. Plus he's got years of service ahead of him, a luxury I no longer have.' He leaned forward, hands clasped earnestly in front of him. 'Things like this, Lorimer, they take a long time to uncover. A bent cop in the pay of a known crim, well, you and I both know that can go on undiscovered for decades.'

'Aye, it happens,' Lorimer agreed with a sigh. He noticed with some relief that Tweedie had dropped the 'sir', calling him by name as though they were fellow conspirators, which, he supposed, they were. 'Bad guy spots a weakness in an officer, greed usually, and exploits it to his own advantage. Think that's what happened here?'

Tweedie shook his head. 'Don't know. But however it started it looks like they're well down the road together now.'

'Watch your back,' Lorimer told the DCI. 'I have a hunch that there may be more than one fish to fry here and that a much bigger name could be involved.'

Tweedie's eyes widened. 'Someone really high up? Anyone we know?'

Lorimer shook his head. 'That's the whole problem. We can't trust a single soul outside the three of us. Could be anyone, could be no one. But ask yourself this: how did a person like Mitchison manage to climb the ladder to detective super in Govan CID without a little help from a friend?'

Lorimer was back at the window staring but this time he was seeing nothing of what was happening below in Helen Street, his mind on the scene years before when he had been told that he was being passed over for promotion in favour of DCI Mark Mitchison, something that had shocked his contemporaries. But there had been one man who may have been instrumental in that decision-making process, a man Lorimer had both respected and liked. Now retired from the force, George Phillips lived a quiet life down the Clyde coast, but, as he stood there thinking, Lorimer knew that he had already decided to intrude on his former boss's tranquil existence.

The house on the corner of the street looked several ways out at its neighbours: round windows pierced the turret that softened the place where a gable ought to have been and massive bay windows on two sides overlooked both the hill down to the main road and the street where more modest bungalows sat, decent and ordinary, the big house across the street almost an affront to their uniformity. Most of the homes had been built post-war and snapped up in a frenzy of men eager to become the new middle classes in an area that was increasingly sought after by the upwardly mobile. The joke was that some of them could hardly pronounce its name: 'Milngavie' sounded strange to their ears; 'Mill Guy', the correct way to utter the name, reminding them of humbler times. Now merging with the affluent suburb of Bearsden, Milngavie was an address that was regarded by many as a highly desirable and respectable middle-class area.

That suited the man who parked his Porsche Boxter in the newly laid brick driveway, the honey-coloured herringbone pattern of the drive pleasing to his eye. Mitchison rummaged in his coat pocket for the house keys and entered the front door, disabling his alarm the moment he was standing in the reception hallway. For a moment he stood listening to the quiet, wishing that there was a welcoming call from the woman who had stayed here for oh so short a time. Charlotte had been charmed by his wealth and the stories of his profession but bit by bit she had seen Mark Mitchison for who he really was: a shallow man whose vanity required constant feeding. Their brief relationship had ended before he'd had time to lead her willingly to the local church and 'make an honest woman of her' (as his mother might have hissed between tightly pursed lips). Putting down the keys on the well polished table, Mitchison sniffed the air. The scent of lavender still lingered, the trace of his cleaning woman, the only female who crossed his threshold nowadays. Not that he lived a hermit's life. There were places he could go whenever the notion took him, high-class prostitutes willing to indulge his fantasies for a fee. Gallagher often paid him in kind for the services he undertook on the gangster's behalf, a perk that Mitchison took without demur. And, of course, there was always Pamela. But it was Mark Mitchison who jumped to *her* orders whenever she called.

Now he maintained a solitary existence in this big house, cooking occasionally but mostly eating out at the local restaurants or driving across the Erskine Bridge to a country club where he chatted up the waitresses in the hope that one of them might succumb to his undoubted charms. That they never did had not stopped his visits, the food and warmth giving Mitchison the illusion of being in someone's cosy home.

He had just closed the wardrobe door after hanging up his cashmere coat when the house telephone rang, breaking the silence with its insistent note.

'Superintendent Mitchison,' he said at once, expecting the caller to be someone from work.

'Good evening, Superintendent,' a laconic voice replied, a voice that made Mark Mitchison suddenly sit down on the chair by the telephone table. 'Thought you might want to have a wee chat?'

'I've told you before,' Mitchison whispered, as if anyone could hear through his thick walls, 'never call me at home. D'you understand what I'm saying? It's not safe!'

'Worried that someone might have put a tap on your line?' the voice chuckled. 'Maybe I've done it already. How would you know?'

Mitchison's knuckles whitened as his grip on the handset intensified. 'What do you want?' he snapped, a scowl on his once-handsome features clearly showing his displeasure.

There was a pause and Mitchison's scowl became a frown of concern. Why had he called his home? And how did he know that Mitchison had just entered the house? He turned towards the front door but the solid wood revealed nothing, simply a barrier to any threat from the outside world.

'I want to talk to you,' the caller replied slowly. 'Car outside across the street. See that you come. Now.'

Mitchison looked at the telephone in his hands but the man had rung off so he slotted it back on the charger with trembling fingers.

What had possessed Gallagher to come here? he thought wildly, looking around in sudden panic. Their arrangement had been to meet in secret places and only when meeting face to face was essential, never to encroach on one another's personal space.

The pale Jaguar was purring by the kerb, keeping its driver warm as Mitchison hurried over the road. He snatched open the car door and slid in, grabbing at the safety belt as the car glided away, Gallagher not even deigning to glance at his passenger.

Mitchison sat on his hands, warming them on the heated seat, suddenly aware of how rigid with cold he had become, wondering if the big man beside him could smell his fear.

They had travelled out of the bright lights of the suburb, past a small Marks and Spencer garage-cum-foodstore and out into the countryside where the Jaguar picked out the road with its full beam when Gallagher spoke at last.

'We have a wee problem, Mitchison.' His statement was followed by a sigh that expressed his exasperation, making the man in the passenger seat stiffen in apprehension.

'What? What sort of problem, Jack?' Mitchison tried for a light-hearted tone but it came out all wrong, a high-pitched whine that betrayed his nervousness.

'The sort of problem that a big-shot guy like you can fix.' Gallagher patted Mitchison's shoulder, making the police officer flinch.

The man turned and glanced at him before focusing his eyes back onto the dark country road that wound up and around the perimeter of the exclusive golf club where Mitchison occasionally played.

'You seem a tad anxious, son. Something on your mind, eh? Something you want to tell your uncle Jack?' The chuckle that followed only increased Mitchison's tension.

'What the hell's going on? You wait for me coming home, you call me, and then tell me there's a problem? What am I supposed to say? "Good evening, won't you come in for a drink?" Not bloody likely! You know we're not supposed to meet up like this!' Mitchison exploded.

Again the gangster flicked his eyes across at the man sitting beside him and this time their eyes met and Mitchison blinked, horrified at the anger smouldering under these bushy brows.

'What?' he whispered. 'What's this problem?'

Gallagher slowed the big car down then took a right turning towards the winding road that led down to the village of Strathblane. Less than a minute later he pulled over into a lay-by sheltered in the lee of a dark pine forest and switched off the engine, killing the lights.

Mitchison felt his body tense as the gangster turned in the driver's seat to face him.

'You really don't know, do you?' Gallagher mused at last.

'Know what?'

Gallagher shook his head and gave another theatrical sigh. 'Well, for a detective you're pretty useless at keeping tabs on your own concerns, Mitch,' he replied.

Mitchison frowned. 'What do you mean?'

'Someone's been raking around in your internet files,' Gallagher stated bluntly. 'Your *personal* ones, no' the polis files,' he added, seeing the shock on the other man's face. 'Like to tell me who that might be?'

'*My files?*' The question came out as a squeak as Mitchison's voice rose in a strained crescendo.

'Aye.' The gangster nodded, prodding a thick finger into Mitchison's side. 'The ones that contain conversations that you and me maybe should both have deleted.' He stared at the police officer but Mitchison melted under his glare and looked away.

'Wanted to keep them for a kind of insurance, did you?' Gallagher nodded to himself. 'Protecting your own back? Aye, I can see you doing something like that. But that was a very stupid thing to do, as it happens.' Gallagher's tone was light but there was no mistaking the menace in his words. 'Turns out someone's been nosy-parkering. Someone with IT skills as good as they come. One of yours, maybe? A young copper fresh out of university? That's what I'm thinking at any rate. My own techie geek stumbled across it almost by accident when he was cleaning stuff up for me.'

'What are you saying?' Mitchison whispered, his mouth falling open in horror.

'Someone's infiltrated our system. Mine. And yours.' Gallagher looked away as though unwilling to look Mitchison in the eye.

'Who . . . ?' The question dangled in the air between them as the two men stared into the impenetrable darkness of the thick pinewood.

'We don't know. Yet.' Gallagher slowly drummed his fingers against the leather steering wheel. 'But when we do find out I can promise you one thing. They won't be living to pick up their police pension.'

CHAPTER THIRTY-THREE

Kirsty Wilson hummed the tune that had been in her head all the way to work. The guy next to her on the subway, music clarinet case stuck firmly between his Doc Martens, had been oblivious to the fact that his MP3 player was not as silent to others as he might have imagined and in between the roar of the rattling train Kirsty could hear the strains of Carl Orff's *Carmina Burana*, one of her favourite pieces of classical music. Despite having heard it countless times in TV adverts and the like, 'O Fortuna' still had the power to send a thrill down her spine.

But it wasn't just the music that had lightened her mood; there was the thought of that old man she'd met again.

Tam McLachlan, her very first tout! Okay, so he had been practically gifted to her through his former association with DS Murdoch, but the old man had been quite happy to enter into a new relationship with Kirsty. She recalled his words as she had questioned him about the bearded man. *He was in the business of stealing souls, not like here where they want to save them. An' remember he's shaved that beard off*, Tam had added, pointing a greasy finger at the images Kirsty had shown him. *Looks different. Younger.*

Kirsty stepped through the doors of the Govan station, eager to follow up on all of this information today, see where it might lead. Okay, by rights she ought to hand everything over to Police Intelligence and the unit that dealt with sources like Tam. But maybe that could wait a bit longer until she had more concrete information.

She was preparing to nod and say a polite 'Good morning' as Detective Superintendent Mitchison approached but something in the senior officer's expression wiped the smile from her face, the humming stopping abruptly.

The scowl that she received even as the words died on her lips made her draw back as though she were about to be struck. But the man strode past, giving her a filthy look over his shoulder as he continued down the corridor to his office.

Kirsty bit her lip. She wasn't aware of any directive that said *no humming* and the senior officer's behaviour struck her as very odd. What on earth had she done to deserve such a look of disapproval? She'd been reasonably content settling in here at the Helen Street police station, trying hard to be part of a new team and thrilled to be close to the major investigation branch that was housed in the same building. Mitchison had greeted her courteously enough on her arrival, she remembered. Not warmly, but she'd thought nothing of that at the time. *A cold fish*, her father had told her when she'd related her first day in Govan. *Never had much time for him*, he had added with a snort. Was it something to do with her dad, then? Wilson was a common enough name, but had the fact that she was Alistair's daughter only just caught up with the senior officer? Was that it? Bad blood between them maybe? Kirsty made a face as she entered the large room where CID officers manned their desks, the various workloads extending day by day.

She shrugged off her coat, hung it on a peg then sat down to open her computer. She was still working on the theft from the Queen Elizabeth University Hospital, 'The Death Star', as Glaswegians had christened the huge building that so reminded everyone of the *Star Wars* film, especially at night when its windows were all lit up against a dark sky. Och, well, Mitchison could scowl all he liked, she told herself; there was work to be done to find this character and loads of data to trawl through for her senior investigating officer. Plus what she intended to do with the things Tam McLachlan had told her.

A shadow fell across Kirsty's screen and she looked up to see a nice-looking young man bending down towards her.

'Boss wants you,' he told her quietly.

Kirsty's eyebrows rose in alarm. The fellow standing there wasn't anyone she had come across before. And why should he be speaking in such hushed tones?

'Mitchison . . . ?'

The officer grinned at her. 'No, not him. It's Lorimer who's been asking for you. I've to take you up there myself,' he added with a grin. 'To the MIT.'

Kirsty leapt to her feet, both astonished and relieved that the message was not from Mitchison.

'Hear you're someone special, DC Wilson.' The young man, who was perhaps a few years her senior, looked at her enquiringly as they set off along the corridor.

'Me?' Kirsty squeaked in disbelief.

'Aye. We were just hearing about the way you handled the Quiet Release case. Well, about a certain car chase and the arrest of a prime suspect?' The detective smiled again, but it was clear that whatever had been said about her had made an impression on him.

'Oh, that ...'

The man stopped and thrust out a hand. 'Forgetting my manners,' he began. 'DC Davie Giles. At your service,' he added with a mock bow, still holding Kirsty's hand and regarding her with more than a passing interest.

Does he fancy me? Kirsty thought. She released her hand and they continued walking along towards the stairs that would take them up to the hallowed corridors of the MIT. Somehow she would need to slip in a mention of her boyfriend, James, before this rather nice guy got any ideas!

'Do you know why I'm wanted ...?'

Davie Giles grinned and raised one dark eyebrow. 'Aye, but I'll let them tell you.'

Several faces turned towards them as Kirsty entered the room that overlooked Helen Street but she had eyes only for the man who stood up and strode towards her, taking her hand in a quick grasp. Turning towards the assembled officers (that included DCI Niall Cameron, she was pleased to see), Lorimer began the introductions.

'Allow me to introduce you all to Detective Constable Wilson,' he began. 'Kirsty was, as I've already explained, instrumental in wrapping up the latter stage of the Quiet Release case.' He turned towards the girl as a few congratulatory murmurs and smiles were directed her way.

'Kirsty, given your intimate knowledge of the case, I'd like to offer you a place on the team during this further investigation.'

'Oh.' Kirsty felt her face redden as a blush of pleasure spread across her cheeks. 'Oh, *yes*!' she exclaimed with such obvious enthusiasm that several of the officers seated in the room burst out laughing.

'What about the actions I've been given in the Queen

Elizabeth end of things, sir?' she asked as the officers settled back down to their own work and Lorimer led her to an empty desk that was, she saw, next to where DC Giles was now sitting.

'Someone else will take that on,' Lorimer told her. 'I want you to help this team make the connections between the various personas this man is using.' He nodded towards the whiteboard at one end of the room where several enlarged photos had been taped. 'He was seen briefly by the neighbour of one of his victims and we have these three images: one from the hospital records that was his official security photo, the CCTV image that Mary Milligan identified and the one I saw on the TV news. We haven't had any further sightings but we do know that his DNA was found at the scene of at least three crimes.'

'The drug dealer on Byres Road, the girl whose sister had motor neuron disease and one of his own accomplices . . . ' Kirsty counted them off on her fingers.

'And Mary seems to be the only one that knows who he really is, more's the pity,' Lorimer continued.

'There's something else that I found out, sir,' Kirsty went on. 'Tam McLachlan, the old homeless man, I managed to meet up with him again. Used to be one of DS Murdoch's touts. He's had dealings with the man we're after. Saw him recently, in fact. Says he's now clean-shaven.'

Lorimer raised his eyebrows. 'McLachlan's told you all of this?'

'Yes, sir. I thought you'd want to know.'

'Right.' Lorimer nodded. 'That's another piece of intelligence we have at our disposal, thanks to DC Wilson.' He smiled briefly, making Kirsty's cheeks redden, then she listened as Lorimer gave out the actions to the rest of the team.

*

Once the other officers had trooped out of the briefing room and they were alone at last, Kirsty looked up at the man who had been a family friend since her childhood. 'Sir, can I ask you something?'

Lorimer nodded.

'See Superintendent Mitchison? Did he and my dad ever have a run-in?'

Lorimer frowned. 'Not to my knowledge,' he replied. 'Mitchison came to Strathclyde about fifteen years ago. Lothian and Borders before then, I believe. And your dad would have told me if there had been a problem, so, no, I'm sure there was nothing between them. Why?'

Kirsty bit her lip and shook her head. 'Och, it's nothing, really, just a thought ...'

Lorimer looked hard at the young woman, his blue gaze making her blink and look away.

'Okay,' he said at last, but Kirsty had the instinctive feeling that her mention of the chief super's name had ruffled Lorimer's feathers and she rather wondered why.

Once Lorimer left her, Kirsty gazed around her, thinking of the men and women that comprised this elite group of police officers. And she'd been asked to join them!

As the strains of Orff's music came back into her mind, Kirsty grinned. The wheel of fortune did turn with some surprises, she thought to herself with a chuckle.

It would take a lot more than luck to find what he was looking for, Solly Brightman thought, tugging his beard thoughtfully. It might be any one of the Scottish universities that had been chosen by their mystery man, if, that is, his theory was correct and the dangerous individual behind Quiet Release had in fact been a drop-out from a medical degree course. It fitted the profile of a man who possessed a keen intelligence but who was seriously flawed, perhaps too arrogant to take instruction from his tutors? Solly had come across that type before, he thought glumly; clever students who refused to work hard in order to achieve the results they needed to stay the course. And there were those who had to cut short their time at university for other reasons: ill health, difficulties with finances, family problems ... Was the man he sought one of those?

Lorimer was right. It was an impossible task but perhaps a careful trawl of his own university's medical faculty might throw something up? He could only ask and hope, after all. And, as his old mother was fond of reminding him, *If you don't ask you won't get what you're looking for.*

Where to begin? Rosie might be able to help, he decided. The department of Forensic Medicine and Science was closely linked to the medical faculty; pathologists needed to be surgeons first and undergo a complete medical training. A few enquiries in the staff club, too, might just nudge some memories of a promising student who dropped out. If he asked the right people. The professor glanced at the two pictures in his hand. Yes, that beard made him look older than his years, he decided, whereas the one that his technical assistant had created for him showed the face of a fellow who might be still in his mid to late twenties. Solly gazed into the distance and wondered. Had this man been here ten years ago, perhaps? There was no way of telling his exact age from the reconstructed image but the professor of psychology was adept at judging the age of his students and he hazarded a guess that the man who had posed as Gordon Smith was now about twenty-seven. There were several senior academics in the medical faculty who would have known him at one time, *if* he had studied here and *if* they had any particular reason to recall him.

Solly smiled tiredly and shook his head. Was it even worth the bother to begin asking such questions? The previous evening Rosie and he had been happily discussing the forthcoming baby, a relief for his pregnant wife after having conducted the post-mortem on yet another itinerant found dead in the city's slums. Shouldn't he be content to wallow in their domestic bliss? His lips twitched as the self-deprecating smile widened. Interesting choice of word, he thought with a chuckle. Wallow, indeed! Well, perhaps an insight into his own thoughts had provided an answer. He loved his Rosie more than anyone in the world, and little Abby, too. But Solly Brightman knew that his world would never be complete without some unanswered questions to challenge his mind.

CHAPTER THIRTY-FOUR

'How did it go today?' Maggie murmured as Lorimer enfolded her in his arms.

It was one of the best times of her day; hearing his car in the drive then the door opening and that voice calling her name never failed to lift Maggie's spirits. And to think it could all have been so different! Had her lovely man been thrust further into that depression, who knows what their future might have been?

'Fine,' he replied then, as Maggie made a face, he stroked her hair. 'Really well, as a matter of fact. We've got young Kirsty seconded to the team and tomorrow we're beginning the preparation for a televised appeal on *Crimewatch*.'

'You've done that a few times before,' Maggie remarked as she laid her head against her husband's chest. 'Will it be you talking in front of the cameras again?'

'We'll see.' He smiled down at her.

'Who else would they want?' Maggie sat up, a quizzical expression on her face.

She saw the shrug and the glance away. Was there still a problem? Did he feel that such a task was too much? Surely not. His hesitation must be down to something else.

'Don't you want to be the one who asks the questions?'

Again that laconic shrug.

'It might not be up to me to decide,' he replied slowly. 'I'm pretty sure it won't matter if the man we're seeking gets to know who is SIO in the case.' He met her eyes with a grin.

'I'm so pleased that you've been asked to stay on in Govan meantime. After all, this was your case to begin with.' Maggie squeezed his arm affectionately.

'Oh, aye, there was no question about that. Like I told you, our new DCC was adamant that I should take the lead on this one.'

'Wouldn't she want to appear on the programme?'

'Too senior,' came the reply. 'Besides, it has to be someone involved with the case. I guess I'm the obvious choice, though,' he murmured. 'And anyone with half a brain could find out what I looked like if they wanted to. The internet these days . . . ' He tailed off, leaving Maggie to fill in her own blanks.

'Well, you always looked good on camera before,' she said stoutly. 'And you've got a clear speaking voice. That makes such a difference.'

Just today Maggie had spent hours assessing the juniors in their speaking tests, anxious for the wee quiet ones whose little speeches could hardly be heard over a bus ticket or the kids whose broad accents made their words difficult to comprehend.

Talking posh is fur snobs, Ronnie Carmichael had snorted when she'd attempted to correct his grammar. In vain Maggie strove to teach them the advantages of speaking correctly, but some children persisted with *I seen* and *I done*. Once there had been a split in children's language, the playground patois and the classroom speech completely different, but nowadays kids didn't seem to want to sound as if they came from the same sort of background as some of their teachers and spoke the same way all the time.

Poor Olga Travis, a new pupil whose father had relocated the family to Glasgow's West End from Berkshire, stood out a mile whenever she opened her mouth. But Olga had scored an A this afternoon, her talk both lucid and interesting. And the rest of the class had listened and applauded the girl at the end, something for which Maggie Lorimer had been very grateful. They weren't bad kids at all, she reminded herself, they just had that pack mentality, something that kept them from trying to step away from what they regarded as the right way to do things or the normal way to speak. Next week she had planned a session on letting them pretend to be TV newsreaders and she wondered how many of them might try to emulate the Scottish presenters they heard night after night.

Lorimer sat back with a sigh. It had been a long day and his wife's home-made chicken broth as a late supper made him realise that he had not eaten much since breakfast. Yesterday's lunch with Niall Cameron would probably not be repeated until such time as they were celebrating the arrest of the man they sought. Yet he felt satisfied with the team's progress. Many of them had ideas about the personality of the person who had seduced the nurse in the Queen Elizabeth and stolen the key to the drugs cupboard, the poor woman finally confessing to how it had really happened. And since the interviews with several hospital personnel were already to hand, a picture was beginning to emerge.

The suggestion about allowing the British nation to see the picture of the man was not the only thing that had been put into motion, however. Lorimer had also been keen to have the team's approval for the inclusion of Professor Solomon Brightman in this investigation, something that still required the agreement of the DCC.

He smiled at the thought of Solly being back on the case. He'd taken the initiative to have the photo of their mystery man graphically altered to show him clean-shaven, a small matter but it showed that Solly was keen to make progress once again. It had been the professor of psychology who had insisted all along that money was at the root of the entire business when they had been carrying out the original investigation into Quiet Release. It would be good to have the man's input once more, especially as Lorimer knew that his friend had never stopped thinking of their fugitive or the tentative profile he had been building.

The staff club was not one of his usual haunts, or at any rate hadn't been for several years now. Once upon a time he had gone there in the hope of bumping into Dr Rosie Fergusson, the pathologist he had met at a scene of a crime and who had sometimes drifted in after work to chat to some of her peers. Their unlikely coupling had raised several eyebrows, not least those of Rosie's acquaintance who had deemed the shy, bearded psychologist entirely unsuitable for the bubbly blonde. But his gentle persistence had paid off and their marriage was now one that others sighed over as something to envy.

This evening it was dark by the time Solly had crossed the main road and headed into the old building where he knew he might find several of his academic friends deep in conversation over a beer or whisky.

A teetotaller by choice, Solly found it hard at times to persuade his friends that he did not and would not partake in any of their drinking sessions and tonight he hoped that he would not run into any of the older crowd who spent evening after evening drinking at the club until closing time, many of them single folk who had only an empty home waiting at the end of a day.

So it was with a little misgiving that Solly spotted Dr McLaren, the emeritus professor of medical science, as he took the pint glass of orange squash from the barman. Yet surely this was just the man who might give him a clue as to the identity of the mystery man?

'Ah, young Brightman! Not often we see you in here,' McLaren called out, beckoning Solly across to the table where he was sitting with another man.

McLaren looked what he was, a bewhiskered academic in tweeds, an empty pipe on the table in front of him, his gimlet eye catching Solly's as he sat beside them. Since the smoking ban had taken effect, McLaren had been known to suck the stem of his pipe before lectures, pointing out to the students that his lungs were in excellent condition, thank you very much!

'What are you having, Brightman? Not just that watered-down stuff, surely, man?' McLaren said in a tone of disgust. 'You're not even driving home, bless my soul! What about a wee dram to warm you up before you cross the park, eh?'

'No thanks, Henry,' Solly replied, 'Fine just as I am, you know.'

'Hm, hm, well, I'm off for another. Peter? Another Islay malt?' he asked the man sitting opposite Solly who nodded his thanks as McLaren rose laboriously to his feet and headed towards the bar.

'Don't think we've met,' the other man said, holding out his hand. 'Peter McAree.' He smiled, his soft Irish accent a delight to the psychologist's ears.

'Over from Dublin?' Solly asked.

'That I am. Second time around.' McAree laughed. 'Lectured here back in 2007. Were you here then?'

Solly nodded. 'I've been here quite a while. London before

231

that but Glasgow is my home now.' He smiled. 'Are you in the same faculty as Henry?'

'Oh, I lectured in general medicine back then,' McAree told him. 'But got the call from Dublin and went back home for a few years.' He sighed. 'My wife was from over here,' he said, dropping his gaze. 'Died last summer. Cancer,' he added quietly.

'Oh, I am sorry. What a terrible thing to happen,' Solly murmured, thinking of his own precious Rosie and how stricken he would be should anything happen to harm one hair of her head. 'Children?' he enquired.

'Two,' McAree told him, taking a sip of whisky. 'Boy and girl. Both at school over here now. Hillhead Primary. Bit of a wrench to leave the old house behind but we've rented it out meantime until my tenure here is finished.'

'You're not in Glasgow permanently, then?'

McAree shook his head. 'More's the pity. Dublin's home but I love this place.' He gazed around him and for a moment Solly understood what the man was saying. It was not this old-fashioned wood-panelled room that held an appeal for the Irishman but the university itself, a place so full of atmosphere and centuries of learning that Solly sometimes fancied he could feel the ghosts of scholars gliding past as he walked through the cloisters.

Henry McLaren came back to the table and set down the two whiskies.

'There you are, Peter. What time do you have to pick the nippers up tonight?' he asked, looking at the pocket watch suspended from a gold chain across his waistcoat.

'They have a drama class after school,' McAree explained, glancing in Solly's direction. 'Let's their da have a wee half before I collect them and head back home. We're in a nice flat in Woodlands Road. Very handy for all of us.'

Solly smiled at the two men and then caught Henry McLaren looking at him over his bushy grey eyebrows.

'I sense you are here for a particular reason, young Brightman,' McLaren stated, wiping the moisture from the end of his moustache. 'Am I correct? Do I divine a purpose in that knowledgeable countenance?' he asked, a pair of shrewd eyes crinkling at the corners.

Solly smiled and held up his hands in a gesture of surrender. 'Can't fool you for a moment, Henry,' he laughed. 'Yes, there is something I wanted to run past you. In fact, either of you might be able to help me.' He glanced at Peter McAree who was eyeing him with undisguised curiosity.

'It'll be a police thing,' Henry told McAree behind his hand with a smile at Solly. 'Our professor here is forever giving them profiles of their most dangerous criminals!' He gave a mock salute in Solly's direction. 'Am I right, Brightman?'

'Absolutely, Henry,' Solly nodded. 'Tell you what,' he began, drawing out the plastic folder from his briefcase, 'before I give you any details, let's see if you can identify either of these men?'

He took out the two images and placed them side by side on the table, facing his two companions.

Henry studied them carefully, picking each one up in turn then replacing them on the table, then shook his head. 'No,' he said at last. 'Good memory for faces but hellish with names, not that it matters. Don't think I ever saw either of these chaps in my life.'

Peter McAree bent over the images, looking from one to the other, then gave Solly a curious look.

'It's the same man, isn't it?' he said at last.

Solly nodded. At least one of them had spotted that, he thought.

'There was a student ...' McAree stopped for a moment, teeth chewing his lower lip. Then he shook his head. 'Such a long time ago since I was here. Such a lot has happened, too,' he continued. 'But that face does conjure up something, Professor Brightman. And I'm sure he was in one of my classes about ten years back,' he continued, pointing at the clean-shaven image.

'Really?' Solly's eyes widened in sudden hope. 'You think he was here? Studying medicine?'

McAree nodded. 'Yes, I'm pretty certain he was someone I actually taught. But you know how it is ... so many students pass through your life that it's impossible to remember them all.'

Unless there is a good reason for remembering them, Solly wanted to add but he kept these words to himself as Peter McAree downed the rest of his drink and stood up to take his leave.

'If you should remember ... ?' Solly handed the Irishman his card.

The lopsided smile told him that it was doubtful but McAree took it anyway and bade them both goodnight.

'Nice fellow, that,' Henry McLaren commented as they watched the door to the staff club close behind him. 'Tragedy about the wife. Far too young,' he added with a sigh.

Solly nodded his agreement. It didn't bear thinking about. But he had seen enough to realise that McAree had managed to pick himself up enough to chat to friends after work and take time to place his two youngsters in a drama class, something that would benefit them as they came to terms with their loss.

'Must be off to my own wife,' he said at last, pushing the half-finished glass of squash away from him. 'Thanks for looking at these pictures, Henry. And if you can let any of the others know that I'm researching this man, perhaps they would call by my office?'

'Certainly will,' Henry McLaren agreed. 'And will you be telling us just what this fellow has done to quicken your interest in him?'

Solly simply smiled and shook his head. 'Oh, I think you may know about that soon enough,' he replied. 'Especially if you are in the habit of seeing *Crimewatch* on television.'

He was gratified to see the man's bushy eyebrows raised at these words.

'Goodnight, Henry.'

'Off you go, young Brightman,' the older man replied gruffly. Then, with an unmistakable twinkle, added, 'Good hunting!'

CHAPTER THIRTY-FIVE

Mark Mitchison screwed up the memo in his hand and threw it savagely at the waste-paper bin, swearing volubly when it missed its target.

Bloody Lorimer! The man seemed to have a charmed life! Not only had he escaped from the fire of a demented gunman but now he was back from Castlebrae, to all intents and purposes fit for work, and had actually been appointed to take on this case! DCC Flint had not disguised the apparent glee in her voice when she had told Mitchison that his services upstairs would no longer be needed. And now, this! The memo had been about *Crimewatch*, the national programme that made regular appearances in the hope that a wider audience would assist the police in their search for the perpetrators of several serious crimes. And it was Lorimer who had been asked to appear! Mitchison ground his teeth in a rage. Damn the man! It ought by rights to have been his own face appearing on the TV screens of millions of viewers, not a broken-down detective who had crumpled under one case, albeit an incident that had posed real danger, something that Mitchison chose to forget whenever he bad-mouthed Lorimer.

As luck would have it there was a slot on the next programme, a high-profile case in Leeds having been solved so would no longer be aired. The opportunity to show the Glasgow case had been snapped up with alacrity by the *Crimewatch* producer. And now Lorimer would be heading down south to the studios, no doubt lapping up all the media attention.

His fingers trembled as Mitchison thought of the results that might follow. Yes, he wanted to have the case solved, of course he did. But if there was one thing that galled the detective superintendent it was not being able to take the credit for it. Besides, that job upstairs in the MIT should have been *his*, not Lorimer's. Surely that had been on the cards? Hadn't his pillow talk promised as much?

And that was not all that had enraged the superintendent: the new DC, Alistair Wilson's girl, couldn't be the IT person who'd been at his personal files, although she'd been his first suspect. A short trawl of the personnel records showed that Wilson hadn't obtained a technical degree at all but had been enrolled in some sort of catering or cookery course at Glasgow Caledonian. And she hadn't even completed it, deciding instead to leave and join the police. No, there was someone else in here that had infiltrated his files, someone he was determined to find and hand over to Jack Gallagher's mercy.

Mitchison's mouth moved in a crooked smile: *mercy* would never even come into it!

As he buckled his seat belt and prepared to settle back for the flight, Lorimer glanced around him at his fellow passengers. Most appeared, like him, to be on a business visit and the suits and briefcases (mostly in overhead lockers now) were a dead giveaway. Beside him an older lady sat, a folded copy of the *Herald* in one hand and a propelling pencil in the other. She had smiled vaguely at him as she had taken the aisle seat but it seemed to the detective superintendent that she preferred to concentrate on the crossword on the newspaper's back page.

A solver of puzzles, he thought with a smile. They had that much in common, but his travelling companion would never know it.

The taxi to the studios whisked Lorimer away from the airport, the driver talking all the time about the weather and how awful it was that Wales had lost the rugby game against their nearest neighbours the previous weekend. Lorimer listened and made some sympathetic noises but his thoughts were on the Scotland–Wales match earlier in the month when the score line had changed four times in a nail-biting second half before the final whistle that had signalled a Welsh victory. The result had been a disappointment for the brave Scots lads but it had been a scintillating game to watch. When would he next have time off on a Saturday afternoon to enjoy one of his favourite sports? Lorimer pondered as the taxi driver swung through the gates of the studio complex.

The place itself had changed a little since his previous visit a few years back, although the presenter was a different person, a smiling blonde lady whom he would see later in the day. First there were the talks with the local police officers seconded onto the programme, then he would have a late lunch before meeting with the producer and finally the sound engineers.

Lorimer was met at the reception area by a uniformed cop who nodded at him.

'Superintendent Lorimer, sir?' he asked, his Welsh accent

redolent of the valleys and music . . . always music for the Welsh; their very speech seemed to be designed for song, Lorimer told himself as he shook the man's meaty hand.

'Sergeant Dai Thomas,' the officer told him. 'They were very glad to fit you in tonight's programme, sir. And it sounds an interesting case from the little I have heard.'

Sergeant Thomas was eyeing him with undisguised curiosity, obviously hoping that Lorimer would like to relate some of the story here and now. But the detective superintendent from Glasgow was too wise for that. Should he begin to discuss the case too much, there was the danger that he might leave out a pertinent detail later on, thinking it had already been revealed. And it was vital that the public caught only the essential points of the appeal.

'Quite right,' Lorimer replied smoothly. 'It's an interesting one, all right.' And left it at that, ignoring the light sigh of disappointment as Thomas led him through the maze of corridors to the room where the task force had set up their base.

The day passed quickly, Lorimer moving between meetings with the Cardiff cops who had to be given the detailed outline of the current case and why it was so important that the appeal was made at this point in their enquiries. The producer wanted to know the same things, of course, but his remit was to ensure that the Glasgow detective kept exactly to his allotted time and didn't run over. There were several cases to show the public that evening, though perhaps none as high profile as the one that Lorimer had brought them.

All over the country people would be tuning in to see this programme; some eager to know the salacious details, as if the real-life crimes were a form of entertainment, others wishing that there was something, even the tiniest thing, they could do to help solve them, and of course there were those looking to see if their face or name appeared, ready to flee further away from the glare of the public spotlight.

The team at the MIT had pondered over what to call the renewal of the Quiet Release case and in the end Lorimer himself had come up with Operation Death Star, after Queen Elizabeth University Hospital's nickname. It had raised a few smiles but the fact that the man they sought was a fugitive from the QEUH made sense. So, backstage the talk was all about Operation Death Star, although the actual presentation would not reveal their code name for the current investigation.

'Three minutes to go,' the sound engineer's voice told Lorimer through the microphone tucked neatly in his ear. He was ready and waiting in the studio, seated at an angle beside the blonde presenter who would be introducing him and asking just a couple of questions before Lorimer delivered his part of the story to the nation. Then she would conclude the detective superintendent's part in the programme and move seamlessly on to the Crimestoppers' numbers that would appear on screens all over the United Kingdom.

Lorimer concentrated on what he was about to say. The way that the script had been agreed upon was very close to what he had written out before coming down today so he felt no nervous tremor within, simply a desire to speak clearly and with conviction. He saw the man with headphones standing at one side of the studio, counting them down.

'Tonight we focus on a dreadful series of crimes that were carried out in Glasgow, many of which took the lives of elderly or vulnerable people. With me is Detective Superintendent William

Lorimer from Police Scotland. Detective Superintendent, can you tell us a little about this case?'

Kirsty and James sat side by side, holding hands, eyes glued to the television screen. They were recording the programme for Alistair and Betty Wilson who were still in the US, but both were eager to see it.

Kirsty felt the squeeze on her fingers and turned to give James a brief smile as Lorimer began to speak. But her focus was soon on the figure seated in that Cardiff studio and her shoulders tensed, waiting to hear what he would say.

'Last year we apprehended several people who were involved in an end-of-life scam called Quiet Release. Relatives of sick or elderly people were targeted, and paid large sums to have the victims dispatched by lethal injection.'

The camera panned in closer until the viewers saw only a head and shoulders shot.

'This was an illegal organisation that sought to make money from the miseries of other people. It must never be confused with any overseas organisation that is legally set up to serve these who *choose* to end their own lives,' Lorimer told the camera, his face set. 'These victims had no choice.'

Peter McAree sat back in his chair, a mug of tea in one hand. It had been a long day but now the kids were both asleep and he could enjoy an hour or so of television before clearing up the kitchen and heading off to his own lonely bed.

He listened as the dark-haired cop spoke of the misery inflicted on so many folk denied the chance to say a last goodbye. At least he'd had that before Kathy had succumbed to the cancer that had taken her away from him far too soon. It was a small crumb of comfort in a world that was for ever changed.

'We have some forensic evidence that links one man to the scene of several crimes,' Lorimer continued. 'This man is known to have posed as a medical professional and has been using different aliases, one of which was Gordon Smith.'

The man peering intently at the small television set in an upstairs room at Glasgow City Mission was watching in silence but Jenni Lothian, the woman volunteer sitting next to him, saw his mouth open as the name was spoken. Who was this Gordon Smith? And why had poor old Tam turned so pale?

'We have several pictures to show the viewers this evening. Two are recent photographs and one is a graphically designed image that shows what our suspect might look like when clean-shaven.'

One by one the pictures of the man that the police sought were brought up onto the screen, then all three were shown in a row for comparison.

Jack Gallagher's fist closed around the whisky glass, its crystal indentations cutting into his skin. 'Charles Graham,' he whispered. 'Well, well, well . . .'

This was not on their agenda. Mitchison had hindered the reopening of the Quiet Release case but was it too late now to stop this investigation going any further?

The furrows between his eyes deepened as he watched and listened and began to think hard.

*

The images to be shown to the nation's viewers were only there for a few moments but they remained superimposed on the screen in a smaller area as the camera returned to the police officer.

'There is a substantial reward being offered for information that leads to the arrest of this man,' Lorimer continued, his blue eyes staring straight into the camera, his voice full of determination. 'Please, if you know who this is, call us now.'

The mug of tea lay on a side table as Peter McAree sat forwards, hands clasped together.

'Oliver . . . ' he began, nodding at the three pictures of the man who had once been his student. 'It was *Oliver* . . . ' But try as he might, the fugitive's complete name eluded him.

'Tam, are you all right?' Jenni Lothian put her arm about the old man's trembling shoulder. But he simply sat there staring at the screen, lips parted as though all sense of speech had gone, oblivious to the kind hand stroking his arm.

The man whose photo had appeared on the TV screen narrowed his mouth into a grim line as he pressed the remote and switched off the programme, consigning it to darkness. He had lingered too long in this city, he thought, getting up and pacing towards the big picture window that looked over the river. Should have taken a trip somewhere else by now, spent some of his earnings on a ticket to Barbados or Cuba, anywhere he might escape from the clutches of people like that detective, William Lorimer.

What if anybody had seen that programme and identified him? So many people in this city *could* identify him. *And would*, a little voice taunted him; the prize of £10,000 would tempt almost any of these drugged-up creatures.

And how would Gallagher react once he knew that Charles Graham was just another bogus identity for the man who had taken so many lives in exchange for hard cash?

But maybe, just maybe, Jack Gallagher was the very man to help him out in a crisis like this?

The phone lines were buzzing with several calls from different appeals and Lorimer knew it would be a long night as he sat with the Cardiff police officers backstage. The programme's format dictated that one whole hour would elapse until the *Crimewatch Update* that informed the viewers of the immediate responses to these appeals. Lorimer had been here before, waiting tense and hopeful for that one call that would bring his team information. It was a formula that had a good success rate but there were also unsolved cases from years back, the perpetrators of some crimes never brought to justice.

'His name is Oliver, but I can't recall whether that was his first or last name,' Peter McAree explained. 'I was his tutor at the University of Glasgow and he was a first-year medical student. Failed his exams, though I remember he was good at the practical side of things,' he told the telephone operator. 'I'm so sorry I can't be more helpful.'

Tam felt hot tears trickle down his wasted cheeks. It was no use him calling this programme. They wanted a name to put to that face and that was something he simply did not have to give them.

But if that man was still here in the city, perhaps there was a way of finding him before the police did. His chin rose in a moment of resolution. If Jenni let him he would wait to see the later programme, find out if anyone had called in with a real name. Or not.

And then, perhaps, he would find a way to carry out a little vengeance of his own.

He glanced around the well-furnished flat, a luxury he had given himself and something he was reluctant to relinquish too soon. The name on the estate agent's records was the one he had given Gallagher. Charles Graham had indeed been a real person, one of his earliest victims, and the dead man's identity was something he enjoyed possessing as though the final joke was on the deceased. All of his official papers in connection with the house sale were in Graham's name too: insurance, stamp duty, council tax ... He sat back down, clasping his hands together behind his head. Nobody would find him here. Nobody would look for a quiet businessman in this place, would they? The down-and-outs would never even see a programme on television so they were no threat. And as for Gallagher ...? He smiled and closed his eyes. *Gallagher and Graham; Graham and Gallagher* – both had a certain ring to them. Perhaps the Glasgow gangster would admire his new partner all the more if he learned the extent of his work to date? After all, what could one lone detective do against the might of Gallagher's empire? Especially when the man had already infiltrated the higher echelons of Police Scotland.

'Sorry, sir, we had a shedload of callers but at least we got one name.' Dai Thomas heaved a sigh as he accompanied the tall Glasgow cop back to the main door of the studios.

Lorimer nodded. 'And that gives us something to follow up,' he replied. 'Never know how many memories these photos might jog and there is still time for calls to come through to Crimestoppers once folk have a chance to think about them.'

'And the reward.' Thomas smiled. 'You'd be surprised how many old lags come out of the woodwork to claim a sum like that.'

Oliver – Lorimer turned the name over in his mind. It was an unusual Christian name for a Scot. But perhaps one of his parents had come from south of the border where the name was more popular? Or, he thought, was it actually the man's real surname? An Irish university lecturer had phoned in the information, apparently. And, as he settled down in his hotel bedroom for the night, Lorimer's thoughts turned to another man whose work centred around the university close to his home.

The ping of the email arriving was not heard by either Rosie or Solly as they slumbered on, the information sent by Peter McAree sitting on the professor's iPad, one single blue dot marking it as unread.

Through the night there would be several people who would lie awake, however, considering their next move as the stars wheeled overhead in the black February sky.

CHAPTER THIRTY-SIX

'Did you see *Crimewatch*?' Niall Cameron asked.

'Oh, aye,' Paul Doherty replied. 'So that's your man, is it? The one that got away?'

There was no swift reply and Doherty nodded to himself, wondering if Niall Cameron was already regretting the clandestine investigation they had carried out.

'I always watch it,' he continued, more to break the silence than to become involved in a conversation about the previous evening's TV programme. 'Like the look of that guy, Lorimer. Wasn't he your boss a while back?'

'Aye, Lorimer's one of the good folk,' the reply came. 'I could tell you plenty of stories about his cases . . . that'll have to wait for another day, though. Just wanted to check and see if you'd come up with anything else meantime. On that other matter,' he said, the words deliberately vague.

Doherty smiled. You never knew these days who might be listening in on a phone call and Niall Cameron was evidently taking no chances.

'Nothing more to report. Yet,' he told his friend. 'I'll see you soon, though, whenever there's anything new. Take care.'

Paul ended the call and tapped his lips with one cold finger. The stream of emails that he had uncovered had dried up rather suddenly. And, while he could not yet prove anything, he did wonder, despite all his care and expertise, if someone out there had found that these files had been hacked.

'There will be records,' Solly was telling Lorimer. 'Peter says that this student was one of his about ten years ago. So there must be records somewhere with that name. Don't you think?'

The detective superintendent listened to the professor's voice and he smiled as he thought of the cases that they'd worked on together. Calm, quiet Solomon Brightman, the man who pondered long and deep about the personalities of offenders, sounded almost gleeful because he had managed to fill in a piece of this jigsaw puzzle.

'Peter McAree assures me that he can give you a description of the boy. Well, he's a man now, obviously, but Peter remembers him as a youngster.'

'I'll get the team onto that right away,' Lorimer promised. 'I'll call you as soon as we have more intelligence on him.'

There was a thoughtful expression on the detective's face as he ended the call and glanced up at the departures board in Cardiff airport. He had already texted the team about McAree's later call. *Oliver*, he'd written. Unable to sleep after the drive back from the studios, Lorimer had googled the name Oliver, and of course it was Oliver Cromwell's that had come up time and again on the screen of his iPhone.

He'd amused himself by looking at famous quotations attributed to the man who had wanted England to become a republic. *He who stops being better stops being good*, was one such and made Lorimer wonder if the Lord Protector's personality was not just austere but flawed. *Subtlety may deceive you; integrity never will.* Was that something he had learned from experience? His ruthlessness in doing away with King Charles and his followers had been almost manic. Then there were the others that made Lorimer think about the Puritan who had come all the way to Scotland in his crusade against royalty and its trappings. *God made them as stubble to our swords.* His thoughts had turned to this other Oliver, the elusive fugitive who had killed God knew how many people. How ruthless and arrogant was he? And was there the possibility that, like his namesake, he would founder because he had been blinded by the certainty of his own cause? His face became grim as he remembered that final quotation, one that had made him see Cromwell as simply another psychopath in a long line throughout history:

Necessity has no law.

CHAPTER THIRTY-SEVEN

He had always eschewed the January sales, preferring to wait until the moment new stock arrived in the better shops, the discreet pastel shirts and glowing silk ties beckoning him into their portals. It was a mark of sheer snobbery, he knew. Who would guess that the clothes he wore had cost so much? Only other connoisseurs of the finer things in life, he told himself. The man who had once called himself Gordon Smith gave a sigh as he stood by the window of the shop, his figure shaded by the huge archway of Royal Exchange Square. Below him on the frozen ground sat a beggar clutching his ragged polystyrene cup, grey hood covering God only knew what vermin crawling on his filthy head. The rheumy eyes were staring up at him, he could tell without looking down. Desperate for a fix. Ready to smile and show a mouth full of rotting teeth and whisper his plea, 'Any change, mister?'

There was no sense of the disparity between himself and this object of misery. Hard work and cunning had got him to where he was today: a man with money and plans for more, much more, to fill his several bank accounts. Whereas this mongrel seated on the cold pavement had chosen to fill his veins with poison simply for a fleeting rush of glory.

A quick glance at that face made him pause for a moment. It was an absurd idea and he despised the creature whilst seeing a potential use for him. Given a wash and a decent set of clothes, this man might pass for himself. The sound of the beggar coughing his guts up made him smile faintly, the decision made. Putting an end to his life would no doubt be a mercy. But what little life he had left might be orchestrated by another's will.

Eyes were indeed staring as he turned his head.

'Spare any change?' the hoarse voice asked, the lacklustre tone devoid of any hope.

He bent forward slightly, but not so close that his expensive overcoat would come into contact with the beggar.

'I can give you more than that,' he said quietly. 'Meet me by the taxi rank on George Street in ten minutes.'

Then, leaving the beggar open-mouthed and speechless, he entered the shop having decided on which items he was going to purchase.

There was no sign of the tramp when he emerged from the shop, a rectangular carrier bag slung from one shoulder. Had he scared him off? Or, when he walked back up Buchanan Street and turned into George Street, would he find him waiting, eager for whatever he was going to provide?

The fire inside him had long since been extinguished but the memory of it still called insistently. A fix, just one more fix and he'd be all right. The world could turn on its axis again and everything would be sunshine and blue skies instead of these slushy streets and dark clouds lowering overhead. The guy had looked a right toff. Probably wanted to do the business, even with a manky person like himself.

Rick frowned, his dirty hair obscuring his pale blue eyes. Someone with money like that could surely do better. Was he sensible risking a taxi ride with this stranger? But sense had long ago deserted him, the craving obscuring his better judgement.

Once upon a time he'd been strong and fit, a man who'd borne arms for his country, taken orders and obeyed them to the letter. And what good had it done him? An honourable discharge and back home with a leg wound to find that there was no place for him here any more; army housing was only for those who were still serving Queen and country. It hadn't taken long for the wife to shove off with the kids, leaving him in the bed and breakfast accommodation on his own, depressed and frustrated, fair game for the dealer who had offered to make him feel better.

Rick shook his head as if trying to clear away the bad memories. He was living in the here and now. He'd survived the winter so far but the hacking cough had given him a warning that he was surely on borrowed time. His thoughts churned as he stumbled on the uneven paving stone in the narrow lane, a shortcut to his destination.

And there he was. Standing a little back from the line of black cabs, looking for all the world as if he were waiting for a gorgeous woman to slip her arm through his and waltz off to one of the expensive eateries in the centre of Glasgow.

As he approached, he sensed rather than saw the man watching him, a peculiar feeling that made him shiver and stand still just for a moment.

But the handsome face that turned towards him held a warm smile and a hand was being raised to hail the nearest taxi.

'Get in,' his new friend commanded and Rick obeyed, choosing the seat back to back with the driver, heaving the seat belt across his chest, happy to comply with whatever this man had in mind.

'Botanic Gardens,' he heard the man say in a loud voice, the sort of commanding tone that reminded him of his superior officers.

As the taxi drew away from the kerb, Rick glanced at the man, noticing that he had settled back in the corner, as far away from Rick as he could manage. He sniffed, feeling the dampness around his cold nose, then wiped his sleeve across his face. He probably smelled bad too, though his senses were so dulled that he was oblivious to any odours nowadays.

'What's your name?' the man asked at last, turning to stare at him.

'I'm Rick,' he grinned. 'Richard Aitken.'

'Richard, eh? *Richard Aitken*,' he said slowly, as though savouring the two words.

'Who are you, mister, and where are we going?'

'Didn't you hear me?' For a moment the handsome face held a trace of a sneer then he looked away from the beggar who was clutching the seat with both grimy hands. 'I told the driver to take us to the Botanic Gardens. Don't you know where that is?'

'Aye.' Rick nodded, feeling suddenly foolish. But his curiosity was piqued. Why were they going there on a cold day like this?

'What's *your* name, mister?'

The handsome man tilted his head to one side as if he were considering his answer and in that moment Rick knew that this man's identity would for ever be a mystery.

The man stared at him with a strange look in his eyes that made Rick flinch. He'd seen men cringing in terror, men blown to bits, but he had never been looked at like this, as if the very devil were seeing into the depths of his soul.

Then, looking away, the man spoke quietly, his words chilling. 'You will call me "sir".'

It was almost too easy. The man had agreed to everything he'd said, the suggestions becoming commands as the balance between them shifted.

The day at the Botanics had ended with him paying out for a decent meal and getting his latest victim into warmer second-hand clothes and a pair of new boots, but there was no way he was going to give him anything more until the tramp had come up with what he wanted in return. *Another identity.* After all, the persona of a former soldier might come in handy. Yet it took time to coax all of the information he needed from men like this, ensure that there was nobody in their past who could interfere. The dangling bait of drugs was a powerful incentive, he'd found, though there was never any temptation to thrust the fine point of a needle into his own veins. That was for losers, he told himself, his mouth turning in a moue of disgust.

Looking out over the city from his penthouse flat above the River Clyde, the man who presently styled himself as Charles Graham smiled thinly. Once Rick had outlived his usefulness he would take pleasure in putting the former soldier to sleep. It was a service to society to rid it of these unpleasant elements, he reasoned.

As the image came to mind of the man bent with that hacking cough, he clenched his fists, desiring the moment when he would watch the last drops of life drain out of the tramp.

CHAPTER THIRTY-EIGHT

The hostel near the river was always overcrowded, those who came first got a place to sleep was the rule and no leeway was ever given to those who could not pay. Tam McLachlan handed over the correct amount for his night's stay to the thin-faced man behind the counter, receiving only a threadbare towel and a dismissive grunt in return.

It had been a hard day on the streets, ignoring the main thoroughfares in favour of the cobbled alleyways that crossed the city. He'd filched some leftover fish and chips from a waste bin at the back of one of the bars, the paper greasy and cold, but a prize for a starving man. It was no use sitting on the pavement, begging; that would only attract the attention of the man who'd once befriended them. If he'd had more sense, Tam would have skedaddled out of the city, maybe hitched a ride across to Edinburgh, but something had stopped him; a feeling of dogged determination that might yet prove to be his downfall.

Tam climbed up into the bunk, eyeing the door as he turned onto his side. The rooms were always open, a rule that everyone adhered to partly for their own safety. A closed door could mean that someone was shooting up or that one of the temporary residents was at a different sort of risk, the hostel manager taking no chances with either.

Tam pulled up the blanket until it reached his nose then pushed it down again at the sound of footsteps approaching his room. He heaved a sigh, relieved that he'd got here first to take the upper bunk, everyone's preferred option. Lying awake and listening to another man's night-time noises was worse when it was accompanied by the creaks of bedsprings from above.

'Aw right?' a voice asked, its Glasgow accent drifting across the narrow space between the door and the twin bunks. It was a rhetorical question, something that did not require or expect an answer, simply a stranger laying down a marker in his territory.

Tam glanced at the dark-haired man, noting that he was a fair size, not someone to be messed with, he decided, pulling the blanket up again. He was satisfied that the newcomer wasn't anyone he'd come across, but that rough voice branded him as one of a kind. His kind. With a bit of luck he'd go to sleep and give him a bit of peace.

Rick folded his towel and placed it under the pillow then, pulling off his boots, he placed them against the wall, far away from any thief who might steal them in the night. The guy had been generous, he thought, smiling at the yellow nubuck and thick laces. These would do him for a good few years.

He laid back on the bed but almost as soon as his head hit the pillow, he began to cough and had to sit up again.

Rick's smile changed to a scowl as the pain grasped his chest in a vice-like grip. He wasn't fit for another winter on the streets, he thought, as he held a stained and ragged cloth to his mouth.

He rolled onto his side, staring at his new footwear.

If he were honest, these boots would likely see him out.

Tam was awakened by a groan. He blinked, running a furred tongue across his dry lips and realising in the haze of sleep still clinging to his mind that the sound was coming from underneath him. Bloody guy below, coughing his guts up! He'd been disturbed several times during the night but had done nothing, fearful of complaining in case the other man had decided to pull him out of the bunk and wrestle him to the floor.

He closed his eyes again, willing sleep to return, drawing the blanket over his nose to keep out the chill air.

A creak from below signalled the man beneath getting out of his bed, then Tam sensed rather than saw the shadow looming over him, heard the ragged breathing.

'Got any gear?' The question was whispered close to his face and he could smell the man's stale breath.

Tam feigned sleep: maybe he'd just go away if he continued to stay quiet beneath the worn covers.

'Got any gear?' the voice rasped. 'Can you no' hear me?'

Tam felt the covers being pulled back and he opened his eyes to see the dark-haired guy staring straight at him. They regarded one another silently, the dim light from the corridor illuminating the man's height and bulk so that the old man knew a moment's panic. *It was him!* ... But, no, that was impossible, Tam told himself, rubbing the sleep from his eyes.

'Piss off, son,' he said at last, hoping the other man would give up and go back to bed.

'Whit kind o' answer is that, eh?' A belligerent note had crept into the stranger's tone and Tam pursed his lips. Last thing he wanted was to draw attention to himself: a fracas in this room would only lead to trouble.

'Naw, son, if I hud cash fur ony gear d'you think I'd be dossing in a place like this?'

The man backed off, loosening his grip on the handful of blanket. 'Jist askin',' he murmured. 'No harm in that, is there?' He had turned away from the top bunk now and Tam watched him warily.

'Jist ask—' The word was cut short as the racking cough began again and the man bent forwards, clutching his arms around his chest.

Tam pulled the blanket over his own mouth; God alone knew what sort of infection this fellow was harbouring and he certainly didn't want any share of it.

'It's no' gear you're wantin', son, it's a doctor,' he said at last when the coughing subsided into a rattling wheeze.

'Too late fur that, pal.' The man leaned against Tam's bunk. 'All I c'n do is ease it a wee shade, know whit I mean?'

'Aye, son,' Tam replied, a sudden wave of shame making him feel a rare sympathy for the younger man. So many street people were riddled with this disease that rotted their lungs, something he'd been lucky to avoid so far. He sat up, wrapping the blanket around his body.

'Huvenae seen you before, huv I?' he asked but the other man was too weak from coughing to do more than shake his head in reply.

'Was hoping . . . ' The words tailed off as he was caught in another spasm of coughing so that Tam could only guess at the rest of what he was trying to say.

'Hoping I had some gear on me?' He gave a short laugh. 'Aye,

that wid be shining bright!' he exclaimed. 'Last gear ah saw—'
He stopped short, remembering the needle and Seamus's cold
body.

'Ye've had some?' The man was upright once more, a gleam in
his eyes as he breathed over Tam's bed.

Tam shook his head. 'Bad stuff, pal. You don't want tae know.'

'Aye, ah dae.' The eyes bored into his own, the familiar look
of desperation something that Tam McLachlan recognised only
too well.

'Kill't a pal o' mine,' he insisted, staring back into those fever-
ish eyes. 'You. Don't. Want. Tae. Know,' he repeated.

'Ach, well, maybe ah'll get lucky somewhere else.' The words
fell out of the man's mouth followed by a sigh. 'Met a fella who
might give me stuff ...'

'Nobody *gives* you stuff, son. They *sell* it.' He shook his head.
Poor soul was deluding himself.

'Aye, but mibbe the price isn't jist cash,' the other man said
slyly. 'Mibbe whit I c'n give is better 'n that.'

'Aah! Don't want tae know things like that, son,' Tam said
disgustedly.

'No-o. Not that.' The man turned to lean over him and gave
a giggle. 'Who in their right mind would want a body like mine
onyway? Naw, lang past my sell-by date fur that nonsense.'

He gave a little smile and tapped the side of his nose. 'This
guy only wants to find out about people. Like he's interested in
hearing what your name is, where you used tae stay, things like
that. Takes all sorts, eh?'

'Polis?'

'Naw.' The man shook his head, then an expression of doubt
flickered across his face. 'Naw. Ye can smell a polis. This guy
wasnae like that.'

Tam sat very still.

'Does he have a name?' he ventured.

The silence drew out as his room-mate shook his head and smiled down at the older man.

'Naw. Ma name's Rick. But ah dinna ken the ither fellow's name.' He paused and screwed up his eyes as though this was something that had just occurred to him. 'I've jist tae call him "sir".'

Glasgow City Mission was open for business as usual and that February morning there was a free cup of tea and a slice of warm toast for Tam McLachlan and his companion.

The wind had blown them along the road that ran parallel to the river, sweeping them in the direction of the city centre building where so many vagrants had found a little piece of sanctuary. Tam sidestepped the puddles that had formed during the night, his old boots hardly dry from the previous day's torrential rain.

'New Caterpillars, eh? Where d'ye nick them?' he asked, greedily eyeing the yellow boots on his companion's feet.

Rick grinned at him. 'Man ah telt ye about bought them fur me, didn't he? Cannae complain about that. No gear, mind you, but he did say ... '

'What? What did he say?' Tam's question shot out.

'Never mind,' Rick replied. 'Ah've tae meet up with him wance I c'n give him some information.'

'Oh, sure! Like what? The numbers of the next Euromillions ticket?' Tam sneered, dodging another huge tract of rainwater that had spread across the cracked pavement.

'Naw. Information about my life. I telt ye, right? He wants tae know about last place I stayed in, dates and stuff, awright? I need tae get a hold o' some things like ma passport an' that. Jist need tae lay ma hauns on them.'

'What's he like? This fellow?' Tam asked.

'He's different. No' like they dealers. Gallagher's goons, know whit ah mean?'

'The ones that stand outside the nightclubs? Or the wans that kick shit out of folk when they dinna pay their dues?'

'Naw.' Rick slumped along. 'Ah dinna speak tae folk like that,' he replied, a huffy note in his voice. 'But there are guys who come aroon the dosshooses an' the hostels an' that. Waitin' fur tae see who's off tae the benefits office.'

Tam eyed him sharply. He'd seen men like that before, thin, weasel-faced young guys with cold eyes, hands in their leather jacket pockets, handling a blade like as not. They preyed on the down-and-outs, taking their little bit of benefit money and turning it into the only currency that mattered.

'Ma new pal's not wan o' them, I can assure you,' Rick declared.

'Jack Gallagher keeps tabs on every dealer in the city. Are you sure this man isn't on his payroll?'

Rick shrugged. 'He's no' the type. Well spoken, nicely dressed an' 'at.' The younger man paused for a moment as though considering. 'Och, ah don't know. Don't want tae know either,' he sniffed. 'All I know is that he promised me something in return for what I could tell him. Okay?' He turned and scowled at the older man.

'Aye, good on, ye, son. Hope it all works out for ye.' Tam nodded and pointed towards the door of the city mission a few yards further on. 'Comin' in for a wee cup o' tea?'

A plan was beginning to form in his mind. It would be risky to be seen keeping company with this guy Rick, but he needed to know what arrangements he had made to meet up with the man who had promised so much.

Promises that had led only to death.

CHAPTER THIRTY-NINE

All across the city the members of the MIT were hard at work following up the lead that had been presented after *Crimewatch Update* and DC Wilson found herself dispatched to a dusty room in the bowels of the University of Glasgow where hard copies of student files had been kept for more than a decade.

'We keep meaning to put them on discs,' the archivist apologised. 'But it's like the Forth Road Bridge: just when you finish painting the whole thing you have to start all over again. Never enough staff,' she had muttered.

Kirsty sneezed as she turned over the pages of a lever arch file. She was seated in a chair in a corner of the room, the file perched on her lap, and already her back was beginning to ache. The names of students who had completed their course were recorded in a different place; what she was looking at were the new entrants to the medical faculty who had come one late September to have their photographs taken and become part of the great heaving machinery of the admin department. She recalled her own enrolment at Caledonian, the Polaroid camera in the hands of a student, the flash making her blink and the laughter as she had protested that the resulting image wasn't like her at all. And there had been the clubs and societies all vying for her to join them, Freshers' Week an endless round of parties and meeting strangers who might become friends. Had Oliver whateverhisnamewas been like that? Had he come to uni with high hopes of becoming a successful doctor? Or was there already a flaw in the young man's character? Something that would lead him to become a mass killer?

She continued to run her finger down the names, glancing at the tiny pictures affixed to the details of each student's current address, date of birth and educational background.

She sat up straight, rubbing the base of her spine with a stifled moan. If folk only knew about this part of police work! The actual slog of finding out tiny but important facts was never something that these TV dramas portrayed. She sighed and bent forward to her task again. Nobody would watch them if they included stuff like this, she told herself gloomily.

The name jumped out at her as if it had been highlighted in fluorescent marker pen. OLIVER NIMMO.

Kirsty gasped and, mouth open, read the few facts that had been included with the undergraduate's registration. Oliver Nimmo, born 25 December 1989, had given an address in Campsie Gardens, a residential area on the outskirts of Bearsden, suggesting that the student had lived at home. What a find! Her head whirled as she removed the page, already wondering if Nimmo's parents were still there and if they had any knowledge of the journey their son had taken after his failure here at the university.

A Christmas baby, Solly thought to himself as he opened the attachment on his computer screen. That was interesting. Had the child felt denied a proper birthday, perhaps? Resentful that when other kids celebrated theirs with parties and balloons, little Oliver never could invite friends back to his home because it was Christmas Day? He would be very keen to talk to those who had taught the boy at Bearsden Academy, yet that task had already fallen to the officers from Govan who were making background checks.

Kirsty sat next to DC Davie Giles as she drove through the Clyde Tunnel, heading to the north side of the city. She suspected that he had asked to be paired with her but hoped he wouldn't smile in that lazy, flirtatious way that he had when she'd first been summoned upstairs to the MIT.

'Think we'll find the old folks at home, then?' he asked conversationally as they rounded a corner and slowed down into Campsie Gardens. 'No phone line for that name. Maybe they're long gone.' He shrugged.

'What did I say the number was?' Kirsty asked, a frown appearing on her brow.

'Thirteen,' Davie replied. 'What's the problem— Oh, I see. No number thirteen.'

'Sometimes people skip that. Superstitious,' Kirsty mumbled. 'But the DVLC definitely gave the car owner's details as number thirteen, so where the heck is it?'

The two detectives were sitting next to a patch of overgrown ground between two old-fashioned bungalows, the sort that had been popular just after the Second World War, their sloping slate roofs like pointed hats atop a rectangle of white walls that made them look like cartoon characters with two windows for eyes and a door for the mouth.

'There's eleven and fifteen,' Kirsty went on. 'D'you reckon it was a mistake and it's actually one of them?' She eyed the weedy plot that might have been large enough to place a bungalow, the tall, dried stalks of thistles and last year's willowherb having taken over the patch.

'Only one way to find out,' Davie replied, unbuckling his seat belt. 'Let's start with that one. Car's in the drive,' he added with a wink as if to let Kirsty know that his powers of detection were up to scratch.

There was no immediate answer to his knock on the glass door but Kirsty could see shadows moving beyond the hallway and soon a figure approached and opened up.

'"No cold callers", it says.' A young woman holding a stained muslin cloth was looking at them angrily and pointing to a small sticker that was indeed meant to act as a deterrent.

'DC Giles, DC Wilson, Police Scotland,' Davie began, taking the initiative and flipping open his warrant card.

'Oh, my God, what's happened!' The woman's hands flew to her face.

'We're looking for a Mr and Mrs Nimmo, ma'am,' Kirsty told her firmly. 'We have the address of number thirteen Campsie Gardens.'

'Oh.' The woman frowned and shook her head. 'But surely you knew?' She looked from one to the other, a bewildered expression on her face.

Davie and Kirsty glanced at each other for a moment then the sound of an infant crying made the woman turn away. 'Look, you'd better come in. Think you've had a wasted journey, though.'

Davie and Kirsty waited in the front room where an array of baby clothes had been spread across a large mesh fireguard.

'Babies,' Davie began, wrinkling his nose. 'Smelly wee things, aren't they?'

'Och, not all of them,' Kirsty protested.

'Got any yourself then?'

'No, I haven't as matter of fact,' Kirsty replied crossly, though Davie's grin told her that he was simply teasing her to get a reaction. 'But I'd never rule them out of my life altogether.'

She hesitated for a moment. Now was the time to put this fellow straight. 'James and I regularly babysit for Professor Brightman and his wife, you know who I mean? Dr Fergusson?'

'James . . . ?'

'James Spencer. My boyfriend. We live not far from the Brightmans,' Kirsty explained.

'Well, that's me told then.' Davie nodded with a weak laugh.

'Aye,' Kirsty said firmly, then she stood up as the woman came back into the room.

'Mrs . . . ?' she asked politely.

'Marsden. Hannah Marsden. Don't tell me you're actually looking for the people who used to live next door? The Grahams?' she asked.

'No, we're trying to find a family by the name of Nimmo,' Davie explained.

'*She* was Mrs Nimmo,' Hannah Marsden explained. 'But that was before her marriage to Charles Graham. You really don't know what happened?' She looked at them in surprise.

'Perhaps you might be kind enough to tell us,' Kirsty said, trying hard to hide the annoyance she was feeling as the young woman smirked at her.

'Fire next door,' Hannah Marsden said, tilting her head to one side. 'Burned the house to the ground.' She shrugged. 'It was all over the papers. Unlucky thirteen and all that. It was horrible.'

'Were you living here at that time, then?' Kirsty asked.

'No, this was my parents' home. Gerry and I bought it from them when they decided to up sticks and move to Spain.'

'So you'll have known the family?' There was no mistaking the eagerness in DC Giles's voice as he leaned forward.

'Oh, yes. Grew up here as a wee girl. Never had much to do with the neighbours, though. Mrs Graham didn't encourage kids to make friends with her precious son.'

'Oliver?' Kirsty held her breath as she waited for a reply.

Hannah Marsden nodded. 'That's right. Oliver Nimmo. Rumour had it that Mrs Graham was an unmarried mum. Snobby wee woman, so she was, though I really shouldn't speak ill of the dead.'

'She's dead?'

'Oh, didn't I say?' Hannah Marsden looked from one to the other, one eyebrow raised. 'Oliver's parents both died in the fire.'

Lorimer leapt out of the taxi as it stopped beside the entrance to the Govan police station. The plane's delay due to fog had held him up for most of the day and he hurried up the stairs to the briefing room, anxious to be with the team.

The noise of voices met him as he opened the door then a silence fell as he entered the room.

'Apologies for being back so late. Welsh mist,' he explained, setting down the folders he had carried back from Cardiff and regarding them all with interest. There was something in the atmosphere, something about the assembled officers that sparked his curiosity.

'Sir,' DCI Cameron began, 'there's been a development today. I think you should hear what DC Giles and DC Wilson have to tell us.'

*

'According to the official records there was no trace of accelerant,' Davie Giles was explaining some time later once the main part of the visit to Nimmo's old home had been related. 'The fire appears to have been due to faulty electrical wires in a back bedroom.'

'And both parents died?'

Giles nodded to the detective superintendent. 'Yes, sir. The boy was out at an all-night party. Nobody knew where he was until he returned home around five the next morning.'

'Alibi?'

'About forty of them,' Kirsty chipped in. 'It's all in the report here,' she added, pushing a file across the long oval table that was passed from hand to hand until it reached Lorimer.

'You're thinking Nimmo might have started the fire himself?' DCI Tweedie asked.

'Well, his killing spree began somewhere, didn't it?' another voice remarked and the officers watched as Lorimer scanned the file closely.

'Anything's possible,' he said at last. 'Boy's at a party in Glasgow's West End. Lots of music and drink. Maybe even a few spliffs ... These student parties are all music and dimly lit corners. Who's to say Nimmo couldn't have left, set off for home and started that fire then returned to the party before anyone missed him? Did he drive? Would any of the other students remember if he had a car? Campsie Gardens isn't all that far from the West End. Quick run along Great Western Road ... Whereabouts was this party?' He flicked over the pages of the fire report then looked up at his team.

A blank silence met his question.

'Well, that's one action covered.' He nodded towards Davie Giles. 'You and DC Wilson need to find anyone who was at that party and question them about Oliver Nimmo. Did he have a car? Had he arrived in it that night? Was he with anyone else? A girl? A pal?'

Lorimer began to pace back and forward. 'Now that we can place the man at Glasgow Uni during that year we have to find out exactly when he dropped out. Did he complete his exams? Where was he living after the fire? What sort of insurance money was involved? The house was never rebuilt so Nimmo may just have walked away with a hefty amount. Check all his previous bank accounts and any entries in DSS and employment agencies. Find out what you can about Charles Graham. Especially his financial position.' He stopped suddenly and stared above their heads.

'If Nimmo *was* responsible for that fire. If he *did* kill his mother and stepfather. Then perhaps we are looking at a long-term psychopath. And maybe we need to begin even further back than ten years ago.'

Every officer in the room was focused on Lorimer's words as he continued.

'We all know how crucial background information can be in establishing a motive for criminal behaviour. Think of all these sorry tales of abuse and deprivation that bring so many wee neds into the courts,' he said with an audible sigh.

'But Oliver Nimmo was brought up in a privileged home, given a good education and to all accounts – at least, those given by the next-door neighbour – had lived a quiet if somewhat lonely life, right?' Jim Isherwood reasoned.

Both Kirsty and Davie nodded their agreement.

'Okay, then. I think it's time we asked questions of other people who knew him: teachers, fellow pupils and the students who had been in his medical classes, many of whom could be doctors practising anywhere in the world, remember.' Lorimer ran his fingers through his hair and gave a sudden grin. 'Going to have our work cut out, ladies and gentlemen. But then, you're all used to that.'

Lorimer sat still in his office, staring at the clouds scudding past the window and wondering if any wind had chased away that low fog bank over Cardiff. The members of the MIT team had been given their actions and were now delving into the past in an attempt to find out what had happened to the man behind Quiet Release and where his killing spree had really started. *To find a trail to where he is now you must look to see where it all began*, he had told them. But there was one more member of the team he had yet to consult. And he knew that Solomon Brightman would be very interested in the developments that he had helped to set in motion. Together they would find out facts and figures to give them as many leads as possible in their attempt to hunt down this killer.

A killer Lorimer was determined to find and bring to justice at last.

'You involved in this case?' Gallagher asked, picking up the crystal glass and sipping his whisky. He was sitting in the lounge of a golf club not far from Mitchison's home, the lunchtime crowd more intent on having food than going back out on the course where a light drizzle had forced several of the golfers to head indoors.

'I shouldn't really be here,' Mitchison told him, lowering his voice. 'I had to make all sorts of excuses to get away.'

'Better you're here than anywhere else right now,' Gallagher told him with a glare that made the policeman shrink back in his seat. 'I want to know all about that case. The one on *Crimewatch*. Isn't he one of yours? This Lorimer?'

Gallagher could see the man's jaw move under his pale skin, the thin lips almost vanishing as he ground his teeth.

'Not one of mine,' Mitchison snapped. 'He's with the MIT. *Temporarily.*'

Gallagher nodded. 'Same rank as yourself, so no way you can order him to give you any information?'

'What's your interest in this anyway?' Mitchison asked, sweeping a hand across his hair.

'That's for me to know and you to find out. Except,' Gallagher leaned forwards and jabbed a fat finger against Mitchison's chest, 'you don't ask *me* any questions and you don't find out why. Got it?'

Mitchison nodded, his face paling even more.

'This character, the so-called Gordon Smith. Maybe he has more than one name,' Gallagher said, his little eyes glittering. '*Charles Graham*, for instance. And maybe you will pass on anything you can find about him. To me. *Directly* to me. Understand?'

The detective superintendent nodded his reply and grabbed his glass of mineral water, downing the remains in one gulp.

'Think you need something a bit stronger?' Gallagher chuckled. 'Steady your nerves, eh?' He patted the other man's hand. 'Find out what I want and it'll be worth your while. Got me?'

Mark Mitchison stared at the gangster then dropped his gaze in a gesture of defeat. He had become embroiled in the man's affairs for so long now that he had failed to notice when the balance of power had shifted in favour of the drug baron. Or had the detective ever had the power in the first place? he wondered, sneaking another glance at the big man who was fishing for change in his pocket. Had he actually been played all this time?

Tempted by the regular money flowing into his private account? Turning a blind eye once too often to Gallagher's activities? There was this threat hanging over them both; someone had hacked into their private files and so now they both knew that this relationship would be terminated in the near future. But not, it appeared, before Mitchison was to deliver intelligence that only Lorimer's team could give him now that he was no longer in the loop. Even the Queen Elizabeth hospital theft had been taken out of his hands.

He clenched his teeth in a moment of anger. It looked as if Lorimer would be the one to take over from Detective Superintendent Renton, something he'd once assumed would be his job for the asking.

And his own future? Would his helper still be willing to offer him a hand up the ladder of promotion? Or had that all been compromised by this mysterious hacker? Maybe it was time to throw Gallagher to the dogs, cut his losses and move away, take the early retirement that he had considered. Who was he kidding? He could never betray this man now without hurting himself. Mitchison shivered, a blast of cold air coming from the door as two more golfers entered the lounge. He could leave everything behind him, go to live in Spain, perhaps, he thought. A quiet seaside village in the sun.

Mark Mitchison glanced over his shoulder at the rows of optics above the bar and turned back to catch Gallagher's eye as the big man rose from the table, notions of escape vanishing like the mist above the hills.

'Yes,' he sighed. 'And make mine a double.'

CHAPTER FORTY

Lorimer stepped aside in the lower corridor to let the man pass by, averting his eyes so that he did not need to meet the other man's stare. But, to his surprise, the detective superintendent in charge of CID stopped and held up a hand.

'Need a word, Lorimer,' Mitchison began, his tone so clipped that Lorimer looked at him curiously.

'It's about this new operation you've been assigned to.' Mitchison sighed.

For a moment Lorimer experienced a pang of sympathy. This was Mitchison's domain and nobody like interlopers from another division interfering on what they regarded as their own patch. Yet the MIT was quite outside Mitchison's remit and the man running nervous fingers through his fair hair really had no say in who was managing their recent investigation. So why had he chosen to tackle him here? Lorimer wondered.

'This was my case,' Mitchison blustered. 'There are several of my officers still looking for this thief.'

'Stand them down,' Lorimer said simply. 'You got our directive, didn't you?'

Mitchison pursed his lips for a moment then nodded, helpless to do much more since what Lorimer said was true. The MIT operation had now taken precedence over the investigation into the hospital robbery but clearly this hadn't gone down well with Mark Mitchison.

'We need to have whatever is in your current report.' Mitchison glanced up. 'If only to tie up things at our end,' he continued between gritted teeth. 'Think you could facilitate that?'

Lorimer gazed at him, seeing the twisted expression on the other man's face, wondering what was at the heart of this antipathy. Could it be that the man was simply jealous? Had he harboured thoughts of being asked to head up the MIT himself? Or was he following some orders from Gallagher, perhaps? What had made Mitchison turn from the codes of duty that they all followed? Why had he not simply left the service when it had become clear he was not cut out for real police work? And yet how had he managed to attain his current rank? All these thoughts circled his mind as his blue stare made Mitchison look away again.

'We wouldn't dream of being discourteous to your department or to the officers on the case, Superintendent,' Lorimer said at last, his tone deliberately smooth. 'Everything that is being done by the MIT that is relevant to the hospital theft will be made available to you as soon as possible,' he added. 'Now, I really must get on.'

He made to pass by but felt Mitchison catch hold of his sleeve then draw so close that he could almost smell the man's desperation.

'I really need that information soon, Lorimer,' he said quietly, his face suddenly changing to an expression that looked a lot like panic. Then Mitchison let go of his sleeve and marched down towards his own office leaving Lorimer to stare after him.

*

Gallagher put down the phone. So that was what was going on. He gave a small smile of satisfaction. Sure, he'd given them a name: Charles Graham. But none of them was to know that he had been instructing his best forger to make out papers and passport in one that was entirely new. *Richard Aitken.* Gallagher swallowed a mouthful of whisky, savouring the new name as he did. His chameleon friend thought he was one step ahead of them all, didn't he? But the fact was that Graham, or whatever he wanted to call himself, was playing straight into his hands.

For a fleeting moment he wondered who the real Aitken was, the man who'd been selected for his identity, and when his body would be washed up on the shores of the Clyde. But that wasn't his concern. Survival was paramount in this game and one way or another the *Crimewatch* programme had sounded the death knell for his most recent business partner. And it was Jack Gallagher who would decide when that would be.

'Niall, a word, please, if you can spare me a few minutes.' Lorimer bent towards the DCI who was seated at a laptop, and the Lewis man followed him out of the room, unaware that DCI Tweedie was regarding the two men with unconcealed curiosity.

Once in his office, Lorimer nodded to Cameron to close the door.

'Is there any chance that Mitchison has found out about your friend?' Lorimer asked at once.

'No, at least I'm almost certain he can't find him.'

'I don't mean his place of work or where he lives, though that would be a real concern,' Lorimer murmured. 'I mean, could he have found that someone has been into his files?'

'I don't think so, sir,' Cameron replied with a frown. 'My

friend's been very careful to cover all of his traces. Though the stream of information has dried up recently,' he admitted. He looked at his superintendent. 'Why are you asking? Has something happened?'

Lorimer took a deep breath before he continued. 'I'm not sure. It's just ... well, Mitchison's been asking questions.'

'About me?' Cameron's eyebrows rose in astonishment.

'About Operation Death Star.'

'Well, he was the SIO in the robbery from the hospital,' Cameron reasoned. 'What does he want to know?'

'Everything, of course,' Lorimer replied. 'Though I did point out that his case has been taken over by ours. Didn't go down too well, I can tell you,' he added with a grimace.

'You'd think he'd be happy to lessen his workload. Always complaining about budgetary restraints, that one,' Cameron added, raising his eyes to heaven.

'Don't let anyone else hear you saying things like that,' Lorimer warned him. 'Mitchison moves in dangerous circles, remember, and we still don't know what other influences there are.'

'Higher up?'

'I think so,' Lorimer sighed.

'So,' Niall Cameron began, 'do you want Paul Doherty to dig a little deeper?'

There was precious little time for anything else other than running this department and collating all the results of his officers' actions on Operation Death Star, but Lorimer had managed to persuade his old boss to come into the city for a late supper in one of the nicer restaurants, a lure that he had hoped would tempt George Phillips from his usual TV dinner.

As luck would have it Maggie was taking a class of senior pupils to the Citizen's Theatre to see a production of *Macbeth* so at least he wouldn't be leaving her alone on yet another weeknight. After this was wrapped up they would head off for a weekend together, he promised her silently. It was the least that she deserved.

George Phillips had commanded respect back in the old days when Lorimer had joined CID and the detective superintendent doubted that he would ever feel anything else for the man who had taught him so much.

He descended the narrow staircase that led to the basement restaurant off Hope Street and looked around to see if his former boss had arrived. At first glance it seemed as if Lorimer was there before him, but then his eye fell on a solitary figure hunched over a table, examining the menu. Lorimer had to look twice to be sure, but yes, it was George Phillips right enough, though the intervening years appeared to have aged the man he remembered considerably.

'George! How are you?' Lorimer slapped his friend on the back then sat down quickly before the other man could shuffle to his feet. 'Great to see you. How's retirement? Spending all your time on the golf course?' he quipped, trying hard not to show the dismay that he felt on seeing the old man sitting opposite.

'Aye, can't complain.' George Phillips smiled back and nodded. 'Don't manage a whole round these days, mind. Arthritis,' he explained, rubbing his wrist and giving Lorimer a weak grin. 'How about you? I hear you're going from strength to strength. Saw you on *Crimewatch* last night. You did well. Anyway, give me all the news. How're things in Stewart Street? Is Sadie Dunlop still serving up her goodies or have the sugar police stopped all of that?'

Lorimer gave an inward sigh of relief. It sounded as if George hadn't heard about his breakdown and that suited him just fine.

'Actually, I'm in Govan right now. Seconded there at the MIT to oversee a case,' he told his friend.

'Busy place, Govan,' George remarked. 'One of the twenty-four seven offices, isn't it?'

'That's right. Anyway, here we are. It's good to see you,' he repeated, meaning it, although the changes in the former detective superintendent were not so welcome. 'Fancy a drink? Some wine?'

'Ach, can't, these days, I'm afraid,' George answered in a tone of disgust. 'Interferes with my medication.' The old man shrugged and made a face. 'You go ahead, though, don't mind me.'

'Something to drink, gentlemen?' The wine waiter appeared by their table on cue but Lorimer shook his head.

'Just a jug of water for the table, thanks,' he replied.

'Still or sparkling, sir?'

'Just tap water for me,' George sighed.

'That'll do fine,' Lorimer agreed and watched as the waiter took their wine glasses from the table. Once, George would have ordered a bottle for each course and knocked them back with relish but those days were past, it seemed.

'Let's have a look at what's on offer tonight,' Lorimer suggested, turning round and pointing at a blackboard against the wall where the specials of the day were listed.

'Crayfish,' George declared, after reading the list. 'Always fresh in this place. Can't tell you how often we used to come here just for that ...' He tailed off with a bleak look in his eyes.

Lorimer turned back to see the old man take a handkerchief

278

from his jacket pocket and blow his nose noisily. The loss of his wife had hit him hard and it was easy to see how much he missed her.

'Right, crayfish for two. Starter or a main?'

'Oh, definitely a main,' George declared, then looked down again at the menu open in front of him. 'And I fancy the chicken liver pâté to start with. Not sure if there'll be room for pudding afterwards, mind,' he chuckled. 'Don't have the same appetite these days.'

And Lorimer could see why. The man had lost a lot of weight since last they had met, cheekbones visible beneath the skin, his once well-covered frame shrunken. Was he ill? The thought flashed through Lorimer's mind. Once they had ordered their food, Lorimer raised his water glass.

'Here's to you, George. Happy days!' he declared.

It was painful to watch the gnarled fingers clutch his glass, the tremble as he lifted it so obvious. Was his friend suffering from Parkinson's disease? Something had affected him badly and it was going to take a big effort not to show how upset he was by George's present condition.

'How's that pretty wife of yours? Still teaching, is she?'

'Aye, for her sins.' Lorimer smiled. 'Think the job gets harder year by year but Maggie still enjoys it. She's out at the theatre tonight with a party of school kids, as it happens.'

'Good for her. Bonny lass, that. You did well there, Lorimer. Anyway, what brought on a sudden desire to see this old codger?' The canny gleam in his eye was far more like the George Phillips Lorimer remembered of old. 'Nice and all that it is to be invited out for dinner, you're far too busy to socialise in the middle of a week. Something's up, isn't it?' he asked quietly, his gaze fixed on the tall man opposite.

'Yes,' Lorimer admitted. 'It's a tricky situation involving a fellow officer. Someone you know from way back.'

George Phillips stared hard at his friend, never flinching under the blue eyes that met his own. 'Can I guess?' he grunted.

'If you like,' Lorimer replied, taking up his glass and swallowing some cool water.

'A tricky situation, you tell me. Are you saying that a fellow officer has stepped across the line?'

The nod that Phillips received as way of reply seemed to satisfy him.

'Okay, someone has gone over to the dark side, eh? Now, who might that be? And why bring me out on a cold February night to ask me about him. It is a he, isn't it?' he added sharply.

'Yes.'

'And it would be someone known to us both from our time together, someone you didn't trust then, perhaps? Am I getting warm?'

Phillips lifted his water glass, the hand less shaky than before, and looked across at Lorimer.

For a few moments the unspoken name passed between them, then Phillips shook his head and glanced down at his lap.

'It wasn't my decision that he was given my job, you know,' he said at last, taking a drink then laying down the glass again. 'You were the obvious choice. Everyone knew that.'

'So why . . . ?'

'This isn't just about Mark Mitchison taking over from me, when I retired, is it?' George asked quietly. His eyes might be faded now, the skin below them puffy with age, but their expression was the shrewd look of an experienced detective, something Lorimer had valued then and valued now.

'No.'

'So,' George leaned forward and clutched the water glass, 'have you any proof that he's bent? Or is this just one of the famous Lorimer hunches?'

'Oh, we have proof. Don't worry about that. One day soon there will be a case to answer, I can assure you. And it won't be handled by me.'

'Putting it into the official channels then?'

Lorimer met his friend's eyes. 'Not just yet,' he replied softly. 'It will be handed over to Professional Standards eventually. However, there are still some things we want to find out. People who mattered back then. And who still have an influence.'

'Do you think for one minute that I had any say in the choice of my successor?'

The frown on the man's face made him look less like an old tired man and more like the George Phillips of old, a stern officer who had brooked no nonsense within his division.

'No, I don't,' Lorimer replied smoothly. 'I never held Mitchison's promotion against you. But I did wonder if you knew of anybody who might have pulled certain strings?'

The two men sat back in their seats as the waiter brought their starters; pâté for George and lobster bisque for Lorimer. For a few minutes there was a lull in their conversation as they enjoyed the food but at last Phillips laid down his knife and wiped his lips with the linen napkin.

'Lovely,' he said. 'Didn't even manage to spoil my appetite, damn you!' he laughed as Lorimer spooned the last of the soup into his mouth, then wiped the plate clean with the Irish soda bread, something for which the restaurant was famous. 'Let not a drop be wasted.' Phillips laughed again. 'Nice to see you still have a healthy appetite, son.'

They glanced around and, sure enough, a waiter came to whisk away their empty plates.

'Good place, this,' Phillips said. 'Great food, excellent service. Thanks for this,. Lorimer.' He grinned. 'Suppose I have to sing for my supper, now, eh?'

'That would be helpful.'

Phillips sat back and gave a sigh. 'Oldest story in the book, I'm afraid. Woman tempts her boss and then demands that he give her back something in return for sexual favours. Not me, you understand,' he added with a mirthless laugh. 'You remember Pamela Crossan?'

'Chief Superintendent Crossan, now.'

'Aye, well, she was just a DI when she made a play for one of the ACCs back then. Poor fellow didn't know what had hit him. You know who I'm talking about? Eh? Wee shilpit man, probably never had a leg over any other woman than his lady wife in all the years he'd been in the force. Och, no need to look so holier-than-thou, Lorimer. It went on all the time back in my day.'

'Wasn't she with Mitchison at one time?'

'Aye, I'm getting to that bit, son. Hold your horses,' Phillips replied, pushing his water glass forward for Lorimer to refill.

'Ms Crossan knew which side her bread was buttered on, believe me. But she was smitten by Mitchison, so I was told, even when she was having it off with the senior officer whose name we will not mention.'

'He knew about the affair?'

George Phillips gave him a hard stare. 'My guess is that Mitchison did more than just know about it. He used that information to get himself up the ladder.'

'Are you saying he blackmailed—'

'Shh.' George laid a finger to his lips. 'Nothing was ever

proved though there were plenty of rumours then. Still are, by all accounts, or you wouldn't be here,' he observed.

'But the person in question has retired,' Lorimer persisted. 'What good can he do for Mitchison now?'

'Good question,' Phillips replied, taking a gulp of water. 'And that is what you have to answer, my friend. If Mark Mitchison has become corrupt – and I guess we're talking about dealing with some low-life in return for cash? – aye, thought so,' he said as he caught Lorimer's expression. 'Well, you know where to begin, now, don't you? Former ACC Anderson, a sixty-year-old retired senior officer whose wife never suspected him of having that affair. Funny what lengths folk will go to in order to sweep their dirty business under the carpet,' he added thoughtfully.

The smile on George Phillips' face broadened as the waiter brought two huge plates of crayfish and laid them down in front of the men with a flourish.

'Now let's forget business for a while, eh? These beauties deserve all our attention, don't you think?'

The street was almost deserted as the two men stepped out of La Lanterna into Hope Street, the lanterns that gave the place its name shining against the walls. Central Station was close at hand, another reason for his choice of dinner venue since Phillips would take the Wemyss Bay line to Inverkip whilst he waited for his own train to the south side of Glasgow.

'Tread softly, Lorimer.' George caught the tall man's sleeve as they walked along the street together. 'Anderson's wife never knew a thing about Pamela Crossan and if you can be kind, see that doesn't happen, eh?'

Lorimer looked down at his friend, a questioning look in his eyes.

'Poor woman has cancer. Terminal, I'm told. Think she may even be in a hospice by now, so any muck you rake up can only make her last days intolerable.'

'I hear what you say, George,' Lorimer replied. 'And I promise to do my best to keep a lid on that for as long as Mrs Anderson lives.'

Lorimer watched as his old friend pushed his ticket through the slot at the barrier then waved one last time as he walked slowly down the platform to his train. Things changed over time, he thought, remembering the words he had read in the Sensory Garden at Castlebrae. George was an old man now and Andrew Anderson's wife was at the end of her own life, possibly cherishing each extra day that she could spend in the world. He would try to keep his promise even though it meant giving Mitchison more time to escape the hands of justice.

He glanced up at the board displaying the times for trains leaving Central Station, noticing that his own was due to leave soon. All around him people were waiting to be somewhere else, already thinking of what lay ahead of them at their journey's end. For George Phillips it was a lonely bed in his terraced cottage on the coast; for former Assistant Chief Constable Andrew Anderson it might be a sleepless night wondering if his wife would still be alive come the dawn.

With a small sigh, Lorimer felt a sudden rush of gratitude for his Maggie who was always there waiting for him.

CHAPTER FORTY-ONE

'Missus Blackburn!' The boy was bent forwards, yelling through the letter box. 'Missus Blackburn! Ur ye therr?'

'She's no' in, son.' A voice from across the landing made the lad turn around.

'Well where is she, then? She's supposed to be doon at the social club the day. Ma granny sent me tae get her. It's auld Missus Blackburn's birthday.'

The woman standing on her doorstep frowned at the boy, arms crossed under her plentiful bosoms. 'No' like her tae miss a pairty, right enough, son,' she replied. 'Truth is, ah havenae set eyes on her in days. Thocht she'd skedaddled off somewhere.'

'Granny says she's got a cake an' everything,' the boy told her, his face expressing a hint of anxiety. He turned again to Ellen Blackburn's front door. 'D'you think she's maybe no' well? Shouldn't we call someone, like?'

The neighbour stepped across the landing, her furry slippers silent on the concrete, and joined the boy who was again crouched forwards, peering through the letter box.

'There's a funny smell,' he said at last, wrinkling his nose. 'D'you think she's left the gas on or something?'

'Here, let me see.' The big woman shoved the lad aside and bent down until her eyes were level with the rectangle of space. For a moment she just looked through to the darkened hallway then gave a sniff.

'Oh, dear God!' she whispered. 'That's no' gas, son!' she exclaimed, rising swiftly to her feet, both hands already across her mouth.

'Do you notice her hands?'

'Eh?' John Longmuir glanced at his neighbour, PC Angela Fairbairn. 'What about them?' he asked, batting away another bluebottle in disgust. 'Whew, soon as we get out of here, the better. Hate that smell,' he remarked. 'Hate that noise,' he added, meaning the drone from the swarm of flies that were buzzing insistently around the body on the chair. 'Wish the doctor would come and just sign the bloody death certificate. Let us go.'

'I don't think it's just the doctor we need to wait for,' Angela remarked darkly. 'I think this needs to be reported to the Fiscal as a sudden unexplained death.'

'And how d'you get that?' John bristled. 'You trying to do a Sherlock Holmes or something?'

'She was a smoker,' Angela told him, ignoring his remarks. 'Look at her fingers? Stained brown with nicotine. Fifty a day habit or I'm much mistaken.'

'So what?' John snapped. Angela Fairbairn was one of those clever-clever young women who were bound to be promoted over his head sooner rather than later and he felt the resentment already. 'Wasn't the fags that killed her. It was whatever she'd put into that hypodermic,' he told her.

'Aye, but how did she do it?' Angela asked, eyebrows raised.

'What the hell are you on about?'

'The needle. It's sticking out of her left arm. See?'

John frowned for a moment then nodded his agreement. 'Aye, what about it?'

'Well, take another look,' she said patiently in the sort of tone a primary school teacher might use on a reluctant learner. 'It's her left hand that's got all these nicotine stains, not her right hand. So how on earth did a left-handed person inject herself like that?'

It was a question that was to be repeated several times that day and the next until it came to the attention of the MIT along with the toxicology report.

Meantime, a small crowd had gathered at the close mouth, hampered by the blue and white tape that impeded further access into the tenement building, most gazing upwards as if in expectation of seeing a face at Ellen Blackburn's window.

'Maisie Dorran telt me she'd snuffed it,' one wee woman stated, nudging her neighbour.

'Och, no,' the other woman replied, stepping away a little so as not to be on the receiving end of another sharp elbow. 'After a' she's gone through, pair wumman.' She sighed. 'An' a' these bairns ...' She tailed off with an exaggerated shake of the head.

'Shh, here's wan o' they pathological folk,' the smaller of the women announced in a tone of ill-concealed excitement, her well-aimed nudge finding its mark again in the larger woman's side.

'Move along, ladies.' The commanding voice behind them became a uniformed police officer whose very presence made the crowd shuffle aside and scowl.

*

Rosie Fergusson stepped into the street, thankful to be out of the flat and into the fresh air. The smell of death was one that she'd become used to over the years but her condition was making the forensic pathologist nauseous at the slightest thing, never mind a decomposing body. A wee boy, she guessed, thinking how different this pregnancy was from her first with little Abigail.

The body had been discovered almost by chance, and Rosie felt a pang of sorrow for Ellen Blackburn. How much grief had it taken to end one's life like that? The needle had still been in her cold flesh, giving the impression that it had been the woman's choice to end it all after the tragedy that had overtaken her family. Yet it would not be only Rosie's evidence that was needed in what was, on the face of it, a sudden death. That sharp-eyed female officer who had been one of the pair called to effect a forced entry into the old lady's flat had given them all something to think about. Toxicology was also needed and already a small forensic team was taking samples from the cadaver and what might become a scene of crime.

It had been the carnage at the previous year's end that had tipped Lorimer over the edge, Rosie thought, with a sigh. How much more so would it have affected a close family member?

'She's deid, in't she?' a gruff voice asked as Rosie felt a tug on the sleeve of her white coveralls.

'I'm sorry, I can't comment . . . ' Rosie began, turning to see a woman looking up at her.

'She loved bein' the centre o' attention, that wan,' the wee woman whispered behind one cupped hand. 'Wid nivver hae missed her ain pairty, c'n tell ye that fur a fact, hen.' The woman nodded. 'Wis it sudden, like? Heart attack or whit? Youse yins widnae be all ower the place like a rash if it wis an ordinary death though, wid yese?' she observed with button-bright eyes.

'I ...' Rosie hesitated then shook her head again. 'Sorry, I can't say anything right now,' she murmured then moved away but not before the little woman had grabbed her by the elbow.

'Ellen Blackburn knew some bad people, hen. Jist like her evil basturt o' a son. Tell ye whit, ah widnae be surprised if wan o' them had done the auld yin in,' she stated, then, letting go of Rosie's arm, she stepped back before the police officer had to usher her behind the tape once more.

Rosie strode along the pavement, mouth open in a moment of disbelief at the venom in the woman's tone. She slipped into her car and began to strip off the protective clothing, fingers trembling as she pulled back the hood from her blonde curls. It was none of her business what a passer-by might say and yet she would pass this on in her report to the Crown Office and the police. Just in case.

'An attention seeker might well take his or her own life,' Solly told her later once Rosie was seated with a cup of ginger tea to settle her stomach.

'But her birthday party was only days away from the time she died,' Rosie protested.

'And what's your professional estimate of that?'

'Several days, but less than a week, certainly.' Rosie told him. 'I'll be able to be more accurate come the PM. You don't want to know the details,' she added with a wry smile. Her husband might be a clever man when it came to the inner working of the human mind but he was one of the most squeamish people she knew and tales of decomposing bodies and the attendant infestation of bluebottle larvae were definitely not what he wanted to hear.

'Have you told Lorimer yet?'

'About it being Ellen Blackburn? No.' Rosie screwed up her pretty face. 'Don't know how he would take it ...' She gave her husband a quizzical look.

'Oh, I think he's all right,' Solly mused, gazing past her at a spot on the wall, a look she knew well. He was disappearing into his thoughts, but what were they, right now? Thoughts of Lorimer and his breakdown? Or thoughts about the demise of an elderly woman whose life had been soured by her own son's destruction of his wife and young family?

Jack Gallagher smiled as he read the text. The old woman's death would be looked at as suicide, he was assured. But the smile faded as the drug baron admitted to himself that allowing Mitchison the knowledge that Ellen Blackburn's death had been on Gallagher's own orders was a little risky, given the detective superintendent's current jitteriness. Still, having someone like Mark Mitchison under his control was an advantage, especially if it came to the bit that Glasgow's biggest drug boss was prepared to ditch his latest enterprise and throw Graham to the wolves. The pictures on national television were bound to cast up some pieces of intelligence and it was up to Mitchison to find out exactly what they were so that they could both keep one step ahead of that guy Lorimer and his team at the MIT.

'Ellen Blackburn was found dead yesterday morning,' Niall Cameron told him as Lorimer stepped into the DCIs' room. 'A report's gone to the Fiscal's office.'

'Who ...?'

'She was Thomas Blackburn's mother,' Niall explained in his soft Lewis voice, watching his boss's face as the knowledge sunk in.

Lorimer gripped the edge of Cameron's desk as a wave of despair washed over him. *Blackburn!*

The very name conjured up memories of that room, the blood and bits of human remains splattering across his face, the acrid smell of gunfire, that last cry cut short ...

'Why is it going to the Fiscal?' he asked, his voice tight with suppressed emotion.

'She was found with a hypodermic needle in her arm. Tox report shows high-grade morphine. Way over the level,' DCI Tweedie said. 'Not the sort of stuff you'd expect her to obtain from anyone on the streets. Here.' He handed his boss a copy of the report.

'Same quality as the drugs stolen from the Queen Elizabeth,' Lorimer remarked, scanning the pages quickly. 'So are we looking at another case of murder?' His fingers loosened from the desk, the feeling of panic subsiding as the two DCIs continued to discuss the woman as though her family tragedy had never impinged on him in such a personal way.

'That's certainly what it looks like,' Tweedie agreed, 'And the circumstantial evidence suggests that the deceased had no immediate reason for taking her own life. No history of depression.' He glanced at Lorimer as he uttered the word yet the tall man gave no sign of being affected by it.

'No medication given by her GP even after the tragedy ... '

This time Lorimer looked away and the two DCIs saw the colour fade from his face, the tight line of his lips telling its own tale.

'Only thing missing is forensic evidence,' Tweedie told them, tapping his own copy of the current report. 'Whoever was there hid his traces well, but there is still a chance that some DNA might be found. We should know by tomorrow.'

'You're thinking it's Nimmo?' DCI Cameron asked, turning to Lorimer.

'It has to be something we keep in mind,' Lorimer replied. 'There has been enough press coverage about him to give other people ideas like that, but this quality of morphine does suggest that it might have come from the same source as that used to kill the two itinerants.'

'But Mrs Blackburn doesn't fit into any sort of pattern,' Cameron objected. 'She wasn't terminally ill. She didn't have any association with down-and-outs that we know of and she didn't even have a drug habit, according to the ladies in the community who knew her.'

'So, what's the common denominator, then?' Lorimer asked quietly, almost as though he were asking the question of himself.

In the end it was a coup for the first journalist who had arrived on the scene and taken aside a little old lady who had turned out to be a mine of useful information about Ellen Blackburn and her family.

The front page carried a grainy photograph of the grandmother and the heading: **TRAGIC GRAN FOUND DEAD.**

Ellen Blackburn might have enjoyed reading the story of her terrible loss and the sympathetic tributes from some of her neighbours.

But one thing she would have hated was the insinuation that she had been in cahoots with darker forces from the Glasgow underground, the merest suggestion of which led readers to believe that her untimely death was something that Ellen might have deserved.

CHAPTER FORTY-TWO

The present from the patient adviser at Castlebrae had turned out to be a book of poetry. *STRESSED Unstressed*, a clever title reflecting both the rhythm patterns of poetry and the need for people to find some sort of peace within the contents of its covers. Lorimer had already dipped into the book, selecting poems he knew from his schooldays as well as others like the ancient haiku poems by Basho that gave him a sense of how complete the world really was if only one could stay still long enough to meditate upon it. Lorimer sat up, the book in his hand, Maggie slumbering softly by his side. If he was being truthful he was seeking some solace after the revelations of the day. That Thomas Blackburn's elderly mother might have been murdered posed a new difficulty for him in a case that had already too many twists and turns. But the complexity of it was not what bothered the detective superintendent. Rather, he was afraid that when he finally slept, the nightmare images would appear once again to haunt him.

In the end it was the Welshman who said it best: Thomas's poem written at the death of his father summing up what Lorimer felt about the old lady's death in particular and the other deaths that had blighted so many lives in the wake of the man behind Quiet Release.

Do not go gentle into that good night . . .
Rage, rage against the dying of the light.

Dylan Thomas had insisted.

And surely that was what had driven the policeman on: the desire to find a killer that had taken away these final days from his victims.

Lorimer laid down the book on his bedside cabinet and switched off the light. Oliver Nimmo was somewhere out there, he told himself, gazing towards the window. He felt sure that he was still in this city, still intent on harming those innocent, vulnerable folk. Lorimer began to ask himself the same questions that had been causing him several sleepless nights. What was the man's motivation? Was it simply money? Or something more sinister?

Solomon Brightman had begun to piece together a profile of the man they sought and Lorimer was aware that the psychologist was increasingly of the view that the killer had an inner need to take these lives, as if by snuffing out their last breaths he was endowing himself with some sort of power. Solly had referred to the Shipman case more than once and there did seem to be some parallels, but this young man in his late twenties had never qualified as a doctor and Lorimer wondered if that fact alone had contributed to his urge to pretend to be someone in the medical world.

Sleep did come at last but Lorimer's dreams were haunted by pictures in his brain, though not by the carnage of the New year's Eve massacre. Instead he relived the moments when he had discovered Maggie's cousin, Patrick, not long after he had assaulted his wife in a moment of madness, the rage at her connivance to have his brother David put to death too much to bear.

Rage, rage ... Patrick's voice seemed to be calling out as he stood in the dock, Lorimer's dream turning to a courtroom scene where the jury consisted of Mitchison and Pamela Crossan side by side with Andrew Anderson, all laughing and pointing at the accused.

Then he was alone in a dark corridor, the voices stilled, the sound of his own heartbeat loud as he walked slowly down a tunnel, blinking to see the way ahead. The walls seemed to close in, his childhood fear returning as Lorimer plunged deeper and deeper into the blackness.

It's just claustrophobia, a woman's voice told him, and, though there was no woman to be seen, Lorimer knew it was his former patient advisor Christine, assuring him that there was nothing to fear.

Then he was out of the darkness and standing beside a shore, moonlight shining down on the gently receding waves, its susurration a comfort to his ears.

Can you see it yet? another voice asked.

In his dream, Lorimer turned to see a bearded man by his side. He blinked, imagining that it must be Solly, but when the man smiled, Lorimer knew that this was not his friend at all but the man whose image had appeared on the television.

And in that moment of realisation, Oliver Nimmo vanished from his sight.

CHAPTER FORTY-THREE

R ick didn't want to offend the older man, but neither did he have any desire to share his good fortune with his fellow room-mate, no matter what hints and insinuations McLachlan had made about his new friend.

It had taken him almost an hour to trudge along the riverbank, past the casino where folk spent wads of cash just for fun, under the echoing railway bridge and arching flyovers then into the heart of the city. As Rick stumbled through Glasgow Green, shivering now that there were no buildings to shelter him on either side, he kept glancing ahead. The man had told him where they would meet. It was just a matter of being there at the right time and Rick was worried about that. Other men had watches but his had been pawned long ago. He lifted his eyes to the heavens but there was no sign of a sun beyond these grey, rain-filled clouds; it was like most days in February so far and it was hard to tell if it was ten o'clock in the morning or four in the afternoon. But Rick had left the dosshouse when the clock hands there had stood at nine so he should be at his destination at the appointed time.

Sure enough, a figure carrying a parcel under his arm detached itself as if by magic from where it had been slouching against the ornamental fountain and Rick's eager feet hurried along the path to meet him.

The last part had been hard. Concealing himself in doorways and behind industrial bins in darkened alleyways had kept Tam out of sight but here, in the huge swathes of parkland, it was impossible not to be seen. So the old man had hugged the hedges, their darker colour giving him a modicum of camouflage while he kept one eye on the other man's progress.

He'd tried to give him the slip, but Tam was feigning sleep before creeping out and scurrying after Rick.

The old man pressed his body against the wet privet, not caring that the twigs cut into his bare neck. So long as the pair of them did not walk this way, he'd be all right. A shudder made him tighten his shoulder blades. If the killer saw him here ... well, the consequences of that happening didn't bear thinking about.

But the two men had turned away now towards the huge glass house that dominated this part of Glasgow Green.

Tam stepped out from his hiding place and followed the winding path, thinking hard. They could be in there for a while, maybe even share a pot of tea. His empty belly rumbled at the thought. There were other exits, too; that was something to take into consideration. He might lose them both if he stayed here, hovering between the hedge and the doorway.

In the end he decided to skirt around the building, keeping well away from its windows but glancing over his shoulder from time to time just in case two figures emerged from the same doorway.

As luck would have it, there were several empty drinks crates piled up opposite a door marked STAFF ONLY, no doubt waiting for someone to take them away, so Tam slipped behind them, crouching down until he could find a space between the boxes that let him peer out. It was a good vantage point, he decided. Not only could he spot anybody coming from the entrance that Rick and the man had used, but he could see the sweeping path where they would have to walk to reach the other end of the park where buses passed along a main road.

Tam shifted his position a little, stifling the groan he wanted to utter as the rain began to fall, gently at first, then that persistent drizzle for which the west coast was famous, running in rivulets down his neck and soaking his clothes.

He was about to give up, stretch his aching bones and creep back along the path, when he saw them.

Rick was slightly behind the other man, darting this way and that, trying to keep up. Had he been given something to make him so jumpy? Tam wondered. It certainly looked like it; Rick was almost dancing as he kept pace with the man, a stupid grin on his face. And there was something else that was different about him, Tam saw; the ex-soldier was wearing a fawn duffel coat instead of his own ragged jacket.

He had no time to think about this, however. They were practically level with the heap of boxes when the killer stopped suddenly and turned to his companion.

Tam froze, terrified to move a muscle.

If he was found now, everything would be lost.

'You know what to do,' he heard him say. 'Buy everything on that list, d'you hear?'

Tam saw him stretch out a hand and pull Rick towards him by the coat front.

'Use that cash any other way and I'll know,' he growled, then, letting go of the man's coat, he shoved something into Rick's hands and turned away, walking smartly along the path that led back towards the city.

Tam stayed still, his thighs screaming in agony from being forced to stay in a crouching position for so long. Then, as Rick took off towards the other exit, he risked standing up, his eyes still following the figure that was becoming smaller and smaller as it strode along the grey ribbon winding around the acres of green grass that gave this place its name. He would follow him, sure he would, but at a careful distance, hoping that luck was on his side and that he might find out just where this man who had stolen the name Gordon Smith hid away from all these searching eyes.

The reward being offered was immense, Tam told himself, licking his lips as he emerged from his hiding place. Then he began to hug the hedges once again, feet silent on the wet tarmac. The old man ignored the falling rain as he tramped quietly in the wake of the killer.

But it was not the thought of money that kept Tam McLachlan's eyes boring into the back of that distant figure. Indeed, no. He'd kept his share of the drug that had killed Seamus and he intended to use it. What he wanted was to watch the man suffer the way his friend had suffered.

That would be reward enough.

CHAPTER FORTY-FOUR

Sometimes it was hard to remember who he was supposed to be. For weeks he had been Gordy, the good-looking porter who flirted with all the nurses and made easy banter with the patients he wheeled from the wards to wherever they had to be taken. More recently he'd thought of himself as Charles Graham, a businessman who had the ear of one of the city's most influential drug lords. And soon he would have to become used to the stolen identity of Richard Aitken, the man who should be purchasing clothes that would fit in with his plan to escape. It was only now, when he dodged between the puddles on the cracked paving stones, that he felt like the person he really was, Oliver Nimmo, a fugitive from justice whose face was maybe being scrutinised by every police force in the country. That idea did not give Oliver any sense of pride, as he bent forwards slightly, his umbrella heading off the gusts of wind and rain.

Once he would have hailed a passing black cab or waited in a queue at a taxi rank but now he was wary of being seen. He could well imagine the glance that a driver might give him, clocking his face as the wanted man behind Quiet Release and the theft from the Queen Elizabeth Hospital. Keeping out of sight was mandatory these days and for once he did not curse the Glasgow weather since he could hide beneath this large umbrella as he made his way back to his riverside eyrie.

The swishing of the buses masked any other sound as Oliver plodded along the Broomielaw, unaware that he was retracing Tam McLachlan's steps, and that the tramp was, at this very moment, just a few yards behind him. He resented having to walk but, after all, Glasgow Green was not so terribly far from the modern bridges that spanned the Clyde and where so many executive flats now lined both banks of the river. He'd kept himself fit by regular visits to a city centre gym, but that would have to stop now, just in case he was recognised by any of the other members. There was a price on his head, Oliver reminded himself, and there would be plenty of folk willing and eager to turn him in for ten grand, the same amount that he'd been offered to dispatch the old lady.

The price of a hit, he remembered Gallagher laughing when he had asked 'Charles Graham' for that little favour. Yet he had turned down the money, telling the big man that he was happy to do this particular job for free. *Let's call it the first of many*, he had said with a smile as Gallagher had handed him that scrap of paper with Ellen Blackburn's address.

Now, Oliver frowned as he wondered just where his relationship was with the gangster. Had that television programme blown all of his careful plans to smithereens? Several times recently he had tried to contact Gallagher but the man was not returning any of his calls and that alone made him shiver with apprehension. A man like that could easily find ways to get rid of him. And that was why he needed to be one step ahead. Sure, the drug baron had sold him the necessary papers, could probably guess what his next persona would be, but Oliver would be far away from this city soon and only a memory in Jack Gallagher's mind. Rick would do as he was told, just like the others had done, of that Oliver was certain. Dangling the bait of regular drug supply made them do everything he asked. And then, once their usefulness was at an end, well, he'd take pleasure in putting them down like the dogs they undoubtedly were.

Tam walked steadily, keeping a distance between the man in front and himself, happy to allow any other pedestrian to come between them. A young woman pushing a buggy passed him by and Tam peered sideways to catch a glimpse of the baby. But the hood and plastic rain cover made that impossible as the woman wheeled the pram swiftly along, one hand jammed to her ear as she blethered into her mobile phone, the rain making rats' tails of her two-tone hair.

How much did a style like that cost a lassie nowadays? Tam wondered for a moment, looking at the blue streaks amongst the dark blonde hair, all spoiled by the ceaseless downpour. Here he was, dependent on the meagre handouts he could get, and there they were, spending good money for a mess like that! He shook his head then smiled. You're getting old, Tam, lad, he told himself as the woman strode forward and began to overtake the figure with the big golf umbrella.

His quarry stepped aside and for one heart-stopping moment Tam thought that he was going to turn and look behind him. A sigh of relief escaped from the old man's lips as the man continued on his way, still oblivious to the fact that the tramp he thought he'd murdered was now following him.

Tam stopped as the traffic lights turned to red. He would catch up with his target if he wasn't careful, but to lose him now would be disaster.

His luck was in, though, as a cyclist sped along, cutting across the road and back onto the pavement as soon as the pedestrian light turned to green, and he hurried behind the well-dressed man whose eyes were on the cyclist now.

Tam stopped then, waiting for a few moments at the corner, head bowed, cupping his hands around an imaginary cigarette. When he looked up again he saw the figure a few yards ahead, outside a modern apartment block, its glass windows staring out across the river, upper flats boasting balconies that wrapped around the entire corner of the building.

So you've come home, Tam thought with a spurt of excitement as he saw his quarry standing in a doorway, fumbling in his raincoat pocket.

He watched through narrowed eyes, spotting the Burberry lining, seeing the flash of metal as the killer drew out a set of keys and fitted them to the lock.

Then he was gone, swallowed up by the glass door, lost to the old tout who had patiently followed him all the way.

The figure on that street corner did not move, however, but stood still, watching and waiting until a light came on right at the very top in the penthouse flat. Its brightness was dimmed when hands came to tug a window cord, letting a blind conceal the room within. But not before the owner of those hands had appeared, be it ever so briefly.

Tam McLachlan grinned to himself.

Would he inform DC Wilson? Try to get his paws on that reward? He licked his lips. Never had he been given such a sum in all his years of dealing with the police.

'*I know where you live*,' he whispered aloud. And in that moment he felt himself grow a little taller, for such knowledge was power. He just had to figure out how best to use it.

CHAPTER FORTY-FIVE

'What do we know about Nimmo?' Lorimer asked, though in truth the question was purely rhetorical. It was the end of another long day and the team was once again assembled in the briefing room where Lorimer stood at the whiteboard, one hand ready to add all of the new intelligence that had been gathered.

'Neighbour gave us more background.' DC Giles spoke first, glancing at Kirsty Wilson who was sitting next to him as if to elicit her agreement. 'Seems that he didn't get on with the stepfather at all. Right disciplinarian. He kept the boy in most nights, making him do his homework, wouldn't let him out to play with the other kids, that sort of thing.'

'Sounds a right bully,' Kirsty agreed. 'According to some of the older residents we've now spoken to, the wife was terrified of him. The girl next door remembers her as a snobby wee woman who kept her son from mixing with the other kids but children don't always see the truth , do they? She hardly ever spoke to her neighbours, just scuttled out to do her grocery shopping and back home again. Never socialised. Case of abuse, if ever I heard it,' she remarked fiercely.

'Women didn't always have the kinds of resources that are available nowadays.' Lorimer sighed. 'God knows what sort of life the pair of them endured.'

'Until he lost them by fire.'

All heads turned to the far end of the table to see the bearded man who had spoken.

'If Oliver had set fire to the family home then he must have wanted to destroy them both: the stepfather who made their life intolerable and the mother who was too weak to defend him,' Professor Brightman explained. 'Do we know what happened to the boy after that?' he asked mildly.

'Yes,' Lorimer replied. 'Thanks to a lot of hard work by these officers,' he nodded towards the men and women seated around the long oval table, 'we can piece together some of Oliver Nimmo's life. We know he failed all of his exams but now we have more details. According to Peter McAree, Oliver was given a chance to resit them all, special consideration being given in the aftermath of the family tragedy. But he never did. Nimmo dropped out and left Glasgow University for good.'

He turned and scribbled some words onto the whiteboard.

'Here's where he went next.' Lorimer stood back to allow the others to see the name Byres Road written in blue marker pen.

He waited for a gasp of acknowledgement but none came.

'This is where—'

His words were suddenly cut off by Kirsty Wilson who twisted round excitedly.

'—Frankie Bissett was found dead there last year!' she exclaimed. 'I'll never forget that.' She turned apologetically to the others. 'My first day in CID,' she explained. 'So how . . . ?'

'Nimmo rented that flat for a while, probably got to know Bissett and had second-hand knowledge of Billy Brogan. That's a name many of you will know.' Lorimer looked around the room to see several nodding heads.

Brogan was a known dealer, now back behind bars, who had been involved in several cases including Quiet Release.

'We've no evidence to suggest that Nimmo ever had a drug habit himself, however.'

'One thing I don't get, sir,' Kirsty piped up. 'Brogan and his pals swore that they didn't know who it was who had overall control of Quiet Release.'

Lorimer nodded. 'And that may well be true,' he agreed. 'As far as we know it was only Mary Milligan and Frankie Bissett that actually met Nimmo. But there was nothing to stop Nimmo from targeting types like Brogan through his connection with Bissett.'

'Before he killed Bissett,' Kirsty finished off, nodding. 'He didn't want anyone to know who he really was, is that what you think, sir?'

'We may never know,' Lorimer said darkly. 'Until we find him. And that, ladies and gentlemen, is something we will do.'

There were nods of agreement on the solemn faces regarding Lorimer, all intent on what he was saying.

'Then there are records showing the purchase of another flat near Byres Road.' He turned and wrote *Chancellor Street* below the first address.

'That was after the insurance money came in from the burned family home. And, given that it was a modest flat, we can assume that Nimmo had enough funds salted away to keep him going.'

'He'd learned that much from the stepfather, then, sir,' Giles remarked.

'Oh, yes,' agreed the detective superintendent. 'Nimmo wasn't stupid about money. On the contrary, we have bank accounts in his name from about eight years ago showing very healthy balances.'

'And then ... ?'

The psychologist's question made Lorimer smile. 'Yes, you've guessed already, haven't you, Solly? Nimmo withdrew the lot one day and then vanished. Just like that.'

'And changed his name, one presumes?' Solly asked, but that question did not require an answer, the gloomy faces around him testifying to that.

'He changed his name and he changed his address. Am I correct?'

'You are,' Lorimer told him. 'We have the record of when he sold the Chancellor Street flat and to whom but nothing about a subsequent purchase.'

'So, who did he become once he had left Oliver Nimmo behind and long before he became Gordon Smith?' Solly mused aloud.

'We tried to trace some of the other students on his course,' one of the female detective sergeants offered. 'Only came across one guy who's now working as a paediatrician in the Sick Kids here in Glasgow.' She consulted a page of her notebook. 'Dr Martin Jamieson. But happily he was also at that party the night of the fire,' she added.

Lorimer nodded to the woman to continue.

'He didn't remember much about the party itself. Said he'd been collapsed in a heap in a back room. Too much to drink, he thinks. But here's the interesting bit. It was Oliver Nimmo who took him back to the halls of residence afterwards, along with some other blokes whose names he's forgotten. Nimmo had a car, a Ford Fiesta. Jamieson remembered that because his older sister had one just like it. And,' she paused for effect, 'this particular car matches the description of Oliver's mum's runabout.'

'So he could have driven home, set fire to the house and been back at the party in time to drive his mates home.' Lorimer nodded. 'Good work, Claire, that was excellent finding this doctor. I take it you have his details?'

The woman reddened with pleasure as she lifted a black-bound notebook. 'All ready to type up, sir. And Dr Jamieson said he'd be happy to help in any way that he could.'

'Right, what else?' Lorimer looked around the room, aware that these highly trained men and women had been hard at work all day sifting through data, asking questions of the people who might have come into contact with Nimmo over the last few years.

'The only thing that we found that still has his real name is the driving licence,' Davie Giles told them. 'DVLA has it on record that he obtained the licence on 28 March 2007. No endorsements, nothing at all.' He shrugged. 'So we might assume that he's still running around with that to identify himself.'

'Much good that'll do us,' DCI Tweedie grumbled.

'He'd need it if he hired a car, sir,' Kirsty reminded the older man.

Her sudden response made Lorimer smile. DC Wilson was growing in confidence now and he was glad to see that she was not afraid to challenge a more senior officer in the cut-and-thrust of this briefing where every scrap of information had to be put together and scrutinised if they were to move forward at all.

'He could have *bought* a car in a different name any time,' Tweedie countered. 'What happened to the Fiesta? Any record of that?'

'Sold it to one of these auction places,' DS Claire Johnston replied. 'And no sign of any purchase by an Oliver Nimmo that we can find since then.'

The psychologist stared into space, stroking his beard thoughtfully. Who did you become then, Oliver? What names did you dream up before you stole Gordon Smith's? You took his identity and you took his life. Then a faint smile played about his lips. Perhaps Oliver had stolen the identity of another dead man, one who had made the boy's life a misery.

'Have you tried the name Charles Graham?' Solly asked.

'What do you make of him so far?' Lorimer asked as they stood together in the car park outside the Govan police station, sheltering under Solly's huge umbrella.

'Oliver Nimmo?' Solly replied thoughtfully. 'He's an interesting one, right enough. Has followed a recognisable behavioural pattern so far as I can see. But I think he may have deviated from what I might call the "usual script".'

'Oh? How's that? Because of the end-of-life scam?'

'Actually, no,' the psychologist told him. 'That is inventive in its own way, of course, but it does show both the desire for money and power – two great motivators for anyone bent on taking lives. And I doubt if the man ever had a qualm of conscience about that,' he added grimly.

'So, what makes him so different?'

Solly was silent for a moment as though gathering his thoughts to put them into words.

'His association with down-and-outs,' he said at last. 'Why did he take the identity of that chap Smith? And where did he meet these men? Hm?' He looked thoughtful as the pair watched the hired taxi approach. 'I can understand him working in medical types of jobs, keeping close to the sorts of victims he was targeting. But what brought him into contact with Smith and that other man . . . ?'

'Seamus O'Halloran,' Lorimer reminded him.

'Yes. Something else for your team to find out, I think.' He smiled then looked up as a silver Skoda drew up at the kerbside. 'Keep me informed about any new developments, won't you?' he said, closing the umbrella and shaking it before running the few feet towards the taxi that would whisk him back to the university.

'You, too!' Lorimer called out, waving his friend away.

It was an interesting thought, right enough, and one that several officers were already investigating. How had the killer met these rough sleepers? And why had he wanted to be in their company in the first place? Was it simply to steal an identity? Or was Nimmo on some sort of a crusade to bump them off as he saw fit?

It was later that day, as twilight crept over the city, that Lorimer did indeed have a new piece of information to pass to his friend.

The lab report from the scene of crime at Ellen Blackburn's flat confirmed something that he had already hoped to see. For, despite every sign that he had tried to clean up after himself, there were some traces of DNA that matched those already stored against the Quiet Release killer, the man whose real name they now knew was Oliver Nimmo.

310

CHAPTER FORTY-SIX

The telephone rang just as Paul was about to turn on the alarm for the night.

It had been a busier day than usual, several folk asking about new laptops and one man actually buying a reconditioned Hewlett Packard machine.

'Hello?' He was glad that this would be the final call of his day. 'Hello?' He spoke again but there was no sound forthcoming then a barely audible click as the caller hung up. Wrong number, perhaps? Paul wondered. And yet he really should be a bit cautious, he told himself, considering the sorts of things he was doing as a favour for his friend, DCI Niall Cameron.

Dialling the four digits that ought to give him the caller's number did not help, however.

'Number withheld,' a recorded female voice told him.

Someone selling stuff, he decided. A call centre where they got their bonuses by the quantity of numbers they'd rung.

Paul stretched out a hand to activate the alarm but at that very moment a shadow passed the window and stopped outside the door. Surely it wasn't another customer at this hour? He glanced at his watch, frowning. The final of the pub quiz would be starting soon and they needed their team captain to give the other three the benefit of his encyclopedic knowledge.

The door crashing open was not what made Paul back up against the wooden counter, it was the black-clad figure whose face was hidden beneath a balaclava.

'Stop!' Paul cried out, one hand up to protect himself, but the figure lunged forwards, a baseball bat raised in the air.

Years of training made Paul duck instinctively, bent into a crouching position. Then, hands held flat, he lunged out with his right leg, a cry of defiance on his lips.

The intruder groaned as Paul's outstretched foot made contact with the fellow's groin.

In two swift moves, he chopped downwards, felling the gasping man to the floor. A thud, as his head made contact with the side of the wooden counter, then silence.

It was over in less than a minute, the dark-clad figure at his feet, Paul scarcely breaking sweat.

Glancing towards the street, Paul saw the deserted pavement. *What if there was someone else out there in the darkness, waiting to help his mate?*

He slammed the door shut and bolted it top and bottom before grabbing hold of his mobile and pushing in the number.

'Niall, it's me. Something's come up and I think you need to be here now,' he explained.

He looked down at the prostrate form at his feet, prodding it with a tentative shoe.

'And maybe bring a couple of uniforms to take away an unwanted visitor.'

Jack Gallagher was not best pleased when Joe McGarrity's mobile refused to answer any of his calls. He ought to have been in and out of Doherty's shop by now, the gangster fumed. How long did it take to pressure a wee nyaff like Doherty and find out if he was behind the hacking job?

He had asked around, of course, and every time the answer had been the same: Paul Doherty. The computer expert from Paisley was the likeliest person to have infiltrated Gallagher's personal email account, in the opinion of his own IT man. A bit of digging had also uncovered the fact that Doherty had been at university with none other than DCI Cameron, one of the MIT team who had been nosing around into the drug baron's affairs. He'd sent in one of his best heavies to do the job, confident that Doherty would by now be a quivering wreck.

But what if things had gone wrong? What if a worse fate than a simple beating had befallen the geek? Gallagher's jaw tightened. He wanted him alive to find out if he was indeed the hacker he sought, and the name of anyone to whom he might have passed information.

If Joe had messed up there would be hell to pay, he thought, grinding his teeth in rage at the possible scenario. A body to bury somewhere and questions being asked about the sudden disappearance of the IT whizz could cause him no end of grief.

Jack Gallagher sat hunched over the telephone, willing it to ring, one fist clutching a crystal glass that contained the remains of his third single malt. He needed to hear Joe's voice, wanted to know that everything had gone to plan. But, as he sat there in the quiet of his study, Jack Gallagher felt the hairs rise on the back of his neck and shivered, recognising a definite sense of foreboding.

He could hear the ringtone again and this time Paul bent down and searched the man's jacket pocket, pulling out a silver-coloured mobile that stopped abruptly as he peered at its tiny screen.

'Someone wants to talk to you, pal,' he remarked to the inert shape lying on his floor. But there was no response and Paul Doherty looked thoughtful as he waited for the police to arrive.

'Are you all right?'

'Never better.' Paul grinned as they watched the red tail-lights of the squad car disappearing down Paisley High Street.

'Gave me a wee start, right enough,' he admitted. 'And it was a surprise to see his face when your lot took off that balaclava.'

'Same fellow that bought the laptop earlier on, you said?'

'Aye. Expensive way to do a recce,' Paul replied. 'Still, we can hazard a guess about who was really paying for that bit of hardware, can't we?'

'Gallagher?' Niall Cameron asked, his dark eyebrows raised.

'My thinking exactly,' Paul agreed. 'Here.' He handed Niall the mobile phone. 'Someone was trying to call our visitor,' he said, looking at DCI Cameron's face. 'Think I might be able to find out who that was if you give me a minute or two.'

Niall Cameron's face broke into a grin. 'Are you trying to tell me you haven't already looked up the number?' he asked, feigning astonishment.

'Had to keep an eye on chummy, there, didn't I?' Paul replied, his laconic smile not fooling the detective for one moment.

'Okay, let's have it,' Niall said, following his friend into the back shop where a laptop sat open, its screen already lit up.

Niall Cameron stared over the man's shoulders as Paul tapped commands into the computer then watched as rows and rows of data were scrolled onto the screen.

'Aye, there it is.' Paul Doherty sat back eventually to allow his friend a clear view of what he wanted him to see.

'It *is* Gallagher,' Niall said softly, then whistled through his teeth. 'Well, well, well. Not quite the outcome he was hoping for this evening, was it?' he chuckled, giving his old friend a pat on the shoulder. 'Good work, Paul. This should help us a lot. And I promise you, we'll nail that man yet!' He nodded as Paul began to print off the page.

'You'd better come back to the station with me, though,' Niall went on. 'We'll need to ask you to complete a statement for us. Is that all right?' He looked at the disgruntled expression on the hacker's face. 'I mean ... you didn't have a hot date or anything, I hope?'

'Nah, nothing like that. Just ... ' He shook his head, despairingly. 'Och, it's too late now anyway.' Paul sighed, looking at his watch. 'We would have beaten that team from Cross Stobbs easily,' he muttered with a frown. 'Ah, well, maybe next year.' He sighed again. 'The lads will give me pelters for not turning up, mind. Having to scratch on the night of the quiz final will cost me more than a couple of rounds.'

'Joseph McGarrity,' Cameron told his boss. 'One of Gallagher's heavies. Thought you would want to know, sir.'

Lorimer's eyebrows rose a little as he heard the name. 'Gallagher, eh? Don't suppose McGarrity's asked for a solicitor yet?'

'First thing he did, sir,' Cameron told him. 'And guess who he wanted?'

'Not wee Colin Patterson, by any chance?' Lorimer asked with a grin. Patterson was known to the police as someone who was so close to Jack Gallagher's organisation that there was a joke about the patter of tiny feet every time the five-foot-four solicitor came to the rescue of one of the drug baron's neds.

'They're just waiting for him now, sir.' There was a pause as Cameron let his question go unspoken.

'You'd like me to be there?'

'It would be a help, sir,' Cameron said, his diffident reply concealing what he really wanted to say: *Everyone knows how good you are at making them talk.* 'I won't be there, myself,' he said instead, looking sideways at the man sitting in the passenger seat. 'I have to be somewhere else right now.' He glanced at the gate to the imposing property where he was parked.

'Have to go out. Sorry,' Lorimer bent to kiss the top of Maggie's head. 'Don't wait up.'

Her smile was tinged with something that he hated to see, a mixture of regret and resignation that smote his conscience. This job, what is it doing to her? he thought as he shrugged on his winter coat, searching in its pocket for the car keys.

Then he was out in the cold, the wind slapping his face as if in revenge for leaving her there alone.

Crime pays was the phrase that came readily to mind as DCI Niall Cameron pressed a buzzer on the stone pillar beside the high metal gates. The house beyond was a turn-of-the-century villa, its pale sandstone gable pockmarked where ivy had been torn away. The rest of the property was hidden behind ten-foot-high hedging but the upper storey was still visible against the darkened skies, its slate roof pierced by several small dormer windows, possibly the habitation of live-in servants back in the pre-war days when such things were the norm.

Their surveillance of the house in this leafy part of Pollokshields had paid off at any rate and the MIT team knew quite a lot about Jack Gallagher, including the fact that he lived alone. There were always lackeys to come when he called, of course, and Cameron had taken a good look around to see if any of their vehicles were parked nearby.

'Think he's at home?' DCI Tweedie shivered beside him as Cameron waited patiently at the gate.

Cameron looked down at his older colleague. Tweedie was so close to retirement, he reminded himself. And he could have opted for an easy ride. But finishing off his career with the chance to nail Jack Gallagher was something that his fellow DCI badly wanted.

The crackle of the intercom told the two men that there was someone at home.

'DCI Cameron, DCI Tweedie, Police Scotland,' Tweedie said, bending close to the metal strip. 'We would like to speak to the owner of this property,' he added slowly, clearly savouring every word.

There was a pause then the sound of a cough. 'Let's see your ID,' a gruff voice demanded. 'Hold them up to the top of the gate.'

It was only then that the two detectives noticed a small CCTV camera set into the side of the stone gatepost and each of them drew out his warrant card in turn, holding them up as directed.

Then a metallic click sounded, allowing the left gate to open a fraction.

Cameron pushed it wide and glanced at his companion.

'Stick a stone or something in that space,' he suggested, then whispered, 'It would be nice to know we could get out of here again quickly if we need to.'

Tweedie shoved a small rock with his toe and wedged it between the two iron gates. 'Good thinking. Wouldn't like to be stuck inside that fortress,' he said, as the two men looked up at the imposing house.

A light came on as they stepped towards the doorway, flooding the entire garden, its lawns and empty flowerbeds sloping down towards the perimeter hedge and the street beyond.

'Big place for one man to live,' Tweedie muttered as they climbed the stone steps then stood on the marble floor of the portico. 'I'd swear that this porch is bigger than my front room.' He glanced around the massive space with its double rows of pegs set into the half-timbered walls and the old-fashioned wooden settles on either side. In one corner an octagonal table made of brass supported a large ceramic planter containing several house plants, its contents lit by a green and pink glass lamp suspended from the white painted ceiling.

'Original art deco,' Tweedie whispered, nudging Cameron's elbow to make him look up. 'Bet that cost him a bob or two.'

Both men looked ahead as a shadow approached the opaque glass door. Then it swung open and the man they sought was standing there, staring at the pair of them.

Gallagher's eyes were sunk in folds of flesh but the baleful look that he directed at the two officers was enough to remind them both that this was a dangerous individual who would stop at nothing to continue his nefarious affairs.

'DCI Tweedie.' He held up his warrant card at the same time as Niall Cameron but it was at the younger detective that Gallagher's stare was directed, a stare that continued for several moments as though this gangster was trying to commit the man's image to memory.

'What brings two senior officers to my home at this time

of the evening?' Gallagher asked, his thick accent belying his attempt to appear deliberately posh.

'One of your employees was involved in an incident earlier this evening,' Tweedie told him.

'An' what's that got to do with me? *Gentlemen*.' He added the word with a sneer.

Cameron had never taken his eyes off the man since the door had opened and now he could see that telltale rise of his shoulders that denoted an increased nervousness. We've got him rattled, he thought with a sudden sense of satisfaction.

'Joseph McGarrity is in custody at this moment, Mr Gallagher,' Tweedie told him. 'And we would be grateful if we might come in for a wee minute to discuss several things with you.'

Cameron suppressed a smile. Two could play at that game and Tweedie's overly polite words were met with a frown and a grunt.

'Better come in, then.' Gallagher stepped aside and turned to walk back along the hallway, leaving the detectives to shut the front door behind them.

'In here,' he told them, turning towards a door leading into one of the bay-windowed rooms that faced the road.

Cameron continued to stare at the gangster, curiosity as much as anything else making him scrutinise the man's body language. Gallagher had turned away from the two police officers to pull the curtain cord, drawing the pale golden velvet drapes across the length of the bay window. Cameron could see that his back was hunched and, as he turned back, the big man suddenly seemed smaller and older, shuffling forwards and slumping into a chair.

'What d'you want?' he growled, regarding them under bushy

eyebrows for a moment then slipping one hand into his trouser pocket.

His mobile's in there, Cameron realised. You've been trying McGarrity's number several times already, haven't you?

'Just a few questions, Mr Gallagher,' Tweedie said smoothly. 'We wondered when you had last spoken to this employee of yours.'

Cameron saw the man's eyes flit between the two detectives then rest on his own face.

'What's that to you?' he asked, the chin raised in defiance, the tone belligerent, his face becoming scarlet with temper. But it was all show, Cameron knew, the sort of bravado that wee boys in the playground put on when they know that they've been outwitted.

'Mr McGarrity called you here at home, didn't he?' Cameron asked quietly.

'Is that a fact?' Gallagher sneered. 'So, what if he did?'

'That's not the only thing that interests us, sir,' Cameron continued, remembering to keep his tone as neutral as possible (a trick he'd learned from Lorimer). 'It's the telephone calls that you made to *his* phone that brought us here,' he said, fixing the man with a stare. 'Made us wonder why you were so eager to hear from Mr McGarrity this evening. Checking up to see if he had done a wee job for you, perhaps?'

'Don't know what you're on about!' Gallagher snapped.

'Oh, I think you do, sir,' Cameron replied. 'In fact DCI Tweedie and I are hoping you will be good enough to accompany us both to Govan police station to discuss this further.' He turned to his neighbour. 'Isn't that right, DCI Tweedie?'

'Just, so,' Tweedie replied with a nod. 'So, if you'd like to get your coat on, we'll be happy to take you with us.'

'What? You serious?' Gallagher blustered. 'I've no intention of coming anywhere with you two!'

'Oh, I think a little chat down at Helen Street would be preferable to being charged with obstructing the police, don't you?' Tweedie asked, turning to Cameron who nodded his agreement.

Gallagher's face was becoming redder and redder, the rage he undoubtedly felt becoming harder to contain. Yet he rose from his chair, snatching away the arm that Tweedie laid on him, and marched out of the room, the two detectives following in his wake.

Niall Cameron placed his hand firmly over the gangster's fist as it slipped into his pocket.

'I'll take that if you don't mind, sir,' he said in a tone that brooked no argument.

Gallagher shot him a filthy look.

'Your phone, sir?'

With a barely audible snarl, the burly man drew it from his pocket and placed it into Cameron's outstretched palm.

'Thank you, sir.' DCI Cameron nodded, stepping back as Gallagher headed towards the door followed closely by Frank Tweedie.

Joe McGarrity was sitting, head in his hands, when Detective Superintendent Lorimer saw him in the interview room.

He was a well-built fellow. Lorimer could see muscles rippling under the thin jacket, a plethora of tattoos snaking from both sleeves and covering his wrists, and his admiration for Paul Doherty suddenly increased. Earlier, the detective superintendent had been introduced to the IT expert and had felt the firm handshake. Nobody's fool, he'd thought at the time, glad that all Doherty's martial arts training had been put to good use.

'Detective Superintendent Lorimer entering the room.' One of the two officers that had accompanied McGarrity from Paisley glanced up at the new arrival then stood to let Lorimer take his chair.

The tape had evidently been running for a few minutes so that McGarrity could give his personal details.

Joseph McGarrity looked up at the tall man who was drawing in his chair to sit opposite, a baleful expression on his bruised and battered face, the result of his falling against the counter in Doherty's shop.

'Ah want ma brief,' he demanded, placing both meaty fists on the table between them.

'Is Mr McGarrity's solicitor in the building?' Lorimer asked the officer by the door.

'Just coming along, sir,' the uniformed officer replied. 'Mr Patterson,' he added with the faintest trace of a grin.

The door opened wide to admit another officer who ushered in a small rotund figure that waddled in and planked himself down in the seat next to his client.

'Mr McGarrity's solicitor Mr Patterson is now in attendance,' Lorimer intoned for the benefit of the video recorder.

'Your client has been charged with attempted robbery and intention to commit assault to severe injury,' Lorimer explained.

Patterson bristled visibly. 'Then how come he's the one with the bruises?'

'You mean despite having worn a balaclava?' Lorimer asked with a grin. 'And coming at his target armed with a baseball bat?' He turned his blue gaze on McGarrity. 'That's correct, isn't it, Joseph?'

McGarrity looked down at once, his entire demeanour changed at Lorimer's words. 'Aye,' he replied, the quiet note of hopelessness accompanied by a shrug.

'So, what do you expect me to do?' Patterson girned. 'Waste of my time coming in here, if you ask me!' he snapped, rising from the table. 'Thought you wanted representation, Joseph.' His small mouth pursed in annoyance as he glared at his client.

'Och, they've got it a' wrapped,' McGarrity said. 'That shop's hoachin' wi' CCTV cameras.'

'Not quite,' Lorimer said softly but in a tone so steely that Patterson sat down once again. 'There is still the question of who put you up to this, Joseph.'

The man looked down, his hands now clasped loosely beneath the table, his refusal to look up and those slumped shoulders telling their own story. He wasn't about to name names. There were too many other hard men in Gallagher's employ that would pose a problem for McGarrity's own family. Men like Thomas Blackburn, Lorimer thought with a sinking feeling in his stomach. Blackburn would have known this man in front of him, worked alongside him doing Gallagher's bidding. How had it felt to have lost a pal, no matter how rotten that pal had been? Something like sympathy filled the detective superintendent's heart as he sat staring at that bowed head. McGarrity was no stranger to the Scottish prisons, one of whose cells he'd be in soon enough. And yet it could have been so different for this man. A bad choice early on, bad company, lack of education ... all of the things that Lorimer and his own colleagues had avoided. Was life simply a matter of luck? Where you were born some sort of fluke or a predestined selection by some capricious Fate? He sighed and shook his head.

'We've got recordings of the telephone calls made between you and your boss, Joseph,' he said softly. 'We know that it was

Gallagher who sent you out tonight. Make it easy for yourself, eh? Tell us what we want to know and maybe the judge will be a bit more lenient when he hands out your sentence?'

But the man opposite kept his head lowered and his stubborn refusal to meet anyone's eyes told them all that silence was his final answer.

CHAPTER FORTY-SEVEN

Patterson had hung around only long enough to sit in with Jack Gallagher and hear the telephone recordings. In themselves, they were damning enough. The conversation between Gallagher and McGarrity clearly indicated that the drug boss had instructed his hired thug to break into Doherty's shop.

'Bring me everything you can,' Gallagher's deep voice ordered at one point. 'Anything like memory sticks or the guy's own laptop, got it?'

But the plan had gone awry from the start, Doherty defying the dark-clad figure armed with a baseball bat who was no match for the martial arts champion.

Gallagher's expletives had increased in ferocity as the calls had continued to go unanswered, his rage only too apparent to those listening to the recorded messages.

In the end it was a different solicitor who had come to the Govan station, one whose credentials impressed most Glasgow juries and whose fees only his wealthiest clients, like Gallagher, could afford. It was scant satisfaction for Tweedie and Cameron to see the drug boss locked up for the night in the certain knowledge that come morning he would be out on bail, free to carry on his business as usual.

'Will he get off with this?' Maggie Lorimer asked as they lay in bed, her husband curled into her side, one arm across her stomach. He had talked into the wee small hours until his eyelids drooped but still sleep seemed to elude him.

'Maybe. He'll say that McGarrity was overdoing a job that he'd been asked to do. Claim that he was only wanting to put the frighteners on Doherty. Or something ...' Lorimer yawned. 'I don't know. Maybe we'll find a way to pin this on him. But I think McGarrity's prepared to take the rap for his boss. We'll see ...' He closed his eyes and soon Maggie could hear the soft breathing that told her he was asleep at last.

She looked at his profile on the pillow next to hers: the dark hair flopping across his forehead, his features softened and all strain taken away from those closed eyes now that he slept. He looked like her young lover once more, she thought with a pang.

Sleep well, my love, she thought, not daring to utter the words aloud for fear that she should disturb him.

Sleep was eluding Tam McLachlan as he huddled down in the basement of the building. Somewhere up above the man he sought would be slumbering on some fancy bed with a thick duvet and silken sheets, no doubt; luxuries that Tam longed to snatch from him. This would be the night when he would form a plan, Tam told himself, imagining the way he wanted his story to end. That was the easy bit. He fingered the plastic box hidden in the inside pocket of his ancient coat. *A bit of fire in your veins*, he promised. *Just like you gave to Seamus.*

*

Upstairs, Oliver Nimmo had already made his plans. The three suitcases full of his favourite clothes and shoes were packed and labelled, ready to go. And soon he would follow them, away from this cold city where wind and rain beat down on him day after miserable day. He had transferred the bulk of his money to an offshore account, leaving enough to carry out his ideas. Every airport would have a picture of the man being sought in connection with Quiet Release so he had abandoned any notion of flying out of Scotland. The same probably went for trains: the transport police would be everywhere, Oliver imagined, smiling as he settled down for what he hoped would be the last time in his penthouse flat. Richard Aitken would enjoy a few days of pleasure impersonating the man who had picked him up off the Glasgow streets. But he'd eventually find the drugs where Oliver had planted them. And then there would be one less voice to tell his part in the story.

Buying the car had been a risk but the chap in the showroom had not batted an eyelid when he had offered to pay cash and the dark blue BMW was innocuous enough to be ignored by any nosy copper. He yawned then turned over onto his side, willing sleep to come. Nobody would think twice about a businessman called Richard Aitken crossing on the North Sea ferry, he thought, as he drifted into a dreamless sleep.

Tam had crawled all around the spacious garage, terrified of setting off some alarm or other, but this basement area appeared to be devoid of any such contraption. Each of the vehicles was currently parked in numbered bays and it hadn't taken the old man long to figure out that they corresponded to their owner's flat. He grinned as he lay beside the killer's car; trust him to have a double space that equated to the ownership of that upstairs flat. The penthouse, of course, nothing but the best for *him*, Tam thought bitterly. He'd made his money out of the misery and fear of so many people and was reaping his filthy reward.

Well, he'd have a wee surprise before too long, if Tam McLachlan had anything to do with it.

His thin face was creased in a grin as Tam ran the blade of his penknife between the tyre and wheel, imagining the dismay on the man's face when he discovered the damage. His smile faded as he thought of the young woman who had tried to befriend him. DC Wilson was a nice lassie, all right, there was no denying that. But she didn't have the rough edges of her predecessor, Murdoch. Tam chewed his bottom lip, wondering what the detective constable would say when she knew what he had done, then realised with a pang that Kirsty Wilson's approval actually mattered to him.

He would not know sleep tonight, Jack Gallagher had decided, sitting upright in the police cell. Wouldn't give the bastards the satisfaction, nor would he eat any of the breakfast they might deign to offer him. The gang boss ground his teeth together as he thought about the previous night and that pair of smirking detectives who had dared to take him from his home. The cheek of them! If he could teach them a lesson they'd not forget in a hurry ...

Gallagher sat up a little straighter as the thought came to him. It was beautiful in its simplicity, of course, like all the best ideas. The cops wanted to find that man on *Crimewatch*, but when they did Gallagher would make sure that it was only his dead body they would discover. What was that saying? *Dead men tell no tales.*

It was a pity, though. The scheme had had so much to commend it and he had actually liked the guy, Graham, or whatever his real name was. All those poor suffering souls ready for the chop ... Ach, what a fortune they could have made together! Still, he'd got rid of Ellen Blackburn and that was something.

A shadow passed the window outside and he turned his head to see the moon uncovered by the shreds and tatters of hazy amber-tinged clouds. Gallagher shivered then looked away but something made him turn his head once more as though the bright sphere had uttered a command.

You're being watched, Gallagher thought, an involuntary shudder passing through his body. And, for the first time in many a long year, he experienced a hollow feeling that a more sensitive creature would call despair.

CHAPTER FORTY-EIGHT

The morning dawned calm and bright after the storms of the previous days, the moon a faint echo of its night-time splendour, fading against forget-me-not blue skies. February was drawing to a close now, the children back at school until Easter but still they needed to wrap up against the chill, frost rising white on the grass verges as they walked along the road.

Tam McLachlan had not lingered in that draughty basement to watch the anger in the younger man's face as he discovered the damage to his car but was waiting nearby, watching carefully, hidden by passers-by as they made their way to work or school, just an old man leaning against the fence, reading his paper.

The arrival of a large liveried taxi made Tam lower his paper and look at the door to the flats. He frowned as he saw the vehicle had blocked the entrance from his sight, realising that he'd have to move further along the street to see what was happening, a risk he was reluctant to take. What if he should be spotted? Would the killer then guess that these slashed tyres were the work of old Tam? A person he thought had been dispatched to the hereafter.

Tam's feet hurried along until he was beyond the level of the front door.

And then he saw him.

At first he had looked away, thinking it was a mistake. Then his smile grew into a grin. Despite the woollen hat pulled down over the man's hair, Tam McLachlan thought that he recognised that Burberry coat and figure carrying the large suitcase: it was him all right. The taxi driver and another man in a duffel coat were helping him, shoving the cases into the van then sliding the doors shut.

He saw something pass between the driver's mate and the man he sought then Tam squinted a little, seeing the familiar figure step back, hands in pockets, then his vision was impeded by the passing traffic and so the old man saw only an empty pavement as the taxi drove away.

Tam watched the vehicle turn left after the traffic lights and head towards the motorway. But where was he taking the man's stuff? Further into the city? Out east or south towards the border? Or would the big taxi take the Kingston Bridge and head for Glasgow International Airport?

He ducked behind his newspaper once more, peering cautiously around its raised pages.

The killer would be back inside now. What was going through his mind? Would he call a repair service? Try to fix the BMW? Or were these suitcases a sign that he was planning to leave the city for good?

Tam looked skywards. He had lost his faith in the goodness of mankind a very long time ago but some things still lingered.

'Dear God,' he whispered. 'Just give me a chance to finish him off, eh?'

Then he shuddered as a chill ran down his spine. *Asking to kill a man!* Tam hesitated for a moment then spat on the ground.

*

'A deal?' The well-dressed Asian man with the refined Glasgow accent raised his eyebrows in surprise.

'Aye. I'm not likely to get off this one unless we do something drastic,' Gallagher replied.

'And what, exactly, do you want me to do?' The lawyer looked at his client, dark brown eyes taking in his client's dishevelled appearance.

'Get hold of Lorimer. There's something I've got for him. Just so happens I might be able help him with a different case,' Gallagher told him, meeting the other man's stare with one of his own. 'Tell him I can find the man they want from that *Crimewatch* programme.' He nodded at the solicitor. 'Or just say two wee words: "Quiet Release".' Gallagher began to grin. 'That'll make them sit up.'

'You're kidding me!' Frank Tweedie thumped the desk as he began to stand up.

'Lorimer said *what* . . . ?'

Niall Cameron gave a long sigh. 'I don't understand it either,' he admitted. 'Just told me that he was going to let Gallagher go back home. Said we'd blown the IT cover between him and Mitchison. But I tell you what,' he added, lowering his voice, 'I think Lorimer's going to announce something later on. He had that look in his eye.' Cameron nodded sagely. 'He's nobody's fool, that one, believe me.'

The front room of the Pollokshields mansion still had its curtains closed against the daylight that should have been streaming in but Jack Gallagher did not appear to be bothered. Or, Lorimer thought, he wanted to keep this meeting as clandestine as possible.

Had Mark Mitchison sat here, sipping tea from one of these china cups he could see in the glass-fronted cabinet? Ready and willing to do the gangster's bidding?

'Mr Lorimer,' Gallagher began, 'please sit down. Excuse the state of the place. Not my cleaning lady's fault.' The false smile on his face reminded Lorimer instantly of a crocodile surfacing from muddy waters.

Lorimer sat, his back to the window, opposite the door that led into the hallway. Should one of Gallagher's men come in then he would be ready for him. Though, in truth, he doubted whether there would be another person present while Gallagher revealed his secrets.

'You and I are men of the world, Mr Lorimer,' Gallagher continued, slumping into a thickly upholstered settee and folding his arms across his chest.

We are? Lorimer thought wryly, wondering where this preamble was going to lead.

'Let me tell you something,' Gallagher went on. 'My old man had nothing, not a bean to his name. Never owned his own house, was always one step ahead of the rent man, couldn't even keep decent shoes on his kids' feet.'

'My heart bleeds,' Lorimer remarked, his sarcasm aimed at rattling the man across the room.

Gallagher frowned. 'You might laugh, but I don't suppose *your* folks were exactly millionaires, eh?'

Lorimer's slight shrug was all he needed as a reply.

'Thought not. Ordinary people, eh? And yet their son was at university and went on to be a senior officer with the polis. No' bad, no' bad at all. Guess they feel proud of their boy now, eh?' Gallagher asked, a slight sneer in his voice.

Lorimer remained silent. There was plenty this gang boss did *not* know about his personal life and he was glad of that. Mark Mitchison had evidently failed to fill Gallagher in on all the facts of Lorimer's early life; his father's death from cancer when he'd been a mere boy, his mother's sudden death when he was barely eighteen.

'No comment? Eh?' Gallagher chuckled. 'Bet that's a phrase you've heard often enough, Lorimer.'

Lorimer glanced at his wristwatch. 'Perhaps you might get to the point of why we are here, Mr Gallagher,' he said wearily. 'I've a lot to do.'

Gallagher sat forward, eyes crinkling in their folds of flesh. 'Aye, and more than you can think.' He nodded. 'See that man you were on about in *Crimewatch*?'

Lorimer tried not to let a flicker of interest enter his blue gaze as he waited for Gallagher to proceed. The man was obviously enjoying spinning this out to its conclusion, a conclusion he was beginning to doubt really existed, despite what Gallagher's lawyer had told him.

'The one that did for all these sick old biddies?' Gallagher gave a mendacious grin. Then it faded as he received no response from the detective superintendent.

'What if I was to tell you that I know the man. *Personally*,' he added, arms unfolding as he leaned forward,

'And in what capacity would that be?' Lorimer asked.

'In what capacity ... ?' Gallagher's mouth opened for a moment then closed again. 'See, here, Lorimer, if I say I've got information then that's what I mean!' he snapped. 'Happens he came to see me. Out of the blue.' Gallagher looked away, a sign that Lorimer noticed immediately as avoiding telling the whole truth. 'Wanted me to be involved in a business proposition. Told him to go to hell. Naturally.' Gallagher attempted another grin but once again he failed to meet the detective's eyes.

'How often did you meet this man?' Lorimer asked in bored tones.

'How often? Just the once,' Gallagher growled. 'But he gave me his name, all right?' He sat back and folded his arms once again, evidently satisfied that he had performed what passed for his civic duty.

'He seems to go under a few different names,' Lorimer offered.

'Aye, but I bet your lot don't know this one. Or what his phone number is.' Gallagher nodded his head, eyes twinkling.

And I'm sure you're dying to tell me, Lorimer thought, though he would deny the man the satisfaction of actually asking.

Instead he began to rise from his seat and pulled his coat around him.

'Hey, hold on a wee minute, I haven't told you yet!' Gallagher protested, one hand out as though to stop Lorimer from leaving. 'It's Graham. Charles Graham.' The words dropped from his mouth as he stood in Lorimer's way. 'And here's his number,' he mumbled, pulling out a piece of paper from his trouser pocket. 'My solicitor said you'd be wanting that as well.'

Lorimer took it from him and, folding it once without even glancing at the number, he stepped aside and headed for the door.

'Do I not even get a thank you?' Gallagher blustered as he followed the tall man through the reception hall.

But Lorimer did not turn around to look at the man again. And, when he closed the door behind him, Gallagher's curses were ringing in his ears.

The vibration from his mobile made Oliver Nimmo hesitate as he picked up the coat where he had flung it over a chair. There were very few people in his life that would be calling him and he was not sure that he wanted to talk to any one of them. However, the landline number on the tiny screen was one that he recognised so he pressed a button then put the phone to his ear.

'Charles? You've been trying to get me.' Gallagher's jovial tone made Nimmo sit down suddenly, a flicker of hope in his breast. *Gallagher could get him another car!*

'You been avoiding me, Jack?' he asked, keeping his tone as light as possible. Had the gangster seen that *Crimewatch* programme? Did he know who he really was?

'Been away, son,' Gallagher bluffed. Then Nimmo heard his throaty chuckle. 'Wee bit of the sun. Had to get out of here for a bit. Hate February,' he added.

'You never mentioned a holiday ...' Nimmo asked suspiciously.

'Last minute deal,' Gallagher said. 'Five star place in Tenerife. You should see my tan!'

Nimmo exhaled a long sigh. His luck was in! Gallagher had been away for a break, that was all. And there was no reason why he should have told him that beforehand.

'How are you, Charles? Any more progress with our little deal?'

Nimmo sat down heavily, pushing aside Rick's duffel coat, his thoughts spinning. Gallagher was assuming that everything was still on course. And, if that was true, then he must use this to his advantage.

'Actually, Jack, I've a favour to ask. Wonder if you could lend me a car for a few days? Something I need to see to,' he murmured.

'No bother, son, no bother at all. Want me to bring one to you?'

Nimmo stiffened. He'd deliberately avoided giving out his

home address, something that Jack Gallagher had seemed to approve as good sense. But now ... had something changed ...?

'Charles? Are you still there?'

'Yes,' Nimmo replied, his mind in a whirl of uncertainty. Could he trust this man? Or was he about to walk straight into some sort of trap?

'What sort of wheels're you after? A big van or something fast? Just you name it, son. I can have it delivered right to your door.'

'That won't be necessary, Jack. A decent car with a full tank is what I'm looking for. See if one of your men can leave it in Houldsworth Street, opposite McDonald's, key in the glove compartment. Say in about an hour from now?'

'Got a nice red Mondeo,' Gallagher suggested. 'That do you?'

'Sounds fine,' Nimmo replied, his heart beating as he listened for any trace of duplicity in the man's voice. But Gallagher seemed to be genuine enough. It was simply that incident with the slashed tyres freaking him out.

'When will I get it back?' Gallagher asked. 'Time we had a wee discussion about how we take this new project forwards.'

'Oh, not too long,' Nimmo assured him. 'Couple of days at the most,' he lied, glancing towards the bathroom where he could hear the sound of Rick taking a shower.

As he cut the call, Oliver Nimmo heaved a sigh of relief. In two days' time he would be boarding a ship heading for Amsterdam then travelling north to the hotel in Copenhagen where his baggage would be waiting for him to begin his new life as Richard Aitken. The Danes were a pragmatic lot, he had decided. And he was sure that lots of them had relatives who were beginning to be a burden to them.

*

The Glasgow gangster's crocodile smile widened as he put down the phone. It would take Lorimer and his cops more than an hour to locate Graham. And there were plenty of reasons why Jack Gallagher wanted to find him first.

CHAPTER FORTY-NINE

The MIT team had been encouraged by Lorimer's report though each man and woman had been given the chance to ask the necessary questions. Was Gallagher to be trusted? With Gallagher having given Lorimer the name Charles Graham, the wanted man's dead stepfather, did this mean that Nimmo was already hiding behind yet another alias? And, even if what the drug boss told Lorimer was true, why had Oliver Nimmo approached someone like Gallagher in the first place?

'It can only have been to extend the activities of Quiet Release,' Lorimer had said at last. 'There is no other logical reason why Nimmo would want to get into bed with a dangerous man like Gallagher. Makes sense on several levels. Drugs readily available from Gallagher's own operations. We know he's got that part of the city sewn up,' he added with a grimace. 'Gallagher has his own heavies to do his dirty work, but what if he could use a different way of getting rid of folk?'

'Like Ellen Blackburn?' a voice suggested.

There was a silence as all eyes turned to look at the detective superintendent. How would he respond to that name? They all knew that she was the mother of the man whose gun had ended the lives of that family.

'We have forensic evidence that ties our killer to her death,' Lorimer agreed calmly. 'If that proves to be Nimmo and if he was working for Gallagher we might ask ourselves why he wanted her dead.'

'Neighbour told us that the old woman had been boasting about coming into money,' one of the team offered. 'Our guess is that she'd been milking Gallagher and he was fed up with it.'

'Drastic way to deal with an old lady,' another detective commented.

'That's Gallagher's style,' DCI Tweedie growled. 'Takes no prisoners, that one. Cross the man and he's brutal. It's how he's always operated. Keeps his thugs on a tight rein, too. Might have rubbed off on Thomas Blackburn,' he added, looking Lorimer straight in the eye.

The detective superintendent did not flinch. What Tweedie had said was probably true. Blackburn had wasted his entire family out of spite. The wife had cheated on him and he had chosen to sacrifice the little children rather than let her get away with that. For a moment he stood still, remembering. The smell of blood, the idea of the woman seeing her two boys slain before he'd shot her in the face, the expression in Blackburn's eyes as he'd stood in that room ...

'Aye,' he said at last. 'You're probably right. McGarrity's cut from the same cloth as well. He'd have done some terrible damage to Paul Doherty if our IT expert hadn't also been a black belt.' He nodded, trying to raise the mood in the room. 'Now, we go all-out to find Nimmo, otherwise known as Charles Graham.' Lorimer turned to the whiteboard where the facts of the case were listed. 'Maybe this time he's been a shade too clever for his own good,' he went on. 'Shouldn't be too hard to find a surname like that here in the city. And our technical department is already looking into that mobile number. So let's see if we can run him to ground with what we've got.'

Once the room was empty Lorimer closed the door and walked to the window, leaning his hands on the sill. There was a strange sort of calm in his head, a kind of clarity as if he had come through a dangerous place and found sanctuary on the other side. Had Frank Tweedie been deliberately testing him back there? Did he want to see if the man who was heading this case was up to the job? The link with Blackburn couldn't be ignored, of course. He'd been a known hood, one of Gallagher's hard men, experienced in wielding a firearm. And he'd chosen to put an end to his own life rather than face the consequences of justice.

Well, perhaps Jack Gallagher was playing a different sort of game; trying to evade the power of the law and still dominate the evil forces that ran through this city. He'd had Mitchison in his pocket for long enough, but now it was time to put a stop to that relationship and crush the gangster's empire once and for all.

But first they would have to find Nimmo before he disappeared into yet another new identity.

CHAPTER FIFTY

He barely glanced at the man on the bicycle as he passed him by, the cyclist heading towards the Squinty Bridge. There was something carefree in the way that man sped along that Rick might have envied as he trudged along the main road, hands in his pockets, new coat collar turned up against the chilly air. But the man wearing these unfamiliar clothes was too deep in thought to notice anybody else. It was harder than he'd expected, pretending to be someone else, despite the flashy wallet and the credit cards that he'd been told he could use.

He looked down at the pavement, thinking hard. He'd been instructed to sit quietly in the restaurant and wait to see who arrived in the red car. If the driver left it and walked away then he was to give it ten minutes then stroll across to see if the key had been left in the glove compartment. It would take five minutes to bring the car to the front of the hotel where he was to leave it. Then he could do whatever he liked. But his fingers trembled against the object in his pocket as if the drugs were willing him to open them up.

Rick was oblivious to the other people passing him by, even the steady footsteps of a ragged old man on the other side of the street who had kept him in his sight ever since he had left the flat a few minutes ago.

McDonald's was not empty – several tables occupied by women with pushchairs, post-school-run mums meeting for coffee and chat but it was easy enough to order food and drink then select a table close enough to the window without being seen from across the road. There was a block of flats with designated parking bays for residents and that was where he'd been told the Mondeo would be parked. If he sat quietly and did not draw any attention to himself then all would be well, Rick decided, his confidence returning as he waited to be served. He could do this. His fingers strayed to his pocket, the reassuring shape of the package of drugs making his heart beat just that little faster. Stupid moron had left it where anyone might have been able to find it, he thought. Imagined he'd been so clever; probably didn't know how desperation made an addict search anywhere and everywhere, even in the unlikeliest of places.

For a moment Rick's confidence faltered. Had that been deliberate, then? Had he been meant to find them? Then he grinned as he remembered the man's parting words before he'd left the flat wearing Rick's duffel coat. *Enjoy the facilities*, he'd said. And he'd laughed. Hadn't that been a way of telling him to help himself to his reward?

As luck would have it, two workmen pushed into the restaurant as Tam hesitated by the entrance, making their way forward and standing in line behind the figure in the raincoat. Tam seized the moment and walked behind them, standing as close as he dared, hidden by their bulky figures. He had to keep this man

343

in his sights, he'd told himself over and over, but the smell from this place had been too much to resist, hunger gnawing at his stomach, gnarled fingers counting the coins in his pocket. He shifted his position as the man he sought walked away, carrying a tray. Then he saw him choose a table facing the window, his back to Tam, coat collar still turned up despite the heat in this place. It was easy after that to place his order, hovering behind the workies, then to sit near the wall, hidden from view.

Tam munched the burger and slurped his tea, desperate for the food as much as to keep the killer in his sight. What was he up to? Why had he sent all these cases away in that van? And, as he watched the man in the raincoat apparently staring intently at a spot across the road, he was curious to find just what he was waiting for.

'They traced Gallagher's call to Lancefield Quay,' Cameron told him as he stood at the door of his room. 'Upstairs flat. We've spoken to the concierge. Says it's owned by a Mr Charles Graham.' The excitement in his voice made Lorimer's mouth twitch into a smile.

'Great work. Let's get everyone mobilised,' he commanded, striding across the room and whisking his coat from the coat stand.

Lorimer's heart beat faster as he drove the Lexus away from Helen Street towards the Clyde Tunnel. A quick dash along the Clyde Expressway would lead him onto the area around Finnieston that had become the latest cool place to stay in a city that was forever reinventing itself.

A penthouse flat! Just how much money had Nimmo been making from his scheme? And how many lives had been cut short for him to enjoy that sort of luxury? Lorimer gritted his teeth in sudden rage against the criminals who exploited innocent people merely for gain. He'd seen so much of that and it might have coloured his outlook on humanity but for the other sorts of people in his life.

His thoughts sped with the car as he descended into the gloom of the tunnel, a journey Maggie made twice daily to work, but a place that never failed to give Lorimer a sense of foreboding. His claustrophobia always made him cower a little in the driver's seat, as though the arched ceiling was pressing down, conscious of the weight of water from the river above. Then he was out again and swinging around the bend that led to the Expressway, the Clyde to his right, the Riverside Museum sitting innocently on its banks.

There were several squad cars there already when he arrived, figures swarming into the building as he parked the Lexus on the kerb.

The concierge was standing in the hallway, a look of bewilderment on his face as Lorimer approached.

'I've already given them the key . . .' he explained as Lorimer displayed his warrant card. 'What's going on . . . ?' He tailed off as Lorimer headed for the stairs, a shake of his head his only answer.

'He's gone. Cleared out,' DC Giles declared to the detective superintendent as he ascended the final stairs and saw the officer standing at the open door of Nimmo's flat.

Lorimer noted the detective's gloved hands and overshoes. This might well be a crime scene and they were taking no chances to contaminate an area that could be of interest.

'Think we're too late, sir,' Giles added as a white-clad DC Wilson emerged from the hallway.

'Looks like he's packed up and gone,' she confirmed, her mouth turned down in disappointment.

'Think Gallagher tipped him off, sir?' Giles asked.

Lorimer gave a sigh and shook his head. 'I don't know,' he replied truthfully. Was the gangster giving them something with one hand and snatching it back with the other?

'Let's have a look inside, anyway,' he muttered, taking a pair of latex gloves from his coat pocket and drawing them over his fingers.

Lorimer was not prepared for the light streaming into the large square room, its windows wrapped around one corner of the building. Standing there, he gazed down at the river, seeing the white arrow-shaped foam from a police patrol boat as it approached the bridge. To his left he could see the city laid out in shades of grey and chrome, towering glass blocks winking in the sunlight, a mishmash of the old and the new rubbing shoulders.

How had Nimmo felt gazing down on all of this? Was he carried along by a sense of power? A feeling of being in control of the figures scuttling below like so many tiny ants? Turning, he took in the bare walls, the empty bookshelves and the lamps unlit on dusty tables. What sort of person could live without a single painting on his walls? Perhaps Solly might be able to give an answer to that one, Lorimer thought wryly as he scoured the place with his eyes. There was a switch still turned on in one double wall socket: a sign of a hasty tug to release an adaptor, maybe? The television set was on standby mode, he found. So, maybe Nimmo wasn't all that careful about flicking off the electricity at night? Had he been as deliberately careless with the wiring in his old home? he wondered, thinking of how that fire might have started.

He gave the room one final sweeping look then went out into the hallway to find the other rooms.

'That's his bedroom, sir,' Kirsty offered as he appeared. 'We checked the other rooms but they're all empty. Obviously didn't intend to have anyone staying overnight,' she said. 'Unless they were sharing his bed.'

'Any sign of conjugal bliss?' Lorimer asked, his tone dry.

'No, sir. Looks like he was here on his own. No spare toothbrush.' She risked a grin then made a face. 'No toothbrush at all. And all his shaving kit's gone as well. However,' Kirsty stepped aside and pointed into the en suite bathroom, 'see what we *did* find.'

Lorimer looked into the bathroom and followed her gaze.

The shower had been recently used and the wet tray was swilling in dirt.

'Looks like he's been somewhere muddy,' she observed. 'Does that make any sense?'

'Get that bagged,' Lorimer told her. 'Soil scientist might use it to find a location we know nothing about.'

There were fitted wardrobes lining one entire wall of the bedroom and when Lorimer pulled a chrome-coloured handle, a pair of bifold doors opened to reveal only a few garments suspended on wire hangers. Green coveralls hung side by side with a navy jacket, standard uniform for a community nurse. But it was the pristine white coat that held the detective's attention. Never worn, he thought, running his fingers down the length of the garment. And not the sort of thing that a doctor wore these days anyway. But had Oliver Nimmo ever experienced dreams of grandeur about donning this coat and parading the corridors of a hospital? That was another question that Solly might well wish to ask when they at last ran this man to ground.

This was a public place, Tam thought to himself; somewhere that the killer would not want to be drawing any attention to himself. The idea that was forming in his mind took shape just as he saw a sudden change in the man as his back stiffened and he sat up straighter, evidently alerted by something beyond the restaurant windows.

Tam stood up and looked. A big, thickset man was getting out of a red car. He looked all around him then closed the driver's door and walked downhill towards Finnieston Street. For a moment Tam sensed a hesitation in the man's body language then he saw him rise from the table and turn in the direction of the gents' toilets, his back still towards the old man.

Tam fingered the box in his pocket. It was now or never, he told himself. It would be a matter of timing, that was all. One swift stab and he'd fill the bastard's veins with the poison that had killed his friends.

Rick yanked the tourniquet with his teeth, drawing it tighter around his arm. There was no tremble in the ex-soldier's hand as he inserted the needle, just a feeling of calm that he was about to receive the bliss he'd been craving.

A moan of relief escaped his lips as the drug began to flow through his veins. Then, everything changed, the fire engulfed his senses and he felt himself slipping backwards, backwards . . .

His body made contact with something solid and Rick felt his legs give way as the waves crashed upon the shore and the sky rained down with blood.

Tam McLachlan stared in horror at the man on the floor, seeing the rag bound around his arm, a different spent needle discarded on the floor.

Rick's eyes were wide with shock, the gurgling sound from his lungs soon followed by red tinged froth escaping from his open mouth.

'Rick? Son ...' Tam knelt down for a moment to feel the man's pulse then drew back, the instinct for self-preservation kicking in.

'I ... I thought you were ...' he whimpered, gazing down at the new raincoat and the smartly polished shoes. 'I was going to ...' He trembled, thrusting the container back in to his coat pocket. Then, rising to his feet, Tam McLachlan shook his head in despair. The memory of Seamus made his mind whirl with sudden possibilities.

'Dear God Almighty, what has that bastard done to you?' the old man sobbed, drawing a hand across his eyes.

There was no answer from the inert form on the toilet floor and Tam staggered backwards, hands feeling for the door, his shaking legs stepping away from the sight before him.

'What was all that noise?' a dark-haired woman asked as Tam approached their table.

'Someone no' well,' the old man muttered, shaking his head as he passed the group of women, giving what he hoped was a casual shrug and walking out of the restaurant, collar up, head down, wondering if there were any treacherous cameras whirring above him.

Someone would find the body lying sprawled on the cold hard tiles, he told himself. They'd just assume he'd overdosed. Not been murdered with the stuff that the killer had given him. Just like he'd done with Seamus.

'Charles Graham,' the voice said. 'That was all the identification I could find ... No, I haven't touched his actual body ... Just pulled out a wallet ... Had credit cards in it. No, no cash ...'

'Nimmo's dead.' Niall Cameron met them halfway down the stairs of the block of flats at Lancefield Quay.

'What?' Lorimer stopped on the final landing, staring at the DCI's red cheeks. 'When?'

'A man identified as Charles Graham was found in the toilets at McDonald's,' he said breathlessly. 'About ten minutes ago. Looks like he's taken an overdose.'

'Taste of his own medicine,' Lorimer mused, shaking his head. 'Well, let's get along there and see for ourselves.'

The police tape was being rolled across the entrance as they arrived, two uniformed officers called out from nearby Cranstonhill office.

'Sudden death, sir,' one of them explained when he saw Lorimer's ID. 'Cleaner found him in the toilets. Looks like a junkie.' His lip curled in distaste.

'Thanks.' Lorimer gave the man a nod. 'But it's someone known to us, as it happens. So we'll just have a look in there for ourselves,' he said, pulling on the latex gloves for a second time that morning.

The dead man was lying against the door, head sideways, mouth open in an expression of astonishment.

But it was his eyes that made the tall detective shiver as he hunkered down before him. The man looked as if he had been staring into the jaws of hell in the moment he'd taken his final breath, the utter terror clear for anyone to see.

'Oh, dear God ...'

Lorimer saw Cameron turn away, hand across his mouth. It was a sight that neither man would forget for a long time to come.

'That isn't Nimmo,' Lorimer said at last.

At that moment the door opened again and they saw DC Wilson entering the men's toilets.

Lorimer heaved a sigh. How quickly things could change. From the sense of relief they'd had in knowing they had at last captured their quarry, he had then experienced a sense of anti-climax to find that he'd taken his own life. And now to find that the killer had evaded them yet again . . .

Kirsty Wilson was standing behind the other officers, hardly able to see the body lying on the floor. But then, just as Lorimer and Cameron moved aside, they heard her gasp.

'That's not him!' she exclaimed, catching hold of the wall to steady herself.

'Aye, we know,' Lorimer said. 'God knows who he is or how he came to have Nimmo's wallet and these credit cards in the name of Charles Graham,' he added with disgust.

She gazed up at Lorimer and shook her head.

'He's got away again, hasn't he?' she asked, her voice quiet with despair.

CHAPTER FIFTY-ONE

More than an hour had passed since the car should have arrived at the front of the hotel and Oliver was pacing back and forward in the confined space of the room, one hand on his mouth as he chewed on a ragged fingernail. Gallagher had let him down, he thought. Or else his lookalike jakey had slipped his leash and vanished.

He peered out of the hotel window high above the city. The morning sky had darkened with leaden clouds that threatened rain or worse. Could he risk walking back along to Finnieston where the red car was waiting for him? Or call for a taxi again? It should have been easy enough to demand that reception call a cab for 'Mr Aitken' but what if every taxi driver in this damned city had already been alerted to look out for him? Would they be able to see though his current disguise, he wondered, glancing at the discarded duffel coat lying on the bed as he walked up and down the narrow strip of carpet between the window and the bathroom door. And, was there anything else that he might do to his appearance that would throw them off the scent?

The thought was barely in his mind when Oliver stepped back

and knelt down to unlock his travelling bag. There would be no going back from this change, he told himself grimly, fingers closing over the razor in his washbag.

'Set a thief to catch a thief,' Gallagher had chuckled to himself but he was no longer smiling as he laid down the phone. Not only had Graham failed to turn up and collect the Mondeo but some sort of fracas was happening at the fast-food restaurant, his man informed him, polis everywhere. The driver had made himself scarce after that, leaving the unlocked car where he'd parked it, hoping that nobody would search it and find the keys.

Gallagher ground his teeth. It was time to find out exactly what was going on, he thought. And there was only one man who could fill him in on that.

'No, Gallagher. I can't do this any more.'

Jack Gallagher took note of Mitchison's words but he could still hear that note of uncertainty in the policeman's voice. He was a coward; Gallagher had known this all along, used it to his advantage often enough, but the trouble with fearful men was their inclination to run straight into the arms of the very people he wanted to avoid.

'Lorimer's on the case,' Mitchison continued desperately. 'And I know he'll not let go of it until he finds that "friend" of yours.'

'Just fill me in on the current situation, Mitch,' Gallagher asked, keeping his tone as reasonable as he could manage, despite the rage he felt boiling inside. 'What's going on over at Cranstonhill?'

'Some junkie overdosed in McDonald's toilets,' Mitchison replied. 'Haven't had an ID on him yet but I'll keep you posted if you like.'

Gallagher nodded silently. That would explain why Graham had failed to pick up the Mondeo. He shrugged. Things happened.

'Okay, Mitch, just keep track of Lorimer's whereabouts, won't you? Let me know what else is going on.'

There was a pause then the policeman's voice came back, quieter this time.

'You heard what I said, Gallagher. This is the last time you call me. We're done here, and this time I mean it.'

Jack Gallagher's mouth opened in surprise as he heard the click ending his call. Bloody fool had hung up on him!

The gangster laid down his mobile and closed his lips in a decisive line.

Nobody told Jack Gallagher when it was time to quit. Not even when it was a senior police officer trying to call the shots.

He heaved a sigh. Mitchison had finally got cold feet, then. Too afraid that Lorimer would find out about his relationship with old Jack Gallagher, was he? And perhaps Lorimer already knew more than he'd been letting on, Gallagher thought, remembering the hacked email account.

Mitchison would crumple under the scrutiny of someone like Lorimer, he told himself. It was time to make his last farewell to the fair-haired cop.

You didn't say no to Jack Gallagher and live to tell the tale.

For a few moments he gazed out at the gathering clouds obscuring the sun. He'd give it a couple of hours then call Detective Superintendent Mitchison again. And this time it would be Jack Gallagher calling the shots.

He keeps changing his identity, Lorimer had told him and Solly wondered how that would affect the killer. Was he play-acting?

Had that small child who'd been bullied by his stepfather retreated into different personas? They'd all done it as kids, playing outside, taking on identities of superheroes and the like. *Pretend I'm Spiderman and you be the baddy ...*

But this was a grown-up man he was seeking and his changing identities were indicative of more than pretending to be someone else. He actually took the lives of those people. Solly gave a shiver. What sort of person could slip into a different identity time after time, leaving a body behind him? *A man who's killed his own mother*, the answer came into his head at once.

The down-and-outs were simply expendable people who served a double purpose; Nimmo could steal their identities and also put them to sleep for good. And, he wondered, was that something that would be the killer's undoing? The yearning desire to take a life?

'Can I speak tae a Miss Wilson, please?'

'Who's calling?' the lady on the police switchboard at Helen Street asked.

'Tell her it's Tam,' the man answered. 'She'll know where tae find me. Tell her it's to dae wi' what happened in McDonald's.'

Tam put down the telephone and looked up at the barman with a nod. 'Thanks, pal. I'll jist wait ower there for my friend, awright?'

The old man shuffled across to a corner seat where a couple of glasses were waiting. The wee lassie would come as soon as she heard, he was confident of that. He took a long drink from his pint of beer. *She'd better*, a voice reminded Tam. It would be DC Wilson who'd be picking up the tab for this after all.

*

Kirsty had not come alone, Tam noted with a frown. The good-looking lad in her wake was obviously a copper, the way he looked intently at him, making Tam's eyes slide away under the fellow's scrutiny.

'Who's yer pal?'

'Just call me Davie.' The young man offered his hand but Tam ignored it and turned to Kirsty.

'How come he's here?'

Kirsty smiled. 'Come on now, Tam. You can't expect me to run around after you on my own, can you?' Her smile faded as she leaned towards the old man. 'Listen, Tam. Whatever you have to tell me stays right here. For now. Got it?'

The old man heaved a sigh. 'Aye. Ah'm gettin' too auld fur this lark ...' He glanced at the man sitting beside Kirsty. 'Gonnae make yerself useful, son? Get in a round, eh?'

'It's fine, Davie,' Kirsty assured him. 'Tomato juice for me, thanks. And see if there are any hot pies?'

Tam waited a moment until he was sure the police officer was out of earshot.

'Kirsty, hen,' he began. 'I was there. At McDonald's.'

'You? How ...'

'Wheesht!' Tam beckoned her closer. 'Guy I met in the hostel. Knew he'd been with that man your lot are looking for. Followed them, didn't I?' He gave a self-satisfied grin and lifted the glass again. Then, wiping his hand across his mouth, he said, 'Aye, and I found out where your man lives.'

'We know that, Tam.' Kirsty looked cross, the old man could see.

'Well, good fur youse,' he countered. 'But I bet youse dinna ken the name o' the fellow who died in there, in that toilet ...' He sniffed and sat back, shaking his head at the memory of Rick's last gasps.

'Thocht he wis yer man ... the guy oan *Crimewatch* ... but it wisnae. He wis dressed in his claes, richt enough, but it wis Rick, no' the man I had been tailing ...'

'Rick? Is that the dead man's name?'

Tam nodded. 'Short fur Richard, like. Richard Aitken. Saw his name oan the hostel register, didn't I?'

'Tam, you're a beauty! I could kiss you!' Kirsty exclaimed.

'Naw, hen, dinna dae that. Ah smell too bad fur ony lassie tae kiss me.' Tam grinned. 'Jist pick up the tab, though, eh? And mind that reward they've been offering an' all.'

'Well, that's not outwith the bounds of possibility,' Kirsty agreed. 'If we do apprehend our suspect thanks to this information ... well, you never know.' Her eyes grew serious once again. 'Is there anything else you can tell us? Anything you noticed while you were there?'

The old man closed his eyes for a moment, conjuring up the scene once again then nodded.

'Aye, there was something funny goin' on with a car,' he said at last. 'See, he needed a new set of wheels ...' Tam chuckled then began to tell Kirsty about his small act of sabotage.

His eyes followed them both out as Kirsty and Davie left the Big Yin, the barman bringing a tray of drinks and a plate full of hot pies to his table.

'You won the lottery or something, Tam?' the barman asked, eyebrows raised.

'Well, stranger things huv happened, son,' Tam chuckled, picking up the first pie, the hot grease running down his fingers. 'Stranger things huv happened,' he repeated.

*

'Sergeant Richard Aitken, Queen's Own Scottish Borderers. Discharged several years ago. Divorced then fell on hard times.' Lorimer shook his head. 'It's an all too familiar story, I'm afraid. Ex-soldier slipping through the cracks.' He said no more but the detectives watching him did not need to hear Lorimer's words to guess what was on his mind. One more military man failed by the country he had signed up to serve.

'Nimmo's got to be holed up somewhere. We've checked out the red car that the old man mentioned. Keys are still in the ignition so it looks like he was right: it was left to be collected.'

'Nobody's lifted it?' DC Giles queried.

'Not yet,' Lorimer replied. 'We've got an officer keeping an eye on it right now, though. Wherever it goes we'll know about it. Oh, and there's one more thing you must know,' he added. 'DCC Flint wants to be kept in the loop. In fact, she insisted on coming over here once we had a sniff of an arrest.'

A murmur broke out amongst the assembled officers. If the DCC was to be present did this mean that they were getting closer to the man who had given Aitken these lethal drugs, adding yet another name to his list of victims?

'There's a pattern emerging,' Lorimer told them, raising his hand for silence. 'Nimmo befriends one of these men, finds out all about them and manages to obtain sufficient documentation to pass himself off with their identity.'

'He was keeping bad company,' Tweedie suggested. 'Gallagher has plenty of contacts amongst forgers and the like.'

'You're right,' Lorimer agreed, 'and my guess is that's exactly how Nimmo has managed to get falsified documents in Aitken's name. Rick Aitken wouldn't have been carrying credit cards with the name Charles Graham unless Nimmo had decided on a new identity. I wonder if Gallagher knew about that? Maybe it's time we put a little more pressure on Mr Gallagher.'

'I'm sorry, I already told you ... ' Mark Mitchison's nasal voice tailed off as he listened to the man on the other line.

'Heard what you said, Mitch. Can't blame you, son. But never let it be said that Jack Gallagher doesn't pay his dues. Cash this time, I think. Too risky to use that account of yours, eh? What d'you say? See you back at your place?'

There was a pause as the detective considered the man's words. It was tempting. And Gallagher was right. He owed him, after all the risks he'd taken.

'Things are really busy here right now,' Mitchison tried to explain. 'Nearly everyone in the MIT is out at a murder scene.' His voice dropped to a whisper and he turned round but his room was empty, the door firmly shut.

'That junkie I told you about earlier. Don't have all the details yet but I think it concerns your man, Graham.'

'He'd dead?' Gallagher cried.

'No, he got away all right. But sounds like he left a body behind him. I'll know more later but that's all I can tell you just now.'

'How soon can you make it?' he heard Gallagher ask. 'Don't want to hang around with all this cash on me.'

Mitchison licked his lips. He could say no, probably *should* say no and refuse this final payment, but he knew that he wouldn't.

'Couple of hours, maybe?' He looked at the clock on the wall of his office. 'Say three o'clock?'

'Time for afternoon tea, then.' Gallagher spoke with a chuckle. 'Call me back before you leave, okay?'

But, as he clicked off his phone, Mark Mitchison shuddered.

And it was nothing to do with the shower of hailstones battering against his office window.

'Graham?'

'This is Richard Aitken here,' Oliver told him, wondering if the sudden silence meant that Gallagher was nonplussed. Then he heard a chuckle.

'Ah, Mr Aitken, is it now?' he laughed. 'Uncle Jack here. Just wanted to let you know what's been happening back home.'

Oliver listened as the gangster outlined the situation at the pick-up point, his face becoming darker with every word.

'Looks like your alter ego copped it,' Gallagher said. 'Nice try, though, son. Like a man who can keep one step ahead of the busies. Now, how are we going to get that car over to you, eh?'

Oliver glanced at his reflection in the mirror, startled for a moment to see the unfamiliar shaven head looking back at him. The eyes were too large, the outline too stark, he thought in a moment of disgust. But he'd pass for a casual bloke, all right. Not the man they were looking for.

'Mr *Aitken*? You still there?'

'Yes, just wondering the best place for your driver to leave it this time.' Oliver paused then gazed down at the tiny figures walking to and from the hotel entrance, the miniature shapes of cars slowly disappearing from sight.

'Crowne Plaza car park,' he said at last. 'But leave the keys for me with the front desk, okay? I can pick them up later.'

'That where you are right now, son?'

'No,' Oliver replied swiftly. 'But I can be there soon enough.'

Jack Gallagher smiled to himself as he put down the phone. He knew a lie when he heard one. And he'd been right. One quick call to the Crowne Plaza had confirmed it for him, though

360

of course reception would not divulge the room number of his 'nephew', Mr Richard Aitken. *Did he want to leave a message?*

No, Gallagher had told the girl, *I want to surprise him*. And that, at least was true.

The man behind Quiet Release was not the only person who would have to be silenced, Gallagher thought as he drew the gun from its soft chamois leather covering. He smiled as his fingers closed around the weapon. One shot to the forehead, one to the heart. That was the way to signal his disapproval. And to leave a message for whoever cared to read it that Jack Gallagher didn't suffer fools gladly. His hitmen had been instructed to drive the Mondeo to the car park then wait in their own car till the quarry appeared. They'd been promised twice the normal rate. And that would be money well spent to rid him of the man whose image was plastered all over the damned country.

Mitchison had also outlived his usefulness and the cop's jitteriness spelled nothing but bad news for their relationship.

Gallagher's thoughts were interrupted by the shrill sound of a phone demanding his attention. Mitchison, he thought with a grim smile. Right on cue. Then he laid down the gun and strolled over to the desk where his new mobile lay winking in a shaft of weak sunlight.

'Got the last one,' the technician nodded, tapping her headset. 'Landline call to the Crowne Plaza. Looks like he's getting careless again,' she grinned. 'Or maybe Gallagher wants us to know who he's calling?'

'Lorimer did say that was a possibility,' her neighbour admitted. 'We'll hear soon enough, I suppose. Just need to keep tabs on him, though.'

*

DCC Caroline Flint grinned as she drove her four-by-four across the city. She would be glad of a little action and just hoped that the baby buggy she'd borrowed from one of her young colleagues would do the trick. Posing as an innocent bystander was something she'd done years ago in the Met during her time as an undercover cop and it gave her a frisson of excitement to know that she was part of this operation here in Glasgow.

Some of the MIT team were already stationing themselves close to the hotel that Gallagher had called, their technical staff having pinpointed the location, and she only hoped that their quarry would take some time to emerge from wherever he had been hiding.

'Mitchison's been talking to someone on the south side of the city.' The IT expert touched her earphones. 'Newly registered number. But we should be able to trace the location okay.'

'I'll tell Lorimer,' her neighbour said, getting up and heading along the corridor.

Lorimer tapped a finger against his lips, thinking hard. Who was calling Mitchison? And who in his circle would have recently purchased a new mobile phone? A faint smile reached his eyes and they widened as he remembered that Jack Gallagher's old mobile was still in the possession of Police Scotland, a piece of evidence that he was determined to use against the drug boss.

The signal was coming from the south side, all right, and so Lorimer had decided to head to Pollokshields to confront Gallagher once more. He pressed his lips together and sighed, remembering his promise to George Phillips. Poor Mrs Anderson.

She might well have to find out about her husband's part in all of this mess before taking her final breath. But that was something to be considered later. Right now he had to find out what was going on between Gallagher and Mitchison.

It was as if the very thought of the man had conjured him up as Lorimer headed along the bottom corridor towards the staff car park.

Mitchison looked less than happy to see him, his face downcast, the Burberry raincoat unbuttoned, silk tie loosened from his shirt collar.

If ever there was trouble written on a face, thought Lorimer, then it was this man's.

For a fleeting moment their eyes met and Lorimer recognised the look that Mitchison gave him. It was fear; sheer, naked fear. But what had caused that look? he wondered, stopping suddenly and grasping the man's sleeve.

'You all right, Mitchison?' he asked. Then he let go, the man starting back as though Lorimer had stung him.

'Going home,' the other detective superintendent mumbled. 'I'm not well.'

Then, before Lorimer could pursue the matter further, Mitchison was out of the door and heading towards his car.

Lorimer frowned. Something was wrong, that much was clear. And he would bet that it was nothing to do with a sudden illness, though the man's face was pasty and strained, right enough. More likely that Gallagher's phone call had summoned the detective to Gallagher's Pollokshields home, Lorimer decided. Well. He'd meet them both there soon enough, he thought, watching as the Porsche sped around the corner of the dual carriageway and headed off.

*

There was no sign of Mitchison's car outside the large house in Pollokshields and for a moment Lorimer wondered if he had been wrong. Had Mitchison really fallen ill? Or had he stopped en route, letting Lorimer arrive there first? He tapped the steering wheel, thinking hard. Would he flee as soon as he spotted the Lexus? The thought was no sooner in his mind than he reversed around a corner and waited. But there was no sign of the Porsche arriving and he decided to tackle the gangster himself.

Several rings on the buzzer by the gate told him the truth at last. Gallagher was not at home. And, wherever he had arranged to meet Mitchison, it was not here in the leafy suburb of Pollokshields.

CHAPTER FIFTY-TWO

For the first time in his life Oliver was experiencing a strange sensation in the pit of his stomach. Every other decision he had taken, every plan he had made, had always been accompanied by a sense of confidence in his own powers to succeed. He had never intended to qualify as a medic, had been glad to drop out and manage his own life after putting an end to the people who had hampered him for so many years. And he *had* been a success, he told himself. He had money, property (though it was not looking as though he would ever live in that penthouse flat again) and a future waiting for him after he disembarked from the boat in which he planned to sail away.

So why did he have this gnawing feeling in his guts, a feeling that other, lesser men, might identify as *doubt*?

He had taken a careful look around the car park before sliding into the red car but there was nothing to alarm him. A granny in a black raincoat struggling with a baby buggy opposite was the only other person he could see, the back door of her four-by-four half open. His overnight bag was in the passenger seat next to him, ready to be snatched up the moment he entered the docks in a few hours' time. The trip to Amsterdam was just the start of a longer journey that would take him to Denmark and a new life.

Oliver adjusted his rear-view mirror then turned the key in the ignition. Soon the barrier lifted then he began to drive slowly over the speed bumps and out of the car park.

Glancing behind him the only car he saw in his wake was the big four-by-four, the woman having managed to stow away the buggy. As he rounded the corner and searched for the road sign that would lead to the motorway he failed to see a black car emerging from the front of the hotel, its two occupants keeping the Mondeo in their sights.

CHAPTER FIFTY-THREE

Sometimes the simplest explanation was the right one, Lorimer thought as he headed through Bearsden and took a left towards Milngavie. Something told him that Mitchison was indeed headed for his home as he had said, but he suspected that it was not only the detective's Porsche Boxter that would be parked in his driveway.

The gardens of each house were neat and trim, a few tubs of snowdrops here and there, harbingers of a spring that still felt a long way off. The houses here in Milngavie were a mixture of post-war bungalows and villas, many of them with tasteful loft extensions or conservatories, signs that people were contented to stay put in this leafy city suburb. He slowed down, reading the house numbers, though not every property displayed them, keen to find if he was nearing Mitchison's home.

It was the Jaguar that he recognised first, Gallagher's personalised plate, J1GALL, giving it away.

So. Gallagher had called his whipping boy at work for some reason. And Mitchison had obeyed. What had the drug boss said to make the detective superintendent look so ill at ease? And, more to the point, force him to leave Helen Street in such a hurry.

Lorimer parked a little way beyond the open gates, careful not to block another resident's driveway. There were no other cars parked kerbside at this time on a miserable February afternoon, stay-at-home mums no doubt off to collect their kids as the school bells rang, he decided, his feet crunching on the well-gritted pavement. Pulling up his collar against a bitter wind, Lorimer headed towards Mitchison's house.

A movement made him pause as he approached. Someone was drawing the curtains across the bay window. In the middle of the afternoon? The sky was darkening with the threat of more hail showers but there was still sufficient light as the days lengthened and he frowned, curious to know whose hand had taken hold of the curtains.

Lorimer felt in his pocket for the mobile phone, wondering if he was going to require any back-up. The memory of another bleak day flashed across his vision, armed men standing at strategic points outside a house, his steps leading him upwards to that room where Blackburn had shot the little girl.

He swallowed hard, remembering the way the officers in the MIT all worked as a team. Then, stepping aside, he keyed in a number and waited.

'You know your trouble, Mitch?' Gallagher asked, his eyes narrowing as he glared at the detective superintendent. 'Greed. Simple as that. Couldn't be content to take a wee back-hander now and then, could you? Oh, no, it had to be big bucks for you or nothing else. And what did I get in return?'

'I protected you, Jack,' Mitchison gasped. 'Surely you know that?'

'Aye, till Lorimer got a hold of the case. And then you wanted to scarper. Leave poor old Jack in the shit.'

'It wasn't like that,' Mitchison cried, his eyes widening as the gunman drew closer.

He tried to swallow but his mouth was dry. That silencer attached to the gun told him everything he needed to know.

'You aren't going to do this, Jack,' Mitchison whimpered. 'You're just trying to scare me, aren't you?' he asked, his voice breaking under the strain of watching as the man with the gun came closer and closer.

'Tell me this is just a game, Jack?' Mitchison stopped, and stumbled as his legs hit the edge of his leather sofa.

'Jack . . . ?'

'You shouldn't have tried to screw me, Mitch,' Gallagher told him. 'Wanting to keep some of the information for yourself, eh? A wee get-out-of-jail-free card, was that it? Dub poor old Jack into it and walk away with a clean pension. Was that your idea?'

'That's not . . . I can explain . . . Jack . . . '

Mark Mitchison felt the warm tears begin to course down his cheeks, the expression on Gallagher's face telling him that he had only moments left to live.

'No, Jack, please,' Mitchison snivelled, his legs buckling under him as he watched the dark hole where the bullet would appear. 'Please,' he begged. 'Don't do this!'

There was hardly a sound from the opening door but Mitchison's gasp made Gallagher turn around, the gun in his hand wavering.

'Put the gun down, Gallagher,' Lorimer told him.

He could see the shock in the man's face as Gallagher took a step to one side.

Would he turn the gun on him instead?

Lorimer lunged at him, pulling Gallagher's gun arm upwards, away from Mitchison.

'No!' Gallagher cried out as Lorimer twisted his arm backwards, forcing the heavier man to stumble.

Then Lorimer felt himself falling, pulled by the weight of the gunman onto the carpet.

He made a grab for the hand that still held that weapon even as Gallagher's shoe made contact with his leg.

Lorimer's fingers closed on the gun just as Gallagher began to rise to his feet. Then he rolled sideways as the man bore down on him, a blade flashing above his head.

There was no sound as the gun went off, just a scream of rage and pain, Gallagher slumping to his knees, clutching the wound on his shoulder.

Lorimer gave a sigh as he staggered to his feet. First he made sure the safety catch was on, then, pocketing the gun, he lifted the knife with a clean handkerchief. Two weapons, two ways to kill a man in cold blood.

He brought out the handcuffs and knelt down beside Gallagher who was muttering curses through his groans.

'Jack Gallagher, I'm arresting you for the attempted murder of Detective Superintendent Mark Mitchison,' Lorimer began, his hands busy searching through the man's pockets. There were no other weapons, however, just a shiny mobile phone that he threw to one side as he continued to read the man his rights.

There was no response from Gallagher who was clearly in too much pain to answer back. Lorimer rose to his feet, leaving the man writhing on the floor. It would not be long before reinforcements arrived to take care of the wounded gunman. And for once Jack Gallagher might be glad to see a group of uniformed police officers.

'You okay?' he asked the man whimpering on the ground, a mixture of tears and snot marring his ashen face.

There was no answer, just the stare of a man clearly in deep shock.

Lorimer knelt down and took Mitchison in his arms.

'It's all right, Mark,' he soothed, feeling the man's shaking body as he comforted his fellow officer. 'You're all right now. It's all over,' he said quietly, patting the sobbing man on the back as though he were a child.

'I thought . . . he was going to . . . kill me,' Mitchison sniffed. 'I thought I was going to die . . .'

Then he looked up at the dark-haired detective as though seeing him properly for the first time.

'You . . .' Mitchison said, blinking hard and swallowing. Then he laid one shaking hand on Lorimer's arm. 'Thank you,' he said at last.

CHAPTER FIFTY-FOUR

When the red light flashed on the dashboard, Oliver blinked, then slowed down, hardly believing what his eyes told him. His jaw tightened as he saw the dial had dropped below EMPTY and the light was alerting him to the fact that there was precious little petrol left in the Mondeo's tank, certainly not enough to reach Newcastle in time to catch the ship to Amsterdam.

He swore aloud, cursing Gallagher. He'd been shafted! The drug boss had never intended to help him and, even now, Oliver wondered if there was some ulterior motive behind the red car's lack of fuel.

He pressed the accelerator again and kept to the inside lane, eyes glancing to left and right in the hope of finding a petrol station.

The orange sign indicating a nearby Sainsbury's made him exhale a huge sigh of relief. He'd fill up there and get on his way as soon as he could. No need for a full tank, he thought quickly. Just enough to reach Newcastle and ditch this heap of old junk in the car park. No way was it coming across the North Sea with Oliver Nimmo, he thought with a chuckle, his former self-assurance reasserting itself. Richard Aitken, businessman, would be standing on that boat in just a few hours from now, watching the British coastline become smaller and smaller.

Nimmo shivered suddenly as he got out of the car and released the petrol cap.

The shadow that crossed behind him made him turn and gasp.

Then the shadow became a dark-clad stranger holding a gun to his side.

'Get in the car,' the man hissed, tossing his head towards a black Subaru parked at the next set of pumps.

Oliver opened his mouth to protest and, at that moment, everything changed as a voice cried out, '*Police!*'

Suddenly the forecourt was swarming with police cars, officers heading towards the scene.

It was over in seconds and he felt a sense of relief, watching the gunman being disarmed by a pair of armed police officers wielding automatic rifles.

But then Oliver felt a sinking in his stomach as he saw the woman climbing out of a familiar-looking four-by-four and heading in his direction, her open raincoat now clearly revealing the uniform beneath it.

He looked around, ready to make a dash for it. But all he saw were two more officers closing in on him. In moments his hands were pulled behind him and Oliver heard a snap as his wrists were handcuffed together.

Close up he could see the woman's grey hair and the lines around her mouth but this was no mere granny staring at him with cold, hard eyes.

'Oliver Nimmo,' she intoned, 'I am Deputy Chief Constable Caroline Flint.' She flashed her warrant card close enough for Oliver to read the name. 'I am detaining you as I believe you to be guilty . . . '

Oliver's head swam as he listened to the woman's words cataloguing the crimes he had committed.

Then he felt all the strength leaching from his body as he was led away.

'Well done, lads.' Caroline Flint watched as Nimmo was pushed into the waiting van. She nodded to the officers from the MIT who had accompanied her from the city centre in unmarked cars. Given the green light after the call had been traced to the riverside hotel, they had scrambled the team together, the DCC playing her own part in the operation.

She'd stand aside now, of course, let the MIT team carry out the necessary work back in Govan. But it would be interesting to see what Detective Superintendent Lorimer made of the man who was now heading into custody.

CHAPTER FIFTY-FIVE

'It would be nice to know why,' Solomon Brightman murmured as he ascended the stairs in the Helen Street police station.

'Exactly.' Lorimer grinned. 'And if we manage to find that out you can write another chapter in that new book of yours.'

'New book? What new book?' Solly frowned for a moment.

'*Serial Killers I Have Met*? Not a bad title, do you think? And, let's be honest, you've met a good few in your time, haven't you?'

The professor merely raised bushy eyebrows as they headed towards the corridor where the interview rooms were situated.

Oliver Nimmo sat, head bowed, on a metal chair next to the uniformed officer who had brought him in. The man did not look like a serial killer, the psychologist thought, but then, what was that sort of person supposed to look like? A childhood memory came back to him, an American TV programme he had watched called *The Addams Family* where its members were a mixture of strange and sometimes frightening creatures, at least to a little boy. One episode that stuck in Solly's brain was at Hallowe'en when the Addams children were dressing up to go out to trick or treat. The little girl had not donned a costume, however, and had chosen to wear her everyday clothes instead and it was these words to her nanny that had stayed in Solly's mind.

'I'm going out as a psychopath,' she had declared. 'They look just like ordinary people.'

Certainly Oliver Nimmo looked like an ordinary man. His scalp was shorn, small razor nicks showing this latest, hurried, attempt at disguise. Despite that, there was no denying that he was a handsome-looking individual, and an intelligent one at that. Put him in a hospital and he might well pass for a doctor, Solly thought. He looked up as the two men approached, glancing first at Lorimer then settling his gaze on the bearded professor.

'You're not a cop,' he observed, chin tilted upwards. 'Are you?' His keen eyes flicked up and down as he assessed the new arrivals.

Solly said nothing in reply, knowing it was better to let the man do all the talking, if that was what he wanted to do. Perhaps they would not be here too long after all, listening to the 'no comment' that proceeded from so many lips. But that wouldn't happen, he decided, settling himself into a chair to one side of the room where he could observe but not be looked at so easily. This man would want to crow about his exploits, wouldn't he? Salve his wounded pride by making them listen to all of the horrible details. He watched as that fine head rose in defiance when Lorimer sat opposite and began to speak for the benefit of the video recording.

'Sometimes it's better not to know why,' Lorimer remarked later as they sat sharing a pot of tea in his office. 'Wish I could scrub out my brain, don't you?'

Solly took a sip of the tea and grimaced. It was, as usual, too strong for his liking but he felt the need for something soothing and restorative after that half hour of hell. Nimmo had indeed paraded his 'work', as he called it, to the men in that room, gloating over each and every death that he could remember. And there were several that he seemed to have forgotten, Solly thought in disgust, as though only the juicier ones had mattered.

Why, he'd wanted to ask him, the unanswerable question remaining unspoken. Why had he taken that road to perdition? Why had he killed so many people? For money? For the sense of God-like power that it had given him? Or because it was simply a way of turning himself on?

It was only when Lorimer had asked the question about his parents that Nimmo had become more reticent.

'How, exactly, did you manage to start the fire at number thirteen?' he had asked, his direct blue gaze fixed on the culprit. And Nimmo had told them. How he had used matches to ignite the fibres from some loosened wires, how he had taken the car and sped back to that party. His manner had been gleeful as he'd leaned forward to recount that night ten years ago. And then it had all spilled out, like a tangle of snakes slithering from a hole in the ground.

'Okay?' he heard Lorimer ask.

'I feel as though I want to go home and stand under a hot shower,' Solly admitted. 'You?'

He saw the tall detective stretch out his long legs and sip his tea.

'Ach, he'll never be fit to plead, will he?' Lorimer answered at last. 'Grade A nutter,' he added with a wry smile. 'Sorry. Not very politically correct, is it?'

Solly shook his head. 'I doubt if he will ever see the light of day again,' he agreed. 'And I don't envy whoever has to take care of him for the rest of his natural life.'

'Thanks, Solly.' Lorimer raised his mug in salute to his friend. 'Everything you told us about him was right on the button.'

'Well, only some of it worked out well, didn't it?' Solly nodded, thinking about the last victim, the man who had died in that restaurant toilet. 'And Gallagher? What will happen to him?'

'Oh, he's already been charged with attempted murder. That's one thing he can't wriggle out of.' Lorimer grinned. 'Seeing as I was there,' he added with a sigh. 'And we are pretty confident that we can wrap up his entire organisation now that DS Mitchison has so readily agreed to help us.' He gave the psychologist a meaningful look. 'That's one case that *will* come to court.'

'So, no loose ends?' Solly asked, rising to his feet and preparing to leave.

'Oh, a few, but aren't there always? At least this time we can say we have closed this case for good.'

CHAPTER FIFTY-SIX

'It doesn't have to come to court,' Patrick told his cousin. 'My lawyers have persuaded her to drop the charges.'

'How is she?' Maggie asked. 'Still recovering, I mean ...'

'She's okay,' Patrick conceded. 'Still has a few scars to show but the surgeons reckon that plastic surgery should mend her face. If only I hadn't lashed out ...'

'You had every reason to be angry,' Maggie said soothingly. 'I am sure any jury would have understood.'

'Well, thank God it isn't going to come to that now that we've settled it out of court. She's made a civil claim instead. Hit me back where she knew it would hurt.'

'You're not going to have to sell the farm?' Maggie gasped.

The sigh that followed made her wince. She had such fond memories of the place in the Stirling countryside that her uncle and several generations before him had owned.

'Had to remortgage,' Patrick told her. 'But that's a small price to have to pay for my freedom, Maggie,' he said, lowering his voice.

'And where is she now? Annette, I mean.'

'Ha! Where you might expect. Holed up with some gentleman

friend of hers waiting for her own trial to take place.' Patrick's tone was filled with disgust. 'What did I ever see in that woman? I mean … how could she have paid to have my own brother killed like that?'

Maggie heard the strain in his voice.

'Does Bill think she'll receive a prison sentence?' he asked.

Maggie stifled a sigh. They'd talked about this with the lawyers who were preparing a defence for Annette should she decide to plead not guilty but in the end the woman had admitted her part in having her brother-in-law killed by lethal injection, his inability to resist the stranger's needle due to his enfeebled state.

'He thinks three years,' Maggie said at last. 'Though she could be out in far less,' she added.

'He didn't deserve that,' Patrick remarked quietly and Maggie did not reply. For what could she say about the ending of her poor cousin David's life except that the timing had not been of the man's own choosing: quite different from those who could and did arrange for their own demise in places like Switzerland where such things took place in clinics set up for just such a purpose.

Annette Imrie would return to the outside world once she had served whatever sentence was meted out to her but not to the arms of her once-loving husband as divorce proceedings had already begun.

She had put down the phone but Patrick's words were still ringing in her ears when the doorbell sounded.

Maggie peered through the spyhole at the figure standing outside, wondering who on earth was calling at this time of night. It was after nine o'clock, rather late for any cold callers and she was wary of opening their door to strangers, something that her policeman husband had dinned into her from his earliest days in the force.

For a few moments Maggie stood still, uncertain whether to call out or to wait until the person rang again. She heard a dull thud then a shadow passed across the glass lintel as the figure moved away. Then the sound of a car engine starting up.

She had been holding her breath, Maggie realised, as she exhaled in a sigh of relief. Curious to see if she recognised the car, she slipped the chain then opened the door and peered through the darkness into an empty street. Gone.

Then, just as she was about to close the door once again, she looked down. There, on the lower step, was a bulky padded envelope.

Instinctively she picked it up and read the words scrawled across one side:

DETECTIVE SUPERINTENDENT LORIMER <u>PERSONAL</u>

What had this person left? And why not hand something into the police office? Unless ... with Bill being in Govan for a spell instead of Stewart Street, had he been hard to locate? And who, she thought with a shudder, knew his home address outside the police?

She turned the package over, shook it and heard nothing significant that might have given cause for concern. Then, holding it between her fingers and thumb, she laid it down on the telephone table in the hallway.

Bill would know what to do with it once he was home.

'Just don't explode or anything!' she said aloud then giggled nervously to herself, remembering her second years' storyboards about mad aliens threatening to blow up a distant planet. *Too much sci-fi*, she told herself. And yet ... if it had been anything official, surely a courier would have rung again and an official label been affixed to the envelope? And that word ... personal. She frowned, troubled by thoughts of people who might want to harm her husband, people whose evil intent made them his natural enemies.

'There is no name,' Lorimer said at last after he had taken all of the papers from the envelope and listened to the tape recordings. 'Someone has wanted to make sure that Gallagher doesn't come out of prison for a very long time indeed.'

'Superintendent Mitchison?' Maggie asked.

Lorimer's brow creased as he considered her question. 'No, I don't think it was him,' he said at last. Then he looked across at his wife. She didn't need to know all the horrible details of his job or of the corruption that had rocked Police Scotland in these past few days. George Phillips had emailed him the death notice: Mrs Anderson had finally passed away and her husband's infidelity would not trouble her soul this side of the grave. He'd never be sure, of course, but he could hazard a guess about the identity of the person who'd left this package: was this Anderson's way of saying sorry?

'Does it help to tie up a lot of things?' Maggie asked.

'Yes, it does,' Lorimer agreed, shoving the papers and tapes back into the padded envelope.

'So, that's all finished now,' she sighed, moving closer along the settee and resting her head upon her husband's shoulder. 'You can go back to Stewart Street again.'

She looked up as he tapped the tip of her nose. 'What?' Maggie said, sitting up and gazing into a pair of twinkling blue eyes. 'I know that look, Bill Lorimer. Something's up, isn't it?'

'Not going back to Stewart Street, my love,' he said, watching her puzzled expression. 'I've been offered the job at the MIT on a permanent basis and I told the DCC that I would be accepting it.'

'When?' Maggie asked, her face full of surprised joy.

'Oh, fairly soon.' Then he pulled out a slim white envelope from his pocket and handed it to her. 'But not before we have a wee bit of time to ourselves. Start of the Easter holidays.'

Maggie's eyes widened as she ripped open the envelope and read the travel agent's letter.

'Venice!' she exclaimed, looking at him, lips parted in delight.

'Sorry it's not the warmest time of year, but maybe we won't need to go much further than the hotel room for a few days,' he said, kissing her softly.

EPILOGUE

The breeze blew her blonde hair across her forehead and Rosie swept it away with her free hand, feeling the cold stinging her eyes. Beneath their feet crocuses were springing up, purple, yellow and pale lilac, dotting the green sward, signs of a spring that was coming at last.

Rosie looked down at her coat, knowing that small bulge was hidden for now but, once the blossom had arrived and the flowers were a riot of colour everywhere, she would begin to show the world the child that was growing inside her.

She looked across at her husband, his dark curls tossed in the wind, and wondered just what he was thinking. As he looked back and smiled, Rosie was sure that she could tell.

New life, Rosie thought, new beginnings.

As they crossed Kelvingrove Park her thoughts turned to the man whose post-mortem had filled her with such sadness. That poor man, Rick Aitken, had suffered goodness knows what deprivations in his wasted life. And how lucky their lives were compared to his. She sighed then glanced up at the sky, wondering for a moment at the vagaries of fate.

*

The North Sea breeze had taken all of them inside, all except for the single figure standing staring at the water as though mesmerised by the wake churning white beyond the stern.

Tam McLachlan didn't mind the cold. Wrapped up in this great new coat of his, a tartan scarf twined around his neck, he marvelled at the changing patterns of the waves.

He tugged the collar of his coat around his ears, feeling the soft fabric between his gnarled fingers, and sighed. Who'd have thought it, eh? After all the fuss had died down he had been the one to win out in the end. Young Kirsty had told him to enjoy the reward money and suggested that he take a holiday. Somewhere warm, she'd advised. A cruise, maybe? With enough left over to set up home again when he returned. The folk at the mission had big plans for him, too, courses he could take to help him re-establish a new life.

Funny how money changed things. The folk here on this big ship treated him just as if he were a decent human being, not a homeless man who'd been so recently down on his luck. This wee bit of luxury wouldn't last for ever, of course, but then nothing did. And Tam was determined to enjoy this time as long as possible.

It would be dark soon and then the lights from the ship would cast bright crescents on these foaming crests as the ship plunged onward through the night, taking its passengers away from this part of the world.

Tomorrow he would wake to sunshine and a new coast, a new dawn. He thought for a moment of his old pals and his old life.

Then Tam blinked, feeling the sting of tears in his eyes that was nothing to do with the fierce sea breeze.

ACKNOWLEDGEMENTS

Oh, what a lucky writer I am! During the research for this book I have had the most amazing help from several members of Police Scotland. First may I thank ACC Iain Livingstone who was so willing to enable me to spend time with his officers. The visit to Gartcosh was especially enlightening. DCI Bob Frew, who has been a great help over the years, gave me so much of his time to show me around the MIT at Govan and allow me to ask all sorts of questions relevant to the story. Bless, you, Bob! And, as ever, my former pupil and pal, DS Mairi Milne, has been a huge help supplying essential details. Thanks, Mairi.

The entire team at Castlebrae Police Treatment Centre were fantastic hosts giving me a detailed guided tour of the facilities and explaining everything I wanted to know about the rehabilitation programme, but special thanks are due to patient adviser Helen Orr; manager Paul Grant; Graeme Addison, PR and fund-raising officer; Alison Daly, operations manager; Neil Williams, head nurse, and head physiotherapist, Pauline Johnstone.

Other sorts of medical research have been interesting, too and among those to thank for their assistance are my niece, nurse Helen Jago, whose first-hand knowledge of hospital wards and drug cabinets was essential. Thanks, as always to Dr Marjorie Turner for keeping me right with forensic medical details and to Dr Gary McPherson for his knowledge of Carstairs. (Yes, I now know there are no longer women in the state hospital but for the sake of the story I have chosen to ignore this! Sorry, m'dear!)

Glasgow City Mission is a charity close to our hearts and I would like to thank them for the regular newsletters outlining their extensive work. My imaginary people and place owe a lot to their ethos if nothing else! Thanks are due to Graham Steven for facilitating a visit to their city centre base and letting me see their work there.

Thanks to Eugene Paul Francis Doherty for his generous donation to Orkidstudio that enabled him to win the right to be a named character. Cheers, Paul!

I would also like to thank the staff at Little, Brown, in particular Katherine Armstrong who was my stand-in editor for this book (you are a super editor, Katherine), plus Cath, Stephanie, Clara, Thalia and every member of the Sphere team who do so much to make it work.

Dr Jenny Brown is simply the most amazing person to have as an agent and friend, always supportive, always there to cheer me on or cheer me up. Thanks, Jenny, you are the best!

I am truly fortunate in having so many crime-writing friends and I would like to pay tribute to Lin Anderson, my co-founder of Bloody Scotland, and Alanna Knight MBE (my fellow *femmes fatales*) who give me such encouragement.

Writing is a strange occupation and sometimes means we cut ourselves off from those we love best. I am so lucky to have someone like Donnie. Thanks, my love, for everything you do from cups of tea on the desk, to helpful analysis of the first drafts and putting up with your wife when that red mist descends.

Alex Gray 2016

When Dorothy Guildford is found stabbed to death in her leafy suburban home, all signs point to the husband. But forensic pathologist Doctor Rosie Fergusson is convinced there's more to this case than meets the eye.

While searching for evidence that will put Peter Guildford behind bars for good, DC Kirsty Wilson and the CID team unearth a link with a human-trafficking operation that Detective Superintendent William Lorimer has been investigating for months. But before they can interrogate Peter further, he is brutally attacked in prison.

Lorimer and Kirsty team up to find out as much as they can about Peter, the attack and how it all connects to the mysterious 'Max' who it seems is at the centre of the trafficking ring. But the stakes get higher still when a young Slovakian woman and one of MIT's undercover agents are kidnapped by the very man they seek . . .

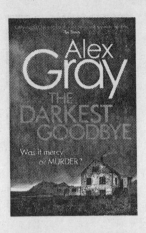

'Brings Glasgow to life in the same way
Ian Rankin evokes Edinburgh'
Daily Mail

When newly fledged DC Kirsty Wilson is called to the house
of an elderly woman, what appears to be a death by natural
causes soon takes a sinister turn when it is revealed that the
woman had a mysterious visitor in the early hours of that
morning – someone dressed as a community nurse,
but with much darker intentions.

As Kirsty is called to another murder – this one the brutal
execution of a well-known Glasgow drug dealer – she finds
herself pulled into a complex case involving vulnerable
people and a sinister service that offers them and their
loved ones a 'release'.

Detective Superintendent William Lorimer is called in to
help DC Wilson investigate and as the body count rises, the
pair soon realise that this case is about to get more personal
than either of them could have imagined . . .

When the body of a red-haired young man is washed up on the shore of the beautiful Isle of Mull, Detective Superintendent Lorimer's tranquil holiday away from the gritty streets of Glasgow is rudely interrupted. The body has been bound with twine in a ghoulishly unnatural position and strongly reminds Lorimer of another murder: a twenty year old Glasgow case that he failed to solve as a newly fledged detective constable and which has haunted him ever since.

As local cop DI Stevie Crozier takes charge of the island murder investigation, Lorimer tries to avoid stepping on her toes. But as the similarities between the young man's death and his cold case grow more obvious, Lorimer realises that there could be a serial killer on the loose after all these years.

As the action switches dramatically between the Mull murder and the Glasgow cold case twenty years earlier, Lorimer tries desperately to catch a cold-hearted killer. Has someone got away with murder for decades?